The Tongue Merchant

Diana —
Enjoy these words. Each is precious to me.
Thanks for putting me in the classroom, where dreams are born.

THE TONGUE MERCHANT

LANCE HAWVERMALE

FIVE STAR
An imprint of Thomson Gale, a part of The Thomson Corporation

Detroit • New York • San Francisco • New Haven, Conn. • Waterville, Maine • London

Copyright © 2008 by Lance Hawvermale.

Five Star Publishing, an imprint of The Gale Group.

Thomson and Star Logo and Five Star are trademarks and Gale is a registered trademark used herein under license.

ALL RIGHTS RESERVED

This novel is a work of fiction. Names, characters, places, and incidents are either the product of the author's imagination, or, if real, used fictitiously.

No part of this book may be reproduced or transmitted in any form or by any electronic or mechanical means, including photocopying, recording or by any information storage and retrieval system, without the express written permission of the publisher, except where permitted by law.

Set in 11 pt. Plantin.

LIBRARY OF CONGRESS CATALOGING-IN-PUBLICATION DATA

Hawvermale, Lance, 1972–
 The tongue merchant / Lance Hawvermale.
   p. cm.
  ISBN-13: 978-1-59414-660-2 (alk. paper)
  ISBN-10: 1-59414-660-8 (alk. paper)
  1. United States. Coast Guard—Officers—Fiction. 2. Murder—Fiction. 3. Caribbean Area—Fiction. I. Title.
 PS3615.R585T66 2008
 813'.6—dc22   2007035766

First Edition. First Printing: January 2008.

Published in 2008 in conjunction with Tekno Books and Ed Gorman.

Printed in the United States of America on permanent paper
10 9 8 7 6 5 4 3 2 1

For Lindsey.
Baby, all I have is this.

Prologue

This is how she hunts him:

She crouches in her Japanese silk pajamas behind the bed in the darkest corner of the cabin, watching, always watching, because they say patience is a virtue and in this case so is rage. Isabella has come to know hate, and her anger is somewhat like the ocean which rises and falls beyond the cabin's tiny porthole. The black Caribbean breathes like a lover in the night, gently caressing the yacht and causing Isabella to sway on the balls of her bare feet as she crouches and waits and clutches the shaft of the mallet in her manicured fingers.

This—this is how she hunts him.

She moves a little when she senses him approaching, anticipating when he will appear and imagining what a relief it will be to sleep peacefully again. Knowing that he isn't going to hurt her. Knowing that she is alone. Thinking of that reminds her of her Uncle Navaro. One night when she was five years old, her uncle struck her with a flashlight so hard and so often that both of their lives were changed forever. Her uncle went to prison. Isabella went deaf.

Silence is her oldest friend.

She can't hear the soft water as it laps against the hull, though she feels its pulse in the bulkhead behind her. Nor can she hear the ruckus of the booze party on the next jetty, though the throb of heavy bass music telegraphs a message through her bones. She is aware of every scent—the polished wood of the cabin, the eucalyptus leaves from the potted tree beside the door, the rabbity stink of her own sweat—and for a moment she wonders if she will be able to smell him coming.

Impossible. He is soundless and scentless and the scourge of her dreams.

Suddenly the water moves. The sea rises without warning, as is its wont, and Isabella loses her balance. She makes a soft sound of surprise—nothing more than an intake of breath as light as a sparrow's wing—but instantly she knows the ruse is over. Somehow her quarry has detected her, somehow . . .

Wait a moment.

Isabella holds her breath when she sees him emerge from the blankets.

He rises up from the white silken sheets, which are tangled in the queer origami native to unmade beds. The black hairs are thick on his legs. Isabella wastes no time, but lifts the mallet overhead and bites down instinctively on her teeth. Because this is how she hunts him. This is how she moves closer, even as he notices her, even as he turns his body to face her, even as Isabella swings the mallet downward in a wicked arc—

The spider never has a chance.

Isabella pulverizes the spider into red and black jelly. The insect bursts like a grape, his remains splattering on her sheets. The impact of the mallet causes the bed to quiver like a living thing, and the boat simultaneously rocks under her feet. But Isabella doesn't notice, for the feeling of exhilaration is too great to ignore.

"Yes!" she exclaims, in her numb-throated way. She's been told that she talks as if her mouth were full of cotton candy. "Gotcha, you evil little thing." She's worked with a speech therapist for the last fifteen years, although right now her deafness is the last thing on her mind. That damned spider has been terrorizing her for days. Scaring the sin and salsa out of her, as her grandmother used to say.

After a few moments to catch her breath, Isabella inspects the messy corpse. She groans. So much for the sheets. Small price to pay, really, for peace of mind. Even still, Nico will have a fit when he finds out she's ruined them. He's supposed to get the boat when the rickety gearshift of their marriage finally slips a notch from S for Separated to D for Divorced and goes grinding down to the scrap heap and out of her life forever.

Screw Nico. Until the yacht is his, Isabella plans on sleeping spider-free.

Stripping the sheets from the bed and bundling them in her arms, she makes her way across the cabin, wondering what the fine is for disposing of an arachnid corpse in the Caribbean. The cops are getting so bitchy about littering these days. On her way to the door, she drops the mallet to the floor, although she never hears it strike.

Neither does she hear the footsteps.

A shadow falls across her shoulder.

She gasps. Spins around. Opens her mouth to scream—

Something hard crashes into her stomach. She doubles over at once, striking the floor so forcefully that it feels as if she's shattered her knees. Her mind clouds with pain. She opens her eyes and sees only a pair of black rubber boots.

The second blow nearly breaks her neck.

There is no sound, only a blur of motion, and then her head snaps to the side and her vision dims.

Get up! she yells at herself.

Panting now, she lunges away. Frantically she scrambles across the room, entombed in her mausoleum of silence, unable to feel her attacker's pursuit because of her own violent cadence against the floor. Her heart is pinched between her ribs. The sheets are coiled around her wrist. And distantly she remembers the last noise she ever heard: her uncle's laughter as he beat her one morning when the Saturday cartoons were playing on TV. No one has hit her since that day.

A hand locks around her ankle.

Even before she can kick or yell or grab the foot of the bed, she's rolled over onto her back, the cabin's single overhead light making a faceless silhouette of her attacker. Isabella's hair is in her mouth and blood crawls over her lips. For one insane moment, she's reminded of the time when she was young and she lay in the forest, letting a caterpillar tickle her face with its feet. That's what the blood feels like. Something with legs.

Move!

Fighting the ache in her stomach, she rocks herself upright and swings a fist.

She connects with her attacker's face but her fading strength betrays her, and then the form is pressing down on top of her and oh Jesus if she is going to be raped then she might as well just let him murder her and—

The sharp object enters just beneath her chin.

What's happening? she wonders. Feels so . . . strange.

There is no pain, just a fountainhead of blood that used to be her throat. Isabella has time to lift her hands to her neck, and then the world goes cold, and she drifts downward, ever downward . . .

Her eyesight is the first to go.

Her vision smolders and turns black, like a stained-glass window sooted by smoke. Darkness envelops her in a way that is reminiscent of the sea on those secret evenings when she slipped away from Nico's bed and waded out for a swim. Of her remaining three senses, taste is the next to abandon her, which isn't really so bad, because she hates the bloody tang on her teeth. Her olfactory receptors are gone before she can inventory them, leaving her with only the feeling of the caterpillar on her mouth and the steady pulse of blood from her throat.

Curiously, it seems to match the rhythm of the party next door, as if the tempo of the music is somehow synchronized with the ebb of her departing soul.

★ ★ ★ ★ ★

Monday
Barometric pressure 30.12

★ ★ ★ ★ ★

Chapter One

With the morning sun reminding my weary eyes of the many benefits of sleep, I stepped from the pilothouse onto the glistening deck, just in time to get an unwanted earful of the ship's PA system.

"Relieve the watch!" the disembodied voice commanded after sounding an ear-splitting boatswain's whistle. "Lifeboat crew on deck to muster! Relieve the wheel and lookout!"

The deck came alive as three dozen blue-clad seamen jumped to their duties. Hawsers whined through metal grommets and boot rubber squeaked on freshly waxed wood. An ensign with a razor-burned chin planted himself in front of me and saluted with youthful precision. "Lieutenant Paraizo, request permission to strike four bells."

"Is it ten o'clock already, Ensign?" I asked, thinking that it felt far earlier than that.

The ensign risked a glance at his watch. "Ten-hundred hours on the money, Lieutenant."

"Very well. Strike four bells. And Ensign?"

"Yes, ma'am?"

"If I were you, I'd invest in some new razors. I'd rather not have members of my crew looking quite so rough as Ahab's ragamuffin whalers."

"Yes, ma'am," he replied, though it was evident by his expression that he had no idea who I was talking about; Melville was evidently not required reading anymore. Not that I truly had room to lecture the ensign on shaving habits. There were days when you probably could've gotten a nice carpet burn by running your hand down my legs. Thank God I was wearing a jumpsuit—officially called our "working blue" uniform—instead of something with a skirt. I watched as the ensign pivoted on his heel. From there my eyes drifted up toward the unrelenting sun, and then out over the signal bridge to the jewel-blue waters of the Caribbean Sea.

The U.S. Coast Guard cutter *Sentinel* plowed a silver furrow through the waves.

I'd been billeted to the *Sentinel* for only a month, but already she felt as necessary to me as my lungs. As the cutter's executive officer, or XO, I was in charge of all personnel, routine activities, and ship discipline, taking orders directly from the captain and juggling all the duties that left him free to do whatever it was that captains did with all the time their lieutenants saved them. Fortunately, my father had taught me how to juggle when I was ten years old. I could now keep five objects in the air at once, at least for a few seconds. But of course the crew of the *Sentinel* knew nothing of this. One more secret piece of myself that I kept safe in the port of my heart.

I spent a few moments enjoying the sun on my skin. The wind was north-by-northwest, providing a gentle uplift for the gulls that seemed our constant companions. I watched them until my eyes began to moisten from the light. I was just about to go below and surprise the enlisted personnel with the locker inspection I'd been threatening, when Captain Maddox leaned his handsome head from the pilothouse door.

"Marcella, wait a sec."

Maddox was the only one on board who ever called me by my first name. And even then only when he was certain that we were alone. He motioned for me to follow him, lines of concern drawn across his normally creaseless face. "I think we might have a situation here."

Instantly the alarms went off in my head. The *tintinnabulators*, I called them, after Poe's lyric about the bells. I hurried to catch up with him, my skin tingling. "What's the matter?"

"St. Noré fishermen found a derelict a mile offshore from Hozumkur. They think there might be a body inside."

"They *think?* What does that mean exactly? Either there is or there isn't."

"We don't know for certain. But we'll be in the area in twenty minutes. I want you to assemble a boarding team and prepare for all contingencies."

"Aye, sir."

"Assign the new chief warrant officer, Higgins, as boarding officer. I want to see how he performs under a bit of pressure."

"Aye, sir."

"Then meet me in the combat information center."

With that, he zigged one way and I zagged the other, and I suppose that was pretty much our relationship in a nutshell. But I wasn't thinking about Kevin Maddox and his green eyes as I jogged double-time to throw together a boarding team. I was considering what he'd said—*They think there might be a body inside*—and how this prospect chilled my skin. Though I'd been trained in martial combat and had fired the cutter's .50-caliber gun at a hostile trafficker's boat, the thought of close-up death still unnerved me. When I spotted Chief Warrant Officer Higgins and lifted my hand to beckon him, I noticed the fine hairs on my arm were dancing.

Inside my head, the tintinnabulators went crazy.

The WMEC *Sentinel* was a 270-foot medium-endurance cutter of the Famous class, capable of a speed of nearly twenty knots. When I stepped into the CIC with Higgins in tow, Maddox had the ship nearly topped out. He was bent over the incoming transmissions concerning the derelict, his wide shoulders pulling his uniform taut across his back. Our section emblem was painted on the wall behind him. Except we don't have walls in the Coast Guard. We have *partitions* and *bulkheads,* and *overheads* instead of ceilings, and *decks,* of course, instead of floors. I'd been a professional sailor since I was eighteen, and my father always laughed whenever I was visiting and called his bathroom the head.

The emblem of the Greater Antilles Section, or GANTSEC, depicted a lighthouse upon a rocky crag. I'd always found this symbol quietly comforting; I guess I liked the idea of being someone's candle in the dark.

Maddox stared hard at the monitors. "Has the derelict given any overt sign of movement, Mister Kyoto?"

The radarman shook his head. "Negative, Captain. She's dead in the water."

"What do we know about her?" I asked as I stepped up beside him, crossing my arms over my chest and cupping my elbows in my hands.

"Only what the fishermen reported," Maddox explained. "Which isn't much. We've no numbers yet, only the ship's name. *Lady Lynn Rob.* Apparently she's a pleasure craft, most likely out of Hozumkur. One of the fishermen boarded her, allegedly saw what he thought to be a body, and then hightailed it back home and called the local cops, who radioed us immediately. We should beat them out there by a few minutes, but only just."

Maddox went on about jurisdictions and who was responsible for what, but I could no longer hear what he was saying. My breath had snagged in my throat the moment he spoke the derelict's name.

No. Not the Lynn. *That can't be right.*

"Say that again." My fingers slowly tightened on my arms. "What's the name of the vessel?"

"St. Noré is calling her the *Lady Lynn Rob*. Or so they're saying."

Oh, God.

"Lieutenant Paraizo?" Maddox fixed me with a look of concern, his usually sharp stare losing some of its edge. "Are you familiar with that boat?"

It took a moment for the paralysis to melt. "I may be, Captain."

"And?"

And nothing, I thought. *Nico and Bella are A-okay, and everything's fine.* "I have some friends in Hozumkur who own a yacht by that name. I was the maid of honor at their wedding." God knew why I threw that in, but it just came out.

Maddox stared at me for a few seconds. "I don't suppose there can be many vessels in the Virgin Islands answering to the moniker of *Lady Lynn Rob.*"

"No, sir. I suppose not."

Maddox turned back to the RD. "Mister Kyoto, keep your eyes on that vessel. Don't let her out of your sight." He bent himself to the task at hand with a new urgency, as if he sensed the swelling tide of my fear.

I imagined I could feel those dark waters rising up around me, threatening to cut off my air. I was an expert swimmer and had once trod water for six hours straight, yet I nonetheless felt like I was drowning. Ordering Higgins to stay on my heels, I rushed back out under the sun, desperate for room to breathe.

Crests broke on the water's surface as we closed the last few miles to the drifting boat, the scattered whitecaps reminding me of the gray curls that were starting to appear in my father's hair. Standing near the wire lifelines that marked the perimeter of the ship, I estimated the wind speed according to the Beaufort scale at force 3, or somewhere between seven and ten knots, with two-foot waves making soft applause against the ship's hull. Small-craft advisories aren't issued till you hit force 6. Hurricanes happen at 12.

Though the barometer was falling slowly and they'd predicted strong winds and rain by Wednesday, for now the sky was mottled by only a few guileless clouds high overhead. Everything around me seemed just as it should have been, except for the fact that we were en route to investigate a vessel on which I'd been a guest only a month before. I stood on the forward part of the weather deck known as the forecastle. Seafarers have always pronounced it *foc'sle*. The first cadet at the Academy's "swab summer" who says *boatswain* instead of *bosun* is either laughed at or cuffed behind the ear, depending on the mood of his superiors. Lucky for me, I'd read enough pirate novels by the time I enlisted to command at least a passing knowledge of the lingo.

Come on, Bella. Be out shopping somewhere. Or getting your nails done. Anywhere but on that boat.

The *Sentinel*'s great steel breast rose and fell against the sea. In the distance I saw the saffron outline of St. Noré, one of the smallest and most socially exclusive islets in the Antilles cluster. St. Noré lies fifty-four miles east-northeast of the city of San Juan, Puerto Rico, and fifteen miles from the much-lauded shores of St. Thomas. Between the cutter and the island was a fair rendition of my childhood home; I'd been born in Miami to a white vice cop and a Latina expatriate, and between the three of us we managed to navigate just about every square mile of water between Nicaragua and the Sargasso Sea. Little by little, the tides of fear began to retreat. Such was the power of this, my truest medicine.

There's a special loneliness to the Caribbean. I'd always felt that way, as if this particular part of the ocean possessed a soul of its own, and my friend Bella Murillo understood me perfectly.

The Tongue Merchant

I'd known Isabella for nearly five years now, and the optimist in my blood refused to admit to my brain that she might have fallen into harm's way. I let the motion of the moving ship unwind the knots of tension in my muscles, telling myself I'd find Bella her usual safe and saucy self.

But that was Marcella Paraizo for you. They say the Eskimos have forty-nine words for snow, because they see so much of it. Me, I have four dozen words for hope.

"Visual confirmation!" came the cry from above.

We adjusted course accordingly, and by now all ninety-eight hands aboard the cutter had been apprised of our situation. They worked their stations efficiently, relaying rapid-fire messages in sailor shorthand, bracing themselves for the dire possibility that the derelict might be a tar baby; last week a trafficker's bomb off the Cuban coast had killed four members of the patrol boat that had been sent to investigate the vessel. Sometimes it's a scary world out there.

The more I thought about Bella falling prey to such monsters, the angrier I became. When the dam finally burst, I leaned over the railing and shouted down to the boarding unit: "Mister Higgins! Belay that!"

He snapped his head up at me. "Ma'am?"

"I'm taking over as boarding officer!" Before he could reply, I was on the run, letting the anger build to a nice boil in my chest. I rarely noticed anymore when that second, more dangerous part of myself seized control from the optimist. From my mother, the quasi-famous Alejandra Chavez-Paraizo, I'd inherited not only the Hispanic half of my genes, but also more than my honest share of daring. My mother had been many things during her life, a revolutionary foremost among them.

Hers was the voice I heard when I grabbed the body armor from the storage locker.

Don't you let them hurt any more good people, gatita.

"I don't plan on it," I whispered.

I followed the bulletproof vest with the fancy equipment belt called *ballistic nylon*. I loaded the nylon with a can of pepper spray, a flashlight, a pair of handcuffs, and an expandable steel baton formally known as an *impact weapon*. Then I retrieved my personal sidearm, a Beretta M92 nine-millimeter semiautomatic pistol, checked the load, and rammed home the clip as if the action were as natural to me as brushing my hair. I stashed two extra magazines in the nylon, donned a blue ball cap printed with the Guard insignia, and of course I couldn't forget my sunglasses. It was hard to look cool when wearing working blues and bulky black boots, so a woman had to take her fashion statements where she could find them.

"Chief Higgins," I said, sliding down the ladder to where the team was gathering near the inflatable boat we'd use to cross from the cutter to the derelict. "Your boarding bag, please."

Higgins nodded without question and handed it over. The slender black satchel contained the miscellaneous forms and equipment we always carried when conducting an open-seas boarding operation: check-off lists, various hand tools, mirrors, a camera, and a Narcotics Identification Kit, or NIK. That's one thing about the armed services. We're nuts for our acronyms.

RHI, for example. Our rigid-hull inflatable boat was a deep-V, glass-reinforced unit with plastic hulls, to which was attached a multicompartment buoyancy tube. It was a state-of-the-art skimmer, much more durable than the rubber rafts of old. We'd use the cutter's special four-point bridle apparatus to deploy the RHI when we drew close to our target.

I looked up and saw the yacht only sixty feet out, bobbing directionlessly on the soft jags of foam. At a single glance, I knew that it was indeed Nico and Bella's pricey fourteen-meter cruiser.

Damn. So much for luck.

Nico always called it their floating bedroom. Last time I was aboard her, Bella and I had gotten drunk on Puerto Rican rum to celebrate her birthday, and by midnight my hands were too sloppy to make proper sign language and her vision too blurry to read my lips. We ended up laughing ourselves to sleep.

Swallowing the memory, I waited for the go-ahead from Maddox, and then ordered my team into the water. We cut the RHI loose from its moorings and a moment later we were skimming the water's surface, the bills of our hats drawn low over our eyes in defense against the sun. I sat at the prow of the boat, one hand resting on the butt of the gun.

"Give me some more speed, Mister Saunders!" I hollered over the din, even though prudence dictated a slow approach speed. But blame that one on my genes as well. The one thing my mother never asked me to be was cautious.

A fine mist blew over my face and cooled my skin as we closed in on the yacht, which was just as I remembered her: a graceful Sabreline 47 with flat shear lines and flaring bows, painted dolphin gray, her name printed in flaxen yellow on her stern. She ran forty-seven feet from bow to transom with a draft of four and a half. Soon the RHI was bobbing against the swimming platform at the yacht's aft section, and I wasted no time in belaying us and shouting my usual salutation: "I'm Lieutenant Marcella Paraizo of United States Coast Guard! Prepare to be boarded and inspected!"

The Guard has regulations in such situations, things about announcement protocol and cautious advances—vital bits of our standard operating procedure we always follow to the letter, to make sure all hands come back alive. I suppose it all went back to an old mariner's adage: never test the depth of the water with both feet. Wise, I guess. But hope has its own momentum. I suddenly found myself leaping from the inflatable and scrambling up the side of the *Lynn*, shouting Bella's name.

I searched the forward cabin first.

With the pistol held in a two-fisted grip close to my body, I dropped low and pressed my back against the cabin. "Ackerson! Ortiz!"

Both men scurried up the rope ladder and dropped down beside me. Something in my face must have alarmed them, because they worked the bolts of their guns.

I did the same with mine. "Ackerson, you've got the stern. Ortiz, take the cabin roof."

"The roof?"

"Get your ass up there, Mister Ortiz!"

"Aye!" He holstered his pistol, put both hands on the cusp of the roof, and hauled himself up.

By then I was already slinking down the starboard side of the deck that wrapped around the cabin, having glanced through the ports and found the forward vee-berth empty. So much for regulations. I probably should've ordered an initial safety inspection, or ISI, to ensure that we weren't walking into an ambuscade or about to be blown to ribbons by a vengeful coke dealer with a remote detonator. But the fires of my anger had burned away my better judgment, a fact I'd have to answer for once I made it back to the cutter. But I wasn't thinking about the consequences as I hustled along the *Lynn* in a soldier's crouch. The boat knocked up and down as a fitful pack of white-jowled waves set their teeth upon the hull. I had no trouble compensating for the gentle rocking; I couldn't dance worth a damn, but I had sealegs you wouldn't believe.

"Saunders!" I shouted at the inflatable.

"Ma'am?"

"Any sign of structural damage?"

He spent a moment appraising the boat, then yelled, "None

The Tongue Merchant

that I can see, Lieutenant!"

Okay. So the *Lynn* hadn't been damaged, and from the looks of things topside, she hadn't been pillaged for parts. So cross thieves off the list of perpetrators. As I passed the windlass and started down the shallow stairwell that led to the main stateroom door, I was no closer to producing a logical theory than I'd been ten minutes ago. Maybe Bella and Nico had fought. They'd been doing that a lot lately. I could almost picture it: Nico gets pissed because he wants to take the boat out fishing with his whore-mongering friends. At least, that's what Bella calls them. Whore-mongers, fish-killers and pot-smokers. So Nico gets a little crazy when Bella says it's her turn with the boat. Nico says something about being glad they're separated because he can't see how any member of the male species could live with such an iron-toothed bitch. To which Bella simply closes her eyes because she can't hear a word he's saying when she's not looking at him, and Nico knows this and it pisses him off all the more, so he settles the issue in his normal juvenile manner by casting off the mooring lines and letting the million-dollar toy float away.

There. That sounded true to character for both of the parties involved. I was warming to my hypothesis when I reached the bottom of the stairs.

The heavy mahogany door was partially open.

Damn again.

The state of the door was bad for one significant reason: Bella never slept in a room without trusting in the security of locks. Doors, windows, whatever—she wouldn't spend the night anywhere unless she was certain no one could sneak up on her in the night. Her anxiety was a direct product of her deafness. She'd been abused as a kid, and had no intention of letting anyone catch her by surprise.

I put my face to the skinny space between the door and the

jamb. "Isabella!"

No response.

No kidding, Einstein. She can't hear you. In the intensity of the moment, I guess I forgot.

I sidled closer and tried to see as much of the room as possible. I took a hand away from the Beretta only long enough to yank off my shades. They hung around my neck on a leather lanyard. I brought the gun up close to my face and squinted into the gloom.

"Nico? Nico, it's me, Marcy."

I wasn't really expecting a response, which was why it surprised me when I heard a soft but definite sound from the other side of the door.

"Nico, are you there?"

The sound had been so brief that was I unable to place it. A boot sliding across the floor? A waiting assailant clearing his throat? My own overwrought imagination?

The radio at my waist crackled: "See anything, Lieutenant?"

Keeping my eyes on the interior of the cabin, I grabbed the radio from my belt and thumbed the call button. "Give me a minute, Saunders. I'm entering the main living compartment."

Ensign Ackerson made the top of the stairs just as I was holstering the radio. I put a finger to my lips, silencing him, and waited for the sound to return.

Nothing.

"Enough already." Goosebumps of anticipation crawled over my skin like insects. Gathering a five-fathom sigh, I shoved the door open with my foot, led with the pistol extended in front of me, and swept into the room.

The brain is a funny thing sometimes. Though the eyes may transmit the truth of what they see around them, the brain sends the message on a detour before we're able to make sense of it. During its circuitous sojourn through the mind, the message becomes garbled, or watered down, or anesthetized, and we end up misinterpreting what we see. That's how it was when I saw that Bella had been redecorating the cabin. She'd torn the sheets from the bed, most likely to make way for new ones of a more flattering color scheme. She'd upended the eucalyptus tree, certainly intending to remove it and perhaps replace it with something more manageable, like a fern. And she'd evidently been in the midst of painting, because like a total klutz I managed to step in her red paint, and how Nico would freak when he learned I'd tracked the stuff all over his floating bedroom.

Dear sweet Jesus.

The next thing that hit me was the smell, drifting up from Isabella's ruined body.

Chapter Two

Half an hour later, the place was crawling with cops.

We towed the *Lynn* back to her home port. Located the proper slip at Marina del Sol in the city of Hozumkur. Moored the yacht. Cleared her decks and put up a cordon of yellow tape. The police descended. The medical examiner. The forensics people. The crowds. Maddox radioed our findings back to base at San Juan. The sun continued to rise in the sky. The gulls still flew. The earth still spun.

Yet to me, the world was motionless.

Frozen between ticks of the clock, I stood on the busy pier, arms crossed over me like a makeshift shield, cradling my elbows. I'd lost my cap somewhere in the tumult. Thankfully I still had my shades. My eyes needed someplace to hide.

"Lieutenant?"

Numbly I turned my neck, finding it surprising that human voices still sounded the same. You'd have thought everyone would be speaking gibberish on the morning the planet went crazy.

"Lieutenant Pa . . . ray . . . zo?"

"Puh-*rye*-zo," I said, emphasizing the phonetics of each syllable.

"Sorry, ma'am. Paraizo. Right. I guess that's why I was a phys-ed major. The English language and I don't always see eye to eye." He fastened a smile to his plowboy's face and held out his hand. "My name's Kyle Straker. *Sergeant*, if you'd rather

The Tongue Merchant

keep things sort of rank-to-rank."

I studied his freckled hand as if I were seeing it through a telescope. Everything seemed to be so far away. Except, of course, for the phantom smell of my friend and the vision of her smeared in her own sticky blood. Desperately I shoved the image away and concentrated on the man in front of me.

"You hanging in there, Lieutenant?"

I shot out an icy hand and shook quickly. "I apologize, Sergeant. I'm just a little . . ."

"Hey, no need to say anything at all. Believe me, I understand." He took a step closer, and I tried to distract myself by evaluating him, checking out the cut of his jib, as we say. He was about my height—around five-nine—and I doubted there was a pinchable inch of fat anywhere on his body. He looked like he could probably play some solid shortstop, as he seemed nimble, a guy who always won his girl a prize by throwing at carnival milk bottles. He wore a blue pullover under his sport coat, his badge on a lanyard around his neck. His faith-worthy, somehow small-town looks reminded me of an instructor I'd had my sophomore year at the Academy. The one who had taught me semaphore, and how to communicate with signal flags instead of words.

Vaguely I wondered if Kyle Straker could read my tacit flags of anguish.

"Do you mind if I ask you a question or two?" His voice was a bit like my brother Micah's, bright and somewhat boyish. "It's an awful mother of a thing to do right now, I know, but if I don't get this little notebook filled up, my boss sort of gets his intestines in a Gordian knot, if you know what I mean."

I couldn't help but warm to Straker's attitude, if only just a little. I forced myself to loosen up and let time start ticking again. If nothing else, maybe the hypnotic act of answering his queries would drain away a bit of the poison, which was still so fresh it felt as if it were eating a hole through my stomach. "What would you like to know?"

"How about we sit first? Sound okay? There's a bench over there. I've reserved us a couple of seats, front row center. Come on."

Gladly I let him lead me away from the *Lynn*. Or the *scene of the crime*, I guess you'd call it. Thinking about that caused me to picture Bella surrounded by a chalk-outline aura like you see in the movies, and it was a minor miracle that I even made it to the bench without collapsing.

This is too, too much.

No, it's not, gatita. *There's no such thing.* My mother always called me the Spanish word for *kitten* when she was passing along advice. *Nothing is too much if you're strong.*

"So . . ." Straker waited for me to sit, then settled down a foot away from me. The sun was huge in the sky, as it always seemed to be in the Antilles. Straker had to squint against it, which made him look even more boyish than before. "How long've you been in the Coast Guard?"

"Is that relevant?"

"Oh, maybe. Probably not. Just seemed like a safe place to start. So how long?"

"Since two weeks after I graduated high school."

"And when was that?"

"Never ask a woman to reveal her age, Sergeant."

"*Ageless,*" Straker said, penning the word boldly in his notebook. "Good enough for me. Married?"

"Never."

"You live here in Hozumkur?"

"San Juan."

"Yeah, okay. That makes sense. A lot of Guard personnel hang their hats over there, don't they? Been there once or twice myself. There's an aircraft mechanic in the Rio Bayamon Housing area who owes me an ever-growing poker debt. We usually play here on St. Noré, but I've paid him a visit, given the scene the once-over. Nice place." He gained a little respite from the sun when a single, renegade cloud dared to interrupt the otherwise seamless sky. "Can I ask you something that has absolutely no bearing on this case whatsoever?"

Case, I repeated in my head. *Isabella is now a case. Jesus.*

"Sure," I replied, thinking what the hell.

"You have a very distinctive voice. Were you born in this area?"

I nodded.

"Care to elaborate?"

I shrugged. "My father lives in Miami. He's a police officer, and about as white-Anglo-Saxon-Protestant as they come. He's got this scratchy sort of mountain-man voice. My mother used to say he was part werewolf." Just thinking about my father made the tension seep through my pores, the poison dilute in my stomach. All at once I felt a little saner, a little more *me.* Dad's always been my best tonic. "And Mom, she was so Nicaraguan that she probably sang 'Salve a tí, Nicaragua' in her sleep. That's the national anthem. But she had a terrific voice. Great singer. Probably could've been a world-class alto, had her life turned out differently. So I guess what I'm saying is blame it on Dad."

"I like it," Straker said. "Your voice, I mean."

"Thanks. And thanks for asking the bullshit question."

"My pleasure. Feel any better?"

"Yes, thank you." Thinking about my parents did that to me. So mark one up for Sergeant Smoothtalk. "Now who killed my friend?"

Straker held up a hand like a roadside construction worker with a sign that said STOP. "Let's not get ahead of ourselves.

We'll take this one step at a time. You were the first one to see the body?"

"No. The fishermen . . ."

"Of course. But as far as Guardsmen . . ."

"Yes, I was the boarding officer. I was in command of the operation. I went in first."

"Touch anything?"

"No. *Hell*, no."

"Was anyone in the cabin after you left?"

"Not that I'm aware of."

"Her name was Isabella Murillo, that right?"

I nodded once.

"She was married."

"Is that a question?"

"Not really. Her husband's name is Nicholas?"

"He goes by Nico. He's a scuba instructor. They were separated."

"You were good friends?"

"Nico and I? Hardly."

"I meant you and Mrs. Murillo."

"Oh. Well, we didn't exactly see each other as much as we'd have liked, but yeah, I suppose Bella and I were pretty tight. You know how it goes. We'd made promises to keep in touch. But things happen."

Straker listened to me with a thoughtful expression, spending a few silent moments either taking notes or pretending like he was. Out on the pier, the paramedics emerged from the *Lynn*, bearing a stretcher between them. There was no human being on the stretcher, only an oblong black bag as distant and meaningless to me as one of the moons of Jupiter. Thinking about Isabella made my own problems—namely tomorrow's appointment with Dr. Avundavi—seem equally distant and moon-like in importance. "Can I ask you a few questions now, Sergeant?"

"Expect nothing but lies."

"Is that a no?"

He smiled. "I'm terrible when you turn the tables on me. But go ahead and ask."

I spent a few moments collecting my thoughts. I had so many questions I didn't know where to begin. But I suppose most of my demands were aimed at God—like, *Why do You let such horrible things happen?* and *Who put You in charge, anyway?*—so they'd have to wait. For really the first time, I met Straker's gaze. He had eyes like lagoons. "Did you see her down there in the boat? Isabella. Did you see . . . what they did to her?"

On the pier, the medics were transferring their package to a black van.

"Yes, ma'am, I did. I guess I'm the guy in charge around here, more or less."

"Was she . . . ?" *Raped?* I thought, but couldn't say. *Beaten? Violated?*

"She died from a single stab wound to the neck. The injury probably punctured the carotid artery, and I'd say that she passed away only seconds later. It's just a guess, but I'm betting that she died around midnight, though that hasn't been confirmed."

"I understand. What else?"

"What do you mean?"

"I don't know . . . was there any evidence of what happened? Were there any footprints, fingerprints, hair samples, any reason why someone would do this? Did your people find anything, some kind of clue or something? Clothing fibers? Or whatever it is that cops on TV are always looking for. Anything like that at all?" I turned on the bench so that my body was facing his, my cheeks flushed. "God, Sergeant, *who the hell murdered my friend?*"

"Hey now, breathe a little bit, okay? We're working on it. I know it sounds feeble and doesn't do you a bit of good right now, but you're going to have to trust us. Can you do that? At least for a little while?"

As if I had any choice. What I wanted more than anything was an extended leave of absence, a bottle of something tough, and a bath so hot it scalded my skin. And maybe my father's shoulder when nothing else did the trick.

" 'Scuse me for a second," Straker said abruptly, and got up to meet a uniformed cop who came from the direction of the black van. They spoke in tones too low for me to hear, though I held my breath in an effort to discern what they were saying. The intensity of my own curiosity startled me. As if by clinging to straws I could somehow keep my head above water.

Too late for that now.

"So," Straker said casually when he returned a minute later. "You were interrogating me. And I was preparing a fresh batch of lies. Please, continue."

"What did he say?"

"Who?"

"That cop. I was watching your face. He said something important, didn't he?"

"It's *all* important, Lieutenant. We consider every tiny detail as if it were the secret for how to turn lead into gold. It's all alchemy at this stage, every fragment of it. Nothing's solid at this point, just little bits and pieces. And the devil and dirty police work are in the details. Now, there are a couple of other matters I'd like to clear up . . ."

Before I fully realized what I was doing, I reached over and took Straker's hand. Forget the fact that he was a stranger; sometimes we simply need to hold on to another's warm flesh and let the science of emotional osmosis do its thing. "Please, Sergeant." My voice sounded faint and airy to my ears, like wind blowing over sand. "I'm about one good hiccup away from breaking down right here in front of you, and then these sunglasses will no longer be big enough for me to hide behind. Anything you can tell me at this point, anything at all, will help me tremendously."

"This won't."

"Humor me."

"I'm being completely serious here, Lieutenant. Let it go."

I just stared at him, waiting.

A brief conflict raged on his face, as duty battled desire. He must have taken pity on me, because eventually he caved. "You may tell no one of this, understand?"

I could barely nod.

Straker sighed and said, "They cut out her tongue."

These moments happen. Disaster, accident, crisis—call them what you will, but they bear a lucidity so pure that it seems as if everything is happening in high-resolution, exquisite slow motion. You're sitting in a white hospital hallway, waiting for the doctor to appear and tell you that your car-wrecked child is either alive or dead. Or you're hunkered down on the courthouse steps on the day you came to talk about divorce, wondering how nobody really took it seriously anymore when the preacher said let no man put asunder that which God had allegedly ordained. Or you're attending the funeral of someone who was a jigsaw piece of your puzzled soul, a single casket the centerpiece for all the world's rain.

The last time I felt this way was the morning we buried my mother. Except of course there was nothing to bury. No body. Just a goddamn box.

I sat at a table amongst the columns that supported the bright fabric awning of an open-air dining verandah. The restaurant was called Dominique's. The columns were of sandalwood, carved with bas-relief dolphins and the occasional, vaguely licentious mermaid. The waiters wore cotton shorts and pineapple-shaped name tags. Resting on the table in front of me, beads of condensation creeping down its sides, was a glass of raspberry tea I hadn't touched. Just across the street lay Marina del Sol, and everything about it seemed frozen in photographic stillness.

"I'm sorry as all hell about this, Marce," Deb said, tracing the moisture on her glass.

"Not your fault."

"I've never known anyone who was murdered before."

"I have." My voice was surprisingly bereft of emotion. I couldn't take my eyes from the pier. Debbie Newcombe and I had adjourned to Dominique's as soon as Captain Maddox granted liberty for three-quarters of the crew. The *Sentinel* would spend the evening off the St. Noré coast, giving our media specialists time to deal with the press and giving me, I suppose, time to attend to Bella's business. Starting thirty minutes ago I was officially on eighteen hours of shore liberty which would expire at 0745 tomorrow morning.

"Has her husband been notified?" Deb held the rank of petty officer second class, grade E-5 to my hard-earned O-3, but I never thought of her as enlisted personnel. We were the same age, and over raspberry tea and commiseration all women are the same rank.

"I dispatched Ortiz to find him," I explained, breathing in the smell of fried scallops that carried on the breeze from the kitchen. The thought of eating still made me a little queasy. "Last I heard, Nico had rented a flat downtown. He'll probably show up here any minute now." And that was a prospect I was dreading with every iota of my being. Nico Murillo wasn't one of my favorite men on planet Earth—not even cracking the top one hundred, to be honest—but I'd already dealt with enough shock and suffering for one day. Namely my own. I had no desire to see Nico fall to pieces.

"Anything I can do to help until then?"

Though Deb's tone was thick with concern for my well-being, I barely heard her. My eyes were still playing over the pier, where everything appeared to be happening with uncanny deliberation. This sluggish passage of time provided me the opportunity to inventory the entire area, from the south end of the dock to the northern tip, where the vast wooden pilings were under constant harassment from the waves. First of all there was the *Lady Lynn Rob* herself, safe in her slip once again, her shiny nickel-plated brightwork winking in the sun. Evidently she'd been loosed sometime in the middle of the night. We'd found her a mile from shore. At this point I had no idea if she'd floated out there naturally on the current, Bella already dead inside, or if she'd been piloted there while Bella was still alive, the murder taking place at sea. And if Sergeant Straker knew one way or the other, he hadn't seen fit to say. His people still dawdled around the boat, packing up their gear and taking a few parting snapshots of the—

—*scene of the crime*—

—yacht and surrounding environs. Other vessels rested on either side of the *Lynn,* lurching in the clutches of the water. The first of these, due south of the *Lynn* and separated by a wooden expanse of about twenty feet, was a catamaran painted Congo green. A tattered Union Jack snapped fitfully in the breeze from the boat's stern, which meant that the vessel was either registered to a British owner or belonged to an Anglophile who thought the local debutantes were attracted to men with cultured English tongues. Which they were.

"Marce? You still with me?"

I smiled automatically and gave her hand a quick pat. "Life is too short, Deb."

"I know."

"We need to start making the most of it."

"You're right."

"Gather ye rosebuds, and all the rest."

She returned my smile, if a little weakly. "You okay, babe?"

"Not a damn bit." I let my eyes go where they wanted to go, which was back to an inspection of the dock.

There was nothing out of the ordinary with the catamaran. In fact, she appeared to be vacant. The vessel immediately north of the *Lynn*, however, was anything but desolate. At least half a dozen people perched atop the boat's cabin, watching the ongoing drama with beer bottles between their knees. A couple of them were shirtless. Only one of them wore shoes. From my vantage point across the street, I thought the oldest of them looked no more than twenty-five. I took a quick count: four men, three women. They were draped about their vessel like sun-drunk animals, the residue of a recent party littering the deck around them. One of them said something I couldn't quite hear, pointed at the *Lynn*, and a few others braved their hangovers to laugh at his quip.

In the amber of time in which they were trapped, I was able to note their every detail.

One of them caught me staring.

Almost as if he'd sensed the probe of my stare, a bronze surfer-type turned his head and happened upon my eyes. I was too far away to see much of anything beyond the fact that he was Asian and wore his hair in a buzz-cut on top, with a long black mane hanging down to the center of his back. He held up his hand and gave me the peace sign.

I looked away.

"Would you rather just be alone?" Deb asked. "I only wonder because you don't seem to be in the needing-a-shoulder-to-lean-on mood."

"I don't really know. Maybe so. Half of me wants to stick

around until Nico gets here, just because I feel sort of obligated, but the other half wants to find a hotel and call room service for about three gallons of dark chocolate ice cream."

"That, or a bottle of scotch."

"Or both," I suggested.

"Yeah. Or both."

We smiled at each other in that tight-lipped way we humans have when smiling is the last thing on our minds. She stroked the back of my hand a few times, stood up, dug some gnarled bills from her pocket, and dropped them on the table. "Call me if you need a drinking partner."

"Or an ice cream partner," I said.

"That too." Her thin smile remained fixed to her face until she turned around.

I didn't even watch her go. Instantly my gaze swung back out toward the pier.

South of the vessel bearing the Union Jack was a long jetty that supported the headquarters of the Hozumkur Rime & Reel Yacht Club, haven for the rich and politically astute, and thus antithetical to everything I believed in. The building had been artfully designed to appear as an aging fishery, with weather-worn plank siding, faded paint, a faux-rusty stovepipe chimney, and strategically placed nets, gaffs, marlinspikes, and barrels. The dual front doors were currently propped open by a barnacled anchor that had probably never touched water.

Standing directly between the yacht club and the *Lynn*, looming like a silent titan, was the pier's most curious landmark: a sixty-foot-tall clock tower everyone called Jehovah. I didn't know the story behind Jehovah, only that it was an exact, albeit smaller, replica of London's lovable Big Ben. Lingering before it were two men wearing the kind of pants you see advertised in *GQ*, smoking cigars and eyeballing the happenings aboard the *Lynn*.

The street that stretched lazily alongside the marina and separated Dominique's from the pier was called Ochoa, supposedly named after a priest who'd sailed with Columbus. I remembered my mother teaching me that charming young Chris Columbus was both a rapist and a flesh-trader, but he made up for these shortcomings by being a thief and a murderer. If you want a sympathetic ear to hear the sundry glories of Manifest Destiny, don't go looking in the West Indies.

Nevertheless, Ochoa Promenade was my kind of street. Lined on both sides by towering palm trees and populated with antique dealers, rare book shops, perfumeries, and several *hacienda*-style taverns, Ochoa offered a cultural sanctuary without the touristy flamboyance found on the rest of the island. The air tasted fresh here and smelled of salt and buttered shrimp. There was a meringue lightness to the wind. The sunlight dappled the palm fronds in such a way that they appeared to be cast of beaten gold.

"*¿Algo más?*"

I shook myself from my careful study of the pier and found a waiter looking down at me, his hands pressed together in front of him as if in prayer.

"No, thank you," I replied in Spanish. "I haven't really gotten started on this one yet." I took a sip of my tea, which by now was watery and warm.

He bowed his head, monklike, and turned to leave me alone.

"Wait a minute," I said, on instinct.

"*¿Sí?*"

"Is this restaurant open twenty-four hours?"

"Sometimes it feels that way to me, I spend so much time here. We close at two in the morning and open up again at ten a.m."

"I see. And one more question. There was a . . . an *accident*

The Tongue Merchant

at the marina. I was wondering if you might have seen anything that—"

From across the street, someone started screaming.

I reached the pier at a blind run, but by the time I got there, Nico Murillo was already lost.

He was puddled on the boardwalk, bent over with grief to such an extent that it seemed as if his bones had turned to water. His normally winsome features melted into an almost childlike grimace of pain, and even as I closed the last few feet which separated us, a tremor passed so powerfully through his body that he seemed to be in the grip of a seizure. A female uniformed cop was standing flatfooted behind him, a hand over her mouth. Obviously she hadn't a clue as to how to handle a man who'd just learned that his wife was dead. Fortunately Kyle Straker was there. He sank down to his knees and put a hand on Nico's trembling shoulder.

"*Get the hell away from me!*" Nico shrieked, recoiling from the sergeant's touch. Bright tears crystaled his eyes.

And then I was there.

"Nico, God, Nico, I'm sorry. . . ." I dropped down in front of him and found his hands. It took him a moment to realize who I was, but when he did, he clutched me and started talking nonsense in high-speed Spanish. I didn't catch it all. Something about a train.

"Nico, I'm sorry, I am so, so sorry. . . ." Looking at him like this—lower lip trembling, eyes awash in tears—was almost more than my already burdened shoulders could bear. In slow and steady English, I said, "You've got to be strong—you hear me?—because Bella would want that, she'd want us to be okay and not to worry because she's in a better place now—right?—she's up there looking down on us right now, telling us that everything's going to be all right, even if it doesn't seem like it right now."

I wasn't sure how much effect my words had on his sorrow, but he nodded vigorously and gripped my hands with a new intensity. He sniffed back the snot that had begun to run from his nose, still nodding. Over his shoulder, Sergeant Straker was talking into a cell phone.

"They're going to find the people who did this," I promised, as much to convince myself as anyone else. "They're going to find them and make them pay."

In Spanish, Nico said, "I pray to God they do," and I was just about to pull him into a much-needed hug when a woman in an island-print skirt ducked under the police tape. She was probably twenty years old, with giant silver hoop earrings and shoes I figured probably set her back at least what I make in a week. She almost shouldered me out of the way, so eager was she to get her arms around Nico. Physically displaced, I had no choice but to stand up and step away.

Nico embraced her fiercely. She spoke softly to him, consoling him, stroking the side of his tear-streaked face. I stood there feeling awkward while she asked Straker if she could take Nico away for awhile. He nodded, but said he'd have a few questions to ask them both before the day was through. Almost before the last word had left his mouth, she put an arm around Nico's waist and helped him under the police tape.

I could only stare at them and wonder why I felt so slighted.

Straker stepped up beside me, tapping his phone against his chin. Together we watched the woman lead Nico toward her waiting convertible. As soon as he was in the car, Nico bent over the dashboard and folded his arms over the back of his head. The woman started the car and drove away.

"I hate my job," Straker said after awhile.

"Quit," I suggested. With that one word, the last of my

strength drained from my body.

"Someday." He didn't take his gaze off the retreating car.

Something about Straker's manner caused the tintinnabulators to give a little tingle. I turned and looked at him, my eyes narrowing to what felt like dangerous slits. "What are you thinking, Sergeant?"

He didn't respond.

"That Nico did this? That's what you're wondering, isn't it?"

"I'm not wondering anything at this point, Lieutenant."

"I don't believe you."

"The case is still in its opening phase."

"Isabella is not a *case*."

His eyes found mine. "Go home, Lieutenant. Get some sleep. Let us do our job. I promise we won't muck it up beyond standard police regulations for muck-ups."

I tried to ignite the fires of my stare, but all the heat had left me. I felt betrayed, my bravado gone when I most needed it. "Nico did not kill his wife."

Straker looked like a spy about to infiltrate a foreign embassy. "We'll see."

Chapter Three

Unable even to summon the energy to seek out a hotel, I returned to my quarters aboard the cutter and fell like a—

—*dead woman*—

—sleepwalker upon the cot. My small, metal-walled cabin was in its normal state of suspended anarchy, the neatness so precariously maintained that at any given moment all my earthly possessions would surely tumble from where I'd secreted them with practiced skill. The closet was little more than a locker in disguise, filled with too many jars of boot polish and not enough sandals and silk underwear. When I settled onto the cot, I had to shove away the most recent copies of *Elle* and *American Flyfishing*. The two magazines fell to the floor atop each other in a sudden flurry, like competing wrestlers.

The last of my sparks turned to embers, cooled by weariness if not by peace of mind.

"Oh, Bella." The words were as light as moth wings on my lips. Already my eyelids were drifting, opening wide when I thought of Nico being suspected of murder, and then drifting once more. It was only three in the afternoon. Strange, it felt like the deepest vault of night. I wondered how long it would take the DA's office to set its goons on Nico's tail. I was afraid that if I slept too long, I'd wake up to find my friend's husband the prime suspect in her murder.

We'll see.

Usually it's my mother's voice that comes to me when I pause

The Tongue Merchant

and listen to my soul. But it wasn't *mi mama* I heard this time, but Kyle Straker. From what I knew of homicide investigations, which went no further than television renditions and the occasional novel whenever I stole a little time to read, the police would have to be fairly certain of at least three things before drawing any conclusions about a suspect: motive, means, and opportunity. And surely Nico had no motive. From what I knew of Nico and Bella's ramshackle relationship, they seemed to be past the point of rescue but certainly not at each other's throats.

I cringed into my pillow. *At each other's throats.* That certainly wasn't the best turn of phrase, considering the circumstances of Bella's death.

So Nico had no reason to commit murder, as far as I could see. As for means and opportunity, those were concepts too intricate to be explored in my current condition. Maybe when I woke up my compass would stop spinning. The last solid thought I had before slipping into the welcome vapor of sleep was far from comforting: *But whoever it was that killed her—Nico or someone else—why, dear God, did the bastards cut out her tongue?*

That damned dream again.

I awoke with a shudder, shaking myself to my senses just before the doctor of my nightmare sealed me up in a full body cast, sans breathing holes. About once a month my dream-self suffocated, and I'd jolt awake wearing a wetsuit of sweat.

I leaned on my elbows, thinking about my Secret Saboteur.

Tomorrow afternoon I had an appointment back in San Juan with my doctor and sole conspirator. Dr. Avundavi was a civilian. No one other than God knew I was seeing her. Not the Guard, not my father, not Kevin Maddox, nobody. Nor did they know of the Secret Saboteur which had said hello to me one morning from the softness of my left breast.

"Easy now," I said to myself, aware of the nervous fluttering in my throat. There were few things in life that truly frightened me; I was the daughter of a freedom fighter and had inherited a certain grittiness that scoured away the usual fears and anxieties. But there were some worries, cancer principal among them, that couldn't be rubbed away. Dr. Janice Avundavi was a breast-cancer specialist and as discreet as they came. If the Guard ever found out about my condition . . .

I wiped away thoughts of tomorrow's appointment with a full-force memory of Isabella.

The more I considered it, the more I knew that Nico was in trouble, and the angrier I became at whoever had so violated my friend. They had killed and mutilated her, and heaven knew what else that Straker wasn't telling me. Had she been raped? Robbed? Who the hell could've done such a thing . . . and why? *Why?*

The sour taste in my mouth was so bitter that I got up and dashed to the head so I could hack the phlegm into the stainless-steel sink. My knees felt made of cork, as if at any moment they'd pop from the pressure and send me toppling.

"Steady as she goes," I admonished myself, clutching the rim of the sink.

Bad advice, gatita. *Keeping it steady doesn't always dry the tears.*

Maybe not. But that was the infamous Alejandra for you. Never one to let crying get in the way of justice. Which reminded me of a verse from the Guard anthem, "Semper Paratus."

From Barrow's shores to Paraguay
Great Lakes' or Ocean's wave,
The Coast Guard fights through storms and winds
To punish or to save.

That last line kept whispering at me, sometimes in my mother's voice, sometimes in my own. But for the most part it was Bella's voice I heard, talking in that wonderful, foggy way of hers, burning away the last vestiges of sleep and keeping the

The Tongue Merchant

anger at a good boil in my belly.

I checked my watch. 5:15.

I still had fourteen hours until shore liberty ended and the *Sentinel* departed for base. The ship meteorologists were tracking a tropical depression off the coast of Antigua, 180 miles southeast of St. Noré. Maddox was under orders to return the cutter to San Juan before the system turned into a storm. Fourteen hours, then, to track down Nico and find out who the hell Isabella was involved with that might have wanted her dead.

As crazy as that sounded.

Crazy or not, the clock wasn't waiting around for me to lace up the stitches of my resolve. So as sagging as it was, I was going to have to get moving. It was either that or let Nico go down for something that I wasn't about to believe he'd done.

I'd stowed my Beretta in small-arms storage, which was probably for the best. In my current state, I couldn't be responsible for what happened if I ran into Bella's killers. I braved the clutter of my locker to find the uniform we call our tropical blue long. An authorized liberty uniform, tropical blue is a lot snazzier than our working blue, with navy slacks and a short-sleeved white shirt with epaulets. I've always liked the way I looked in these duds. Give me a smart-edged uniform over a dress and heels any day. I'd never really been fond of the hat, but I guess you can't have everything.

I skinned out of my jumpsuit and grabbed the pants.

Technically we're not permitted to be in uniform unless we know that the Guard approves of the actions we're taking while wearing it, but I didn't think they'd mind if I wore official colors while sniffing around for my friend's murderer. After all, I was only upholding our creed: to punish or to save.

Right now, punishment was all I had in mind.

St. Noré was not my home.

I lived fifty miles away on the palm-dappled island of Puerto Rico, which sometimes felt like the nexus for every cruise ship, treasure-hunter, deep-sea fisher, and honeymooning couple in the western hemisphere. The sunshine was so constant in these parts that it had faded my memory of snow. The last time I saw a snowflake, I was a cadet at the Academy in Connecticut.

As my apartment was back in San Juan, I had no means of ready transportation in Hozumkur. I owned a 1962 Lincoln Continental. A convertible with suicide doors. Dad had rebuilt the car and surprised me with it when I graduated from the Academy. Right now I would've given my next paycheck to be sitting behind the Linc's leather-wrapped steering wheel, because I always felt *centered* there, and centered was a feeling that currently eluded me.

"Taxi!"

The cab was a shiny new Volvo with an open sunroof, painted octopus pink. Technically it was a *público*, or a shared taxi. The driver must have been ninety years old. He wore a straw hat and a Hawaiian shirt that looked like the veteran of several dozen hardcore luaus.

He smiled crookedly at me in the mirror. "Destination, please?"

"Downtown, I guess."

"Shopping center?"

"No, nothing like that. I don't want to go to the mall." Not that I knew *where* I wanted to go, exactly, or where to begin. Odds were that Nico hadn't returned to his flat, but was being consoled somewhere by the woman in the hip-hugging skirt. As far as I knew, Isabella had remained in their old house during the separation, but I was pretty certain that the cops would still be picking at the place like aardvarks at an anthill, so I wasn't about to go there. Later, perhaps.

Of course, where I really wanted to go was back to the *Lynn*.

Though I had no desire to revisit the horror I'd found in the master stateroom, something compelled me to return, look around, maybe see something vital that I'd missed. But the cops would never let me inside, and I wasn't about to cross the legal line just to follow a half-brewed hunch.

"Destination, please?" the cabbie said again.

Then inspiration struck. I considered it only for a moment before I decided that I had no better option. "Take me to Lionese Avenue, in the Artisan's Quarter. And hurry."

The sun was turning to butter on the hotplate of the western horizon, and I wanted to find Saul before dark, because Hozumkur transformed with the coming of night like a thirsty vampire rising up from a casket. There was a local legend about the *jipia*, spirits of the dead that walked the night and stole fruit from kitchen tables. A favorite pastime of the college kids here on summer vacation was to dress up in fantastical *caret-as* masks and run around drinking, vandalizing and fornicating in the name of the *jipia*. I had no desire to be without a guide when the freak show began.

Besides, I hadn't seen Saul Tunlunder in what my father would have called a coon's age. Saul was a professional potter who specialized in salt-glazed stoneware, purveying his crafts on the Antilles tourist circuit and making enough to keep himself in Bavarian chocolate bars and bottled water drawn from melted Swiss snow, both being delicacies he personally imported in bulk. Saul owned a studio—or *bottega*, as he called it—in the heart of the city's bohemian Artisan's Quarter.

I bounced around in the backseat of the cab, aware of the sprightly polka on the radio but not hearing it, noticing the hustle of city life around me but not seeing it. Between Bella's death, my possible medical crisis, and my splintering relationship with Kevin Maddox, I had more than enough fodder for thought. We passed streetside merchants hawking kingfish and

British tabloids, pauper mariachi bands playing for coins, and even a troupe of mimes dressed as matadors and fighting invisible bulls, but nothing shook me from my trance until the cab lurched to a stop at the bottom of a small hill on the corner of Lionese and Conquistador. The depression in the street served as a natural tributary for a constant gurgle of waste water that trickled into the gutter. It seemed innocuous enough, at the time.

The driver punched the meter and read off my fare.

I flipped through the small mess in my pocketbook, tipped him enough that I didn't feel like a total jerk, adjusted my hat—my *cover*, as we say in the military—and stepped out onto the darkening street.

At least, it would have been darkening, if not for the antique lanterns and modern sodium-vapor lights flickering to life around me. A string of blue and green bulbs hung from the portico of a watchmaker's shop. A line of bronze torches illuminated the sidewalk in front of a bookbindery. Women in halter tops and men in polo shirts wended rather aimlessly down the streets, passing in and out of bars and trendy discotheques, all of them nameless, faceless, made different only by the variety of their colognes. Jazz music as rich as brown sugar sprinkled itself down the avenue.

I slipped between the bronze torches and headed for the *bottega*.

Saul's studio was housed within an unassuming building of freshly painted brick, the sign out front carved by hand from a single section of teak. Saul once told me that teak and greenheart were two woods often used in wharf construction, as they were more resistant to weather and those nasty little marine borers which dissolved lesser woods. Saul had paid a bundle for the sign. He probably imported that, too.

Two men were standing beneath the sign when I approached.

The bigger of the two had his thick finger pointed in the face of the smaller, who was gesticulating defensively and looked about two seconds away from bolting. The shorter man wore camouflage pants and had half a dozen turquoise rings in each ear. A pair of headphones hung listlessly around his neck.

". . . a worthless slice of squidshit is what you are!" the giant was railing as I drew near. "Something that floats to the surface and contributes absolutely *nada* to the ecosystem. Even the single-celled *dung-eaters* don't touch that stuff."

"But it was an accident!"

"Your conception was an accident. Somebody should've mentioned to your mother the sundry benefits of partial-birth abortion."

"Take it out of my pay!" The little man's voice became a falsetto of panic. "Please, for the love of Mary and the saints, I need this job . . ."

"A quick blitz to the teeth is what you need. Or a back-alley lobotomy. Now get lost."

"Please, boss . . ."

"Get out of my face before I feed you your own eyelids!"

"Hey, Saul," I said, stopping a few feet away from him. "Bad day?"

Upon hearing my voice, the look on the big man's face turned into one that Zeus might have worn had someone filched his last lightning bolt when he was looking to hurl one.

"Zo?"

I couldn't help but smile, in spite of the many tribulations that made smiling an effort. Saul's expression was simply too much. "You keep going on like that, they're going to have to use a seismograph to measure your stress level. Should I keep a lookout for potential witnesses while you finish dismantling this poor guy?"

"Who? This sack of eel guts?" Saul glanced at the man in

question. "Naw, Zo, we're cool. Corky and I here were just discussing a few of the problems with today's younger generation. Weren't we, Corkster?"

"Yeah, boss. Sure."

"And Corky agreed, sycophantic little piss-licker that he is, that if he doesn't stay off the smack while he's on the job, first I'm going to rearrange his bowels with my size-fourteen, custom-made, ostrich-skin boots, and second, I'm going to call the cops and testify against him the first chance they give me. Isn't that right, Mr. Cork?"

"Something like that," Corky muttered.

"You better listen to him," I advised Corky. "I've seen him work. The only things he sculpts better than clay are the faces of those unfortunate few who incur his wrath. But other than that, he's a real teddy bear." Which was certainly true. Though he'd never admit it, Saul had a soft spot for street urchins, and he'd give just about anybody the chance to make something of themselves. Keep dumping on him, however, and you couldn't make a more fearsome enemy if you slighted a Mafia don on his daughter's wedding day.

Corky peeked up at Saul like a dog expecting to get kicked.

"You hear what the lieutenant said?" Saul asked him, the plowshare of his voice digging a furrow through the otherwise tranquil air.

"Yeah, boss." He nodded ardently. "I heard it all. And I promise I won't screw up again, I totally promise, for Chrissakes . . ."

"And don't take the Lord's name in vain!" Saul planted his hands on his hips. "Now get back to that garbage hole you call a home, sleep off the dope, and be here not one damn second past eight in the morning. *Go!*"

Corky stumbled back, spun, said another thank you, and hurtled down the street.

The Tongue Merchant

Saul turned to me and grinned like a kid. "Sure is good to see you, Zo."

"Ditto," I said, and then I was being enfolded in his arms, my face against the slalom of his chest. Saul's passion was art. His hobby was bodybuilding. His hair was cut close to the scalp of his planet-shaped head, his cheeks smooth and a little red. I'd always thought that he seemed elemental, as if the collar of his T-shirt were the caldera of a volcano, with a mountain below it and everything above it fire and wrath.

He was positively the most unlikely potter this side of the equator.

"You okay?" he asked, holding me at arm's length.

"The truth?"

"Always."

"Isabella Murillo is dead."

Though the softness in his eyes didn't change and his fingers remained light on my shoulders, his shovel-shaped jaw hardened appreciably. He stood there without knowing what to say.

"She was murdered. Last night, or early this morning. I found her in her boat. *Me*. I walked in on her and found her . . . lying there like somebody's doll they'd forgotten to put away before going to bed. *I stepped in her blood, Saul*. She had it on her lips, her chin, so much . . . so much I don't know where it came from. And the cops think Nico did it but I'm not so convinced, and by now they're probably halfway to getting a warrant to search his house and maybe arrest him, and here I am trying to hold myself together long enough to find out what's going on. So there. You could say it's been a goddamn awful day." I winced as soon as the word left my mouth. "Sorry."

Saul didn't move. Mountain ranges eroded with more alacrity.

"Say something, please."

Finally he gathered a cavernous breath and let it stream slowly through his nostrils. "Does Nico know she's dead?"

I nodded.

"Where is he now?"

I shrugged.

"The pigs are after him?"

"Not yet. But soon, I think."

"But you don't think he did it."

I shook my head. Suddenly I didn't feel capable of speech.

"He can be a real dickhead sometimes," Saul allowed.

I silently agreed.

"But he didn't necessarily off his wife just on general account of his dickheadedness."

"Sugarcane," I said simply.

"Huh?"

Swallowing the pellet in my throat, I tried again. "Bella's father. Ernesto de Casals. He passed away a couple of years ago, but his estate, De Casals International, owns half the sugar industry in Puerto Rico. Plus that big resort hotel in San Juan. The board of directors is acting as regent for his company, but Bella inherits when she turns twenty-five." Or was that twenty-six? I couldn't quite remember. I knew she was almost six years my junior—the big three-oh was looming over my head like the sword of Damocles—but I'd lost track of when her inheritance came due.

"So what's your point?" Saul asked.

"I'm not sure. But as long as Bella and Nico were still married, which they were, then Nico would get everything if she died. I just realized that on the ride over here. I guess a multimillion-dollar corporation is a pretty strong motive in the eyes of the police, isn't it?"

But Saul was shaking his head. "You're forgetting something, Zo." He motioned toward the *bottega*. "We'll talk about it in a minute. It's getting dark. You want to come inside? I make a bastard of an espresso."

"There's no time. Now what is it that I'm forgetting?"

"Abdías de Casals. Isabella's little pill-popping, slut-jumping, rat's ass of a brother. Kid spends his dead daddy's *dinero* faster than you can row those skinny little racing boats. And I've seen you row. I'm not certain, but I bet Abdías gets the cash upon his sister's death. Not Geeko Nico. Though neither one of the scumbags deserves it."

I spent a few moments digesting this latest bit of information. I'd never met Abdías, but Bella had mentioned him, and the picture I'd constructed was one involving rowdy Latino music, societal soirees, polo matches, and the occasional dance with the darker side of Hozumkur. I wondered if Sergeant Straker knew about Isabella's little brother.

"You going to tell the pigs about Abdías?" Saul asked, practicing a bit of potter's ESP.

Well, was I?

I only vacillated a few seconds before the inherent avenger in me grabbed the wheel. "No. Not yet. I think I want to talk with him myself. Do you have any idea where to find him?"

"Maybe. I don't know. You conscripting me into some kind of shady undertaking?"

"Yeah. I think that I am. You up for it?"

He sighed again. "I really liked Isabella. She was a good woman."

"You do have a car, don't you?"

Saul smiled. The growing shadows made his cheekbones look like plateaus. "Let me lock up the shop. I'll meet you around back. Lieutenant." He saluted me with a snap of his heels, then hurried into the studio, bawling out orders to his staff even as the door was swinging shut behind him.

Which left me alone with Bella's ghost and a fistful of new suspicions.

As I made my way down the boardwalk beside the studio, I

uncurled my fingers and used them to enumerate what I'd learned. One: Bella had been killed, either at sea or set adrift that way, which put the killer at the marina and potentially in sight of witnesses. Two: considering her father's empire, money was the most likely motive for murdering her. Three: the police would consider Nico as their first suspect, at least until he provided a suitable alibi, which remained to be seen. Four: her *hermano,* Abdías de Casals, was a known ne'er-do-well and the possible benefactor of her death. And finally, five:

What the hell was five?

Oh, right. Five: in exactly twelve hours and forty minutes, I would have to return to the *Sentinel* and leave Bella's ghost in the care of Straker and his cohorts. And as long as I was counting black tidings then I could also throw in the Secret Saboteur, not to mention the brewing storm front, which considering the inertia of my bad luck, would surely beat itself into a hurricane by week's end and probably flatten my apartment, total my car, and ruin my best pair of shoes.

Saul came jogging my way, buttoning down the cuffs of a white silk shirt, then tucking the tails into a pair of Versace pants. "Fancy meeting you here," he said as we converged on his car, a black, heart-wrenching Dodge Viper. The license plate read POT GOD.

"Nice ride."

"Art pays."

He unlocked the doors electronically, and two minutes later he was turning on the headlights and we were cruising down Lionese, the stars unseen behind all the colored strobes and streetlamps. Saul touched the CD player, and I was more than a little surprised when the voice of Mel Tormé filled the car. Saul didn't seem like the type. Aerosmith, sure. But Tormé didn't seem tough enough.

"So I was thinking," Saul said, one hand on the wheel, the

other enveloping the gearshift. "Maybe Abdías really did it, he honestly killed his sister. The sick little cock-knocker. Maybe he broke into her boat, because he probably had a key, being her brother and all. That would've made it easy. And of course poor Isabella wouldn't have heard him sneaking around, being deaf, you know? So he does it. He kills her. For the money. Because his lifestyle is too fast to wait for big sis to dole out an allowance from their daddy's till. But he's not worried about an alibi because not only does he have enough lowlife friends who'll lie for him, but he's also got enough highbrow friends who'll pull the strings to keep him in the clear." Saul pondered this theory for a full minute, nodded to himself in resolution, then turned to me. "So what do you think?"

I stared at him. "You listen to Mel Tormé?"

"Skip it, Zo."

"You surprise me, Saul. Macho, bruising guy like you, I never would have thought you a Tormé fan. Barry Manilow, maybe. Or Wayne Newton . . ."

"You're cruising for a fat lip," he warned.

"Wonder what all the beefeaters down at the gym would say if they knew the truth." I struck a contemplative pose. "Saul Tunlunder, man among men, secret Tormé groupie."

"First of all, there's nothing wrong with me liking Tormé. Secondly, you can always get out and walk." He tried to grind me to the mortar of my seat with the pestle of his eyes, but my impregnable smirk was too much for him. He attempted to swallow his grin, failed miserably, and ended up winking at me and shaking his head. "You tell anybody, I'll break your legs."

"May the carrion crows eat my eyeballs if I talk." I traced a cross over my heart.

"Yeah," he said, his grin morphing into a full-fledged smile. "*Viva la* crows."

We both laughed, and spent the rest of the drive pretending the world was okay.

Chapter Four

So this part of town could have been London.

Or Tokyo, or Istanbul, or any other exotic place I'd never seen yet always imagined to be populated by people far classier, loftier, smarter, and snobbier than me.

Snobbier than "I," gatita, is the correct usage.

Yeah. Snobbier than I. Proper grammar and how to field strip a .45. These are the various etiquettes my mother taught me.

"Welcome to swank city," Saul said, turning down a crushed-pebble driveway between a pair of sweeping plum trees. "This is how the other half lives, Zo. Got their silver spoons so far up their assholes they could use them to stir their tonsils."

"Have you been here before?"

"Not by choice, I assure you. I've got a friend, Marcus, he's a bouncer down at the Cubano Club, does a little freelancing at some of the rowdier local shindigs. His partner was out of commission one night, so I did him a favor by helping out at the door, keeping the slugs from mingling with the starlings."

"Here at Abdías's house?"

"Yep. Scrawny shitheel was so whacked on blow that night that he almost let a woman asphyxiate in his swimming pool."

"I take it you're not fond of him."

"Guy's a pimple on the buttcheek of humanity."

"Well, at least you're giving him the benefit of the doubt." I peered out the window as the Viper eased around the circle drive, watching the last pink mouth of clouds get smothered by the black pillow of night. The security lights had already come alive around the perimeter of the property, revealing a two-story, turreted home built to resemble an *alcázar,* or Spanish fortress. Ivy climbed the stone walls. Masterfully pruned topiary adorned the grounds. In the high center of the house's facade was a giant compass window, lit from behind by a live flame.

"What a dump," Saul decreed.

"Shanty," I concurred.

"Hovel," he said, shutting off the engine and hauling himself out.

"Shack." I got out and smoothed the wrinkles from my slacks.

"Izba," Saul said.

I matched his stride as he made his way under a vine-covered archway toward the front door. "What the hell's an izba?"

"A traditional Russian log hut."

"Oh. I didn't know you were so well read."

"I don't read, Zo. I sculpt. Reading is for people who don't have anything better to do with their time, one notch up from watching TV. But one of my patrons is from St. Petersburg. He made a million bucks Westernizing his city when the Sovs got kicked out. But he used to be poor. Said he lived in an izba. And so, like you, I asked what the hell an izba was."

"Glad to know I'm not the only one ignorant of Russian peasant architecture." I rapped on the center of the door. Even as I stood there, waiting, I pictured Bella with her neckline clotted in a choker of blood. Perhaps the man who did that to her was somewhere behind this door. Or maybe I'd already passed him on the street. Perhaps I'd seen his face and hadn't recognized him for what he was. He could be anyone, anywhere, and I was glad to feel that my anger was a full three strides in front of my fear.

To punish or to save. It was becoming my mantra.

The Tongue Merchant

I heard elegant music from inside the house. Bach, maybe, or Mozart. I wasn't really good at all with the classics. But just to get a rise out of Saul, and to keep myself from thinking about—

—*the victim*—

—my friend, I said, "Now there's some true music for you. Real Carnegie Hall kind of stuff. Beats Mel Tormé anyday."

"Mel Tormé kicks ass."

"Saul, it's with reasonable certainty that I can say that no one else on earth has ever before uttered those words."

"You'd be surprised."

"I would? What, is there some fringe cult skulking around on the Internet, holding symposiums on Tormé's prowess as an international ass-kicker?"

"Zo." His voice was like the undertow of the sea. "If you promise to drop the wisecracks, I swear to dance at your wedding. Naked."

"If you're waiting for my wedding to learn how to dance, you may be doing the foxtrot in a nursing home with a woman with blue hair."

"Why's that? Captain Nemo not doing it for you anymore?"

"Let's just say we're not exactly scorching the pavement on our way to the chapel."

"Dumb wave-jockey doesn't know what he's got."

"No comment."

"I ought to tie an anchor to his ass and drown some sense into him."

I was just about to offer the use of several anchors I knew of, when the door pulled open, and there he was. Abdías. I knew him on sight. He wore his hair in a decidedly feminine style called a coquette bob, which I suppose was the latest statement in the language of urban fashion, a tongue in which I was hardly fluent. The ends of his black hair were curled toward his unblemished face, his bangs cut straight across his forehead, framing his intense Hispanic features. Like most natives of the Puerto Rican region, Abdías was of creole descent, predominantly Spanish with several dollops of African, Native American, and western European blood mingling in his veins. His lavender shirt, almost diaphanous, was open at the throat, with a wide linen collar with a scalloped edge. I think it was called a Vandyke. My brother Micah could've told me; he's a model in Miami, and though he prefers casual khakis and loafers, he's obligated to keep up with all matters sartorial.

"*¿Sí, quiere algo?*" Abdías asked formally, looking first at my uniform and then fixing on Saul.

Saul deferred to me. His Spanish had always been spotty.

"*¿Habla usted inglés?*" I inquired, for Saul's benefit.

"That depends," Abdías said, shifting linguistic gears. "You two in the Marines or something?" His eyes went from my lieutenant's bars to Saul's jarhead haircut.

"My name is Marcella Paraizo. I'm with the United States Coast Guard. This is my friend, Saul Tunlunder. I assume you're Abdías de Casals."

His eyes narrowed defensively, although his girlish hairdo only made his expression look comical. "Paraizo, huh? I've heard of you." He cocked his head slightly to the left, causing his pixie tresses to jiggle. He wore a platinum chain around his neck. "Isabella has a friend in the Guard. That you?"

"Yes. I don't believe you and I met at her wedding."

"I wasn't there." From behind him came the strains of a long-dead composer, the flickering of candlelight, and the sounds of dinner guests clinking their cocktail glasses. "So what's this all about?"

I felt my pulse beginning to pick up the pace in my wrist. *What, indeed?* I reminded myself that I had no authority to pursue this amateur investigation, and if I wasn't careful then I was liable to draw the wrath of the very person I sought to unmask. If there was any chance at all that a murderer was standing here before me, I was about to put myself in the crosshairs. My father, a cop to the marrow of his bones, would have counseled me to leave everything up to the police. My mother would have agreed with him and given me a thumbs-up behind his back.

But I couldn't just stand there. I had to speak up. I was just about to wade in, slow and easy, with the speech I'd quietly rehearsed, when Saul blurted, "Your sister's dead."

I winced, held my breath, waited.

Abdías's slender mouth twitched. It was a funny little motion, as if he were a man made of wood, his lips tweaked by a puppeteer's wire. And then an odd thing happened. His chin dropped in slow motion, the corners of his mouth eventually turning down in a grimace of disbelief. But for a moment while his face was in transition, I could've sworn that he was about to smile.

Fifteen minutes later, I was seated beside him on a heavily stuffed Chesterfield sofa, while he dabbed his eyes with a monogrammed handkerchief and his guests stood around with drinks in their hands and stunned looks painted on their faces.

"Murdered . . ." he whispered.

My body was angled toward his, my knees together, hands clasped securely in front of me. I'd taken off my hat. It rested beside me. My hair was pulled back in a bun tight enough to give me the beginnings of a headache. Though my instinct was to take account of the house and its current occupants, I forced myself to attend to Abdías's grief.

"I wish there were more I could tell you," I said, honestly enough. "But the police have just begun to gather the evidence, and they're not about to let me in on anything. I know that doesn't help at all, but . . ."

"And who, pray tell, is the detective in charge of the operation?" someone interrupted.

I looked up. The speaker was a middle-aged man who might have been the captain of a nineteenth-century whaling ship. He was wide through the chest—that part of him we sailors called his *beam*—with heavy gray muttonchops and a pocketwatch chain that gleamed from his belt to his plaid vest. His cheeks were reddened as if by a lifetime of exposure to salt and wind, but there was a solidity about him that assured me that he was no man of the sea; mariners learn to celebrate the impermanent, like the ever-changing caprice of the ocean. This man was all bedrock and immutability.

"Who are you?" I demanded of him, with a little heat. I guess it was that don't-talk-to-strangers mentality, warning me not to disclose any information without a good reason. "We haven't met."

Saul interceded. "He's all right, Zo. This is the honorable Cicero Horne, federal circuit court judge. Your honor, this is Marcella Paraizo, future admiral of the U.S. Coast Guard."

"Pleased to meet you," I said with a slight nod of the head. I'm courteous when I have to be. But I have my limits.

Horne held an empty snifter, which he used as a baton to guide his words through the air. "The pleasure is entirely mine, Ms. Paraizo. Now, as I've yet to hear anything about this most dreadful event you just described, I assume that it occurred only a short time ago."

I wasn't certain if that was a question or not, but I nodded anyway. "This morning. Our cutter was called to investigate a derelict craft. We found . . . we found Isabella inside. I don't believe the police have released her name to the media yet."

"Vexatious," Horne said.

I wasn't sure how to respond to that, so I didn't.

"And the detective in charge?"

The Tongue Merchant

"His name is Straker. Kyle. I spoke with him this morning."

"Ah. Straker, is it? I've had the pleasure of making young Straker's acquaintance. Seems a straight enough fellow. A bit more astute than many in his department. College lad, I'm sure." Judge Horne stood there glowering, now less like a ship's captain and more like a lighthouse, blazing his eyes at me as if trying to penetrate an everlasting fog to locate something hidden in the mists.

"Who did this?" Abdías whimpered beside me. "Who did this to my Isabella? What kind of monster . . . ?" His head dropped closer to his knees.

I dared to put a hand on his leg. His skin was hot beneath his leather pants.

"That's what I'd like to know," said a new voice. "Just who in the world could commit such an atrocity?"

My eyes went from Horne to the man beside him. He wore a smoking jacket and glasses with tortoise-shell rims. There are certain species of turtles around these waters that are on the endangered list, and I wondered if this man was one of those who bought endangered-animal products just because his wallet said he could. He was the judge's age, but leaner, *hungrier,* with a daredevil's face that probably served him well in the bedroom. "My name is Robert Castigere. I do a little stock trading for Abby here. Delighted to meet you." He extended his left hand, as his right was set in a fiberglass cast.

I smiled tightly and shook without standing up. Castigere offered similar sentiments to Saul, then turned his attention back to me. "This Straker fellow have any leads yet, madam?"

"He didn't say."

"I don't suppose he would."

"Cops are funny like that," I said.

"And they sent you to inform the family?"

"No. I came here on my own. Isabella was my friend, and I

guess I wanted Abdías to hear it from someone who cared about her."

"*Who goddamn did this?*" Abdías looked directly at me, his face streaked with moisture. "Isabella never hurt anyone, *anyone*, so you tell me why someone would kill her. Tell me why they would do such a thing to my sister. *You tell me.*"

"Maybe we should go somewhere and talk," I suggested. I certainly wouldn't be able to question him in front of his guests, and I was growing more uncomfortable under their collective scrutiny the longer I sat there. "Can we go outside for awhile? I for one could use a bit of fresh air."

Abdías nodded several times, and while he was rising shakily to his feet, I took advantage of the passing seconds to take note of the remaining three people in the room. First there was an older gentleman Abdías had called Pablo, a servant or butler or some kind of thing, with a sun-wrinkled forehead like that of a lifelong farmer, and a smileless face. Next there was Castigere's companion, a woman with skin so rich and mocha-dark that she probably could have been on the cover of a magazine. She wore a red taffeta dress that covered her down to her ankles, but her arms were left bare: objects of envy to those of us with less-than-perfect complexions and muscle tones. I'd heard the men refer to her as Evangelina. Finally, keeping to himself and evidently oblivious to the goings-on around him, a worker in a sleeveless shirt was replacing a windowpane in the French doors which opened from the parlor onto the patio beyond. He wore a pocketed belt for his glazier's tools. He'd swept a pile of jagged glass to the side of the doors. I wondered about the accident that had broken the window.

"Please." Abdías tottered at my side. "I need a drink."

"Here, take mine," Evangelina said in a voice as luxuriant as her black skin. She handed over her brandy, then pulled Abdías into a chaste hug. "This too shall pass, Abby." Her accent was distinctly Haitian. "The Lord promises as much, does He not?"

Abdías didn't reply. He'd gulped down most of the brandy by the time we passed through the French doors.

"I have to warn you of something," I said, finding myself surrounded by sculpted topiary and Greek-style statues of naked athletes. We walked to the balcony, well away from the room where the guests were no doubt whispering about my dead friend.

"And what would that be?"

"The police are going to ask you to account for your whereabouts around midnight last night. Can you do that?"

"Are you asking for my alibi?"

I met his gaze. The moisture had cleared from his eyes. "Do you have one?"

He was silent for a moment. Then a puzzling grin twisted his lips. "Lady destiny is a fickle bitch sometimes, isn't she?"

That wasn't the reaction I was expecting. "Is that what you're going to tell Sergeant Straker when he asks you where you were at the time of Bella's death?"

"It's not like I can tell him the truth, now can I?" He drained the last of his brandy, then smacked his lips.

"So what's the truth?"

"The truth, Ms. Paraizo, is that adultery isn't much of a sin compared to murder, but having another man's wife vouch for me wouldn't be in my best interests right now."

"Evangelina," I guessed.

We were leaning on the balcony, which overlooked a lighted Shinto garden below the patio. Abdías had unbuttoned his shirt down to his navel and rolled up the sleeves; anything to fight the humid night air. His chest was flat and hairless. He braced himself on the railing and looked down at the artful assembly of stones.

"Castigere will ruin me," he sighed.

Though I felt the perspiration beginning to form along my neck and lower back, I didn't have the luxury of unbuttoning or rolling. One of the rules of wearing a uniform. Promising myself a cool shower, I ignored my discomfort and asked, "Would you like to tell me about it?"

"Not especially."

"Better me than HPD."

Abdías snorted. "Isn't that the truth." He wiped his nose and inhaled noisily. "I hosted a dinner party this evening. About twenty people or so. Just a few friends enjoying a summer evening. Judge Horne, Castigere, and Eva were just saying goodnight when you came calling. Castigere is my accountant. Sort of my business partner too, in a sense. And he manages my portfolio, such as it is. I have a tendency to overextend my resources, if you know what I mean."

I thought about his father's estate and wondered if he was thinking the same.

"Anyway, Castigere and Eva showed up a little after five. I was here by myself until the first of the guests arrived, except for Pablo, of course. Good old dependable Pablo. He can verify me from about seven this morning, when he came to my room to wake me up."

"Pablo wakes you up in the morning?"

"I despise clocks. Every time I turn around, one of them is telling me I'm late for something important. I will never set an alarm, so Pablo rouses me whenever he feels it's appropriate, which is usually around seven." He parted his hair with his hands and glanced over at me. "Did she die badly?"

Immediately I envisioned the blood and the sprawled state of her legs and the bruise on her face the size of a tea saucer and—

"It wasn't easy," I said quietly.

The Tongue Merchant

Abdías closed his eyes, leaned his elbows on the balcony, and hung his head.

"Was Evangelina with you when Pablo came to your room?" I asked.

"Good God, no. I'm not quite so *estúpido* as that. But I'd only been back for a couple of hours. I parked the Beemer in the garage and came in the house from there, in the back. I'd been at her house at Russet Beach all night. Only the two of us. So she's the only witness I've got."

"And Castigere?"

"Out playing poker or screwing American college girls or some such shit. Neglecting Eva, as usual. They own a condo south of the marina. Bobby Castigere and his rich asshole friends hang out at their yacht club, the Rime & Reel, shooting snooker and telling the hookers they're all Hollywood producers."

As he spoke, I peered over his shoulder at the house. Every now and then I could see Saul looming before the window, keeping watch over me like a muscle-bound guardian angel. The repairman at the French doors was in the process of weatherproofing the new glass with a tube of sealant.

"And just last night," he went on, "I was telling Eva about Isabella, and how they'd make great friends. They could go shopping together, sailing . . ." He snorted again. "But now I'll never have the chance to introduce them."

I decided to change tack, hoping that if I trolled the waters long enough, I'd come across a piece of information-flotsam worth all this trouble. "Do you sail, Abdías?"

"Not much. I do a little windsurfing. Why do you ask?"

"When was the last time you were aboard the *Lady Lynn Rob*?"

"Isabella's yacht? Probably a month ago." He thought about it for a second or two, then nodded. "Yeah, just about four weeks, actually. To be brutally honest, Ms. Paraizo, I needed some quick cash, and it was a Sunday night and the banks weren't about to open their doors for me when everyone on the island was at evening Mass. Isabella wasn't home when I went looking for her. I found her down at the pier. She loved that damn boat."

So score one for Saul. He'd been right about Abdías frittering away his allowance and leeching off Bella, which didn't make him a killer, but give me an M and I'll spell you *motive*. Maybe Nico wasn't the only one who might have wanted Bella out of the way to make room for her bank account.

So I decided it wouldn't hurt anything to bring up the idea of the money. Heaven knew the cops would get around to it quickly enough. Letting my eyes linger on the repairman's sinewed shoulders, I said, "Rumor has it that you stand to inherit your father's wealth in the event of your sister's death."

He carefully examined his fingernails. "People talk too much."

"Is it true?"

"What's true, Ms. Paraizo, is that I'd rather have Isabella back than all the gold in the goddamn Caribbean. Maybe next time you talk to God, you can mention to Him that He can have all the money if He just sends my sister back. I'll give my father's estate to the Pope, if that's what it takes . . ."

His voice faded away on that last word, and I didn't know what else to do but let him weep in silence. I've never been very good at human interaction. Aside from the tears I shed this morning, I hadn't cried since they put my mother's box in the ground, which sometimes seemed so far away that it might have happened in a past life.

"It's just so . . . unfair," he said. "Isabella, she never did anything to hurt anyone, or at least I thought she hadn't. But you never can tell, huh? She must have pissed someone off really badly." His delicate fingers were bunched into fists. "They had better not take their time finding out who did this. Those damn incompetent cops. I swear to God I'll ride their ass until they do."

"You say she never hurt anyone."

"Never. Not Isabella. She was a saint, for God's sake."

"So let's pretend for a moment that she did. Who would it be?"

His head dipped even lower. In the darkness his hair was so black it was almost blue. "I really don't know. Other than her and Nico doing their usual twelve-round heavyweight fights, there wasn't much going on in her life. She was just shopping and sailing and waiting for the old man's fortune to drop in her lap. I guess she'd met somebody new, which was a pretty dumb mess to be getting herself into since she was still attached to Nico. But I have absolutely zero room to nag her on that subject, huh?" When he smiled, his teeth were as white as seashells. There wasn't an ounce of mirth in his grin. "But live and learn, right?"

"Isabella had a lover?" That shocked me. I knew that Nico had done his share of sleeping around, but I hadn't thought Bella capable of even *looking* at another man as long as she was still married to Nick the Dick, as we'd dubbed him one night after too much *cañita,* our favorite bootleg rum. Maybe I was naive to think so, but I always considered Bella . . . well, *better* than that. "Are you certain she was seeing someone?"

"Seeing, dating, screwing . . . she was doing something. It was none of my business. Anyway, maybe she'd made an enemy of someone on the board of directors. The senior stockholders are in control of our father's assets until Isabella's next birthday. Maybe one of those pricks knows something about what happened to her."

"Have anyone particular in mind?"

"No. Sorry."

"Come on, Abdías. Give me something to go on here."

"Why should I?"

"Fine. Keep it to yourself. Or tell it to the cops when they come and ask for your alibi. I'm sure they'll be more than happy to ask Evangelina to corroborate your story, and maybe you'll be really lucky and her husband won't be home when they come knocking."

He brooded on that for a minute, then said simply, "Rotto."

"Pardon?"

"Joe Rotto. He and Alonzo Serca are the two directors who always seem to vote against the other three. Rotto has this screwed-up idea about selling off parts of the sugarcane line and using the money to build an oil-shipping trade, which is like . . . how do you say it? Not dancing with the one who brought you to the ball." He sneered. "Ever since the old man died, Rotto and Serca have been pulling the company in all kinds of stupid directions. Real estate, online catalogues, that sort of thing."

Joe Rotto and Alonzo Serca. I stowed the names in my mental filing cabinet. "And Isabella didn't agree with these ventures?"

He didn't reply. His fingers were laced in front of him, his face buried between his arms and his forehead resting on the railing.

"Abdías?"

"I'd like to be alone now, Ms. Paraizo. Do me a favor and ask Pablo to get everyone the hell out of my house."

I watched him without moving, wondering if I should press him. The warm wind blew a few errant strands of hair in my face. Overhead, the stars seemed without number. My father and I used to lie on our backs in the sand and try to count them.

"Goodnight, Abdías."

The only reply I received was that of a lone gull, crying

The Tongue Merchant

forlornly, trying to find its way home in the dark. I headed back to the house without the answers I'd been counting on. I only ended up with more questions.

Such is life.

Just as I was about to step back into the house, I remembered the broken glass. I stopped on the threshold of the French doors and looked down at the repairman. He was sitting cross-legged, wielding a putty knife. He had blond hair in need of a good cut, and wore lace-up boots.

"Excuse me."

He looked up with a pair of brown eyes I thought too soft for a handyman. There was a tiny scar in the center of his chin, like a dimple. He didn't say anything, just sat there and waited and punished me with those eyes.

"Was there an accident here?" I asked.

"You could say that."

"A fight?"

"Folks like this don't have fights. They like to call 'em *altercations*."

"Fair enough. An altercation between whom?"

"I'm just the hired help, ma'am," he said, resuming his work. "See no evil, just work the broom."

That sounded like good advice.

I checked my watch. It was nearly nine o'clock.

Wonderful. Less than eleven hours till I was to report back to the *Sentinel*. Hardly enough time to dig up any facts on the bad blood between Isabella and her corporate foes. Finding myself back in the parlor, I didn't linger with small talk, but apologized to the guests for interrupting their evening, said my hasty goodbyes, and hurried Saul out the door.

"You're moving like your bra's on fire, Zo."

"Want to do me a favor?" I asked as I slid into the passenger's seat of the Viper.

"Why do I get the feeling I should say no?"

"Just hear me out."

"I'm listening."

"I need you to take me back to the marina. I have to take a look at that boat."

"You mean *inside* the boat?"

"Yep."

"Won't happen. The pigs'll have it locked down. You'll have to get a warrant or something if you want to go snooping around inside. And it's just a guess, but they probably won't allow it, no matter how much you turn on your feminine charms when you ask."

"Who said anything about asking?" I replied.

Chapter Five

We sailors have something in navigation called *deviation*. When using a compass, you have to account for several factors that tend to make your needle go a little *loco* on the dial. Like the difference between geographic north and magnetic north, for instance. That's called *variation*. And then there's deviation, which is what happens when your physical surroundings play havoc on your orienteering device. The metal housing around the compass, nearby iron objects, a greenhorn seaman walking too close with a set of keys—anything can cause the reading to deviate.

Result? You miss what you're aiming for, all thanks to the tug of interfering bodies.

As I sat in the contoured passenger's seat of the Viper, watching the city lights turn like blurry pinwheels beyond the window, I couldn't help but feel that I was being pulled from my intended course by forces I couldn't see. Suddenly there were too many participants—Nico, Abdías, his mistress Evangelina and her hubby Robert Castigere, not to mention the mysterious Joe Rotto and Alonzo Serca—all of them exerting their own magnetic pull and putting my normally dependable internal compass into a tizzy.

"You sure you want to do this, Zo?"

"No, not at all. In fact, sneaking onto that boat is the last thing I want to be doing right now. But I don't have much of a choice."

"Like hell you don't. Ever hear of something called minding your own business?"

"Isabella is dead, Saul. And Nico may be a creep, but he didn't murder anyone."

"Then let the pigs figure that out. They might be nothing but Neanderthals, and *corrupt* Neanderthals at that, but they're not going to book the guy unless they've got some rock-hard evidence that he's a killer. That's how the system works. No one can arrest Nico Murillo just on the grounds that he's a gutless misogynist, otherwise he'd already be doing ten to life."

"Joe Rotto," I said.

"Huh?"

"Rotto. Joe. Ever hear of him?"

"Doesn't he manage the Yankees?"

"Abdías mentioned the name when I asked him about Bella's possible enemies. He said that Rotto and a man named Alonzo Serca were always butting heads with Bella concerning the greater good of her father's company."

"So?"

"So I don't think Sergeant Straker wants to hear about how two high-level corp execs might be mixed up in this, which means it'll do no good to tell him about my talk with Abdías. Besides, if I start going on about things like that, word will eventually get back to my superiors, and I know for a fact that they'll reign me in the second they get wind of what I'm up to."

"And what is it that you're up to, precisely?"

"Punishing and saving, Saul. And breaking and entering . . ."

The wind blew out of the city like the dying breath of the sky.

With the sudden departure of the wind, the air around Marina del Sol became striated with long tendrils of silver fog, a sure sign that the temperature had dropped and storm conditions, though still far away, were creeping closer. As Saul slowed the car and nosed up to the boardwalk, the individual strands of mist braided themselves together and pressed more intimately against us. The mist somehow reminded me of a woman putting a finger to her lips to beg her lover's silence.

Speaking of lovers . . .

My friend Bella was an adulteress. I said that to myself again, trying to believe it, while Saul stopped the car and let it idle. Bella had a lover, and she was married. And if she'd kept such a secret from me, then what other little tidbits had she held back? Bella had led a double life, so who could say the kinds of illicit unions she'd entertained?

"This is dumb, Zo."

"Tell me about it."

"We're talking mentally retarded, brain-damaged, U.S. congressman kind of dumb."

"You're great on morale, Saul. I bet your apprentices would work for free if you asked them to, with that kind of support behind them."

"Hey. I am the frigging *monarch* of morale, until I see one of the peckerwoods about to screw up."

"Are you calling me a peckerwood?"

"Dammit, Zo."

I offered him the best smile I could muster and put my hand on his, where it rested on the gearshift. "Don't sweat it, Potter Man. I know this pier. I can find my way around in the dark. And the fog is thick and no one will notice me. I'll just get aboard, take a look around, see if I can find anything I might have missed earlier."

"If something like that was there, the pigs would've already slapped a tag on it and hauled it away to lose it, misshelve it, or let it get stolen from the evidence locker."

"Well, see there? Your faith in law-enforcement officials should convince you that I have to do this. You want our corrupt boys in blue handling Isabella's death? Or a battle-hardened, tough-as-sailcloth military officer?"

He ground his teeth together awhile, then slumped his hilltop shoulders. "Should I come with you? I can, if you want. It'd make me feel better."

"Have you ever broken the law before?"

He touched me on the arm, his gentle, craftsman's hands belying his girth. "All right. You've convinced me, for now. You've got my cell number. Call me if you need anything. And I mean *anything*. Unless they only give you one phone call."

"Funny."

"It wasn't meant to be. The Guard'll have your ass in a cereal bowl if you get in trouble over this. And you know that's true. Call whoever you have to call to keep them from finding out."

"Yes, mother."

"Up yours. Just be safe."

I leaned over and kissed him on the chin. "I'll let you know how it goes."

"Damn right you will."

He started to say something else, but I didn't give him the chance. I slipped from the car and inhaled deeply of the wet summer air, which was laced with a mist that washed out the normally pervasive scents of salt and seafood. I shut the door as quietly as I could, just as Mel Tormé, ass-kicker extraordinaire, started crooning about a lullaby of leaves.

I watched as the Viper's taillights disappeared in the murk like closing eyes.

Then I fastened my hat to my head and made my way to the *Lady Lynn Rob,* feeling something like a thief and wishing desperately for the sound of my mother's voice. It was my father who read me bedtime stories when I was growing up. And my mother who warned me that life was a firefight, and that you had to step lightly when the fog was up, for fear of booby traps and the men who planted them.

Walking as quietly as I could through the darkness, I came upon the *Lynn* from the south, where the catamaran was moored in the adjacent slip. The Union Jack hung like a wet dishrag on its staff. The boat was black and deserted. Though I could see barely twenty feet in any direction, I could hear the sounds of traffic, as well as the occasional jet descending on Hozumkur Municipal and what might have been the twang of country music a few berths down. I was raised in a household where the term *music* was narrowly defined; if it didn't have the words *Creedence* or *Grateful* in the name, it might as well have been an alien language. Dad still took a day of sick leave on the anniversary of Jerry Garcia's death.

But I was certain I was hearing Hank Williams.

Strange. And stranger still was the smell which coiled through the mist.

I swore it was cherry Kool-Aid.

Pocketing these morsels of information for later consumption, I nudged around the catamaran until I saw the plastic yellow cordon which separated the *Lynn* from the rest of the pier. Though mercury-vapor security lamps were positioned at every other berth, their blue lights were gummy through the ground-crawling clouds, hardly bright enough to make any difference. Someone would have to be practically on top of me to notice my stealthy advance, a favor for which I profusely gave thanks to the fog gods.

Two more steps brought me to the warning sign which they'd set up in case the yellow tape wasn't enough to dissuade the curious:

ABSOLUTELY NO ADMITTANCE BEYOND THIS POINT
TRESPASSERS WILL BE PROSECUTED

But the boat wasn't guarded. So at least I didn't have to worry about slipping past a sentry. My bluster goes only so far.

I took an extended stride from the pier to the deck of the yacht, my senses pricked for the slightest untoward movement, my stomach tied in a knot that even an old sea dog would've had trouble untying. I'm a real wizard with hitches, hawsers, ratline, and ropes in general, but I could work no magic on my own nerves, bundled in my belly as they were.

The boat rocked softly underneath me.

I paused, listening, waiting.

She who hesitates, gatita . . .

I bit my lip and walked to the cabin, for better or for worse. If you asked me to list my personal shortcomings, I'd have to write *impetuous* on the top line, although my impulsiveness was often a result of my thirst for justice. I have a tendency to breathe fire when I sense a social inequity, and I've been burned by my own flames on more than one occasion. But that's what happens when you keep a dreamer too long among realists. And a sailor too long on the land.

The stairwell was a lightless rectangle, a black mouth in the night.

Once again I found myself descending the few steps that led to the aft stateroom. I fought flashbacks all the way down. When I thought the visions would overwhelm me, I shot out a hand and braced myself, counting the seconds until the nausea passed. Only a few limp rays of blue light reached the bottom of the stairs, just enough for me to discern the shiny brass knob and keyhole. Two steps later and I was at the landing before the door, which had been sealed with a sticky version of the police line that encircled the yacht. The tape had been plastered completely around the seam where the door fit into the frame, forcing would-be insurgents to cut their way through.

I pulled the keys from my pocket. The keychain was a type of fishing lure known as a spinner, minus the hook. I used the Lincoln's trunk key to slice the tape all the way around the door, careful not to touch anything. I was already risking the wrath of the powers that be. No use in making their job any easier by leaving my fingerprints all over the place.

Once the tape had been cut away, I used the hem of my shirt to test the knob. Apparently the cops hadn't had access to the cabin keys, because they hadn't locked the door . . . which reminded me that whoever had killed Isabella had most likely let themselves in with a key. There was no sign of forced entry, as the TV police liked to say. Who might've had such a key? Nico, certainly, and probably Abdías, too. And if Bella truly had been sleeping with someone new, then I had yet another potential key-holder to consider.

Holding my breath, I pushed open the door and waited for the worst.

But it wasn't so bad. For one thing, it was dark, so I couldn't see the blood. And the smell was also easier to deal with than I'd anticipated. Maybe the forensics people had disinfected the cabin after they were through with it. There was one scent, however, that I could easily detect: eucalyptus.

When I reached for the lightswitch, I noticed that—surprise, surprise—my hand wasn't shaking. At least not yet.

I blinked rapidly when light filled the cabin.

The first thing I noted was that there was no eerie chalk halo to designate where my friend's body had lain, as there might have been in the movies, although the hardwood floor was stained a deep indigo color in that area. Similar splotches were dabbed about the cabin like paint flung from a brush. If I hadn't known this to be dried blood, I might have mistaken it for a simple spill that someone had forgotten to clean up.

I took a much-needed breath, exhaling slowly.

The bed had been stripped. The sheets, pillows, comforter,

lace dust-ruffle—all gone, carted off in plastic bags or maybe paper so the blood which coated them could dry without rotting for lack of air. The bed frame was made of solid hickory. All four posts were scarred and nicked as if worn down by a chisel.

No, that wasn't right. Not chisels.

Handcuffs.

I raised an eyebrow when I realized that Bella had been using the bedposts as anchors for cuffs or chains. If she'd ever had a fetish for bondage, she hadn't disclosed it to me. Maybe her new lover had talked her into it. The slug.

On the far side of the bed was the writing desk Nico had bought in Maracaibo. The desk was made of brazilwood with a single lap drawer and hand-tooled carvings of chameleons on the legs. A leather blotter sat atop the desk, but everything else had been removed. The authorities had claimed the pens, the laptop, whatever.

No help there.

The wardrobe was probably equally empty. The dual doors were open, and from my vantage point at the door, I could tell that at least half of the usual contents had been carried away by forensic snoops hoping to find fibers or body hairs belonging to someone other than Isabella. The wardrobe was still worth a once-over, but I was rapidly losing confidence that I'd find anything vital. Had I come here and risked my career for nothing?

I glanced to the right, saw the eucalyptus tree, and suddenly I remembered—

"Roosevelt."

I said his name without realizing that I'd spoken aloud. If Bella had a better friend than yours truly, it had to be Roosevelt, her pet koala bear. She'd rescued the poor thing from an animal shelter on San Juan. How he got to be there in the first place was anybody's guess. But Bella had a pal who was a vet, and he told her about little Rosy, and two days later the *Lynn* was moored a mile from the shelter and Bella began investing heavily in eucalyptus and mistletoe. That's what the little buggers eat.

Thinking about the koala brought back a memory of this morning. When I'd first entered the cabin all those hours ago, I'd heard a sound, a sort of muffled, might-be-a-footstep kind of noise. Except it hadn't been a footstep, for there'd been no one else in the room. I recalled seeing the eucalyptus dumped over on its side, the dirt from its red clay pot spilled across the floor. Then I'd seen Bella lying there mutilated, and I'd forgotten all about Roosevelt. But the koala had made the sound. He'd been scratching around in the cabin. He'd seen his adopted mother murdered.

"Rosy . . ."

There was no sign of him. Hopefully the police would contact someone who knew how to take care of him. I promised myself to call and check on him first thing in the morning.

In the corner near the eucalyptus was a wet bar and mini-fridge. Both items bore the powdery black residue of a recent fingerprint search. Clinging to the door of the refrigerator was what looked like an exploding crossword puzzle. Magnetic poetry, I believed they called it. There must have been two hundred words jumbled every which way on the fridge. Though Bella lived on a stipend from her father's estate, she worked part-time as a reporter for the *Hozumkur Plebiscite*. She'd always loved the written word, and had bought the magnetic poetry as a birthday gift for someone, but ended up keeping it herself. Nico used it to compose dirty haikus.

Other than that, the cabin was empty.

Oh, there was the shelf with its half-burned candles and the pile of American magazines beside the bed, but I wasn't getting any kind of vibes from them. If there was something to be found here, I was already looking at it.

So now what?

I forced myself to take that first step into the room. The going was difficult, as I had to sidestep the dried blood. The ceiling fan had begun to spin when I turned on the light, and its lazy motion helped to disperse the smell. I walked around the foot of the bed, my eyes playing over the harsh grooves which marred the posts. So this guy, whoever he was, liked it rough. I imagined Nico's reaction if he learned that another man was scuffing up his bed by strapping his wife to it. Nico's temper was right along the lines of those volcanoes you hear about on the nearby island of Montserrat.

I crouched down in front of the fridge.

Though most of the letters were a traffic jam of meaningless semantics, someone had selected and arranged a few of them into a pattern, forming an intelligible if poetically questionable verse.

> Canopy me with your sweet boughs
> Leaf me in kisses and sap my strength
> I root in ecstasy
> You bark in desire
> Where dew lies like white forest blood
> And no one can hear me when I fall

Okay. So Keats didn't have to worry about the competition. But this bad lyric was relevant to Isabella's life. Of this I was as certain as the sea. The police had photographed the poem, to be sure, and had probably already turned it over to the shrinks for analysis. As if psychiatrists knew anything at all about poetry.

I read the words several times, stacking them like gold coins in the vault of my memory, to be taken out and examined at my leisure. Then I opened the fridge, careful to protect my fingers

The Tongue Merchant

with the tail of my shirt. I found nothing but beer and caviar, so I tried the desk. I looked under it, behind it, even tipped it up and checked out the underside of the legs, but the sucker had been neutered by the police. The magazines and the candle shelf were the same. I didn't even bother checking under the bed.

Finally I went to the closet, aware of the dampness under my arms and the way the hands of my wristwatch seemed to be flying. It was already half past eleven. The cutter sailed at quarter till eight tomorrow morning. I had two hours of sleep to last me until then. I had never felt more awake.

I found nothing by pawing through the clothes on the rack. Many of them were still in their protective plastic sleeves, straight from the cleaning service. They were all women's clothes, not a single tuxedo or pair of men's slacks to be found, which meant that either the police had already absconded with them, or Mystery Man had never left anything behind, other than his calling cards on the four bedposts. The top shelf offered no better hunting, just an assortment of old photographs, a box of unfinished *mundillo*—a local style of lacemaking—a bag from Saks full of newspapers, and the saxophone that Bella was determined to master in spite of her deafness. As far as I knew, she'd never gotten beyond an off-key rendition of "Mary Had a Little Lamb."

I dropped down and began rummaging through the shoes, of which there seemed to be roughly eighteen thousand pairs. Bella was the queen of footwear, and there wasn't a shoe store in the Antilles or along the South American coast that she hadn't pillaged like Captain Cook in the cargo hold of a Spanish galleon. I pushed my way around sandals and spikes, Mexican *huaraches* and Italian-made flats, loafers for Sunday strolls and Reeboks for racquetball.

I shook one of the shoes in mounting frustration.

I found a pair of sequined calfskin boots that were relics from Bella's *Urban Cowboy* days, and I had to smile when I came across her Winnie-the-Pooh house slippers. Soon I was surrounded by a moat of shoes and none the wiser for it, and in a moment of flash-fire agitation I grabbed the nearest sneaker and flung it against the back of the wardrobe. *Come on, dammit. Give me a break here.* It felt so good that I did it again with a red stiletto, no longer caring if the neighbors heard me, no longer concerned with anything but throwing and hitting and striking and—

Something fell out of a patent leather oxford.

I watched it fall, like you watch a snowflake drifting in front of your face. It was small and papery and alighted on the toe of a plum-colored pump. For several seconds I was afraid to touch it, as if it might melt in the heat of my hand. Then I snapped from my paralysis and plucked it up to hold before my eyes.

"And who might you be?"

I was looking at a postage stamp. The kind you lick and mash down on your envelope and mail off to Biloxi or some damn place, and then you forget about it. The scene depicted on the stamp was that of a locomotive chugging down a mountain pass, except that the image seemed to be upside down. The text above this inverted train was printed in German. The stamp was held in a slender plastic envelope about an inch and a half square. The envelope bore no markings of any kind. Squinting, I turned the thing over in my fingers, peering at it like a woman at a microscope.

And then I remembered: Nico had babbled something about trains when I was trying to comfort him at the pier. I hadn't known what to make of it at the time, but could he have been talking about this stamp?

"Curiouser and curiouser."

I got to my feet, displacing the shoes which were piled in my lap, cupping the stamp in my palm and wondering who had put it there and why. I knew nothing of stamps. I was not a collector of anything; I've never had the inclination to accumulate while others go without. So I was going to have to ask around if I wanted to find out anything about my unexpected find.

What was that?

I stopped. My fingers closed over the stamp. I didn't breathe. Just listened.

There it was again. Several sounds from the deck above my head.

Someone was on the boat.

Shit. Hustling now, I dashed across the cabin and killed the light, hoping it hadn't already been seen, my heart wild in my chest. A second later the footsteps began to descend the stairs and there was no quick place to duck for cover because the head adjacent to the cabin offered no outside exit and sure, there was the bed, but that was the first place they looked for you when they knew you were hiding from them, so I froze, suspended in a vacuum of indecision, and at the last moment I decided to try for the corner behind the mini-fridge and pray to the fog gods for another spot of invisibility but—

The door swung open. A flashlight beam struck me in the face.

"That's far enough, sister."

In the sudden glare, the only thing I could see was the gun pointed at my head.

Chapter Six

In the next second, several things happened at once.

I shoved my hand in my pants pocket and took a step backward.

Someone said, "Get your arms up!" and moved toward me.

Leaving the postage stamp in my pocket, I quickly raised my arms.

"Don't move!"

I felt my heart strike once, as loud as a gong.

The overhead light came on.

I blinked.

And then the second was over and I was staring down the barrel of what looked to be a .357 revolver. The man behind the gun had a head that was large and round, like a globe. The globe's surface was so broad that the man's facial features seemed to have been distorted by the Mercator projection. His nose was flat and too wide, his eyes spread apart and overly large, the way Greenland is always warped on a world map. He had a polar ice cap of white hair and a plucked mustache along the equator of his face.

"What the hell are you doing here?" He adjusted his legs so that he gripped the gun in what shooters refer to as a Weaver stance. "Who are you? And why are you here?"

"I . . ." My jaws clamped shut before I could give myself away. I could hardly offer him a false name, though the idea certainly crossed my mind. I was betrayed by my uniform, which was only fitting, as I was in the process of betraying it in return. Coast Guard personnel did not flaunt the law with such reckless impunity. "Maybe if you put down the gun—"

"That ain't going to happen, lady."

"This is really just a misunderstanding—"

"Lieutenant Paraizo?"

Kyle Straker stepped into the room.

The pent-up wind rushed out of me at the sight of him. *Thank God.* I may have been looking at a night in jail and subsequent punishment from the Guard, but at least I wasn't facing down the man who murdered Isabella. For a second there I thought I was dead.

"Uh, Lieutenant?" Giving me a look of total incomprehension, Straker stepped around his companion and grabbed my wrist. "Everywhere I go, I seem to find you in the center of the storm. You want to tell me what's going on here?"

I decided to play it cool. No reason to get any more anxious than I already was. "I came here to gather some of Isabella's things."

"Like what?"

"Like her purse, if I could find it. Which I didn't, but I suppose that's because you have it."

"As a matter of fact, we do."

"You know this woman, Kyle?" The map-faced man still held his gun, although he'd lowered it to his side. His voice was like gravel shaking around in a gourd. "Friend of yours?"

"Not yet." Straker's disappointment in me was evident. "Lieutenant, I'd like you to meet my associate, Detective Samuel Raznik. Raz, this is the bullheaded and ever-surprising Marcella Paraizo, United States Coast Guard."

"Very pleased to meet you, *Lieutenant.*" Condescension dripped from every word. "But now, if you don't mind, I'm going to have to place you under arrest. You have the right to remain silent—"

"Raz, wait up." Straker waved him off, but kept his other hand firmly around my wrist. "Let me talk to her for a minute."

Raznik's geographic features went through a seismic upheaval. "She could've been tampering with evidence, Kyle. You know as well as I do that we should haul her in ASAP for being here. I'm not about to turn this case into a circle-jerk because some civilian was messing around at the crime scene."

"I'm not a civilian," I snapped.

Straker fired a look at me, then turned back to Raznik. "She's not a civilian. Okay? Yes, we're taking her in, but no, not yet. I want to make an attempt to sort all this out. Circle-jerks are not my idea of a good time, either. Just give me a minute or two. Why don't you wait up topside? I'll bring her up when we're through."

Raznik smoldered.

"Raz?"

"All right. But let it be known that I leave you two alone under protest. Things like this aren't by the book, you know what I'm saying? Captain'll have our shields if we louse this one up." He held me under the firing squad of his gaze for a bit longer, then holstered his weapon and carried his bulk up the stairs.

"Hell of a way to make a first impression," Straker said as soon as we were alone.

I tried to tug my hand away, but he was having nothing of it. "Par for the course," I said. "I've never been much of a people person. I'm sure that's why I ran away to sea the first chance I got."

"You're in a lot of trouble. You realize that, don't you?"

"More than you know, Sergeant."

"And what's that supposed to mean?"

"May I please have my arm back?" I waited until he decided

The Tongue Merchant

to release me. Massaging my wrist, I sat down on the edge of the bed. It was either that or fall over. Suddenly my career was on the line, and what transpired in the next five minutes would determine my fate as a member in good standing of our nation's maritime defense team. Here I'd been hoping for a promotion to lieutenant commander, and now I was on the cusp of a reprimand, demotion, and probably a transfer to an ice-breaker off the frozen coast of Alaska. "Thanks for giving me a chance to plead my case," I said when I was sure of my voice.

"Don't thank me. Just talk. You say you came here for her purse?"

"Sort of."

"Sort of? Then what were you thinking you might find?"

"I don't know. A valentine, I guess."

"Excuse me?"

Valentine? Hmmm. I hadn't intended for that to come out, yet there it was. Sometimes my heart got ahead of my brain. But now that I'd picked open that old scar, I thought that I might as well let it bleed.

I shifted a bit on the bed, trying not to look as uncomfortable as I felt. "My mother, she was, uh . . . killed when I was a little girl. She was lost at sea when her boat was attacked by the Sandinistas, half a mile from Puerto Cabezas, on the Mosquito Coast of Nicaragua. She'd been smuggling Contra rebels in and out of the country, and . . . and I suppose that's how you die when you're a political dissident. Her boat was hit at night, without warning. I guess she was either shot or drowned."

Straker actually took a step in retreat. He broke eye contact, jamming his hands in the back pockets of his pants. Apparently this wasn't the kind of confession he'd been expecting.

"Anyway, it was February, and I'd just mailed her a valentine I'd made in school. When my father came into my room to tell me that she was dead, the first thing I asked about was that stupid valentine. I wanted to know if she'd gotten it before she died."

Straker closed his eyes.

"So what I was doing here . . . I was looking for valentines. Anything to let me know that Isabella hadn't died as terribly as I'm imagining she did."

Straker ran a hand through his neat Boy Scout hair. After a few seconds of uncomfortable silence, he sat down beside me on the bed, leaned his elbows on his knees, and studied the floor. "I'm sorry about your mother."

"You had nothing to do with it."

"I'm sorry anyway."

"It was a long time ago."

"She must have been quite a person."

"So was Isabella."

Straker nodded. "I'm sure she was."

"I came here, Sergeant, trying to find some reason why anyone would want her dead."

"I know. And call me Kyle."

"Fine. Kyle. So tell me. Am I way off track with this? Can you at least let me know that I'm not completely off course? Was there anything here to indicate why she was murdered?"

"You know I'm not supposed to answer that."

"Then don't answer it. Just speculate."

He rubbed his chin, where a day's worth of blond stubble had formed.

"It's almost midnight," I reminded him. "You came back here for a reason."

"Just a hunch."

"Wonderful. Hunches are my specialty." I turned toward him, so that he was forced to look me in the eye. "Please, Kyle, toss me just this one bone, because I'm really out here on the ragged edge, and this day's been the shittiest I can remember in a long time, and I've got a feeling, all things considered, that tomorrow's going to be a lot worse. So come on. Why did they kill Isabella?"

Straker stared at me so hard that for a moment I thought he was going to pick up with the Miranda warning where his partner had left off. But then he said, "Maybe for ten thousand dollars in jewels."

"Explain." Unconsciously I wrapped my arms around my chest, my clammy palms clutching my elbows. "I don't know anything about any jewels. Tell me what you mean."

"I'd like to, but I'm not allowed to discuss the case. You know how it is."

"You said ten thousand dollars in jewels."

"Yeah. Don't go around broadcasting that, huh?"

"She kept those here, the jewels?"

Straker stood up and went to the wardrobe, as if he was uneasy sitting beside me. "We found a lockbox here in the closet, bolted to the bulkhead. The lid was open, no sign that it was forced. There was nothing inside but Mrs. Murillo's passport and other documents of a personal nature. But Mr. Murillo claims that his wife kept her jewelry in that safe, which totals out to around ten grand. We verified that figure through the insurance company."

"You took this box with you?"

"We took almost everything that wasn't nailed down, and even some of the stuff that *was* nailed down. Like that box. You could only remove it by cutting it out of the wall, or by removing the nuts from inside. Which is exactly what we did."

"Fingerprints?"

"What? So now you're a forensics expert?" He offered me a strained smile. "Sorry, Lieutenant, but—"

"Marcella."

He hesitated, then said, "Marcella. You're not involved in this investigation."

"Funny. It sure doesn't feel that way to my heart."

"Look." He turned away from the wardrobe with a sigh. "You think by hearing everything I know that it will make you feel better? I don't believe so. Want me to prove it? Then here it is, so good luck with it." He held up one finger. "First, we've got no prints other than those belonging to Mr. and Mrs. Murillo, which only makes sense, as this is their rig." Another finger. "Secondly, she was robbed. She was probably forced to open the safe before she was killed. So the motive could've been burglary, as it often is. We interviewed Mr. Murillo and he claims he was making love to his girlfriend all night, a story which she was more than happy to back up. Where am I? Thirdly? Fourthly?" He finally gave up with his fingers and instead made a fist. "Whatever, you'll be relieved to hear that the rape analysis came up negative. The ME says Mrs. Murillo was struck once in the head by a blow so violent that it broke her jaw in two places. And that's a serious shot. Not just anybody could deliver that kind of wallop. But as we all know—"

"As we all know," I interrupted, "Nico used to be a prize-fighter."

"Uh-huh. A welterweight, as a matter of fact. And now he's a scuba instructor."

"Is that significant?"

"Sure, when you consider that the boat was found a mile from shore. You, Marcella, might be able to swim a mile in a choppy sea at night, but not this cowboy." He tapped himself on the chest. "I could maybe make it a hundred yards to save my life, as long as the water was calm and I could see where I was going."

I felt like pressing my hands against my head in hopes that the world might slow down a few paces and allow me to catch up. Everything led back to Nico, which still felt as wrong to me, as *misplaced*, as the Secret Saboteur in my chest. "I really don't believe that Nico stole Bella's jewelry to cover up the fact that he murdered her in a fit of rage, then piloted the boat out to sea and just happened to bring along his diving gear so he could swim back to shore."

"So maybe there was no fit of rage. It was premeditated. He had the scuba equipment ready, had a key to the cabin and one to the safe."

"And talked his girlfriend into lying for him."

"Happens all the time."

"Not in my world."

"Well, welcome to mine."

"*You doing okay down there?*" Raznik shouted from the deck.

"I'm bringing out the rubber hoses right now!" Straker assured him, hollering up the stairs. "I'll have her talking any minute." He looked at me and said, "I take it that you know she was a millionaire waiting to happen."

"What about witnesses?" I asked, ignoring the question.

"Just the craft in the next berth. We're bringing them in one at a time to interview them, but what usually happens is that a dozen people were in the vicinity and nobody saw anything. Typical. They were partying so hard an aircraft carrier could've docked next door and they wouldn't have realized it."

I thought about the people I'd seen sitting on the boat while the medics loaded the—

—*body bag*—

—black parcel into the van. To think that they'd been so close and not seen anything . . .

"One other item of note," Straker said, dropping down in front of me. "And this is the last bone I'm throwing you, so don't ask for anything more. Mrs. Murillo got a whack in on whoever killed her."

"Excuse me?"

"She hit him. With a wooden mallet. Like the kind you use to tenderize meat. We found one with blood on it other than her own."

"That's . . . that's terrific. You've got his blood. That's better than having his fingerprints, isn't it? *You've got his DNA.*"

"Now don't get too enthused. It's not like we've got a tracking beacon that will lead us to his doorstep."

"But you can take a sample of Nico's blood, see if there's a match."

"In time. It may come down to that. We've got to work through a few pesky Constitutional amendments before we'll be authorized to run a genetic test on him, or anyone else for that matter. But it's a start. Now then . . ." He looked nearly as worn down, stomped on, and regurgitated as I felt. His sport coat was rumpled and his shoes were scuffed. "Fair trade. What I know for what you know. So start talking."

"What makes you think I know anything?"

Remarkably, Straker laughed.

"What's so funny?"

"Just you," he said, shaking his head. "One look at you this morning and I could tell you wouldn't let this take care of itself. I should've posted a unit out here, knowing you'd come back." The grin he wore looked good on him. "Now 'fess up, Nancy Drew."

"Okay." I figured it couldn't hurt. Straker had already extended me more courtesy than he'd been obliged to do, considering the circumstances. "But one more thing first. Tell me why they took her tongue."

It was closing in on one a.m. when we emerged from the cabin, stepping out onto the deck of the *Lynn* into a silent cathedral of haze, constructed of clouds instead of brick, mortared with mist

The Tongue Merchant

and resounding with the unearthly choir of the foghorn in the distance. The ever-charming Samuel Raznik leaned against the railing, smoking a filterless cigarette, his underarms black with sweat despite the fairly cool temperature. He stared at me with eyes as black as bullet holes.

Tell me why they took her tongue, I'd said to Straker.

That's what doesn't make sense, Marcella. A thief wouldn't have bothered. Understand?

No, Kyle. I don't understand any of it. So it wasn't a thief. They killed her for a reason.

Yeah. Looks that way. Maybe taking her tongue was a metaphor.

A metaphor? So you're also an English professor?

Straker looked squarely at Raznik and said, "I'm letting her go."

Raznik scowled, pushing himself off the mast and flicking his cigarette butt toward the sea. "Terrific. Just gol-damned terrific . . ."

"I take full responsibility for her actions."

"Damn straight you do."

Straker started to respond, thought better of it, and turned back to me. "You understand the size of the favor I'm doing for you here?"

My mind went back to his words of minutes earlier: *Maybe the killer cut out her tongue as a way of saying she was talking too much, or telling secrets to the wrong people.*

"Yes." Goosebumps crawled over my skin. "I understand. Thank you, Sergeant."

"*De nada.* Now you better skin out before my partner talks some sense into me."

"I will, but I have one more question. Why did the two of you come back? If you'd already scoured this boat from bow to stern, why return now?"

"Kyle . . ." Raznik warned.

"Just following a lead, Marcella. That's what we do. Mr. Murillo told us that his wife had a habit of stashing things like extra money in her shoes. So Raz and I came back to rifle through the woman's footwear, as desperate as that may sound."

"*Kyle.*"

"Now go," Straker said. "I'll call your apartment in Puerto Rico and do what I can to keep you updated, so at least you'll know if we make any arrests. But that's as much as I can do. So scram. You're making my partner's ulcer act up."

The stamp in my pocket suddenly weighed thirty pounds. I was terrified that, if I dallied, Straker would notice my spine bent from the pressure. I wanted to stay, to ask a few more questions, but I was already pushing it. Raznik glowered at me. As I mouthed another thank you to Straker and turned to leave, I knew I hadn't seen the last of Mr. Mercator.

I stepped onto the pier, and almost at once the *Lynn* vanished, the cathedral closing its white doors behind me. Only Jehovah's great yellow clock face was visible, like a sickly moon over my head. Straker and Raznik were arguing as I fled the scene. I heard each of them say my name, and I speculated that Raznik wanted to get a flag officer on the horn and rat on me for what I'd done. There was nothing I could do to stop him from making such a call.

Maybe the killer cut out her tongue as a way of saying she was talking too much . . .

What did Bella know that was so incriminating? If Straker was right and the murderer collected her tongue as a way of shutting her up, so to speak, then plainly there was more to my friend's furtive nightlife than she'd ever let on.

. . . . or telling secrets to the wrong people.

Bella had known something dangerous and had threatened to expose it. She was a journalist. She'd unearthed a damning skeleton, but had been killed before she could open the closet

The Tongue Merchant

door. I wondered about visiting her office at the paper. Would her editor know what stories she'd been pursuing? A better question: would her editor tell *me* about these stories? If I could only convince him that something newsworthy had been transpiring . . .

Belay that. I had to be aboard the *Sentinel* by quarter till eight. And from there it was back to port in San Juan, and so much for tracking down newspaper editors and postage stamps, not to mention Joe Rotto, Alonzo Serca, and Bella's possible lover.

Well, there were those three weeks of leave I'd accrued . . .

I walked across Ochoa to Dominique's. The waiter had told me the place didn't shut down until two in the morning. Good thing. I was strung out, frazzled, and thirsty as hell. Several uppity couples occupied the rattan dining tables, sexing each other up over their wine glasses. Jimmy Buffet was playing on the jukebox. No one paid me any attention as I went to the bar and ordered a bottle of spring water.

"Pretzels?" the bartender asked. "I'm about to trash them. Speak now or forever hold your mustard."

"I'm fine, thanks."

He dumped the pretzels into a wastebasket and left me alone with my ghost.

Bella had now been deceased for twenty-four hours. Her assailant remained unpunished. There was nothing I could do before sunrise that would rectify that. Bella's editor would be home asleep. No dealer in rare stamps would open his door to me. Even the local animal shelter would be locked down for the night, so I couldn't see Roosevelt and promise to get him out of there as soon as the law allowed.

I was helpless. Nico's alibi was still unsubstantiated beyond anything other than the word of his lover. Abdías's alibi was flimsier still, constructed as it were on an adulterous tryst. Both men had a motive. And I was certain that Nico, a former boxer, could've delivered a blow powerful enough to shatter a woman's jaw.

Yet there had to be *something* I could do, even at this sunless hour.

I stopped the bartender the next time he wandered by. "Do you have a San Juan phone book I could look at?"

"Sure. That'll be two bucks for the water."

"Ouch. Two dollars? Is there a water shortage somewhere?"

The bartender just stared at me until I forked over the money.

As soon as he was gone, I dashed through the book. De Casals International, or DCI, was noted in the yellow pages, headquartered in San Juan, and lo and behold: both Rotto, Joseph, and Serca, Alonzo, were listed in the white. I copied their addresses and phone numbers on a tangerine-colored napkin, then made my way to the pay phone to call a cab. It was time, at last, to head back to the ship.

I couldn't imagine what Kevin Maddox would say upon my return, or how I'd lie to him and tell him that everything was working out okay with Isabella's unfinished business. I wouldn't be able to tell him that I was into it up to my neck, and sinking fast. As I listened to the phone ring, something that the handyman had said earlier in the evening came back to me: *See no evil, just work the broom.*

I was one out of two. Working my broom to clean up the mess, but catching sight of new specters of evil every time I turned my head.

★ ★ ★ ★ ★

Tuesday
Barometric pressure 29.57,
falling slowly

★ ★ ★ ★ ★

Chapter Seven

Three bells rang out across the ship, marking half past the hour of five a.m.

I greeted the cutter's officer-on-deck just after dawn, the chill of the morning cool on my cheeks. Clouds the color of mud oozed across the eastern sky. Trapped somewhere behind them, the sun offered us little in the way of daybreak; the orange glow on the horizon was as dim as lantern light. The wind hummed along at force 5, having gathered courage in the night behind the cover of the fog. It whipped our pennants at a brisk twenty knots. The waves had grown in the night, and spray blew up over the prow. Word had just come over. The squall had spilled over Antigua and was brewing in the Leeward Islands, now officially a tropical storm, christened Bartholomew and bearing down upon us.

And my personal compass still suffered from radical deviation.

Though I'd stretched out on my cot upon returning to the *Sentinel*, I hadn't been able to sleep. Not even close. A shower, toothbrush, and change of uniform had been all I needed to hone my mental blade. Regardless of my sleepless night, my body felt as if it still held an edge, which I was going to need, now that I believed that Bella had gotten herself entangled in something perilous. I considered applying for a few days of leave, but did I really want to? Did I truly desire to tie myself up in the very web that had cost Bella her life? Kyle Straker, for all of his gallantry, would be no help at this point. I had nothing substantial to offer him in way of proof. All I'd accomplish by confiding in him was to implicate myself in a bit of petty larceny.

I held the stamp up before my eyes.

Maybe it was nothing. Maybe it was just as Nico had told the cops. Isabella sometimes stored valuables in her shoes. People do weird stuff like that all the time. Me, I keep my cosmetics in a Swisher Sweets cigar box. Bella knew the stamp was valuable and stashed it in the closet, intending to sell it or save it or use it for some other harmless enterprise.

Yeah, sure. And I've got this bridge in Brooklyn.

If I was intent on guiding myself not by logic but only by the sextant of my heart, then I knew full well where it was leading me. The postage stamp was not irrelevant. It made sense. I had other leads to pursue—Rotto and Serca, the identity of Bella's lover, the veracity of Abdías's alibi—but first I wanted to track down the significance of the stamp.

After my initial rounds topside, I returned to my quarters, did a quick number with my makeup to fool everyone into thinking I was still running on an even keel, and attended to the remainder of my morning duties on the cutter's busy deck. We got our first splattering of rain an hour into my shift, but it drizzled out and a bright crack in the cloud ceiling provided enough sunlight that Bartholomew was forgotten. At least for now. Before we made port, I put in my request for leave, which Maddox seemed to think would be approved without reservation. I spoke with him for half an hour in the officers' mess, our topics of conversation calm and clear and free of shoals: the *Sentinel*'s upcoming maintenance cycle, our mutual fondness for horseback riding, my father, the GANTSEC grapevine, and of course the weather. We steered around the obvious breakers and whirlpools, such as Bella's funeral, our own doubts and desires, the way he never held my hand anymore, and I got up from the

The Tongue Merchant

table feeling glazed over. Like a piece of Saul's pottery hardened and glossy from the kiln.

The harbor at Base San Juan was as busy as I'd seen it in months. The city itself is the fourth most active port in the U.S., seeing a million cruise-ship tourists a year and collecting maritime-related revenues of over thirty billion dollars annually. And all of those people and all of that money means trouble. Last year GANTSEC saved nearly three hundred lives and prevented over fifteen tons worth of cocaine and marijuana from reaching Puerto Rican shores. And today was more frenzied than usual. The threat of Bartholomew had everyone scrambling. The cranes and booms moved freight from shore to ship and back again. Electric forklifts buzzed in and out of warehouses. Whistles blew and American rock music blasted from a distant and poorly tuned radio. Port security had its hands full.

I was so busy that the hours slipped away like rainwater from a freshly waxed deck. As ship's XO, I handled enough duties and fielded enough queries from anxious seamen to keep my mind from roaming more dangerous shores. One thing I had to do was acquire a spare pair of boots. Mine were sitting in a Hozumkur evidence room, their soles tacky with Isabella's blood.

I managed not to think about that, but filled myself with my work, as we're all apt to do when our hearts are secretly fragmenting. Reality didn't set its teeth into me until five bells were struck on the afternoon watch, and I realized my doctor's appointment was only an hour away.

Deep in the warmth of my left breast, I imagined I could feel my Secret Saboteur, speaking dire riddles I'd yet to understand.

The Avundavi Women's Health Clinic was a single-story complex spread across ten acres of landscaped lawn so perfect it might have been molded from plastic. The building's roof was of russet-colored, Spanish slate tiles. Flower boxes complemented the windows. Honeysuckle and bougainvillea were the only two plants I knew by name. I've never had much of a green thumb, having played taps over the dead remains of more than one houseplant in my day.

An old-world iron fence, capped with sculpted spearheads, separated the building from the parking lot. The statue at the gate depicted the poet Sappho, the ancients' first feminist. Sappho was garbed in the shoulder-baring robe of a muse. As for me, I was dressed in mufti. It felt good to be wearing my civvies, including a light linen top, tennis shoes, and a new pair of blue jeans, and stop the presses if my hair wasn't loose around my shoulders. We had this agreement, my hair and I. It promised to stay a prisoner of bobby pins sixteen hours a day, so long as it got to escape every now and then, and I promised not to shave it all off and go totally butch for the rest of my career. So far we'd both lived up to the bargain, though we'd had a few close calls.

I'd taken a cab to a bookstore down the street and walked the last block for some mad notion that I might be under surveillance. As if the Guard trailed its officers in spy cars designed to look like floral-delivery vans, just to make sure we weren't keeping secrets from them. Which I most certainly was. I steadied myself and concentrated on the walk to the clinic. Take one step, then another. Pass Sappho and her pen poised above a stone tablet. Stride through the gate and onto the sidewalk. Make a straight line between neat rows of the prickly shrubs that might have been native poinciana, with their fiery blossoms. Stop before the lone coconut palm providing shade at the big glass doors. Take a breath. Put a hand to the doors. Exhale. Head inside.

Dr. Janice Avundavi was only five feet tall if she were wearing shoes, which she seldom did in the rear offices of the clinic,

The Tongue Merchant

which only made me adore her all the more. She had hair as dark and rich as Rangoon silk, black eyes like wells, and two hours into my visit, this tiny, vital woman had guided me through a world that all women pray to avoid—*Sit here, Marcella, and we'll get started. How've you been? I know the room is frightfully cold but the AC's taken control of the building and we're all its hostage. Shift just a little bit to the left, please. There. Have you heard that new Josh Groban song? I love that man, Marcella, but I'll be damned if he's ever replied to one of my letters. I don't know how familiar you are with mammography, but I'll walk you through the process. How's darling Kevin Maddox treating you? Ah, I see. Well, that's a man for you. Beasts in uniforms is all they are. The majority of breast cancers originate in the mammary duct, which is the gland that secretes milk for our dear babies. I breast-fed my first two, but by the time Taylor came along I'd changed my ways. There, now. Sorry it took so long, but I like to take my time with these things. Did I mention that Josh Groban refused to write me? The handsome cretin. Marcella? Are you awake? Sorry to leave you alone like that, but I have an expectant mother down the hall, and is she ever expectant. In another month I'll be the proud doctor of triplets, the good Lord willing and the tide don't rise. I'll see that you get a cigar. Now let's take a look at your results—*

She paused with her hand on the folder and swallowed me with those eyes.

Shit. I knew it was bad without her saying a word.

But she said it anyway.

I got home at dusk. I could feel the weight of twilight in my veins. Everything was sinking. The sun. My spirits. Whatever.

All the way to my front door I thought about the object I held in my hand. It had become a talisman to ward off all the rotten mojo the universe was hurling at me. As long as I concentrated on it, I wasn't susceptible to the voices, so many of them now squawking for my attention that I'd go mad if I gave in to them. So I concentrated on the magic wand I'd gotten from Dr. Avundavi's office.

A tongue depressor.

There'd been a glass jar of them on the counter the way licorice whips used to sit and tempt me at the drugstore. And there was Isabella's ghost, back in my brain for round two, and my gloves not yet even bloody. Her body was lying in a steel drawer somewhere, a tag tied to her toe, spiritless, bloodless, tongueless.

The rage quickened my step as I dug for my keys at the ground floor of my apartment building, which looked out onto never-ending Condado Beach and the vastness of the dusky Atlantic beyond. Tiny triangles of ship's sails dotted the water. Sand as white as talcum ran down to the waves. Everything was its usual beautiful self except for the grim clouds spreading from the east, growing, creeping toward us. Like cancer.

I scowled, shoved the key in the lock, and let myself in, holding my wooden stick in front of my body, like a dagger.

I dropped my purse and didn't stop moving. I crossed the mostly empty living room and punched the button on my ancient answering machine to play my messages but didn't pause to listen, only kept on down the hall and into my bedroom long enough to pull the shirt over my head and discard my bra, and there in the mirror I imagined I could see the Secret Saboteur, while from the living room I heard my father on the recorder saying he just wanted to wish me a good day and he'd try again later, and the sound of his voice gave me the strength to curl my lip at my invisible assassin and turn away from the mirror.

I unfastened my jeans as I entered the guest bedroom, which I used for my work room. On three separate tables lay the ingredients of a full-blown case of flyfishing fever: bobbin

The Tongue Merchant

threaders, several brands of whip finishers, two rotating hackle pliers—one in rosewood, the other in cocobolo with my name carved on the handle—a bodkin and half-hitch tool, and more dubbing brushes than one woman could ever need. An open cabinet held hooks of all sizes, sundry bottles of head cement, and miles of spooled thread in every shade from crayfish tan to mackerel green. Resting on the largest of the three tables was my prize, a Renzetti Master's Series tier's vise. My father enjoys deep-sea fishing as much as the next Miami sportsman, but his passion is trolling the lakes of the Midwest, from Arkansas to Nebraska. He'd taken me out three times a year until I graduated high school, and call me a tomboy if you'd like. Though I hadn't fished in months, I still tied flies as a meditation. It sure beat crocheting.

I cleared a space on my work table and placed my two recent acquisitions in front of me. First the tongue depressor. It looked like a Popsicle stick on steroids. Next, the postage stamp, with its inverse depiction of a steam engine. I played my eyes over the two items, fighting a gravity so strong I had to brace myself on the desk. I knew that the riddle of Bella's death could be divined from these things, if only I could muster the clairvoyance to make it work.

Absently I pushed off my jeans, staring at the stamp, then the stick.

Lost in a hypnotic state, I showered, changed clothes, and noticed that Kevin had called while I was in the bathroom: "Hey, Marce. It's me. Just, uh, just wanted to tell you that you've got a two-day leave. You've earned it. I'd like to see you sometime soon, but . . . just call me, will you? I'm easy to find. I'll be the guy in the big white canoe with *Sentinel* painted on the side." He paused, then: "Take care, Marce. I miss you."

Click.

I pressed ERASE and went back to my stamp.

From an out-of-date encyclopedia I learned that stamp-collecting was known to those who practiced it as *philately*. I probably could've found a trove of information on the Internet, but I didn't own a computer. VCRs were about as high-tech as I got. Somewhere around here I had a record player collecting dust.

I consulted the phonebooks of both Hozumkur and San Juan. Under the headings of "Coin & Stamp Dealers," I found three listings, one back in the 'Kur and two here in town. Maybe if I could learn the significance of the stamp, I'd uncover the trail that led into Bella's backstairs existence. Sergeant Straker—*Call me Kyle*, he'd said—had speculated that Bella's tongue had been taken as a way of saying she should've kept quiet. She was privy to some damning bit of lore, perhaps something she'd discovered in her journalistic pursuits. But did the stamp have anything to do with that? She certainly hadn't been hoarding it for a rainy day. She didn't need the money, not with Daddy's fortune soon to fall like manna in her lap. So why stash the stamp, unless it was connected with the person who murdered her?

I grabbed the phone and dialed the dealer in Hozumkur, a man named Paulo Longoria. No answer. Not surprising, as it was after normal business hours. Undeterred, I dialed the first philatelist in San Juan. I got his voice mail system, so I left my name and said I'd pay him a visit tomorrow morning. My last call was answered by an irascible woman who told me in seething Spanish that her husband was out on a swordfish boat until next Wednesday, and the shop was closed for the evening, and they only dealt in coins, anyway, because stamps were for pretenders—nobody collected stamps anymore but children and imbeciles and her husband was neither one of those, a thoughtless ogre sometimes, but not a child or an imbecile—and about that time I said *gracias* and hung up.

So much for sniffing out the stamp tonight.

The Tongue Merchant

I sat there, surrounded by speculation, tapping the tongue depressor on my knee.

Fine. If I couldn't go after the origins of the stamp, I could certainly make myself a nuisance in the lives of Joe Rotto or Alonzo Serca, whichever one of the lucky fellows I could manage to corner before bedtime. Back to the phone book. I tried Rotto first, just because that was how the alphabet was laid out. He had a house over in the posh Miramar district. I considered calling first, but then decided against it. Best to catch him unawares, so he didn't have time to concoct any more than the standard, off-the-cuff batch of lies.

Damn. There I was, assuming the worst about the man. Though my mother expected everyone to prevaricate and connive as it suited them, my father suspected anyone he met to be the keeper of a vivid inner kindness. Though he was a cop, he believed that humans were, at the core, creations of a higher power and thus sacrosanct. Me, I was already writing both Rotto and Serca off as outlaws to be shot at dawn.

I figured Rotto would have pretty upscale digs, so I put on a dress. I'd bought it in a moment of clearance-sale delirium a month ago and hadn't yet had occasion to wear it. It was sleeveless and V-necked, blue cotton with a light palm frond print. It was crinkle-skirted, and I liked the way it moved when I walked. More importantly, I was going fishing for answers, and looking good was half the lure. Flytiers are constantly experimenting with new patterns, knowing that eventually the right tie will always get a bite. But you've got to know the waters and your craft. A fly run between the fish and the water's surface has got to be translucent so that the light shines through the dressing and catches the fish's eye. I wanted to have a similar effect, though my quarry was far more dangerous than a smallmouth bass.

I put the stamp and stick in my purse, but only after first

removing the pamphlet Dr. Avundavi had given me—*Breast Cancer: Hope after Diagnosis*. A shiver slid down my arms. I flung the pamphlet away and was just about to walk out the door when the tintinnabulators gave a little tinkle and stopped me on the threshold.

Already I'd endangered myself by probing into Isabella's death. From here on out, the waters were only going to get more treacherous. If I kept to these bearings, I could eventually end up facing a killer, and that wasn't something you did unarmed.

I went back to my work room, flipped open a certain tackle box in the corner, lifted the upper tray, and removed the gun. The 6.35 millimeter Walther PP may have been an exotic caliber, but I liked it nonetheless. They tell you not to choose a sidearm which requires hard-to-find ammunition, but I wasn't expecting to get myself in a position where I'd expended the magazine's eight rounds and was scouring the streets of San Juan for a black-market reload.

Knock on wood.

I rapped twice on the door as I pulled it shut behind me.

"I am not a police officer," I said to myself as I turned the Lincoln into a gentle curve that brought me up on the bay. "Or a vigilante, for that matter." I was a career Guardsman with a degree in environmental science and a knack for juggling and tying streamer flies. And here I was, pulling the convertible up the double-wide driveway of a condo owned by a man who may have been, in the dark cave of his heart, concealing savagery. But that's how it goes. One day we're Plain Janes and Ordinary Joes, and the next day we're Hamlet hunting for a murderer at the behest of a ghost.

Rotto lived in the *barrio*, or city district, called Miramar. The house itself was modern and glass, looking out over the yachts

The Tongue Merchant

and powerboats lined up in front of Club Naútico. Two fancy European cars glittered in the drive, with a motorcycle parked near the curb. I saw a windsock marking a helipad on the side of the house, but there was currently no copter in residence. Nor were there any gardens or artsy yard art, just a single, menacing mangrove rising up from a man-made pond in the front yard. A giant radar dish stood on the corner of the house's flat roof. The sky was fading from pink to purple as I nudged the Linc up behind an Alfa Romeo with one of its taillights busted out.

I shut off the engine and sat there for a moment, summoning my reserves.

"No time for nervous breakdowns now," I told myself. "Later, maybe . . ."

Gripping my purse with cold fingers, I got out of the car and made my way to the door. I noticed two things—no, three things—as I neared the house. First there were all the footprints in the dirt around the pool. Dozens of them, between the narrow cement sidewalk and the edge of the house. It looked as if someone had been playing volleyball here, except there wasn't a net in sight. Secondly, a cigarette lay in the crack between two of the slabs which formed the walk. Not a butt, but the entire cigarette, like it had been dropped unnoticed from the pack. I thought about picking it up, but settled for just crouching down and inspecting it. It was long and brown and thin, with no markings other than a triple ring of gold stripes near the filter. Finally, there was the sound I heard as I was standing up. A door. From around the corner of the house.

I turned in time to see a man emerge from a side exit, though in the velveteen twilight his features were difficult to discern. He must have sensed me watching him, because he turned around on his way to the motorcycle. And in that instant I knew him.

Though I couldn't see his face, I felt the depth of those fathomless brown eyes.

Abdías's handyman.

What's he doing here?

"Hey!" I said.

He didn't reply, but walked backward for a few steps, watching me. Then he turned, threw a leg over the bike and—

"Hey, wait a minute!" I jogged toward him.

Looking back at me, his blond hair brushing his neck, he kick-started the bike, gunned the throttle, and sped away. The surly sound of the engine was an affront to the otherwise quiet avenue. I stood on the curb and watched him go, hair trailing behind him, the bike's single headlight opening a tunnel into the night, through which he soon disappeared.

Chapter Eight

I had no time to recover. The front door of the house swung open behind me and a voice like burlap said, "Are ya selling something, darlin', looking to fix a flat tire, or just plain old-fashioned lost?"

I turned around. The light above the door illuminated a small-framed man in cowboy boots and a western print shirt.

"Ya hear me over there?" he called again.

"Yes, hello." I went to him with my hand outstretched, affecting what I hoped to be a smile of the disarming variety. I told him my name but nothing about my affiliation with the Guard, wondering all the while what the fix-it guy from Abdías's place was doing at the home of a DCI board member.

Watch your back, gatita. Things are getting all twisted up around here.

"Good evening," I greeted. "I'm looking for a man named Joseph Rotto."

"Well, then you're doing just fine, darlin', cause ya found him. The pride of Forrt Worth on loan to the grand city of San Juan. What can I do ya for?"

"I was a friend of Isabella Murillo. I'm here on her behalf."

"Is that a fact?" He screwed his eyes to mine. The tiny pocket of flesh above his left cheek twitched almost imperceptibly. After a few seconds, his face relaxed. "Sorry as all hell to hear about what happened to her. I reckon you're here for legal reasons, then. There'll be a mess of paperwork, that's the truth."

"I'm not her attorney, Mr. Rotto. Just her friend. I don't know anything at all about the business side of her life, and that's actually why I'm here. I was hoping you could help me understand a little bit about her father's company."

Rotto scratched his chin, which was as rough as an old roadmap on the floorboard of a pickup truck. He was at least fifty-five years old with a severe haircut and a face baked by a combination of the Texas and Caribbean sun. "Ya legit, Ms. Paraizo?"

"Excuse me?"

"Legitimate. Ya know, are ya shooting straight with me? I only ask on account of all the complications Isabella's death brings to the corporation. There's bound to be a mess of litigation coming out of this, and even *I'm* not sure what belongs to whom at this point. I just want to have your word that Eager-Beaver Abdías didn't send you."

"Abdías? Why would he—"

"Fifty million smackers, that's why. That's what Isabella's shares would've been worth to her in about a month when she turned twenty-six. She'd control forty-five percent of the whole shootin' match. When Abdías hits that same age in three years, he'd get Ernesto's remaining ten percent, giving brother and big sis control of De Casals International. So I'm sure ya agree that those're pretty *grande* numbers up for grabs, now that Isabella has gone and passed on."

I nodded solemnly. "I understand. And no, I'm not working for Abdías, or anyone else, for that matter. To be frank, Mr. Rotto, my only concern is to find the man who murdered her."

"It's Joe." He held open the door and motioned me inside. "And what makes ya think it was a man?"

I stopped on the threshold. "Do you know something I don't?"

"All I know is what I'm told, Ms. Paraizo."

"Marcella. And what is it that you're told?"

He rolled his tongue around in his mouth, then winked. "What are your personal feelings about vodka martinis?"

Joe Rotto's living room was a time warp. Sit down on the leather sofa, close your eyes, and—zap!—you're sucked down the temporal pipeline to the days of cattle barons and Kansas range wars. As the decor was distinctly not my style, I ignored the U.S. cavalry artwork and cowhide rugs and lariat-wrapped banisters, focusing instead on the adornments which covered the south wall on either side of the swinging doors that led to the kitchen. Racked there were several dozen vintage blades. American and British military sabers, mostly, but also more than a few daggers, Scottish dirks, antique bodkins, and other knives. There were some obvious empty spaces along the wall, pegs which sported no show pieces.

"So what about that martini?" Rotto asked. "I make a mediocre one, if ya like to give one a try. But I got more cans of Michelob than Santa Ana had Mexicans at the Alamo, if ya prefer one of those."

"How about a glass of ice water?"

"Yep," he nodded on his way to the bar. "A woman after my own heart. No brew before business . . . and no business after brew." He called into the kitchen, "Carmalita? Keep it warm, honey. I'll be in shortly." He brought me a tall glass and sat down in a chair that looked cobbled together of barn wood and barbed wire but had probably set him back a thousand bucks. "Carmalita's roast beef has started fistfights and ended marriages, Ms. Paraizo, so ya might want to make it short and sweet."

I smiled politely. "I appreciate your taking the time to see me . . ."

"Hogwash. My business day ends at five o'clock. I may not

look like the executive type, darlin', but I'm the biggest corporate boardroom junkie around. Can't get enough of it. Been with De Casals International since I started as an office clerk first year out of college. Now I'm the acting chairman. But I'm not for working myself into an early grave, either. Come sundown, I skin out of that Brooks Brothers bullshit, pardon the French, and get myself into a pair of Wranglers faster than a bluetick dog on a coon. So aside from Carmalita's dinner, I got nothing to do tonight but watch the game and start working my way through those Michelobs." He saluted me with his ice water. "And talk to you."

"Glad to hear it. What can you tell me about Isabella?"

"What would ya like to know?"

"Was she an active participant in the company's affairs?"

"Depends."

"On what?"

"On what you mean by active." Rotto leaned back and crossed his legs so that his pants rode up high on his boots. "Did she attend board meetings, ask for fiscal-earnings reports, that sort of thing? Nope. Not once that I know of. Didn't have an office in the building, didn't have her own bookkeeper to keep track of our progress with her inheritance, which was her right, according to the will. We'd send her all the information on a regular monthly schedule, just so there wouldn't be any question about where the company was going, but she seemed to trust that we were keeping a good watch on her ranch, so to speak."

Something in Rotto's tone told me that he thought I should be extending him a similar trust. But I wasn't so willing. "But Isabella was still somehow involved," I prompted.

"Yep, she sure was. And that, I must say, would be her charm."

"Care to be more specific?"

Rotto stared at the liquid in his glass like a sage seeking an

The Tongue Merchant

augury. "Isabella had taken to writing memos. Woman loved memos. Couldn't get enough of the things. Sent them about to all the important De Casals people, letting it be known both high and low that she had no intention of steering her daddy's wagon train off the trail, if ya know what I mean."

"No, Joe, I'm not sure that I do."

"We're expanding, Ms. Paraizo, or *Marcella,* if you prefer. That's what companies do when they want to remain solvent. De Casals is still making money, sure, but this is the twenty-first century. If we don't expand our operation—"

"Isabella didn't want to expand."

"Tell me something I don't know. Basically, De Casals International is a two-part operation. First there's the sugarcane trade. We're Puerto Rico's leading exporter. Own the fields, the processing plants, the ships, the whole thing from top to bottom. That's ninety percent of our income right there. Then there's the resort hotel Ernesto built just before he died . . ."

"The Croesus."

"Yep, that's right. Biggest damn tower of sin in San Juan. Makes Babel look like a Mormon tabernacle. Got your gambling casinos, your athletic club, cockfighting arena, two bars, not to mention your heart-shaped Jacuzzis and round-the-clock massage staff. Whole hotel is really just one big—"

Floating bedroom, I thought.

"—rendezvous spot for weekend lovers." Rotto took a long drink, then wiped his mouth on his sleeve. "Anyway, up until a year or so ago, that's been the extent of Ernesto's legacy. Then we made an executive decision to explore new areas. Diversify, ya know? We hired some brainy young people to come up with all the numbers, and six months ago we voted to open up a third wing of the company."

"Which is?" I waited, not knowing what to expect.

"Oil," Rotto said, with relish. His lips, which looked perpetually chapped, widened in a grin like that of a new father. "We already owned a modest fleet, and with a few modifications, we could get involved in the transportation of oil out of Venezuela. Let me tell ya, darlin', it's been a long fight, getting through all OPEC's red tape, but the Antilles area is a growing region in need of small-scale oil conveyance, and we aim to provide it."

"Okay, I'll buy that. But why would Isabella be against such a plan? I'm no marketing major, but it sounds like a good idea to me. Has the company been losing money?"

"Sure, at first, but hell's bells, this is business, right? These things take time. My grandfather always said that ya don't rush God giving miracles, or mama cows giving birth. All things come in their own time. We had a truckload of legal work to wade through, palms to grease, regulations to meet, that sort of wasteful stuff, but any of our folks down in the finance department can show ya the charts. We're on the way up, Marcella. Give us another half a year of this and we'll have earned back our expenses and be riding roughshod for pay dirt."

"That may be true, but Isabella obviously didn't think so. Or she had some other reason to doubt the feasibility of the move. Otherwise she wouldn't have bothered with the memos."

"Yeah, sounds that way, huh? But I guess the opinions of her misguided associates were messing with her better judgment."

Uh-oh. I wrinkled my brow. "What do you mean? What associates?"

"The greenies."

He must have read the blank expression on my face, because he immediately explained, though the subject brought him obvious consternation. "I'm talking about those self-styled environmentalists she's been running with behind everyone's backs. The tree-huggers. Those sickos who plant booby traps that kill loggers and sink tuna ships. Now, I don't know how familiar ya are with the fun little world of eco-terrorism, but the baddest of

The Tongue Merchant

the bad is a clan calling themselves the Earth Liberation Front. I've done a little checking up on Isabella's cohorts, just to see why'd she gotten the sudden bee in her bonnet over the company's recent expansion. Seems that an ELF splinter cell has pitched its tent in Hozumkur, and heaven only knows what kind of propaganda they're spreading. But Isabella got mixed up in it, whatever the sam hill it is."

I let that soak in for a few moments. Isabella an eco-terrorist? I wasn't ready to believe that. Admittedly, I was coming to learn that I didn't know my friend as well as I thought I had before all of this started, but I wasn't about to write her off as a left-wing zealot, either. "So let me get this straight. You believe that Isabella Murillo was involved with a sect of environmental anarchists who . . . what? Brainwashed her into believing the transportation of oil was an act of Satan? I'm sorry, Joe, but that just doesn't sound like the woman I knew."

"Oh, she was involved all right." His eyes told me not to challenge him on that point.

"I suppose you have evidence of this?"

"Ya suppose correctly. Like I said, I did some investigating. But ya don't need to get all riled up about Isabella's membership in their little social club." He took a sip and peered at me over the rim of his glass. "I think she was about to turn traitor on them."

I was past the point of being surprised by anything the man said. I just stared at him and said, "I'm listening."

"Isabella was a reporter."

"Yes, I know."

"She was digging up a big story."

"About what?"

"Don't have a clue. But I think she was trying to crack the terrorist operation."

"And this got her killed?"

"Maybe."

"Who was her contact in the operation?"

"An old black hippie woman in Hozumkur."

"And how do you know this?"

"Al Serca and I both hired professional snoops."

"And you think this woman killed Isabella?"

"Yes, ma'am."

"Are you just speculating?"

"Nope."

"You have proof?"

"Yep."

"What kind?"

Joe Rotto smiled. "Did I mention that Isabella was fond of memos?"

He returned from his study carrying a manila folder.

As soon as I saw it, I was back in Dr. Avundavi's office, staring at a similar folder, feeling my fingertips go numb.

I'm your doctor, Marcella. I'm not going to beat around the bush.

That bad, huh?

Potentially, yes. The lesion is cancerous . . .

Oh, God.

Now hold on, Marcella. We've got a lot of options at this point . . .

But I wasn't in the mood to hear about options. The Secret Saboteur was a time bomb, and all I wanted was for someone to hurry up and clip the wires before the clock hit zero. If it hadn't been for Bella's ghost distracting me, I would've been an emotional wreck, so I guess the good Lord hides a blessing or two in even the most horrible packages; in this case that package was a long black body bag cooling in the morgue. Supressing a violent shiver, I sat up straight in my chair and accepted the proffered file.

"It's not much," Rotto admitted, "but it's enough to make a

The Tongue Merchant

man wonder just what Isabella was up to."

I took my time scanning the slim dossier Rotto had assembled, detailing Bella's memo-sending campaign and her possible affiliation with a nameless group of ELF supporters in Hozumkur. Obviously Bella was pissed off about the board's decision to take the company into the oil-transport business, and from what I read, most of her reasons seemed grounded in nothing but tradition. Ernesto had never done it this way, she argued, so why start now? A few of the memos were dedicated to environmental issues, principally the depletion of nonrenewable fossil fuels and the ever-present risk of oil spills, your typical green philosophy. The remainder of the file included a couple of black-and-white photos of Bella and a woman who was presumably the one Rotto had accused of being a terrorist and possible murderer. In one of the pictures the woman's face was obscured by a wide-brimmed straw hat. In another she wore a hooded cloak, reminiscent of something from the Victorian era. Only in the final photo were her features fully visible . . . and I had to admit, entirely arresting. She had the face of someone who eunuchs carried on a silk sedan chair in small countries with funny names, someone adorned since birth in foreign gold and perfumed with things like jasmine and myrrh. Her skin was richly black and unblemished, save for a few fine but not unbecoming wrinkles around her eyes. Her hair was scandalously long and even darker than my own, but threaded with gossamer strands of white. A hand-written notation informed me that I was looking at Isolde Berlin Bancavia.

"She's beautiful," I observed.

"Aren't they always?"

"Have you met her?"

Rotto grunted. "If I ever meet her, it's going to be inside a court of law."

"Why do you say that? Has her organization threatened your

shipping lanes?"

"Not directly, no. But there've been some accidents . . ."

"Involving whom?"

Rotto drained the last of his drink and gave the cubes a shake in the glass. "Ya heard about that series of warehouse fires over on St. Noré eight months back? Two of those warehouses belonged to us. Cost De Casals close to two million in damages and three innocent employees who had the misfortune of being on duty that night. Well, they caught this guy trying to leave the country and brought him up on arson and second-degree murder charges. Name's Jan Voorstadt. Dutch, I think. Anyway, the prosecutors had a table of evidence bigger than Dallas, and they were all set to prove that Voorstadt was in cohoots with ELF by way of its Hozumkur connections. ELF's about the most secretive cabal on the block. Interpol has been collecting dirt on Voorstadt for years, and they still haven't gotten any proof worth more than a bucket of horse piss. Voorstadt, now, he's a dyed-in-the-wool ELFer, probably one of their top agents. And the prosecution was finally set to bust the club wide open. But like my grandfather used to say, don't go loading the wagon before you check the mule." He paused, maybe for effect, probably just because it pained him so much to say what happened next. "The arraignment got hung up on an arrest technicality, and the judge let the man walk."

"Ah. Another triumph for our judicial system."

"Tell me about it, darlin'."

"But what's that got to do with Isabella?"

Rotto indicated the folder in my lap. "Try that last memo on for size."

I flipped past the pictures of Isolde Berlin Bancavia and found one final square of paper, a photocopy of a De Casals memorandum sent to Rotto's office, written in a penmanship I recognized at once.

The Tongue Merchant

Joseph. Just a forewarning. Our friend Voorstadt? Found the connection tying him to Hozumkur. I know me and thee often don't see eye-to-eye, but there are forces, as they say, aligning against us. Keep the ships safe, and buy next Sunday's paper. Isabella.

"This isn't exactly a smoking gun," I remarked.

"Well it's a start."

"Maybe. Was there anything else?"

"Like what?"

"I don't know. Something that incriminates this Bancavia woman? Obviously Isabella found a link between Bancavia, Voorstadt, and ELF. Did she mention anything like that? Any tangible proof? Something she might have stashed in a safe deposit box or left with a friend or anything like that?"

"Darlin', if I knew the answer to that question, I'd have been on the horn with the *federales* the second I heard she'd been murdered. Besides, the cops have already sacked her house, I'm sure. If she left anything hidden there, you can bet they've already found it."

"Yes, I suppose they have." Except I knew they hadn't. An inner phonograph kept replaying the same message in my heart. *The police have nothing. The police have no clues. The police, to put it poetically, have dick.* Kyle Straker would find no such evidence at Isabella's, because she was too damn wily to stash the keys to the kingdom in a coffee can or under the door mat. I may have been surprised by all her many guises—adulteress, undercover journalist, possible eco-terrorist—but I was still safe in the knowledge that whatever mask she wore when moonlighting, she was no dummy.

"Ernesto's daughter knew too much about Bancavia and her friends," Rotto concluded grimly. "And they killed her for it."

And cut out her tongue, I thought, imagining I could feel the wooden stick pulsing out a Morse warning in my purse.

"Ya say ya want to find the murderer? Then go pay a visit to a shop called Bancavia's Antebellum Books, over in Hozumkur. Just make sure your life insurance is up to date. Those people plainly don't take kindly to interlopers."

"And what are you going to do?"

"What I get paid to do. Run De Casals International the best I know how. And that means boating oil from Venezuela better than anybody in the Caribbean. And if that dishonors Isabella's spirit, then I truly apologize, but it's the only way I know to play the game."

And that was that.

Or was it?

I sat there on the sofa, leaning on an armrest in the shape of a wagon wheel, scrambling for something else to ask, that one perfect question that would lock the puzzle in place. But I'd had little practice at interviews like this, and I figured I'd gotten enough new information to keep myself up half the night. The petroleum trade, missing jewels, love affairs, Dutch arsonists, high-risk journalism, million-dollar inheritances, ecological perils, and international terrorism. It was enough to make a person seriously question the fairness of the cosmos, to say nothing of God's sense of humor.

And how the hell did the postage stamp fit into all of this?

Behind my unruffled facade I was tearing my hair out in clumps.

"Well, thank you for sharing your story with me this evening," I said, wondering if that sounded as lame to Rotto's ears as it did to my own. "All I want is to find the person responsible for Isabella's death. You've been a great help."

"Don't know about that, darlin'. I'm not keen on a whole helluva lot about the lady's personal life. I only did a bit of checking up on her to make sure she wasn't part of that whole ELF enterprise. And now . . . now I'll just take one day at a time, I reckon. Not much more a man can expect to do in this day and age."

I responded with something inconsequential, said thank you again, shook hands, and let him walk me to the door, talking about Bartholomew and the precautions San Juan was taking in anticipation of its arrival. There were a lot of hatches to be battened down before that old rogue, Johnny Storm, came a'calling.

Rotto wished me luck, gave me his card and told me to phone him the moment I learned anything, or even if I just needed someone to talk to. The offer sounded genuine.

Even still, I turned around before I was halfway to my car. "Hey, Joe?"

"Yep?"

"Do you mind telling me where you were Sunday night around midnight?"

He studied me as best he could in the balmy darkness. "Do you play snooker, Marcella?"

"Can't say that I do."

"Well, I've got a table in my rec room. I play every night. To unwind."

"And you play alone," I guessed.

"That's right."

"What about Carmalita? Was she or anyone else in the house that night?"

Rotto slowly curled his thumbs over his oversized belt buckle. "Only me and Señor Jose Cuervo, and he ain't much for talking."

"No," I said after awhile. "I don't suppose he is. I'll see you at the funeral."

"Yep, Marcella, I'm sure that you will."

I slammed the door of the Lincoln and gave it too much gas, trying to drive faster than my skyrocketing emotions.

Fat chance of that.

★ ★ ★ ★ ★

Tongs of yellow lightning speared the eastern sky.

When I got out of the Lincoln in front of my apartment building, I clearly saw what was happening in the direction of St. Noré. Already the eastern sky had begun to change. Though the place where I stood was a bubble of stillness and warmth, smelling of sea spray and green living things, 165 miles off the St. Noré coast lay a barbarism so raw that the scents were scoured from the air and the clouds were wrecked like falling houses. I knew those rare winds, had tangled with them in the past and found myself too small for the battle. There was that night in Grenada with the sand bags and the sirens and the rain so hard on my face that I thought my skin would tear apart . . .

Pushing away the memory the way one tucks a wayward hair into place, I left the car out of the garage, knowing I'd need it soon enough, and passed between the giant queen palms to my front door. I crammed the key into the lock with too much force, scuffed my knuckles against the door frame, hissed one of my mother's more imaginative curses, and burst into my house rather like a storm myself.

I dropped my purse on the table and touched the button on the answering machine, knowing it would be the luscious yet lackluster Captain Maddox but stopping cold when I realized that it wasn't.

Instead, I heard the shopworn voice of Kyle Straker.

"Uh, hi, Marcella. Kyle Straker here. You might remember me. I'm the cop who caught you trespassing on police property and was Galahad enough not to haul you in. Okay. So that wasn't very funny. Sorry. But I wanted to let you know . . . I mean, hell, I don't know why I should even tell you this but . . . but this evening we obtained an arrest warrant for Nicholas Murillo. I brought him in myself half an hour ago."

The blood turned arctic in my veins.

"His alibi fell to pieces, Marcella. We have a witness who puts him at the scene at the time of his wife's murder. So . . . damn. That doesn't mean he did it, but it does mean that he lied when he claimed to be with his girlfriend all night. Anyway, something tells me that I'll be seeing you around. Have a good night."

I closed my eyes and braced myself on the wall.

"And Marcella?"

I held my breath.

"I know it doesn't count for much right now, but I'm sorry it had to happen this way."

He hung up, and the wind rushed out of me.

Fortunately I made it to my bed before collapsing.

Chapter Nine

I didn't lie there very long.

Just five minutes, I told myself, my face in the pillow the way it used to be when I was small and the night-things pressed down upon me. *Just five minutes, and I'll either be asleep or I'll have faked the night-things into thinking that I am, and they'll leave me alone.*

I waited for three minutes and couldn't stand it any more. The ghoulish night-things of my childhood had returned, joining hands around my bed and chanting my name like some kind of bogeyman choir.

Enough.

I shot to my feet and retrieved the postage stamp from where I'd hidden it between the pages of my old neglected Spanish Bible, tucked in the Psalms, chapter 46.

Be still, the verse read, *and know that I am God.*

Good advice for manic women like me out here on the wild side.

I remained still for all of fifteen seconds before losing the fight to motion. *Sorry, God.* Quickly I used the bathroom, scowled at my hair in the mirror, snagged my purse, and raced back out to the car. It was nine o'clock at night and Nico was sitting in the Hozumkur city jail. Served him right. After all, hadn't he lied to the authorities? If what Straker said were true—and at this point he was the only person I would trust with my fine china, if I had any china to lend—then Nico had, at the very least, misrepresented his alibi and would most likely be the headline of tomorrow's *Plebiscite*. They'd probably run a photo of him trying to conceal his face with his shirttails, his wrists cuffed in front of him.

The Linc's mastodon of an engine roared on the second try, and I barely checked for traffic before thundering into the street. I needed answers. To this end, I was on my way to interrupt the evening of a perfectly innocent philatelist, just the way Bartholomew was en route to spoil the lives of more than a few undeserving islanders.

Saldaña's Stamp & Scroll was located in the bustling student *barrio* called Río Piedras, where the iconoclastic university spirit was as evident as it was on any campus in the States. The streetlights on the outskirts of the university revealed the island's cultural potpourri: horny creole students bopped in and out of nightclubs, cutting-edge salsa music chasing after them every time they opened the door; angry teenage mulattos with red scarves in their hair chanted slurs concerning the White House, the Drug Enforcement Agency, and *americanos* in general, all to the beat of a conga drum; male prostitutes in elevator shoes hung on the corners; someone was hawking local fruits—papaya, yuca, and oranges—but not selling half as well as the crack dealer in the back of the black Impala; a woman in fuzzy slippers was chasing a dog.

I parked illegally on campus a block away. Better to walk than leave my car around here for the jackals to pick apart. I got a few wolf whistles as I made my way down the sidewalk in front of the coffee houses and boutiques. Most of the businesses I passed had turned around their CLOSED signs hours ago.

Saldaña's shop was a narrow building of locally quarried stone wedged between two rundown student hostels and guarded by a pair of dignified kapok trees. The moon sailed directly over my head, giving me an encouraging half-wink as I approached the building but doing little to dispel the shadows thrown by the kapoks. *More shadows,* I thought. *More nightthings. Terrific.* Peering through the ground-floor windows, I saw stacks of books with weathered dust jackets, but they were piled too high and the room beyond too dark to discern any details of the shop's interior. The door of the building was painted the color of forest moss, with a bright brass knocker cast in the shape of an elephant's head. There was a little metal slot for mail halfway down the door, but someone had tacked it shut.

A tarnished plaque above the elephant informed me in Spanish that Señor Saldaña kept his hours from ten to four, and please pardon the inconvenience but no smoking was permitted inside, *gracias.*

After rapping four times on the door, I paused for the count of one heartbeat, then tried again. Saldaña most likely lived in the apartment above the shop; there was a lighted balcony up there, ringed with pots full of hollyhock and foxglove and spied upon by a ceramic gnome with a tiny watering can. I rattled another series of knocks, louder this time, and threw in a couple of swats with the palm of my hand, because I may be my father's child in most respects but I've got a timer on my patience I inherited from my mother, and you never kept her waiting when there were folks in need of punishment and saving.

I thought about her as I shouted, "Señor Saldaña? Is anyone home?" There was that morning when I was eleven. Dad was already at the cop shop, and I sat at the kitchen table swinging my legs beneath the chair and watching in mute fascination as Mom tried to scrape burned batter from the inside of the waffle iron.

She raked at the stuff with a fork, an unlikely apron around her waist. "Damn thing."

"Dad always uses butter."

"Yeah, *gatita*, I know. But I forgot. It happens. You get old, that's the first thing to go."

"I don't want to get old, Mama."

She stared at me from across the room, her night-black hair touched with a few renegade threads of gray, her fork caked with blackened gunk. A sad smile touched the corner of her mouth, just above her scar. "Hey. You don't want to be old? Then don't spend your life in the kitchen worrying over waffle irons. Just take your dear little daughter out to the nearest pancake house, and save your time for the important things. Like . . . *tickling*." She rushed me, and before I knew it we were both on the linoleum, giggling, surrounded by the smell of charred waffles.

"Señor Saldaña!" I went at the door like a battering ram at a castle drawbridge.

"*Sí, sí!*" came the muffled response from inside. I heard someone rustling closer, a dull light flickered behind the windows, and then a series of deadbolts snapped back and the door was yanked open. A man with kerosene eyes stared back at me.

"Good evening," I said in Spanish. "My name is Mar—"

The door shut in my face.

At once the locks began to slide back into the door.

"Hey, wait a minute, goddammit!" Anger surged through me. Isabella was dead and I went to the nearest window and smacked it so hard that it shook in the casement. "I need to talk to you! Do you understand? It's important!" I gave the window another drubbing, dislodging years of dust from the sash. Inside I could see the man's bent little figure, scuttling back through the books.

He stopped when I struck the window nearly hard enough to break it.

"You give me five minutes of your time, señor, unless you

want to be sweeping up glass until the sun rises tomorrow."

"You stay away from there!" he warned, his voice like a trembling wire. He came to the window, moving faster than I thought him capable of, and thrust one cork-colored finger at my face. "I don't want no solicitors in my place, especially at this time of night."

"I'm not selling anything. Please. I just need to talk to you."

His eyes, too large for their sockets, bulged like eggs. "I don't need no coupon books, you hear? No coupon books, no magazine subscriptions, no life insurance and certainly no damned Avon. That make sense to you?"

"Yes, perfectly." I paused, drew a breath, let it go. "Look, I'm getting tired of talking through this window, okay? I know it's late, but it's tremendously important that I speak with you."

"About what?"

"A stamp."

One bristly eyebrow lurched up his brow. His lips parted. I saw a row of small hard teeth between gums that seemed a little too red. "What kind of stamp?"

It was all I could do to keep from punching my fist through the glass, grabbing him by the lapels of his flea-market shirt, and dragging him bodily into the street, where I'd force-feed the stamp to him and shake him till he told me what I wanted to know. Instead, I touched my forehead to the window. "I have a stamp. I'm sorry to bother you. But I think the stamp is valuable. Perhaps extremely so. I thought you might be interested in it. I was under the impression that you dealt in that sort of thing. Maybe I was wrong."

The man considered me, his chinless mouth moving as if he were chewing up my words, trying by taste to tell fact from fiction. After a few moments of excruciating silence, he scooped his cobweb hair from his face and went about disengaging the locks.

Thanks, God. I don't think I had the energy to lift the knocker again.

"Sorry," he said, standing in the doorway. "Didn't know you was a customer. But it's late."

"I realize that. Do you have a minute?"

"You really have a stamp?"

"I don't know. Why don't you invite me in and we'll see what happens next?"

He nodded. His head seemed too unwieldy for his shoulders. He stepped aside.

I walked into the shop.

The moonlight disappeared as he closed the door behind me.

I thought that my host would turn on a few more lights, but he left the room swathed in shadows, resorting only to a bare bulb which hung from a chain above a desk. The desk itself was immense. Its legs, carved as elephant's feet, gave me the spooky impression that the thing was almost alive, waiting to be granted the final spark of life from this old sorcerer standing before me. With the bulb swinging over his head and dark shapes lunging back and forth against the wall, he looked at me and sort of waved his hands around the room.

"This here's my shop. She don't seem like much, you know, but I've been saving for years, and so maybe she's the best that I can do." His Spanish was so husky, so *earthy*, that I knew he'd never spoken a word of English, the devil-tongue of tourists. He verified my suspicions when he said, "Haven't the time nor the liking for white people. Europeans, Americans, they think they run the world, ever since Christ went and got Himself killed." He made a halfhearted sign of the cross. The rosary looped through his cracked leather belt was made of mismatched plastic pellets. "Me, I only serve customers who know these parts. True collectors, you get me? Men in Buenos Aires, Santiago . . .

sometimes all the way to Barcelona. They want an honest quote, they telephone me, Miguel Saldaña y Hinojosa." Quite to my surprise, he gave a disjointed little bow.

"Pleased to meet you. My name is Marcella."

Saldaña cocked his head to one side, like a dog keen on a sound no human could hear. Something about that posture caused flakes of unease to drift down my throat. I swallowed a few times to get rid of them.

"Marcella. That's from Latin mythology, eh? I know things like that. I read. Read all the time. I come across a lot of old documents, antique manuscripts, that kind of thing. So let's see . . ." He perched one thin hip on the edge of the desk. "Marcella would be the feminine form of Mars." The spectral smile was back on his lips. "God of war."

"If you say so," I said, even though I knew it was true. I didn't have time to butter the guy up. My patience timer was still sitting at zero. I opened my purse. "I recently acquired a stamp that I thought might be of value. I'd like you to take a look at it, appraise it, and tell me exactly what I've got, if anything." I withdrew the small plastic envelope. "Can you do that?"

"You selling?"

"Anything's possible."

He held out his hand, the palm of which was tooled with a diagram of wrinkles.

With more than a little reluctance, I handed over the stamp.

"Very good. So let's see what you got." He rummaged around through the disaster on the desk until he found a complicated pair of eyeglasses. Half a dozen magnifying lenses were affixed to the heavy wire frame, which Saldaña hooked over his ears after first batting back strings of hair from his face. I wondered if he'd fashioned the spectacles himself, as they seemed a rather ungainly bit of engineering. Once the glasses were firmly fixed

The Tongue Merchant

over his nose, he went through a rapid series of motions, moving the lenses on their tiny hinges until he had the two he wanted positioned in front of his eyes. His already bloated pupils now looked grotesque.

"Mmmm . . ." With a surgeon's care, he used a pair of tongs to slide the stamp from its protective cover. He held it up to the light.

I stood there smelling yellowing paper, traces of orchid-scented incense, and old-man's cologne.

"Where did you get this?" he asked, never taking his eyes from it.

"Does that matter?"

"Might."

"What's that supposed to mean?"

He looked up at me sharply, his features ridiculous behind his array of lenses. "This is a very rare stamp, to say the least. I mean, damn, to say the least at all."

"You recognize it?"

"By reputation, yes. It's Prussian. Turn-of-the-century. Except it's defective."

"What do you mean?"

"I mean this here is a very old piece of postage that happens to have been minted upside down, which makes it worth a small fortune. It's a mistake, you see? Got printed the wrong side up, and this is the second time in the last week that I heard about it."

I frowned. "You heard about this particular stamp?"

"It's called an Adelbert. That's actually the name of the train, which they named on behalf of a martyred German missionary. At last count, there were only fourteen Adelberts still in circulation." He traced his finger over the stamp. "Do you know music, Marcella, Goddess of War? Here's an analogy. You want the best violin, you'll probably go hunting for a Stradivarius. Some of the world's most extraordinary violins were actually made by Guarneri—but hardly any of those instruments still exist. And of course a Stradivarius is still remarkable. That's what this Adelbert is. Not the rarest postage around, not a Guarneri. But it's the Stradivarius of stamps." He slipped the stamp back into its plastic cover.

Jesus. What was Bella doing with something like that?

"And this is the second time you've heard of this stamp in the last week?"

"A fact. A contemporary of mine in Hozumkur, a scoundrel he is. His name is Paulo Longoria and he will rob you of everything if you make the mistake of wandering into his shop." Saldaña's face twisted up in revulsion, like a fruit spoiling in the heat. "But rumor has it that Longoria just facilitated the sale of an Adelbert and probably took a commission so damn big that neither of the trading parties will be able to pay their next month's rent. He don't take no prisoners, that Longoria."

All right. I knew I was on to something. A spark of electricity passed down my arms, and suddenly I realized how cold the building was; Saldaña had the air-conditioner throttled wide open, and my thin dress did little to warm me.

Forget the cold. Just keep going. Grab the stupid puzzle piece and make it fit.

"Who was the buyer?" I asked.

"What do you mean? I thought it was you. You got the stamp, right?"

"When was the sale completed?"

"Longoria had been working on it for months. He finally talked someone into selling."

"What are the odds of two Adelberts showing up in the Antilles at the same time?"

"Dismal."

"That's what I thought."

"So did you steal this?" He kept looking at me with his magnified eyes. I could clearly see the tracings of red around his pupils. "You thinking maybe Señor Saldaña is a fence?"

"Who was the buyer?" I asked again, feeling the quickening in my chest. I was finally on the trail and I'll be damned if I couldn't smell blood.

"Can't say. That part of the deal wasn't made public."

"What about the seller?"

Saldaña whisked his tongue over his pallid lips. "That wasn't made public, either, but word gets around. The stamp trade is cutthroat sometimes. Rumors squeak out even when you don't want them to, like farts." He seemed pleased with his simile.

"I'd like a name, please."

"And you're going to go smashing my windows again if I don't give it to you?"

"Please, it's imperative that I—"

"Armande St-Germain," he announced. "I'm telling you this only because Longoria is dogshit and I owe him one. St-Germain is rich and likes to buy and sell things. He collects everything, including people. He's a dilettante in the stamp business, mind you, but he has money to afford to be frivolous. Someone wanted an Adelbert, he had one, and Longoria set up the deal."

"How much did this St-Germain sell it for?"

"God only knows. Enough to ransom a sheik, probably."

"When was the sale?"

"Six days ago."

"Where?"

"Longoria's shop, I would guess. Or maybe out on that battleship that St-Germain calls a yacht. Damned thing is probably still moored around here somewhere. Men like that love Puerto Rican whores and all their diseases, right?"

Armande St-Germain. Where had I heard that name before?

Then it came to me.

"Tennis," I said. "St-Germain is the French tennis star. Retired, right?"

"From Monaco," Saldaña confirmed. "But he's old now, and fat, and he buys racehorses and women and politicians, now please tell me, just what are you asking for this stamp, because I can see that you're no collector and I get an erection just holding the thing in my hand."

I resisted the mad urge to glance down at the crotch of his grimy dungarees, just to see if he was serious. "Sorry. It's not for sale."

"Everything is for sale."

"Not tonight it's not."

He made a sound like an animal clearing its nasal tract. "You think you can bother me at this hour and make me answer your questions and not even tell me where you got this thing? You shouldn't even be walking around with it. Could get yourself into a good mess of trouble, for sure. Fine-looking woman like you, anything could happen to you and your stamp. Anything at all."

So there we were. He stood before his desk with its pachyderm girth, the dirty lightbulb hanging above his head, shelves rising around him with their pigeonholes crammed with papers that would probably turn to dust if a moth alighted upon them. He was hardly five-foot-six, his Rube Goldberg glasses making him seem more freakish than comical. He held the tongs in his right hand, the Adelbert in its envelope pinched between them, his left hand gripping the lip of the desk.

A wooden bird stuttered out of a clock on the wall behind him, cocked once for half-past-the-hour, and rode an unoiled track back into its hidey hole.

"I'm taking my Stradivarius," I said calmly, managing to keep my arms from crossing themselves defensively over my chest, as they tend to do when I'm not paying attention. "And then I'm leaving you in peace. If I decide to part with the stamp, you'll be my first phone call. I don't think I'll have much use for it, and we wouldn't want Longoria to be one up on you. I truly appreciate your seeing me tonight, but I must be going." I took a step toward him, lifting my hand to take the stamp.

He snatched his arm back.

My eyes narrowed dangerously.

"I'm sure we can come to some kind of arrangement," he said quietly.

"Give me the goddamn stamp."

"It should really be in the collection of someone who would appreciate it," Saldaña said, dreamily, moving the tweezers in front of his face like a magic wand. The shadows mimicked the motion on the wall. "You? You didn't even know what you had. Let me at least make you an offer."

"The only thing I want to hear from you," I said, leaning toward him and forcing the words through my teeth, "is a promise to keep from pissing your pants when I kick you in the balls. You're a troll, Saldaña. Now hand over the stamp."

Not bad, gatita.

"You stole it. Didn't you?" The tension drained out of his face, the leer sliding from his mouth. He extended the tweezers toward me as if he no longer had the strength to lift his arm. "You took it from whoever bought it from St-Germain. That's right, isn't it?"

I had the sudden vision of the hobbit, Bilbo Baggins, parleying with the contemptible Gollum in a dank cave. Dad had read that book to me when I was thirteen and recovering from pneumonia. I hadn't thought about it again until today.

I took the stamp back at the same moment that Saldaña, as fast as a rock lizard, shot out his left hand and locked it around my wrist.

"You thieved it, didn't you?"

The light shined through the panoply of lenses and illuminated an injury on his scalp, just over his temple: a fresh abrasion an inch long, not yet scabbed over.

"Let *go* of me." My fingers pinching the stamp, I tugged myself free of his clammy but surprisingly brawny grip, my heart rocking against my ribs. My body went on autopilot and shifted my feet to offer less of a target, while bringing up my fists and feeling my internal engine dump what felt like two pounds of sugar into my blood. Visions of the Walther in my purse flashed through my mind, but I didn't think matters had reached the gun stage just yet. However, I came very close to living up to my threat and blasting him between the legs. "Now back off!"

Strangely, Saldaña chortled. But at least he scampered back a few feet, putting the desk between us. "Boy thieves go to the principal's office," he said in an eerie sing-song. "Girl thieves go to hell or Cleveland."

Not knowing what to make of this odd proclamation but knowing that it was *definitely* time to get the hell away, I backed up till my rump touched the moss-green door, and then hurried outside.

"Bad girls go to hell or Cleveland!" he shrieked.

"Good!" I hollered back, which was really a juvenile thing to do, but hey. This guy was asylum material, and I was just thrilled to be back in the heat and under the moon and still, apparently, in my own universe. For a moment there I thought I'd fallen through a rabbit hole.

"Freak," I whispered in English as I clipped across the street to where I'd parked the Linc.

I slowed down in hopes that my heart would do the same. I thought about what I'd just learned. The playboy philanthropist Armande St-Germain had sold the stamp to Isabella, who had probably dipped into her allowance to make the payment. The odds of there being two Adelberts in the area at the same time were off the chart, so it was safe to assume that the gem I was holding in my hand was the very one which St-Germain had sold. And Bella, no philatelist herself, hadn't purchased the stamp for any normal reason. Otherwise she wouldn't have stashed it in her shoe. So what was she going to do with it? And what, if anything, did her acquisition of the stamp have to do with the story she was working on for the *Plebiscite* and her possible connections with ELF?

Maybe Longoria could tell me. Or Armande St-Germain, if I could find him. In the meantime, though, there was Alonzo Serca and Isolde Berlin Bancavia, and now that I was thinking about it, I also wanted to have a talk with whoever saw Nico at the crime scene and ruined his alibi, because either Nico was lying or this supposed witness was. And of course there was always the Mystery Man himself. He was Bella's lover, and he knew she was dead. Either he was guilty of the crime, or he was mourning her death and unable to make his grief public because it would expose them as adulterers . . .

I almost didn't see the car until it was on top of me.

It was my own fault. I hadn't been paying attention. My nerves were still frayed from my encounter with Gollum, the strings of my anger still strumming, and by the time I looked up, the pair of headlights was only ten feet away. The car came right at me. Its engine howled.

I jumped.

I used to swim a little in college. But rowing was my passion. My senior year at the Academy I was crew captain. We placed second at the NCAA finals. We had T-shirts printed with the Guard logo on the front, and a creepy bit of Nietzsche on the back: *"When one rows it is not the rowing which moves the boat; rowing is only a magical ceremony by means with which one compels a demon to move the boat."*

Well, when I drove my legs against the concrete to provide thrust to my muscles, it wasn't my legs lifting me into the air. The movement of my legs was only an incantation to summon infernal assistance. A demon threw me clear of the car.

I came down on my hands. Instinct kept me from opening my right hand, where I still clutched the stamp. The skin peeled away from my knuckles and sent a bolt of pain all the way up my shoulder. The demon's momentum carried me onto my back, and then I rolled until I collided with the curb.

The car rushed by me.

I grunted for breath, but there wasn't one to be had. The world was airless. Looking up through the white lights that seared my vision, I saw the car's brake lights flare just enough to slow it down before it squalled around the corner. Still not breathing, I forced my head up higher to get a glimpse of the vehicle; in the pallid shine of the streetlights, the car might have been a Camaro or Trans Am, but whether it was blue or black or something in between, I wasn't sure.

The sound of the car faded in the night.

Then my throat opened up and I sucked in a mouthful of air.

"Holy shit." I lay there with my face an inch off the pavement, my dress halfway up my thigh and my purse nowhere to be seen. The tintinnabulators rang so ferociously that I could barely hear my pulse, walloping against the side of my head the way the steel wheels of a locomotive bang against the tracks.

I'd almost been run over.

Intentionally, you think?

"Maybe," I said.

That's not good.

"No kidding." I pushed myself up on my knees, which stung from road grit and friction. I examined my bloody knuckles. Maybe I'd be lucky and they wouldn't need stitches. The palm of my other hand was also abraded, but there wasn't much blood.

I sat there for far too long, trying to keep my head from spinning and the ground from tilting and my tears, goddammit, from falling down my cheeks.

Something caught my eye from the direction of Saldaña's shop.

For a moment I thought I saw a bulbous face watching me in the window, but then it was gone.

Chapter Ten

My hand wrapped in a bundle of tissues and my instincts on red alert, I twisted the Linc through the darksome streets of San Juan, bracing myself for another meeting with someone I didn't know. I was on my way to Alonzo Serca's. My nose was running. My hand was bleeding. I've always kept a little travel pack of tissues in the glovebox; now they served as a field dressing.

They almost killed me.

"There is no *they*," I said aloud. "Coincidences happen, you know."

And that cut on Saldaña's head. 'Spose that was coincidence as well.

"Isabella did not hit that old man on the head with a hammer," I argued.

Straker said she certainly hit SOMEBODY.

"Not Saldaña."

Why not?

I didn't respond, just kept on driving.

I said, why not?

"And I said shut the hell up." I knew things were bad when I was holding a tête-à-tête with myself and actually letting the conversation dissolve into an argument. I pulled up to a stoplight and took a moment to check the time. I wore an Australian diver's watch with an illuminated tritium face. The compass affixed to the dashboard was also luminescent, so I sat there in an eldritch green glow at a deserted intersection with the top rolled down and a saxophone playing somewhere down the street and the palm trees swaying menacingly in the ever-building wind. It was one of those moments. I squeezed my eyes shut until it passed.

By that time the light said go. It was ten o'clock.

I stomped on the gas.

I couldn't shake the sense that I was building up to something, the way Bartholomew was stacking its black clouds like crates of ammunition and stirring up the guns of thunder. That storm and I, we were both coming to a head. Give us a few more hours, perhaps as long as a day, and we'd turn this island upside down.

Alonzo Serca lived in the posh resort district of San Juan. I drove there wondering what my personal Beaufort rating was up to. I must have been at least a force 7, and gaining speed with every revolution of my wheels.

I'd seen buildings like this before. The dude out front in the brass buttons. The porte cochere to keep you out of the rain when you disembark your Jaguar. There was only one thing that surprised me as I pulled to the curb and cast my gaze all the way up to the top of the structure.

I was looking at the Croesus.

Crowning the building were gigantic letters made of blue and silver lights. For two seconds the letters were dark, invisible in the black sky, and then, far on the left, a twelve-foot-tall *C* blazed to life, followed by the *R* and *O*, until the last *S* made an artificial daylight of the night, so hefty was the candle-power of its bulbs. Then one by one the letters dimmed, only to repeat the process in another fantasia of silver and sapphire. The Croesus was shaped like a hexagon, its six sides rising up thirty-two floors and representing the island's only self-contained community. Those inside could seal themselves off from the goods and services of the working world and live comfortably for at least a month before having to come out for air. The first seven floors were comprised of the casino and four-star hotel, the De Casals International emblem skillfully entwined with the trendy Croesus logo that adorned everything from the polarized windows to the water fountains to those little bars of soap they put in your shower. The next three floors, so went the rumor, held the shops and boutiques and restaurants that kept the inhabitants fat and happy. There was a movie theater, two dance clubs. The works. Two of the floors housed staff. The remainder were leased by that one percent of the population that spared all the rest of us the burden of having too much money and still trying to finagle our way into heaven.

I doublechecked the address. Yep, this was Serca's pad. I shouldn't have been surprised, really, since he'd been behind De Casals's decision to erect the bloody thing. Only fitting that he should hang his hat on the top floor. I'd never been to the Croesus and hadn't recognized the street address, but now that I was here, awash in its capitalistic glow, I realized how obvious it should have been.

Follow the money, they always said.

Well, here I was.

Though it was Tuesday and there was a possible land-smasher gathering courage not far away, the Croesus had still drawn a crowd. As I brushed the road-grit from my dress and gave CPR to my poor hair, more gamblers-slash-tourists motored up to the hotel and strode like conquerors inside. Most would drag themselves out by one a.m., their shoulders bent in defeat.

Wishing I'd had time to make myself more presentable, I crossed the street, this time *damn* sure to check for oncoming traffic, passing the doorman at the residential entrance and making my way to the glitzy casino doors. They were of the swivel variety, the better to welcome the hopeful and discharge the impoverished. A man in a loosely knotted tie smiled at me as we cycled passed each other in the door.

I didn't smile back.

Instead, I thought about that wound on Saldaña's head and the strength of his grip when he grabbed my arm and, tugging beneath these worries like the undertow of the ocean, there was the Secret Saboteur, asking me what it felt like to have a breast amputated.

In my mother's voice I told it to go to hell.

The main casino floor was dotted with islands of slot machines and tickering roulette wheels that played host to at least three hundred gamblers, most of whom were tourists and looked that way. Four chandeliers hung from the vaulted ceiling, where I noticed at least a dozen security cameras keeping an electronic eye on every cranny of the room. The music—God, what was it? Chopin or Haydn? I'd always been a procrastinator about getting in touch with the classics, but whatever it was, it filled the room at a subliminal level, not loud enough to distract the amateur card sharps trying to concentrate but still providing a steady pulse to the overall rhythm of the room. On my right was a bar of solid cherrywood which nearly ran the length of the chamber, polished to a sheen and worked by college-age men in shirtsleeves and black ties. On my left was a bank of faro tables, the nearest one presided over by a dealer with skin so unearthly pale that I could almost see his blue veins working underneath. A pair of hands as white as a cadaver's stuck out from the cuffs of his tuxedo as he manipulated the cards. He wore Ray Charles glasses, and a shock of colorless hair dangled down the bridge of his nose like an inverted question mark.

Haven't you ever seen an albino before? Stop staring and start—

"Doing my job," I said under my breath.

I wended my way between the tables.

Though I tried to stay alert, primed for any sign that might set me on the trail of Bella's murderer, I was too bombarded with the casino's circus atmosphere to concentrate. Waiters wove adroitly through the maze, the men wearing black vests and the women black minis; glasses clinked like little bells; there was swearing—English, Portuguese, an upstart bit of French—and tipsy laughter that sounded the same in any tongue. Sirens of victory rang out from a lucky slot. Blue and red chips lay everywhere, in stacks tall and short, in tidy and messy piles, and strewn about the green-felt tables like bones cast by a fortune-teller. Perfumes by Chanel, leather shoes, slots clattering with coins, lights flickering off the faces of wristwatches and the corners of earrings, flesh exposed by scooped necklines, and cocktails bought for strangers who'd be lovers by morning.

Through all of this I swam like a woman in an alien sea.

Where to go from here? I stopped in the center of the room, the people bustling by me smelling of cigar smoke and that elusive scent invoked by desperation. Even those fortunate enough not to be draining their bank accounts were nonetheless dangerous, as if their lives could change for good or ill on the next chance encounter or tumble of the dice.

Behind me, someone was shouting for boxcars.

"Ker-raps!" the croupier sang, "Loo-zer!"

I spotted the elevators and made a break for them.

Just my shoddy luck. A bruiser with a neck like a fire hydrant stood his post at the elevators, his hands cupped in front of him. His eyes picked me up the second I emerged from the mob.

Here we go. Let the bullshit floweth.

"Good evening," I said, trying to bolster my smile. I could see my reflection in the wall mirror. I hoped I looked better than I felt.

The Tongue Merchant

"Evening." He was one of those hybrid types who hovered between Anglo and Hispanic; it was impossible to tell which, though his English was crisp. "Looking for the ladies' room?"

I clasped my purse against myself, attempting to look demure and a bit girlish, when all I was really trying to do was conceal my bandaged hand. "Actually, no. I was wondering if you could tell me where I might find Señor Alonzo Serca. It's really quite crucial that I speak with him."

"I apologize, ma'am, but you'll have to make an appointment. Mr. Serca's a—"

"Busy man. Yes, I know. But, you see . . ." I sidled closer, even more self-conscious than before, now that I was attempting to spread on those feminine charms, which was something I'd never really been cut out for. Not that I was bad looking. There were far homelier women than me in the room, and if you'd have asked my father he probably would've said I was a snowy dove trooping with crows. As a kid I'd never understood what he meant by that. After all, my skin is dusky and my hair and eyes as dark as the inside of a Spanish guitar, but then I hit college and read Shakespeare, so there you have it. And maybe Dad was right. There wasn't a dame in the house that could hold a candle to me, and here I stood, feeling inadequate at flirting.

"I've really traveled a long way," I explained, "and it's been one of those nights. So what do you say"—I shot a glance at the brass tag on his pocket—"*Anthony,* feel like giving a road-weary woman a break she more than rightly deserves?"

"I have my instructions, ma'am—"

"Marcella." I beamed at him.

He nodded. "Marcella. I have my orders. This is Mr. Serca's baccarat night."

"Ah, good. I love baccarat. Show me the way. Better yet," I added when it was obvious he was about to shake his head,

149

"why don't you just tell me where I can find him, and then you can happen to be in the little boy's room when I go looking for him? How does that sound?"

For a second I knew he would acquiesce, but then he turned to stone.

"No way, ma'am. I can't afford to lose this job."

Hell.

"Okay then. How about . . ." Before I realized it, my hand slipped into my purse, past the Adelbert and the evil tongue depressor, and then I had a fifty-dollar bill in my hand, and then it was in his. "Take this, please." I dialed my voice down to a whisper, lacing it with a sense of urgency that I didn't need to feign. "Just tell me where to go and then look the other direction, *please.*"

Anthony enclosed the money in his big hand, his eyes banking left to right, the cords of muscle in his neck stretched taut. "Jesus, lady." He stepped away from me as if I were on fire and throwing off sparks. He said, sotto voce, "He's in the private lounge at the back, the door beside the kitchen. Now get away from me."

"*Gracias.*" I sent him a silent message of sincerity with my eyes, which only made him all the more shuffle-footed, and then I went looking for the kitchen.

Every camera in the room seemed to be tracking me.

Two things occurred to me as I cut between the blackjack tables and dodged waitresses with empty trays and machine-gun smiles. One, by the hang of his suit it was likely that my dear Anthony had been wearing a shoulder holster, and two, if I was going to keep up this fevered investigation, I'd have to invest in a more potent antiperspirant.

Nearly swept away by a tide of Japanese women with cameras around their necks, I found myself dog-paddling for escape, and when I emerged my knuckles were white from clutching my

The Tongue Merchant

purse like a floatation device. But at least I'd made the other side. Three swinging silver portals serviced the kitchen, in front of which was a buffet table in the shape of a Brazilian log canoe, currently being ravaged by piranha-hungry gamblers. And standing discreetly nearby was an unadorned door of burnished iroko. As I approached it, I reminded myself not to look guilty. But the truth was that I felt like a burglar. If it hadn't been for my mother's salt in my blood, I never would have made it.

But as it was, I found the *umph* to put my hand on the doorknob. One second I was a seducer, the next a thief.

"Bad girls go to hell or Cleveland," I whispered, and slipped inside.

Four men stopped what they were doing and stared.

Pinned by the arrows of their eyes, I could only stand there, the epicenter of a spiraling silence that rippled out to the walls.

The pile carpet was ochre-colored, the paint a shade darker. A flat TV was mounted above the wet bar. The ESPN anchormen were wisecracking without sound, the volume muted. There was a ceiling fan, a stationary exercise bike. And the baccarat table. Around which were seated four men. One white. One black. Two Hispanic. Despite their racial differences, they looked identical. Like a team of lawyers discussing a million-dollar client.

Though my father enjoyed cigars, I wasn't so comfortable with the smoke that I could stand here for much longer without coughing. I was taking in the fine details of them—their gold tie tacks, their silk jackets slung over their chairs, their commanding postures—when one of them broke the spell.

"I trust you're familiar with *chemin de fer*."

My eyes went to his face. It was one of the Latinos. He sat in a wheelchair.

"*Chemin de fer* is a card game," he said, plainly amused, studying me through a nebula of cigar smoke. "Specifically, it's a style of baccarat. Please make me a happy man and tell me you're here to play."

Well. Say something. You're the war goddess, after all.

"Alonzo Serca, I presume."

He placed his cards on the table. He wore a vest with a subdued fleur-de-lis print over a white button-down. He looked like someone you'd see in the audience at an Italian opera. Not that I'd been to many operas myself . . .

"I confess," he said, moving his hands in an obeisant manner. "But you have me at a disadvantage. I thought I'd met all of the hotel's visiting royalty. Evidently I was wrong."

"I'm not a guest, but . . ." I stalled. There were too many eyes still staring at me. I took a breath and tried again. "If this isn't a convenient time—"

"Nonsense," Serca said. "We aren't doing anything that can't suffer an interruption by a beautiful woman. Were we, gentlemen? Please"—he beckoned me with a twitch of his fingers—"introduce yourself to my slack-jawed companions."

Somehow I managed to take a step toward the table. The moment I did, three chairs began to slide back, three rumps lifting up in deference to the lady in the room, and I was quick to wave them off. "That's not necessary, really."

They stood up anyway.

"I must beg your pardon," Serca said, still ensconced in his chair, his knees drawn together so close they almost touched. "Believe me when I say that, in spirit, I rose to my feet the moment you stepped through my door."

"That's quite all right," I assured him. I smiled feebly around the table, and the other men resumed their positions.

For some reason, Serca seemed a little too delighted to see me. "And you are . . . ?"

"Paraizo. Marcella Paraizo." I thought about leaning over the

The Tongue Merchant

table and offering my hand, but the situation was awkward enough already. "Sorry to crash in on you like this . . ."

"Not at all. I'm always game for a surprise. Eh, Nat?"

The black man grinned, privy to an old secret.

"Nat here knows my fondness for surprises. Nathan, I'd like you to meet Miss Marcella Paraizo. It is *Miss,* isn't it?"

"Yes."

Serca seemed relieved. "And these fine exemplars of chivalry are Lawrence and Jorge."

I endured more hellos and phony smiles.

"Now," Serca said. "This matter you've come to discuss with me. It's of a private nature?"

"That's right."

"Business or personal?"

"Both."

He nodded as if he expected nothing less. "Gentlemen, I must entreat your good graces. It seems that dame fortune has tonight kept me from falling prey to your collective prowess at cards. Let us disband for the evening and meet again say . . . Thursday?"

Even before he'd finished speaking, Lawrence and Jorge were sliding out of their seats. They agreed that Thursday sounded smashing. They recovered their coats, Jorge downed the last of his bourbon, and then they both shuffled by me, bidding me goodnight.

After they were gone, Serca sat there like a monarch, Nathan a silent knight beside him. Obviously the men were more than allies. Perhaps Nathan served as Serca's right hand, or his chief legbreaker, or his broker, or acted in some other intimate role. He wore a worsted wool suit with a tie done in the traditional black, yellow, and red colors of Uganda—as a Guardsman, I knew my flags. He smiled at me somewhat lazily, the way I imagine a veteran snake-charmer looks at an amateur about to sit down before the basket.

"Do you drink, Miss Paraizo?" Serca asked.

"Not tonight."

"Do you sit, then?" He motioned at the chair vacated by Jorge.

"Thank you." I sat down before the discarded hand of cards.

He studied me with lucid brown eyes. "I don't know you."

"I've never been to the casino before."

"What do you do for a living?"

"I'm an officer in the United States Coast Guard."

"Truly? Well, heavens me. I am honestly impressed. I never would have guessed . . ."

"I'm here about Isabella Murillo."

Serca's face was blank. He glanced at Nathan, who shrugged.

"Isabella De Casals-Murillo," I expounded.

"Ah, of course! Ernesto's daughter. An engaging woman. She—"

"Was killed at midnight on Sunday."

He sobered instantly. "Yes, I was aware of that. You'd be here about the funeral then."

"Actually, I'm here for some answers."

"Oh? If that's the case, then I'm afraid I'm going to be a maddening disappointment to you, as I hardly knew the woman myself. How many times did I run into her, Nat? Five or six at the most?"

If Nathan replied, he did so on a telepathic level I couldn't hear.

"I'm sorry, Miss Paraizo. From what I understand, and this is only what's growing on the company grapevine, Ernesto's daughter had gotten herself involved with . . . well, shall we say the wrong crowd? I suppose her stand on our new oil venture was common knowledge, and we all knew she despised our quaint little gambling house here, but she was also embroiled in things far nastier than I want to consider. I'm not a violent man, Miss Paraizo. Ernesto's daughter had made alliances with hazardous individuals."

"Maybe so." I decided to start throwing things at him, to see what bats I could shake loose from the belfry. "Do you know her younger brother, Abdías?"

"What is it you're looking for, exactly?"

"Information. I know I don't have the authority . . ."

"But as a friend," Serca said, "you've taken it upon yourself to assist the police. I assume that's who you're working for."

"I'm not working for anyone."

"Then why do you expect me to answer any of your questions?"

That stumped me. There was little I could do if Serca refused to play along. I had no court order, no subpoena, nothing more substantial than a hunch and a heavy sense of debt. So maybe Serca would meet my questions with a brick wall. But I owed it to Bella to ask anyway. "I suppose, Señor Serca, I was counting on you simply to be a decent human being."

He moved his hands lavishly. "And so I will make every effort to be."

"Thank you. Now. Do you know Isabella's brother, Abdías?"

"We've met."

"What do you think of him?"

"Honestly?"

"Of course."

"He's an ungrateful young man who refuses to grow up. Not to mention a slave to amphetamines."

Not just anybody could deliver that kind of wallop, Straker's voice said in my head. It occurred to me then that whoever hit Isabella didn't have to be a brute, as I first assumed. Someone wired on crank could've easily been strong enough to break her jaw.

"Do you know the man who manages his money, Robert Castigere?"

"I know everyone remotely involved with my company."

"It's not your company," I reminded him.

He smiled ingenuously. "Do I detect a speck of anger soiling your attitude, Miss Paraizo?"

"Castigere. What do you know of him?"

"Bankrupt, or close to it, from what I hear. And if you put faith in the grapevine, he's racked up quite a debt with certain less-than-credible loan institutions, the result of his unfortunate addiction to cockfighting. He's had to liquidate quite a few of his assets to make up the difference."

"What kind of assets? I assume he holds shares in DCI. Did he sell them?"

"That, my lady, I wouldn't know."

"What was the effect of the warehouse fires on the DCI stocks?"

"Profound."

"Did Castigere sell his shares before or after the ELF attack?"

"I don't remember."

"Good enough. Evangelina."

"I'm sorry?"

"Castigere's wife."

"Oh, yes. The lithe Haitian temptress. God knows how Robert talked her into marrying him. Bribery, perhaps. Robert's such a pretentious snot, don't you think?"

"Isolde Bancavia."

"The name's not familiar to me," he said without missing a beat.

"Miguel Saldaña."

"Neither is that one, I'm afraid."

"Armande St-Germain."

The Tongue Merchant

"The real-estate mogul? What's he got to do with anything?"

"Paulo Longoria."

"Really, Miss Paraizo, this gameshow line of questioning is entertaining, although—"

But Nathan's eyes jumped when he heard Longoria's name. Damned if they didn't.

"—I can't guess where it's all headed," Serca finished.

With considerable effort I made myself look away from Nathan. *Okay. What the hell was that all about?* Poe's bells were clanging out a manic chorus between my ears. "I'm sorry," I said, "but do you have a restroom I could use?"

Serca held my gaze for a count of three, thinking things about me that I couldn't begin to imagine, then he said, "It would be my pleasure." He hit a button on his chair's console and buzzed backward to the wall. He opened a semi-concealed door. "Take all the time you need."

Need? I need about six months and four bottles of aspirin, thank you.

With my purse in hand, I smiled and maintained my ladylike demeanor all the way to the bathroom. But Serca stopped me before I could close the door. He stared up at me with penetrating black eyes. "You've come here hunting heads, haven't you?"

I answered him by shutting the door.

Chapter Eleven

What do women do in the head at times like this?

I almost laughed at that. There *were* no times like this.

There was the sink. A foot lower to the ground than normal. The toilet was bracketed by aluminum hand rails. The whole place was sized for a midget. Or someone bound to a chair.

"Just powder your damn nose," I admonished myself. I touched up my makeup and my hair, because I'd almost been run over and having a demon fling you across the street wasn't great on the old bod. Tentatively I removed the clotted tissues from my hand, washed away the last of the blood, and was glad to see that I was no longer bleeding. Meanwhile there was a little girl sitting at a table in my mind, a thousand puzzle pieces scrambled in front of her and a look on her face that was either the premonition of a scream or a good long cry. Either one would do.

Alonzo Serca spoke the queen's English and he was slick and I didn't trust him.

Abdías de Casals was a spendthrift and now owned his sister's company. He might have had the key to the *Lynn*'s master bedroom and maybe even one to the coffer of jewels.

Robert Castigere was desperate and might have coerced or stolen the keys from Abdías.

And Nathan, otherwise serene as a monk, had reacted to Longoria's name like a cherry bomb had exploded under his ass.

So what had I learned in the presence of these baccarat-playing aristocrats? Well, if Serca considered himself the de facto owner of De Casals International, he had reason to despise Isabella and her politics. But he certainly hadn't murdered her by wheeling himself aboard the *Lynn,* which wasn't exactly handicap accessible. Even if he'd been able to get himself on the yacht, he wouldn't have had a key, and Bella never left a door unlocked at night. Blame that little quirk on her abusive uncle, Navaro de Casals, still moldering in a Florida prison. I suppose Serca could've sent a lackey to do the job for him—Nathan, or maybe someone like Anthony the gun-toting, bribe-taking security guard—and they might have known how to jimmy a lock.

"Nathan knows Longoria."

I said this to myself so quietly the words barely left my lips, on which I was applying a fresh coat of Cover Girl. I'd never been a big fan of lipstick, but I had to fit the part.

"Which means," I concluded, "that Nathan was part of the deal for the stamp."

Could that be true?

More importantly, would I be able to find out if he was?

Good intentions always prevail, Dad liked to say. Jerry Garcia was dead and pushers addicted Miami kids to coke and there was my father saying that good intentions always prevail. God, I loved that man.

I flushed the john to make it sound like I wasn't just stalling for time.

There still remained a few names to toss at my host, in hopes that he'd swing at a wild pitch, but instinct told me that I'd gotten my lucky break for the day. I'd surprised Nathan by mentioning Longoria, which meant—sound the trumpets and beat the war drums—I was officially On To Something.

Feeling inspired, I left the bathroom.

The two men stopped their low-decibel chatting the moment I appeared. Nathan's face was an inscrutable slate, but Serca wore a lazy smile. He had an effortless way about him. The world fit him, and he knew and relished it. His clothes, his market shares, his women—I imagined them all laid out before him like jeweled trinkets in the tent of a Turkish *pasha*. He possessed an aura of what we here in the islands called *personalismo*, a term we use for politicians who project a charismatic and patriarchal air. He touched his control pad, and his chair turned a few degrees so that he was facing me.

" 'And all that's best of dark and bright,' " he quoted, " 'meet in her aspect and her eyes.' "

"You seem intent on flattering me, Señor Serca."

"At all costs, Miss Paraizo. Do you know Byron?"

"His wasn't one of the names I was going to ask you about."

Serca chuckled. "You're not one to dawdle on unnecessary exchanges of etiquette, are you?"

"My friend was murdered."

"And you're here to put things right."

"Something like that."

"Then why come to me?"

"You and Joseph Rotto oversee control of Isabella's company." I sauntered a bit closer. "She didn't like the way you two were running things, and she wasn't afraid to put her beliefs in writing. We both know she had a penchant for memos. It's only logical that I ask you a few questions."

"I suppose so," Serca allowed, offering me a chair that I declined. "Be that as it may, it's my understanding that she was killed in the course of a common robbery. Wasn't she missing a fair amount of valuables?"

His knowledge of the crime shouldn't have surprised me. He had far better resources than I could ever marshal. When he first heard about the incident, he'd probably phoned the Hozumkur chief of police directly and gotten every last detail.

I don't know why I loathed him so, but here I stood, biting back the bile.

"She wasn't killed for her money," I said. "At least not the small amount she kept on her boat. But someone wanted it to look that way."

"Ah. Murder by cliché."

"It happens."

"I've no doubt that it does. Any suspects?"

"Actually, the police are holding her husband in custody."

"I see. That's quite disturbing news."

"What can you tell me about Jan Voorstadt?"

"Nothing, I'm afraid. Did Isabella and her husband truly have that dysfunctional of a relationship?"

"No. Come on, Serca. The name Voorstadt means nothing to you?"

He exhaled dramatically. He tilted his head to one side and propped his knuckles under his chin. "I couldn't help but notice that you've dispensed with the *señor* and reduced me to a simple surname." He grinned briefly, as if to challenge me, but when I didn't respond, he permitted the smile to slip from his face. "Yes, then, I suppose I do recall the name, upon reflection. I read the newspapers, like the next man. Voorstadt is an environmental activist, if memory serves. A violent objector to certain timber and petroleum practices here in the Caribbean. He was thought to be responsible for razing our property eight months ago, but he was acquitted."

"Not exactly. He was set free on a legal loophole." It made my teeth ache just thinking about it. The Paraizos, father and daughter, were no friends of defense attorneys. "Rumor has it that Isabella might have been involved with Voorstadt's people."

"I'm afraid I wouldn't know anything about that."

"You never thought she was consorting with parties hostile to DCI?"

He drummed his fingers against his chair. "I'm having something of a social gathering here at the hotel tomorrow evening. A shameless soiree to celebrate Isabella's spirit, as well as to celebrate life, liberty, and the pursuit of Fortune 500 status. Surprise me and tell me that you'll come."

I blinked so hard I could almost hear my eyes move. "You've got to be kidding me."

"Now, Miss Paraizo." He buzzed his chair around the table to the bar. "You must learn that there are two things in this world of which I never jest. One of those is driving while under the influence . . . and I'll allow you to draw your own conclusions about the origins of that particular declaration." Yet almost in defiance of this statement, he poured himself a belt of whiskey. "The other item which I would never sully with jocularity is the death of a compelling woman." He offered me a quick toast. "Promise to attend and I swear upon dear Ernesto's soul to answer your every query."

Tell him to go screw himself, gatita. *Isabella is too dead for you to be hobknobbing.*

My first impulse was to follow my mother's advice. An angry moon waxed in my breast just thinking about Serca's audacity. But then Bella's ghost gave a little whimper, and I admitted to myself that Serca was probably my best hope for making the Voorstadt piece fit into my puzzle. If there was a link between Bella and ELF, and if Serca had taken extreme action against such an alliance, then I had to hound the man until he slipped. And one way or another, I knew that slip would come. But did I think him capable of orchestrating murder?

The answer to that was easy. I was standing in a thirty-two-story monument he'd built to Mammon. Serca had long ago chosen his god, and around his altar were certainly the ashes of more than one person he'd offered up as a sacrifice along the way.

Through clenched jaws I said, "The owner of your company has been murdered, and you're having a barbecue."

The last remnant of Serca's smile dissolved. "I'll have you know that I spent the better half of the day personally contacting those on the guest list, informing them of recent events and the subsequent change in tomorrow night's atmosphere. Actually, Miss Paraizo, we're going to be honoring Isabella's life, not toasting her death, as you're implying. Nathan here will be at the door taking donations on behalf of some of Isabella's favorite charities."

It was the kind of response I expected. Serca was masquerading his cocktail party as a wake.

Which made it all the more vital that I attend. "All right. I'll see what I can do. What's the dress code?"

"As formal as a funeral, I'm afraid."

"Terrific."

"You do own a suitable dress, do you not?"

"I'll see what I can scrounge up. Can I bring a guest?"

"A date, you mean? I was rather hoping you wouldn't."

"Sorry to disappoint you."

He spread his hands and smiled almost bashfully. "Alas, the story of my life."

Throughout all of this, Nathan sat at the table before the forsaken baccarat game, black eyes crawling over me. He was starting to give me a rash of first-degree willies. Time to make my getaway.

"What time?" I asked.

"Seven. Which means I expect to greet my first guest at quarter-till-eight. You know how people are about being fashionably late."

"No," I said, honestly enough. I began backing away. "I don't know anything about that at all." A few more steps and I bumped into the door. "I'm a Coast Guard officer. I'm always in the nick of time." Without looking I grabbed the knob and twisted it. "See you boys tomorrow."

I fled the room, feeling Nathan's eyes on my back.

I made it home at midnight.

When I walked into the living room and turned on the light, I expected the place to be ransacked. Don't ask me why. Maybe my close encounter with the speeding sports car had been a coincidence and maybe it had been enemy action, but all the way up the sidewalk, listening to the surf against the sand and the howl of the wind as it gathered strength in the east, I'd been envisioning my home in the aftermath of hired vandals.

But the apartment was just as I'd left it. It had a tendency to look ransacked on the best of days, anyway, so what the hell.

My paranoia didn't end there. I checked all the possible grassy knolls: behind the doors, under the bed, in the shower. But there was no assailant waiting in the eaves with a stocking over his head and a piano wire in his hands. If my investigation had upset someone to the point where they were sending people after me with moving cars, well, you'd think an old-fashioned mugging would be the next order of business.

But I was, as so often I seemed to be, alone.

I collapsed on the couch and pulled a pillow over my face.

The Mystery Man was out there tonight, Bella's lover and maybe her killer, thinking his unspeakable thoughts. Nathan, Serca's silent *compadre*, knew something he wasn't letting on. Nico had lied about his alibi. Castigere was a destitute gambler. And tropical storm Bartholomew was closing in.

And more wretched than any of these was my follow-up appointment with Dr. Avundavi tomorrow—or *today*, I suppose—at four p.m. I commanded myself just to lie there on the couch for a moment and think about the big C, because it didn't do any good to pretend it wasn't happening.

Fortunately, Marcella, there are no metastases.

You're speaking Swahili here, Janice.

That means there are no tumors that have spread to other areas. Count yourself lucky.

Yeah, I'll get right on that.

And there's no indication of cancerous growth in the lymph glands.

And the bad news?

Minimal, I believe. We should be able to remove the entire lesion with a lumpectomy.

With my face behind the pillow, I had to grin at that, if only just a little. What kind of goofier word was there in the English language than *lumpectomy?*

You know what my next question is going to be, Jan.

It's a type of surgery where we remove only the tumor and a small amount of tissue.

Surgery?

Followed by radiation treatment, yes.

Will it work?

Ninety percent of the time it does. So if you like to play the odds . . .

If I liked to play the odds, I wouldn't put any money on me finding Bella's murderer.

I made a mental list of things to do when the sun came up in a few short hours: catch a charter to St. Noré so I could (a) see why the hell Nico had fibbed about his alibi, (b) get Roosevelt out of lockup, and (c) crash in on the exotic Isolde Berlin Bancavia, dealer in rare texts and possible pipeline to the terrorist underground. Oh, yeah. I might as well add (d) track down Saul and sweet-talk him into chaperoning me to the pit of vipers that Alonzo Serca was calling a wake.

I yawned enormously, stretching my arms above my head,

feeling every muscle in my body grow taut and then slowly relax—

The phone rang and scared the shit out of me.

I swung upright, my eyes on my purse and the pistol it concealed.

The phone rang again.

Muttering a series of soft oaths, I snatched the cordless off its base and said hesitantly, "Hello?" I expected to hear heavy breathing from the other end. Or a deep-throated threat to mind my own business before it got me hurt.

"Marce? It's Kev."

The wind rushed out of me and I leaned back on the couch, hand on my forehead. "Oh. Wow. Evening, Captain. I thought you were going to be someone talking through a handkerchief."

"I don't follow."

"Forget it."

"Okay . . . you all right?"

I grunted.

"Were you asleep?"

"Never again," I assured him.

"Can you talk?"

"Kevin, what's wrong?"

There was a moment of silence, then: "Damn, Marce . . ."

I sat up straight, my eyes wide open. "Kevin, what's happened?"

I could hear him breathing. Finally he said, "The brass knows what you're doing."

"Huh?"

"About two hours ago I got a call from Rear Admiral Kirkland. You were the subject of discussion."

"I don't understand."

"The admiral was concerned that you might be guilty of conduct unbecoming an officer. He was notified of some,

The Tongue Merchant

uh . . . some strange stuff about you."

"Kevin, what the hell are you talking about? Notified by *whom*, for God's sake?"

"Supposedly an unimpeachable source." He paused, gathering his thoughts, then blundered ahead. "The admiral confided in me that he was contacted by the Hozumkur Police Department. They informed him that you knowingly violated police mandate. Something about trespassing and tampering with a crime scene."

My stomach turned to sludge.

Mr. Mercator had ratted me out.

"God*dammit*," I hissed into the phone.

"Excuse me?"

The nausea turned to anger. "Kirkland's *unimpeachable source* is a pig-headed, chain-smoking, by-the-book primate named Samuel Raznik. He had it in for me the moment he saw me."

"Well, be that as it may . . ."

"Be that as it may *nothing*. Kevin, listen to me. Isabella was murdered."

"Yes, I know, but that doesn't give you—"

"Will you just hear me out?"

"Okay, sure, settle down. I'm listening."

"Where are you right now?" I stood up and began to pace the room.

"I'm calling you from my quarters. Why?"

"Just wondering. Did you know that HPD has Bella's husband in custody?"

"No, I wasn't aware of that."

"But the cops don't know the whole story. I think they've got the wrong person in jail."

"And what makes you think that?"

"Because I found out that—"

"No," he interrupted. "Belay that. I don't want to know. It's obvious that you're making this into some kind of vendetta—"

"Damn right I am."

"—and you're putting your nose where it positively does not belong. And I've got to warn you, Marce, if you keep it up, if you insist on pursuing some half-cocked hypothesis, then you're going to find yourself in a world of trouble. You've got your eye on a promotion, right? Then let me inform you here and now that Rear Admiral Elias Kirkland has his eye on *you*. Am I making myself clear?"

"No, Kevin, maybe you should spell it out for me."

"What you're doing is *illegal*, Marce. And if it's not illegal then at the very least it flies in the face of Coast Guard policy. If you go around breaking the law, you're not only putting your own career in jeopardy, you're risking the reputation of the *Sentinel* and its entire crew. And I will not have the individual problems of one officer become a distraction to the other ninety-seven members of my ship. Now I know that sounds like a heartless thing to say, but I won't sacrifice the cutter's good name on behalf of your personal quest."

I left off pacing to stand before the window, hoping the view of the starless eastern sky would help assuage my ire. Usually I was comforted by the sight of the sky. But not tonight. After awhile I said, "Are you finished with the soap box now?"

"Give me a break, Marcella. We're *adults* here. This is my *job*."

"Yeah, well, it's a shitty time to choose your job over your girlfriend."

"I'm not choosing anything . . ."

"Well I am. Nico should not be sitting in that jail. Whoever killed Isabella is still out there somewhere, thinking he's getting away with it."

"I suppose you have proof of this?"

"Not one speck. But I've got a tabletop full of puzzle pieces."

"Whatever. Look, this is how it is, Lieutenant. I'm ordering you to stand down. Upon Admiral Kirkland's strong suggestion, I am forbidding you to go forward with whatever it is you think you're doing."

I closed my eyes. "Please don't do this to me, Kevin."

"I'm sorry, but if it'll keep you from a court-martial—"

"*Court-martial?* Jesus, it's not like I'm giving state secrets to the Cubans."

"I know that. And to the best of my ability I explained as much to the admiral, but it's his belief that the Guard does not need this kind of publicity at the moment. And I have to say that I'm inclined to agree with him. If the police have a man in custody, then they must have enough evidence to warrant a trial. And if this theory of yours ends up being wrong—"

"It's not wrong. Nico is not the murderer."

"So you say."

"Yeah. So I say. Goodbye, Kevin."

"Marcella, wait."

"What? What is it now?" I was stalking the floor again. "I'm hanging up, Captain, because I don't want to be accused of insubordination, and right now I'm about one good *go to hell* away from that. It's late. I'm going to tie flies until my fingers bleed and then fall asleep exhausted. I'm on shore leave, remember?"

"And you're still an officer in the Guard, *remember?*"

"Yeah. Don't I know it."

"And if you want to stay that way—"

"And if I want to stay that way, I'll learn to ignore all the unjustness in the world, because our vow of punishing the bad guys and saving the underdog only counts when our reputations aren't on the line. Goodnight, Captain."

"Marcella, I just don't—"

I pressed END, and the room was silent.

I stood before the big bay window, counting the beats of my heart. The telephone slipped from my icy fingers. My hair, in a rare state of abandon, hung wildly in my face. Eventually the anger reverted to nausea, and I was left feeling more solitary, more coldly alone, than I had since my mother went away and never came home.

"Court-martial," I whispered.

The words seemed to hang in the air long after I spoke them.

★ ★ ★ ★ ★

Wednesday
Barometric pressure 28.32, falling rapidly

★ ★ ★ ★ ★

Chapter Twelve

The rain finally came in the morning.

I awoke to the sound of it pattering a poem against the bay windows which looked out over the shore. Not a downpour yet, but surely a harbinger of torrents to come. Though it was daybreak, the sky was dismal, as if a cast-iron kettle had been dropped over the world, trapping us in here with our new and incorrigible neighbor, Bartholomew. Dazed by murky dreams that were already losing definition, I sat up in bed and stared through my disheveled hair at the doom which continued to encroach from the east.

Wet palm fronds slapped at the glass. Down at the waterline, the beach was vacant.

Slowly I climbed from the well into which sleep had thrown me. It took a moment to make sense of my surroundings, despite the fact that I was nowhere more spectacular than my own bedroom. But even that didn't seem familiar anymore.

Are we awake yet, gatita?

"Hell, no." I plopped back down and hoisted the covers around my chin, a ward against the night-things and their leering eyes.

Storm's coming.

Yeah, so it was, in more ways than one. The best place for me was right here amongst these pillows, several good books within easy reach on the headboard, the bathroom not too far away, some rum in the cupboard. Screw Nico and his problems. And

Serca and Joe Rotto and all the rest of them. They weren't worth the heat I'd face from the Guard if I kept pushing it. And pushing was, of course, my nature. So it wasn't easy just to lie there and pretend that none of it had happened, that none of it really mattered. But sometimes we have to ignore the mountains and hope the winds of time erode them into molehills.

Five minutes passed.

I tried to keep my eyes closed. But every few seconds a new face appeared in the darkness. First Abdías, who may have been just enough of a weasel to con me into thinking he was innocent. Then the seedy stamp dealer, Saldaña, who seemed a little unbalanced to begin with, and certainly lusted after the Adelbert. Then Castigere the gambler and ill-fated patron of cockfights. Who knew what kind of trouble he was in? And finally the man called Nathan, who was either mute or fantastically shy. Either way, something about him made me shiver.

But they were all history, right? No longer my concern. Whatever grand conspiracy they were so precariously maintaining, a delicate cipher that clumsy old me couldn't quite decrypt, they were going to go on doing so without interference from either Marcy Paraizo or, apparently, the cops.

The rain went on and on. The ceiling fan turned. The hands of the clock crept toward seven.

"Shit."

I climbed out of bed.

And went down to the sea.

I always came here to sort things out, albeit not usually in the drumming rain. I'd thrown on a windbreaker and pulled the hood over my head. Hands in my jacket pockets, I stood there in my bare feet and sweatpants with the surf flowing around my ankles. This was my place of solace. The beach was my confessional and the ocean my priest. Yet this morning the usual seren-

The Tongue Merchant

ity was invaded by thoughts of court-martials and dead friends and the—

—*tumor*—

—sickness in my body. My compass continued to deviate, distracted by all of these false poles. Even as I stared out over the water, the wind picked up speed and blew the hood from my head. I made no effort to replace it, just waited there with the rain prickling my face. Was Kyle Straker awake yet? Was he drinking his coffee, maybe, and thinking about the story of marital strife he hoped to elicit from Nico? Were they nailing plywood sheets over the windows on St. Thomas in preparation for disaster? And more importantly, had I already come into contact with the Mystery Man, or was he still out there somewhere, thanking God that Nico had taken the fall?

My mother was nominally Roman Catholic. I don't think she ever confessed her sins to a man of the cloth once she turned eighteen and was free of her parents' religious shackles. When it came down to it, she only had faith in the tangible, and in the love she felt for her family. Dad was the one who taught me how to pray, though I seldom took the time anymore.

A sudden gust caused me to take a step backward to keep my feet.

I took that as a sign and almost laughed.

If I were going to pray to someone, then it should have been the old Taíno god, Jurancán. The Taíno were the indigenous people of Puerto Rico. Jurancán was the god of the hurricane. And though the last Taíno tribes had been wiped from the earth by smallpox, slavery, genocide, and several other European imports, the hurricane deity lived on. And he was, as a rule, pissed off at humankind.

A minute later my hair was a soggy mess. By that time, my heart had chosen its path. The mountain was never going to fade away into a molehill. In fact, it was turning out to be a volcano, and the pressure was only building. Very soon now, very soon . . .

I turned around and marched through the wet sand. The surf chased after me, as if it wanted me to stay.

"Not today," I breathed.

Court-martials and cancer be damned. I had no choice but to risk the former, and there was little I could do right now about the latter. As I hurried up the weather-scarred stairs to my apartment, a new and reckless sense of mission aligning my compass, I had only two things on my mind.

Punishing whoever committed this act. And maybe saving myself along the way.

I chartered the first boat I could find to St. Noré.

It cost me a hundred bucks and the captain spent the entire two-hour trip complaining about how he could make twice as much on tourists with fishing poles. But no one but a madman would be out for blue marlin in these conditions, and though I told him as much, he never stopped grousing. If it wasn't Bartholomew then it was politics. Apparently he was an unswerving *independentista,* a supporter of Puerto Rican self-governance, and the United States could take its commonwealth bullshit and eat it on their hot dogs and apple pie. I listened with half an ear. Political games were the island's national pastime. Guys like this wouldn't know what to do without government controversy.

Overloaded with rhetoric, I was happy to make landfall. We docked at a pier a mile south of Marina del Sol, for which I was silently thankful. I had no desire to see the *Lady Lynn Rob,* nor did I want to be spotted anywhere in her vicinity. I'd crossed the line once already. No sense in testing the limits of my fortune. It would certainly come to that soon enough.

You sure you know what you're doing, gatita?

The Tongue Merchant

"No. But I'm going anyway."

That's my girl.

I paid the captain with some of the cash I'd gotten from an ATM after leaving the house. Not knowing what to expect of the day in front of me, I'd prepared for every contingency. I wore khaki pants with a weatherproof weave and the best pair of hiking boots I owned. I had my pine green windbreaker, my diver's watch, and a palm-sized, short-wave radio to keep tabs on the weather. I carried the radio in a nylon belt pouch, just like some kind of silly tourist, along with the Adelbert, the tongue-depressor, four hundred dollars, a few effects I usually carried in my purse, and the Walther. My hair was in a ponytail, looped through the back of a Miami Dolphins cap. Drawing the hood over head and cap alike, I hustled down a taxi.

The cab had only one functioning windshield wiper, and it was working overtime, like a manic metronome. Discharging droplets of rain, I scooted across the tattered fabric of the backseat and said, *"Lléveme a Avenida Matisse, por favor."*

The driver nodded and squirted the little car into the street, barely missing the bumper of a honking delivery truck. Drivers in Hozumkur are no better than those in San Juan. The narrow streets are cratered like the beaches of Normandy, and everyone behind the wheel is marginally daft. Rare is the vehicle free of nicks, dents, and other war scars. If you haven't spent much time here, I wouldn't recommend driving yourself through either city unless you're a Hollywood stuntman, an airbag test driver, or perhaps considering suicide.

Beyond the window, the city was as doleful as the sky. The sun was dead and buried in a mausoleum of clouds, and a certain grayness permeated everything from the storefronts to the faces of those who clipped down the street under their umbrellas. The bright colors of their raincoats seemed smeared and blurry in the downpour. I was reminded of a painting by

Monet, but I couldn't recall the title. Matisse Avenue lay in the heart of the tourist district, which meant that two-star hotels were shouldered between restaurants and souvenir shops in an eclectic hodgepodge of architectural tastes, each designed to attract attention, or make a statement, or set a mood conducive to shopping. With a three-story brass foundry on one side and a balcony-laden, Mediterranean-style boardinghouse on the other, Bancavia's Antebellum Books almost went unnoticed.

I tipped the driver a five for getting me here alive, then stepped out into the rain.

It was only coming down harder. What had started out as a sprinkle last night had turned into serious business. With luck, the core of the storm would peter out before it reached us, or divert its course, as they were sometimes known to do. But the way it looked now, we were in for a deluge.

"Here we go." Holding my hood around my face so that the wind couldn't swipe it, I headed for Bancavia's in direct defiance of an order from a superior officer. Even as I approached the building, I knew there would be consequences to pay.

I hit the steps in front of the bookshop at the same moment as a man in a camouflaged boonie hat and black galoshes.

"*Disculpe,*" he apologized as we narrowly avoided a collision.

My breath hitched in my throat when I recognized him.

"You!" I froze him with my eyes.

Abdías's handyman wiped the water from his face. When he realized who I was, his body tensed like a wild animal about to bolt.

"I've got a gun in my bag," I warned, dropping my voice an octave. "If you take off running, I'll shoot your kneecaps off."

He looked at me for several seconds before he said, "I don't believe that."

"Try me."

"Maybe I will."

The rain continued to pummel us. Neither of us said another word.

"Who are you?" I asked when I could stand it no longer.

"Would you like to go inside?" He nodded toward the store. "I make a better impression when I'm not drowning."

"*Answer the goddamn question.*"

"Leo," he said quickly. "My name is Leo."

"All right, Leo. What is it that you're doing here?"

"My job, I guess."

"Which is?"

"I fix things."

"Like broken windows in French doors."

"Yeah. Among other things." He bent the rim of his hat, trying to funnel the water out of his face. His blond mane was matted against his neck, and I noticed there was a rugged touch of gray at his temples. And of course there were those eyes of his, as dark as stones mined from warm earth. "Hey," he said. "What do you say we call an armistice, just for the sake of getting somewhere dry?" He gave me a half smile.

But I wasn't so easily pacified. There was too much at stake to ignore the blatant fact that this man—Leo, he called himself, and I wondered if that were an alias—kept turning up every time my inquest took a new turn. Crossing my arms over my chest, I said, "For more reasons than one, *Leo*, I'm not in the mood for games, or for wasting my time with pointless conversation. I'm on what you might call a tight schedule here. So spare me the runaround, no matter how charming it may be."

He held up his hands as if to ward off my barrage. "Take it easy, lady, it's just—"

"My name is Marcella."

"Yes, I know. I heard you introduce yourself at Mr. Casals's house."

"Do you work for Abdías?"

"I'm his repair guy. And his gardener. And a damn fine one, too, if I might add. What I can do with azaleas and snapdragons you wouldn't believe. Now can we please get in out of—"

"And you were at Joe Rotto's house to . . . what? Spy on him?"

Leo studied my face, still wearing that wisp of a smile. The rain rolled off his hat like a waterfall. "You sure surprised me, showing up there like you did."

"I'm tricky that way. And you have a habit of avoiding the question."

His smile faded. "See no evil," he said. "Just work the broom."

With that, we stood there like a pair of fools in the punishing rain, with the water surging down spouts and rushing down gutters, and the distant ricochet of thunder.

"Get inside," I said, feeling charitable and deadly at the same time. "We'll talk."

A tiny brass bell tinkled like a pixie's chime when we entered the shop. I stepped through the doorway, and in so doing crossed the threshold of Isabella Murillo's secret life.

She came here as someone else, I thought, putting all my senses on alert, ready to receive the slightest impression of her passing, the smallest indication that all was not as it seemed. *She made private liaisons here and spoke in whispers to wanted men. She knew something horrible.*

Though Leo's sudden appearance made it difficult to concentrate—after all, he was just one more crazy bit of magnetism that made my compass spin—I did my best to absorb the details of the shop, for any one of them could have been my Rosetta Stone. I added another entry to my list of life-altering C-words. Cancer. Court-martial.

Clues.

Unlike the interior of Saldaña's store, Bancavia's Antebellum

The Tongue Merchant

Books was a study in anal-retentive behavior. The furniture, though antique, was meticulously maintained, with one large Shaker reading table surrounded by shelves, and each shelf carefully labeled alphabetically according to the titles it held. Most of the texts were pre–Civil War, although a black steel shelf near the window displayed several newer volumes bearing the name of I. B. Bancavia; apparently the shop's proprietor was also an author. I wondered about the contents of her books. Memoirs? Fiction? Or how-to instructions for aspiring eco-terrorists?

"Nice place," Leo observed. "Reminds me of one of those Dickens novels I've always meant to read."

I conspicuously ignored him.

The room was small and quaint and, I had to admit, certainly cozy. The rug which covered most of the floor had probably been purchased at the bazaar down the street, in one of the shops that specialized in handcrafts from Tehran. A spiral staircase in the corner led up to a balcony and what looked like an office. I saw a desk up there, an oil painting or two on the walls, and a free-standing Japanese screen, the kind you always see people dressing behind in movies but no one ever owns in real life. Instantly I thought of Bella. She loved all things Oriental. She had pajamas made from the product of actual Japanese silkworms.

I wondered if there was a connection.

Before I had time to consider it, a door opened up in front of me.

Separating me from the door was a heavy counter made of what looked to be wood of the guayacán tree. I remembered Saul telling me that guayacán was so dense that it wouldn't even float. The great slab of guayacán was inlaid in the popular intarsia technique, with a pattern of lighter woods forming a Mexian-style mosaic on the countertop. Standing on the other side of the counter was a woman from a fairy tale my father used to read to me at night.

Her hair was a storm. Supremely black and tumbling over her shoulders, it was woven with random braids and tiny wet curls and beads of pink and white coral, like the headdress of a pagan priestess. A necklace of shells rested on her throat, her sable skin glistening with body oils that smelled faintly of hyacinth. Though her slender fingers were adorned with silver and she wore a scrimshaw bracelet on either wrist, her arms were otherwise bare all the way to her shoulders. Her dress seemed more like a sateen sheet she'd taken from her bed and wrapped around her waist for decency's sake. It was the palest purple shade, accented with rather risqué vermilion streaks.

Don't get distracted, I cautioned myself. *School's in session. Eyes to the front of the room.* That was really unnecessary advice. If I were any more alert, my heart would have pinged like a sonar.

"*Buenos días,*" the woman said in a voice like something that should have been on the other end of a phone-sex service. "*¿Busca usted algo en particular?*"

Very gingerly, I exhaled. Bella's ghost dwelled in this place, haunting the walls as surely as the wind blew outside. What furtive alliances had been made here? What promises made?

"*¿Habla usted ingles?*" I asked.

The woman smiled broadly, revealing teeth as white as the shells at her neck. "Only when I have no other choice." She gave a flicker of her fingers, as if to say that perhaps she was only being facetious. "Welcome to my salon. And allow me to ask you again, are you looking for anything in particular?"

My mind jumped a few hurdles. "Well, yes and no."

"Mmmm, sounds intriguing." She placed her hands palms-down on the countertop. Beside her was a turn-of-the-century cash register, and a carved wooden sign that politely requested in three different languages that patrons refrain from smoking.

The Tongue Merchant

Oddly enough, at the far end of the counter, I saw an open pack of cigarettes.

"We're not tourists," I said, to get things started.

"Perish the thought," the woman replied.

"My name is—"

"Leo," he said, stepping up beside me and swiping the dripping hat from his head. "I'm Leo Kavisti. Sorry about tracking in all the water . . ."

"Think nothing of it. I'm simply glad to see some business on this frightful day. I do believe that I'll be forced to retire somewhat early this evening, what with the hurricane making such an absolute ruin of things."

"It's not a hurricane," I said, a little too loudly. I shot Leo a bullet from my eyes, then looked back at Bancavia. "It's only a tropical storm. The National Hurricane Service will only upgrade it to hurricane status when the winds exceed seventy-four miles an hour."

"Is that so?"

"Yes, ma'am, it is." I stepped to the counter, offered my hand, and introduced myself.

She hesitated before shaking. I watched her eyes as my name soaked into her brain and fired a few synapses. A second later she concealed her thoughts with a smile, but I'd been too ready, too damn circumspect. She knew who I was, and I'd caught her in the act of trying to pretend like she didn't.

"I am Isolde," she said. "Bancavia, of course."

"Yes, I've heard of you. I've come here, Isolde, because . . . well, you and I have a friend in common."

"Indeed?"

"Did I mention my name is Leo Kavisti?" Leo interjected, pressing himself to the counter and holding out his hand. "You've got a really upscale establishment here, Mrs. Bancavia, a real cosmopolitan but comfortable kind of atmosphere, if you know what I mean."

"Thank you very much. You're too kind. And it's *Ms.* Bancavia, I'm afraid. Or Isolde, if you prefer."

"Yeah, I do prefer. Isolde. I like that. Isn't there some old myth about a woman named Isolde?"

"I certainly hope so." She favored him with a wink.

"Be that as it may," I said firmly, wondering why the hell Leo wouldn't just keep his mouth shut and make my life a little easier, "there's this friend of mine . . ."

"Yes, you were saying?"

"Isabella de Casals-Murillo."

Isolde batted her kohl-dark eyelashes.

"You do know her, don't you?"

If there were any air left in the room, it had gone too thin to breathe. I was already so nervous my teeth were shaking, and add to this several other heavy-duty distractions: Leo Kavisti had blown in with his own satchel full of secrets, the woman across from me knew and supported eco-arsonists, and we were standing in a room that had somehow led to the death of my closest friend. I cupped my elbows so tightly that my fingers began to ache.

Then something happened I hadn't anticipated.

Isolde turned and ran from the room.

Chapter Thirteen

"Go!" I shouted at Leo. "Get outside and check around back!"

I didn't wait for his reply. I vaulted over the counter, hitting the floor just as a solid *click* came from the far side of the door through which the pagan storm-maiden had vanished. I twisted the knob, but she'd thrown the deadbolt.

"Dammit!" I heard movement in the room beyond.

Behind me, the brass bell tinkled as Leo raced outside into the rain.

"Isolde!" I banged my hand twice on the door. "Isolde, I just need to talk to you."

"Get out of here, please."

"I can't do that. I'm sorry. I have to ask you some questions."

"I don't have any answers."

"Well that makes two of us. Now I'm not here to hurt you, I just need to sit down and speak with you about Isabella. Sort of woman-to-woman, if you know what I mean."

"I have nothing . . ." Her voice cracked. She was crying. "I have nothing to *say.*"

"Isolde, if you don't let me in, I'm going to have to kick down the door, and believe me when I tell you that I'm trained for that sort of thing. I've gone to school for it. I got top marks in door-kicking class." I waited, but apparently my charm was getting me nowhere. "Isolde?"

Nothing.

All right. There is a time for humor, and a time for busting down doors. I think it says that in Ecclesiastes somewhere.

I took two steps backward.

Careful.

"Yeah, I know." Isolde might have murdered my friend, and she may have been waiting back there with the same weapon that had done the job on the *Lynn*. I drew out the pistol, jacked back the slide to put a round in the chamber, and held the weapon in a two-fisted grip. "I'm coming in now, Isolde."

She made no reply. I could no longer hear her weeping. Maybe she'd slipped away.

Gathering a stabilizing breath, I lifted my foot, tensed the muscles in my leg, aimed for that weak spot just below the knob, and—

—*oh shit what have I gotten myself into?*—

—slammed my heel into the door.

By some fluke in the great karmic lottery, I got lucky and the deadbolt ripped a chunk from the doorjamb. The door swung open. I sank to one knee and swept the Walther from left to right. The door *whacked* against the wall and bounced back at me. I stopped it with my left hand but kept my right firmly on the gun, the barrel of which was now pointed across the tiny room at the woman slumped in front of the picture window.

I swallowed the buildup in my throat. *Easy now.*

Isolde Bancavia sat in a seventeenth-century Derbyshire chair, distinctive even to a simpleton like me because of its carved top rail and rigid square uprights. Her legs folded beneath her, Isolde stared from the window, brush strokes of rain smearing the glass and making it impossible to see more than a few feet into the street beyond. She held a handkerchief to her mouth. Even from here I could see that her hand was shaking.

I lowered the gun.

Isolde never even looked over at me.

"You should have opened the door," I said.

She squeezed her eyes shut at the sound of my voice.

"I think you're in some kind of trouble here." I stood up and zipped the pistol back in my pouch. "And I think that I'm the only person who's willing to help you." I made myself take a few steps across the parquet floor. "So you can either talk to me or my friend Kyle Straker down at HPD. It's your call."

I felt like a schmuck for tossing out such an ultimatum, but the feeling didn't last for long. I was chancing the ruination of my career by coming here. Schmuckiness I could live with.

"Please leave." Her eyes never moved from the window.

"Can't do that." I crossed the room and sat down on a hickory chest. There was a folded afghan nearby, and I took the liberty of picking it up and offering it to her. "Here. Watching you shake like that is making me cold."

She blinked a few times, finally glanced my way, and dashed a hand over her eyes. She accepted the blanket with a shaky smile. "Thanks."

"Don't mention it. Now what do you say we talk about this the nice way? *A la buena,* as they say."

"You think I killed Isabella."

"I didn't say that."

A fresh tear, bright as a diamond, tracked down the dark curve of her cheek. "Are you with the police?"

"I'm with no one. I'm pretty much running solo nowadays." And boy, wasn't that the truth? I shifted around on the trunk so that I was facing her more intimately, my knees only a few inches from her chair. "I'm just Isabella's friend, looking for some answers. Maybe you can understand. Now what I'm about to ask you may not sound like it makes any sense—"

"*None of this makes any sense.*"

"You're telling me."

"Isabella was a beautiful person," she said with such acute

emotion that I could see the diagram of her feelings stenciled on her face. "She was shining, and emancipated, and ungovernable. She was just so goddamned *free*. Every day I spent around her was like opening a treasure chest. She was human gold, Ms. Paraizo. I counted myself lucky even to hold her fancy for an hour."

This sudden outpouring caught me unprepared. Before me sat a woman of vast and abiding passions, and I was only beginning to see the slightest glimmer of them. Like Bella, Isolde seemed hard to contain. You'd have better luck trying to catch the north wind in a bottle.

"I liked her too." It was all I could think of to say.

Isolde nodded, as if she understood what I couldn't put into words. Sniffling through a smile, she said, "I met her at a Wagner performance on St. Thomas. The show was *Die Walküre,* and we found ourselves sharing a mirror in the ladies' room. They have such cramped restrooms at the amphitheater, we just seemed to . . ." Isolde dabbed the corner of her eye and brushed away a few wayward strands of the tempest which had fallen into her face. "Isabella was something of a valkyrie herself, just like a character from the opera. Wouldn't you say?"

"She was certainly amazing." Though I agreed with Isolde's comparison, I couldn't help but feel a pang of jealously; she apparently knew Bella on a level I never had. Of course, I was always off playing Lady Ahab somewhere, trolling the seven seas in search of a vision I could never quite define. But that was no excuse for letting my friend turn into a valkyrie without me. I'd been seeking my personal Atlantis ever since I was old enough to understand the necessity of hopeless quests. And though I still believe tremendously in both the value and folly of searching for unattainable places, I've paid the price for my convictions.

I was just about to embark on the where-were-you-at-the-

The Tongue Merchant

time-of-Bella's-death speech when Leo walked into the room through the door I'd destroyed. He looked like a man who'd just escaped a drowning.

"There's no back door," he announced. "Just an alley with one huge, unavoidable mud puddle." His arms hung flaccidly at his sides. Water dripped from his nose.

Considering the circumstances, it struck me as odd that I'd even have the notion to smile. It must have been nerves.

Isolde almost leaped out of her chair at the sight of him. "Here, let me help you." She hurried to the adjacent bathroom, each movement as ethereal as a ballet dancer across a stage. She returned with an oversized towel, which Leo accepted with gratitude. "I'm sorry to have put you through all of this," she said.

"Not a problem." Leo ardently toweled his hair. "I've always liked the rain."

" 'Tis a bit more brutal than a summer shower, I'm afraid."

He dried his face, then got started on his arms. "Have you ever been to Thailand?"

Puzzled, Isolde shook her head.

"I spent a year there one week. Longest seven days of my life. Never stopped raining. Seemed like forever. Everything was wet, everywhere you went. I slept wet, ate wet dinners, made love to wet Thai hookers." His smile was bewitching and well-timed. "Just kidding. About the hookers, that is, not about the rain."

I could see that his affable manner was having its intended effect. Isolde visibly relaxed, asking if he'd like a second towel and even saying something about coffee.

"Sounds positively grand," he said. "Modern man's cure-all elixir. How about it, Marcella? Would you like a wee dram of joe?"

Though this interview wasn't going at all as I'd envisioned, I thought it best to play along. There was a lot more swimming around beneath the water's surface than this particular angler could see. In the last three days I'd come to realize that dealing with people who were protecting deep secrets was a lot like fly-fishing. The trick of tying a successful artificial fly is the ability to create the illusion of life. The fly has to move like the real thing to fool the fish into taking the hook. And that's what I was doing, making like a fly to deceive my quarry into thinking I was nothing but a harmless busybody, mourning her dead friend.

"Coffee?" I said, having never been a big fan. "I'd love some."

Isolde held her smile rigidly in place and tried to spread the creases from her dress. "I admit that I have nothing but Puerto Rico's own Alto Grande, one of the three finest coffees in the world. Forgive a woman her petty vices."

"Certainly. My own weakness is black licorice. Coffee sounds good. I'll take mine *con leche*." I probably wouldn't be able to stomach the stuff without the milk.

She turned to Leo. "And how would you like yours, Mr. Kavisti?"

"It's Leo, remember? And I'd like it *negrito con azúcar*, of course." He grinned broadly.

Isolde returned his lighthouse smile. Leo liked his coffee black and sweet.

It was all I could do to keep from groaning.

"Tell me about the Earth Liberation Front," I said half an hour later.

By now Isolde had rebuilt her composure to such an airtight degree that not the slightest flicker of recognition escaped her at the name. We were seated on barstools she'd pulled up to the counter after first turning around the CLOSED sign in the front window. We'd spent the last thirty minutes talking about

The Tongue Merchant

the local sugarcane trade, premium coffee beans, and of course the approaching storm. The Secret Saboteur and I were due back in San Juan late this afternoon for our rendezvous with Dr. Avundavi, but if the weather took a turn for the worse in the next few hours, I'd have to get out fast if I had any hope of finding transportation back to San Juan. The only boat pilot I knew who was maniacal enough to drive through a hurricane—a former gun-runner named Wicker Falco—had refused to ferry me until I promised to take him trout fishing. And since I'd sooner floss my teeth with concertina wire than waste a good trout weekend on the seedy likes of Falco, I was determined to outrun the storm.

"I'm not sure I understand what you mean," Isolde said over the rim of her mug.

"No offense, but I think maybe you do. Yesterday I spoke with someone who suggested you might occasionally liaison with members of ELF."

"I don't believe that's possible."

"And why not?"

"Because, Marcella, if one is a *member* of an organization, then that implies a certain level of structure within the ranks, and most likely a central core of command. Perhaps even a physical base of operations."

"Your point?"

"From what I've been able to piece together," she continued, "the Earth Liberation Front is not an organization. Rather, it seems to be better defined as an *activity*."

"I don't follow."

"Simple," Leo said, his elbows propped gamely on the countertop. "To remain intangible, ELF can't consolidate authority. So they leave it up to small cells and dedicated individuals to carry the flag in ELF's name. That's probably why they've been so damn hard for the FBI to pin down. They have no corporate HQ."

I stared at him, trying to penetrate his motives, which he was obfuscating with such skill. "And you're some kind of guru of eco-terrorist squads?"

"Just a concerned citizen, that's all."

I gave him a specimen from my Derisive Sneer collection and turned my attention back to Isolde. "So you admit to having knowledge of ELF."

She took a long sip, then nodded. "Yes, I suppose so. I see all types passing through this port. I've had the pleasure of making the acquaintance of a variety of people representing innumerable philosophies. And one or two of them would probably label themselves as no-compromise environmentalists."

"Have you ever facilitated exchanges between ELF members?"

"There are no *members* . . ."

"Yeah, yeah, I know." I waved it away. "The group doesn't exist, no one takes orders from anyone else, and the whole organization is a myth. It's irrelevant. The truth of the matter, Isolde, is that I don't *care* about ELF. In fact, I probably tend to *agree* with the better part of their principles, if not their methods. But what I do care about is the fact that Isabella was murdered, the wrong man is in jail for the crime, and whoever stabbed her to death is still out there."

Though Isolde recoiled a bit at my tone, she summoned up another reserve of defiance and tipped her chin back just enough to make me want to sock her in the jaw. What can I say? The world's grindstone was wearing me down, and it was Darwin's law from here on out.

"Just talk to me," I pleaded. "Please. There's too much at stake."

"I would like to help, I assure you. But I don't see how this conversation has anything to do with . . . with Isabella's death."

"You knew her?" Leo asked.

Isolde's nod was so slight I almost missed it.

I leaned closer. "Did you introduce her to someone claiming ties to ELF?"

After a moment, she whispered something inaudible.

"Isolde . . ."

"Yes," she said through her teeth. "Yes. That's why she came here a few months ago. To the bookstore. We'd spoken briefly on St. Thomas, and that's how she knew where to find me. She was a writer. A reporter. And a very gifted one. She learned of my connections through her research on the streets. That, and fate, brought her to me."

"And what did you tell her?" Leo wanted to know.

"Wait a minute," I said. "You're telling me that Bella was snooping around for information on terrorism, and that's how she ended up here?"

"Essentially, yes."

"What does that mean, *essentially?*"

Her coffee forgotten, Isolde folded her hands securely in front of her. "It means, Marcella, that our friend Isabella Murillo didn't contact me in regards to the environmental movement as a whole, but rather"—she paused, flicking her tongue over her lips—"but rather to obtain data on a specific figure in the eco-radical movement."

"A specific figure?" Leo asked. "Who?"

"I know who," I said, the words barely escaping my lips.

They looked at me expectantly.

"Jan Voorstadt."

This sudden insight turned my skin to a sheath of ice.

"Voorstadt was indicted on arson charges," I explained, "after burning down several De Casals warehouses in the name of the Earth Liberation Front." My mind hurried through a new set of gymnastics. How had Bella learned of Voorstadt in the first place? And why did she want to dig up the dirt on him? Was she trying to expose ELF for the sake of her trade as a journalist, or—and this thought sent renewed ripples of nausea through my stomach—was she trying to contact him about taking action against Joe Rotto and Alonzo Serca? Was Isabella going to hire Voorstadt to conduct terrorist acts against the De Casals oil industry?

And had meeting Voorstadt gotten her killed?

"Uh, Marcella?" Leo touched me on the arm. "You need to get some air?"

"I'm fine."

"Could've fooled me."

"Isolde, I . . ." Suddenly my hands wanted to fidget, and I had to clasp them together in my lap to keep from giving myself away, if I hadn't already. "I need to know if Bella ever met with Voorstadt. It's very important."

Isolde put her fingers to her mouth, the lights of realization kindling her eyes. "Oh, my. You don't think that man had something to do with her death, do you? If I were somehow responsible for what happened to her . . ."

"She met him then?"

"I'm afraid so."

"When?"

"A week before she passed away. Or ten days perhaps. You don't think—"

"What did they talk about?"

"I don't know."

"Where's Voorstadt now?" Leo asked.

"I don't know that either."

I was churning now. Finally the gimbals were beginning to hold my compass steady. "Did Bella ever mention the name of Joseph Rotto? Alonzo Serca? They were acting as regents for her company until she inherited full control. Do you recall ever hearing those names?"

"No. No, I'm sorry. They mean nothing to me."

I wondered if that were true. In the last few days I'd honed my people-perception skills to a new and frightening edge. Now those skills were telling me not to accept everything Isolde Bancavia told me as if it were the voice from the burning bush. I needed more proof of her veracity than her own word.

I stole a glance at the pack of cigarettes at the far end of the counter.

Leo asked, "You haven't seen this Voorstadt scoundrel lately?" She shook her head.

"Do you know him well?" he probed.

"Hardly at all, actually."

"Do you think he might have murdered Mrs. Murillo because she was threatening to expose him? Maybe he'd committed some other crime that hadn't been pinned on him yet and she was using her contacts at the paper to get the story. Is that a possibility?"

"I suppose so," Isolde admitted, beginning to sound as if she were losing the fight to exhaustion. "But as a general rule, ELF activists are concerned solely with sabotage. Or *ecotage*, rather, and they abhor any kind of harm to human life."

"Real angels then, are they?"

"They are men and women of honor, if that's what you mean."

"There's not much honor in burning buildings down and sinking oil ships."

"Do not apply your own schema of ideals to all of mankind, Mr. Kavisti."

"I'll keep that in mind."

I stood up.

"What's wrong?" Leo asked.

I turned around, my eyes trawling the shop. What *was* wrong? I knew I was missing something important, but my damned deviating compass had caused me to overlook it. I drifted toward the front of the store.

"Marcella?"

I toured the bookshelves, reading each title, and when that exercise proved fruitless I crossed the room and tried another shelf, this one packed with collections of personal letters and journal entries from men and women two hundred years dead. I brushed my fingers against a stack of yellowed newsprint. And that made me think of newspapers, and maybe if I got in touch with Bella's editor he could set me on a proper course, but that was just another distraction and not what I was looking for right now, but something else . . .

Leo got to his feet. "Uh, Marcella, is there something you're not telling me?"

"Perhaps it would be best if you two called on me again later this afternoon," Isolde suggested. "You can understand that I'm feeling a little overwhelmed by all of this. You did kick in my door . . ."

I reached the big windows and stopped cold. The rain slashed at the glass, turning the street beyond into a watery blur. The wind blew a tin can down the sidewalk.

"Marcella?"

I took one of Bancavia's books from the black shelf and opened it.

Leo stepped up beside me, but I barely noticed. I was too busy reading.

"What is it?" he wondered.

I scanned half a page, flipped through a few more, and read another sample. All the while the goosebumps rose on my arms and a strange new feeling grew in my chest. It was the feeling of a puzzle piece finally sliding into place.

"Poetry," I whispered.

"Yeah, so?"

I looked up at Isolde. I'm not sure which emotion was more evident on my face, surprise or disgust. " 'Where dew lies like white forest blood.' "

She frowned. "Pardon me?"

" 'And no one can hear me when I fall.' " I held up the book. "Those were two of the lines I found in the cabin of Bella's boat. You wrote them, didn't you?"

She put her hand over her mouth and answered me with her eyes.

"You. You're the Mystery Man. You were Isabella's lover." I had detected a special affection in Isolde's voice when she spoke of our mutual friend, and on an intuitive level I'd sensed something more. Even so, I was still shocked when enlightenment finally hit me. Bella had been involved in a sexual relationship with another woman. That wasn't the sort of thing your best friend was supposed to keep from you.

Isolde closed her eyes and lowered her head.

"Now," I said, "do you want to tell me what you were doing around midnight on Sunday night, or should I just start speculating? Believe me, I'm getting pretty good at it."

Isolde didn't say a word.

Outside, the wind cried out like a lost child.

Chapter Fourteen

"She called me that night," Isolde said meekly.

"When?"

"Nine. Perhaps ten o'clock. She said she was meeting someone."

"Who?"

"I don't know. But I certainly asked. I admit to an irrational degree of jealousy."

"What do you mean?"

"I was afraid that . . . I was worried she was seeing someone else."

"Such as?"

"It's childish, really. I had little on which to base such a suspicion, but I thought she might have been mending things with her husband but didn't want to tell me for fear of breaking my heart. Not that she hadn't already done that a dozen times before . . ."

"So she was meeting Nico? He was supposed to show up at the *Lynn* Sunday night?"

"That would be my assumption."

"And you went nowhere near the boat that day."

"That is correct. Though unquestionably I wanted to. There was nothing I more desired than spending time with her that evening, but she made it quite clear that we wouldn't see each other until the next morning."

"So you stayed home that night."

"Yes. My apartment is just upstairs, humble as it may be."

"Anyone vouch for you?"

"Only Audrey Hepburn, I'm afraid."

"I'm sorry?"

"I stayed up watching *Breakfast at Tiffany's*. That was our favorite movie, Isabella and I. We would watch a little, make love, rewind what we missed and do it all over again. She would insist on eating popcorn in bed, and I was too much of a fool for her to tell her no. Sometimes, Marcella . . . sometimes I wanted to hold her more than I wanted to breathe."

Upon hearing those words, uttered with such plaintive devotion, all I could do was sit there in my ordinary clothes, stranded in my unromantic life, and fight the sudden heaviness in my chest. It felt as if someone had placed a stone upon my heart. I'd die content one day if I was loved half as much.

"I can't believe I'm having this conversation," I said with a dry mouth. "But I do have one more question. Where did Bella meet with Voorstadt?"

"Here. Upstairs. In my room. I waited down here, reading Maya Angelou and trying not to hear what they were saying."

"Thank you. Come on, Leo. Get your hat. Let's give this woman some peace."

"So what do you think?" he asked when we were on the steps in front of the shop.

I pulled the hood over my head and took several long samples of the air, letting the oxygen clear my mind the way the rain was cleansing the street. Entwined inside of me were the paradoxical feelings of elation and disillusionment. I was thrilled at having pieced together the first fragments of my friend's mysterious death, but I was simultaneously dispirited. If Bella had kept from me the fact that she was sleeping with another woman, then how many other secrets had she withheld, like a miser woman with a hidden stash of Spanish doubloons . . . and how many of those forbidden coins would I have to discover before I could point my finger at her murderer?

So she was bisexual. Get over it, gatita, and get moving.

And that, I realized, was why I'd seen no proof of Bella's lover in her cabin. The clothing had been there, all right, but it belonged to a woman and had consequently gone unnoticed.

Overcome by the simple need to clear my mind, I lifted my hand and let the rain patter against my palm. "Did you ever wonder how many drops actually fall from the sky in a storm?"

Leo scratched his head. "Uh, did I miss something here?"

"I used to think millions. When I was a girl I assumed there must be even *trillions* of them, but now . . . now it wouldn't surprise me if it was only just the same raindrop, reborn the moment it hits the ground, falling over and over again with no one the wiser." I glanced at him obliquely. "Does that make any sense?"

"Not one damn bit."

"I didn't think so." I shoved my hands into my windbreaker, shook out of my trance and surveyed the street. Other than a ragamuffin dog with a sodden red bandana around its neck, the avenue was deserted. I saw no pedestrians, only several featureless faces behind storefront windows, as patrons and shopkeepers alike stood behind the glass and marveled at the cascade. From somewhere down the street, a church carillon sounded out the opening notes of "That Old Rugged Cross." The bells seemed muted, subdued by the storm. Or maybe that was just my imagination. "What I need to do right now," I said, "is check out the cigar shop on the corner."

"Cigar shop. Right. You're just one surprise after another."

"And what about you?"

"Me? Oh, I'm just standing here hoping I don't get pneumonia. Can we go now?"

The Tongue Merchant

"We?"

"Yeah, you and me, as in us. Plural. If you don't mind."

"You seem awfully interested in the events surrounding Isabella's death."

"So I'm inquisitive."

"And I'm suspicious."

"No reason to be. I'm just curious. And you want to know why? Well, for starters, a fortune is on the line, everybody wants a piece of it, and the woman who was supposed to enjoy it is dead. Not only that, but it looks like she was covering up a good chunk of sordid info, and it's clear to this *hombre* that she died on the verge of disclosing said info to the world. The police think her hubby did it, but at least half a dozen other questionable characters stand to benefit in a major way from her death. And that complicates matters in a serious way. Add to the mix our resident wild card, formally known as Lieutenant Marcella Maria Paraizo, age twenty-nine, daughter of Detective Harry Paraizo of the Miami PD homicide division and record-setting rower from the United States Coast Guard Academy, from which she graduated *magna cum laude* and promptly turned down a scholarship for a master's program at Yale in order to serve as a defender of her country's interests in the Caribbean Sea."

I didn't even give him an incredulous glare, just shook my head. "Handyman, my ass."

I headed down the street to the cigar store.

"Truth?" Leo said as we neared the Landbrook & Swaine Tobacco Emporium on the corner of 4th and Matisse.

"I think it's about time."

"Joseph Rotto hired me."

I kept walking. Rotto had mentioned that he and Serca were both employing people to check up on Ernesto's children. It seemed that Leo was Rotto's informant. I wondered who was working for Serca. Probably Nathan.

"I do slave labor for a private security firm in the Keys. Joseph suspected Isabella and Abdías of conspiring against him. Isabella, at least, was unhappy with the way Joseph was running things, and she made no bones about her feelings. As for Abdías, well, he might have been going along with her, for nothing other than the selfless and altruistic reason of supporting the woman who controlled the cash flow. I managed to get myself employed as a groundskeeper to keep an eye on him. I can tell you all the finer nuances of eavesdropping. It's an art, believe me."

"What company?"

"Excuse me?"

"Your security firm. What's the name?"

Leo pinched a grin between his lips. "You think I'm lying, don't you?"

"Whatever gave you that idea?" I pushed my way through the door of the cigar shop.

I didn't bother scouting the place, dialing my radar down a notch and concentrating on the object of my search. I wasn't here looking for clues, but rather a certain brand of cigarettes. I went straight to a wall rack which sported at least twenty different brands, most of them foreign and all of them exorbitantly priced.

"Hammersmith," Leo said from over my shoulder.

"Hmmm?" I ran my fingers along the packages.

"The name of my boss. Klaus Hammersmith. It's his company. Real nice guy, Klaus, except when the Buccaneers lose to Chicago, and then he's as pissy as a wet cat."

The proprietor was emerging from the back of the store with a *May I help you?* on his lips just as I found the motherlode.

I tore into the pack and pulled out a cigarette.

"Having a nicotine attack?" Leo asked. "I didn't peg you as a smoker."

I held the cigarette up to the light. Long and slender, brown, with three thin gold bands near the filter.

"Got you," I muttered. "You liars."

"Come again?"

"Rotto and Bancavia." The warmth of fresh anger drove away the chill of the rain. "He told me he'd never met her. And she basically said vice versa. But they *knew* each other. She'd been to his *house.*"

"And you know this how?"

"I found one of these very same cigarettes on the ground out in front of Rotto's place, right before I saw you scampering away like some kind of crook. And what are these things, Turkish? They're twelve bucks a pack. I doubt it's the most common brand smoked in San Juan."

"Maybe so. But it could still be a coincidence."

"There's no such thing." I paid the shopkeeper and asked for a telephone to call a cab.

"And what do you mean *scampering?*" Leo said, trailing after me. "I'll have you know I make it a personal point never to scamper. *Scurry,* maybe, and *scuttle* if I'm certain no one's watching, but never *scamper.* At least not in public."

I hardly heard a word he said.

Both Rotto and Bancavia had lied to me. Just the thought of it caused my fingers to curl into talons. And not only did they know each other, but their relationship was such that Isolde actually came calling at his home, which implied a deeper familiarity between them. And that begged the inevitable question: *What the hell were they up to?*

"Forget the taxi," Leo said. "I've got a truck."

"Congratulations."

"I mean I can give you a ride. And I can help you out. If you want."

"I don't think I'd do so well with a partner."

"Who said anything about partners?" He took the phone out of my hand and hung it up. "Look. It's obvious that you and I could both benefit from a détente and a friendly exchange of information. Especially now, if what you say is true and my patron is involved in some kind of cover-up. I'll drop you off wherever you're going, and along the way we can compare notes. How does that sound? And I'll charge you a lot less for the ride than one of the local highwaymen who call themselves cabbies."

"Not a chance. You work for Rotto, remember?" *And he's suddenly my prime suspect,* I mentally added. "But thanks for the offer."

"What if I told you that I don't care if I'm working for him or not? Would you believe me if I said I was more concerned with seeing justice done than earning a paycheck?"

I evaluated him for a few moments. Leo Kavisti, private eye. He seemed a little too anxious to betray his meal ticket. If Rotto was paying him good money, and I had little doubt about that, then I wasn't about to lend him my unconditional trust, regardless of the seeming sincerity in those charcoal eyes. I decided to give Dad a call the first chance I got, just to check out Leo's background story. And then a chilling possibility occurred to me. If Rotto had taken a hand in Bella's murder, then Leo might have been his trigger man . . .

I didn't need the ringing of the tintinnabulators to tell me to watch my step with this one.

"Okay, you win." I resigned myself to the next pitfall destiny was sure to deal me. But everything was happening too rapidly to worry about that now. The hours were falling faster than the rain, and I still had heaven and earth to move before my afternoon appointment with Dr. Avundavi. "You tell me everything you know about Joe Rotto, and I promise to keep my gun in my bag. At least for now."

"Swell. My kneecaps are breathing sighs of relief." He held open the door for me, and the rain slanted into our faces. "So where are we going, anyway?"

"To jail," I said, and headed out into the wind.

"I had to ask," I heard him mutter as he lowered his head and followed me into the storm.

"It must have been tough," Leo said as he drove, "finding her like that."

"You have no idea."

"You don't think so? Maybe I have more of an idea than you think." He gripped the wheel of the pickup with both hands, keeping his eyes on the rainy street. He wore a turquoise pinkie ring, like the kind you buy from roadside Navajo stands in New Mexico. A pale band of flesh lay across his wrist, evidence of a watch he normally wore. He looked like I imagine certain country-western songwriters look when they hear someone else singing one of their tunes on the radio and getting all the credit for it. Every so often he'd toss a glance at the rearview mirror, but all there was to see behind us was the rain. "When I was thirteen I found my brother in the back of our old man's locksmithing van. He was lying in a pile of ten thousand keys with a garden house in his mouth. He'd taped the other end to the exhaust pipe."

Oh, damn. I started to say something, but I guess I couldn't get the words past the foot in my mouth. The heat rose in my cheeks.

"Sorry," he said, giving me a false smile. "I don't know where that came from. I haven't mentioned that to anyone for years."

"No, *I'm* sorry. I didn't know . . ."

"Hey, no harm done. It was a long time ago."

His tone sounded genuine enough, and all I could manage in return was a commiserating look and a half-assed apology. Then I surprised myself by reaching over and touching him on the leg. "Really, Leo. I shouldn't have presumed you didn't understand. But I'm not that great with people sometimes, you know?"

"Marcella, you're talking to the grand potentate of social-skill deficiency. I'm the king of a country called Gauche. Ever hear of it? And as such I hereby vow to remain unoffended by any interpersonal faux pas you commit in my presence, regardless of its size. On one condition."

"Name it."

"You let me call you Marcy."

I raised my eyebrows.

"It's not so formal, see? A woman named Marcella sounds too stately to be sitting in the cab of an '81 Silverado with the duct-tape patches on the seat. Makes me nervous. Now a Marcy, on the other hand, that sounds like a girl you can take to a doubleheader on a Saturday afternoon and not be worried when you spill peanuts in her lap."

I had to laugh at that, if only just a little. The truth does that to you.

But instead of confiding in him my private fetish for coyote-fur fishing lures, I decided it best to stay on my charted course. I had enough deviations to worry about without Leo Kavisti fooling with my compass. "You've got yourself a deal. Whatever you say. So now tell me who broke the window."

"Window?"

"At Abdías's place. When Saul and I showed up there Monday, you were installing a piece of glass in the doors that led to the patio. At least I thought that's what you were doing, though now I know you were actually spying . . ."

"Oh, the window, right. There was a minor scuffle in the

The Tongue Merchant

house just before you arrived. Why? What difference does it make?"

"None, probably. But I've learned a lot in the last three days, mainly to take nothing for granted. So who was doing the fighting?"

"I didn't hear much of it. But that Castigere guy, I think he was harping on Abdías for being his normal improvident self. And then the judge—Horne, I think his name is—he sort of plays the white knight and comes to Abdías's rescue, yelling at Castigere for mismanaging the kid's money. And I'm walking through the garden with my arms full of the dead tree limbs I'd been sawing all day, and I hear Castigere say something about only being able to manage the money if there was actually money to manage, or something like that. Then I suppose the two of 'em got in each other's faces, and the posturing led to a brandy snifter being tossed across the room."

"Did they fight? Physically, I mean."

"Perish the thought. Guys like that don't really ever get their hands dirty. But they've both got short fuses, and every now and then, they up and explode. They each think they've got to act like the kid's father, just so they can get a little of the moolah from him. It's sick, really. But Abdías is generous, and he throws the stuff at 'em just to shut 'em up."

"So who pitched the snifter?"

"Well, now that you ask, I'm not entirely sure, but I think that the judge was the thrower, and Castigere was the throwee. But he ducked, wily bookkeeper that he is, and then I'm summoned to keep my eyes and ears shut and sweep up the evidence of their tantrum."

"I see."

"Any other questions?"

"Yes. Have you ever met Alonzo Serca?"

"Dude in the wheelchair? Yeah, I saw him at Rotto's once.

He was pulling up in his limo just as I was leaving. Had a torpedo with him that was either his bodyguard or his spirit guide. I couldn't tell which."

"Nathan," I said, repressing a shudder.

"That his name? Nathan, huh? Whoever he was, he was wearing some kind of voodoo charm around his neck, so I thought it best to light out from the back door. I didn't want him taking offense at my presence and sewing up a mojo doll with my face on it. Not that I believe in all that islander witchcraft mumbo-jumbo, but the possibility of somebody poking needles into an effigy of me is something I don't want to take a chance with."

"They call it sympathetic magic," I told him. "And I doubt that Nathan is a practitioner. But he may be into *espiritismo*. Basically that's a local flavor of spiritualism. Does the name Paulo Longoria mean anything to you?"

"Nope. But the chair's not for real, you know. Serca's disability, I mean."

That got my attention. "Alonzo Serca isn't really a paraplegic? He's faking it?"

"Oh, no, I wouldn't go that far. But Joseph told me that his partner had been in rehab for years now, and though he isn't exactly Baryshnikov on his feet, he can get a little ambulatory when he has to."

"Then why keep up the pretense of being paralyzed?"

"Heck, beats me. Guy's embarrassed to try and shuffle around in front of his peers, I guess. Thinks it's classier to ride the steel stallion than to hobble along like an old man on crutches. Besides, he still goes whole-hog for every outdoors fad that comes along, just like a lot of rich, middle-aged, weekend warriors. Joseph's got pictures of the two them parachuting, weight-lifting, scuba diving . . ."

"This is it." I pointed toward the black brick edifice which housed the Hozumkur municipal offices. I was so lost in

The Tongue Merchant

contemplation that I'd almost permitted Leo to drive right on by. "Pull up around back. The entrance to the police department is in the rear of the building."

Leo did as I instructed. After shutting off the engine, he looked over at me, and for one weird second it was almost like I was inside of him—*he's seen his brother dead and he's killed in self-defense and he's been married once but things never last for men like him and even though the world's going down the crapper he still believes in trying*—and then the moment closed up like the petals of a flower in a sudden freeze. He said, "Thanks for trusting me."

"I have a thing for lost causes."

"I'm serious."

"Me too."

We let the rain drum the truck for awhile, then he put a hand on the door. "We're here to talk to her husband, aren't we?"

"He didn't kill Isabella, Leo."

"What makes you so sure?"

"My heart. For what that's worth."

Leo opened his mouth to respond, then apparently thought better of it. Instead, he shrugged and climbed out. He waited for me to run around the nose of the truck, then we jogged for cover with our heads low, like soldiers ducking enemy fire.

I sat in a lifeless room with concrete walls and fluorescent lights full of dead bugs. The place was as muggy as a swamp. The uniformed cop who'd ushered us here had said the air-conditioner was so old they were calling in an archaeologist instead of a repairman. I'd laughed as best I could.

I sat on the lip of a folding metal chair with only three of the four rubber caps on its legs, having somehow found myself the center of everyone's scrutiny. Kyle Straker sat on my left, his shirtsleeves rolled up and his tie askew. He was allowing me to question Nico in hopes that I might be able to bring about a confession and save the taxpayers the expense of a lengthy trial. He was taking a chance on me, and I owed him one for it. On my right was my pal Sam Raznik, his ample neck spilling over the edge of his too-tight collar. Leo stood behind me by the door. Next to him was the uniformed guard with all the jokes. And directly across from me, weariness riding his shoulders like a gothic gargoyle, sat Nicholas Murillo, wearing orange coveralls and a look of such childlike confusion on his face that I almost felt ashamed for my freedom, as if I were taunting him with it. His lawyer, a bespectacled Puerto Rican with an NYU tie tack, glowered at us over his client's shoulder. Nico seemed small and shrunken in the attorney's shadow.

"*¿Quieres hablar?*" I asked him.

"In English, please," Raznik blurted. "Not all of us savvy *Español*."

Somehow I refrained from scowling at Mercator, though I briefly considered giving him the finger. I haven't flipped anybody off since junior high. Fortunately for all of us, self-control prevailed. I consoled myself with the thought that if the Buddhists were right about reincarnation, then I was sitting next to a future earthworm.

"Nico," I said slowly, for the linguistically impaired among us, "do you feel like talking?"

Nico's eyes jittered, a caged animal observed by scientists with sharp instruments. He shifted in his seat. When he reached for the glass of water they'd provided for him, I knew everyone in the room was watching the palsied shaking of his hand.

"Go home, Marcy," he said.

"You know I can't do that." I clasped my hands on the table in front of me and leaned an inch closer. "I came here to ask you some questions, and it's for your own good. So if you don't mind . . ."

"I *do* mind. Already I tell them all they ask."

"That's true," Straker confirmed. The young sergeant had pouches like little handbags under his eyes, making him look ten years older. I wondered if he'd slept since the last time I saw him. "Mr. Murillo's been the epitome of cooperation. Unfortunately, we've got motive, means, and opportunity, and most importantly a witness whose sworn statement undermines his alibi."

"And who is this witness?" I fired the question at him point-blank, figuring that the time for tact had long since passed. "Does he or she have a name?"

"That's police business," Raznik informed me.

"It's all right, Sam . . ."

"Bullshit it is." Raznik wagged a fleshy finger at his partner. "This woman has absolutely no business being here. I know that, and you know that, and you can be damn tootin' the captain knows that too."

Please, I thought, sending Raznik a telepathic plea. *Just give me this one break.*

Instead of launching a return volley on my behalf, Straker jerked his head toward the door, prompting Raznik to labor himself out of his chair for a private confab. The two of them huddled close and talked inaudibly, so that I couldn't make out a single word. Then, much to the delight of the recent spy I'd become, I noticed Leo standing a few feet away from them, looking fabulously bored with the whole affair. Thus I knew that he was eavesdropping the hell out of them.

Thank you, Leo. Or whatever your real name is.

I made the most of the next few seconds by tilting myself even farther over the table and saying emphatically in Spanish, "Give me something to go on, Nico, you bullheaded bastard, so I can get you out of this mess, because right now I'm the only chance you've got."

The lawyer's mouth twitched.

Nico swallowed hard.

Then he bent toward me and whispered a single word: *"Zapatos."*

Shoes.

How long it took for those few syllables to make sense to me, I couldn't say. But it seemed like continental drift moved with more speed than my overworked cerebellum. Shoes?

When I finally caught on, I cursed myself for being a numbskull and said rapidly, "Oh, right, yes, I'm with you, I found them, the shoes, and I know what's inside, I've got it right here with me, but what was Bella going to do with it? Why did she buy it from St-Germain in the first place?"

Nico's face became a drastic mask.

"Nico, dammit, you're going on trial for *murder.*"

"*Nathan,*" he hissed, the word coming out like the discharge from a taser. "All I know is that she spent a fortune on that stupid stamp, just so she could give it to someone named Nathan, probably one of her new lovers who collects the damn things."

Nathan. I knew he'd been hiding something. I'd seen it in his eyes when I spoke Longoria's name.

"Why, Nico? Why was it important that Nathan get the stamp?"

"She didn't say, and I didn't ask. It had something to do with a newspaper story, I think. We weren't talking very much at that point in our relationship."

"But she didn't at least say—"

Nico suddenly leaned back, his eyes alerting me to the detectives' return. They resumed their seats, and I tried to look casual even though I'm sure that only made me look all the more like a woman who'd just sold the launch codes to the Russians.

"I don't s'pose you talked a confession out of him," Straker said good-naturedly.

"My client has nothing to confess," his attorney was quick to point out.

"Could be you're right," Straker allowed.

"So this witness," I said, desperate to keep things rolling in my favor, "they put Nico at the marina at the time of the—"

—*slaughter*—

"—incident?"

Raznik's frown only deepened when Straker nodded and said, "His name is Tommy So. He owns the rig in the berth next to the one leased by Mr. and Mrs. Murillo. You remember when I told you about the party late Sunday night? It seems that one of the party-goers *did* see something, after all. Tommy So was one of the last people we interviewed. He alleges that Mr. Murillo was in the vicinity, just before the *Lady Lynn Rob* pulled out to sea."

"We consider Mr. So a profoundly unreliable source," the lawyer said.

"Why is that?" I asked.

Straker explained. "It's true that Tommy So has been in and out of trouble for possession of narcotics, mainly marijuana, but that was wiped from his record when he turned eighteen. He supposedly had a full-ride scholarship to some whizzer school like Caltech, but he ended up a beach vagrant. Since then he's been in the clear, at least as far as convictions are concerned, and I'm sure his testimony will be viewed equitably by any jury we put him in front of."

Tommy So? Vaguely I recalled seeing a roguish Asian man watching the activity aboard the *Lynn* the morning after the murder. Had he actually seen Nico that night? Was Nico still lying about his own whereabouts, and if he was, how could I possibly get him to tell me the truth? Isolde had said that Bella was meeting someone at the boat that night. Was Nico that someone?

And through this raging river of thoughts slipped a single, crucial current: *Why was it so critical to Bella that Nathan receive the stamp?*

I'd known that Nathan had been hiding something the moment I spoke Longoria's name.

But *what?*

Straker's phone whistled, and I took advantage of the distraction to draw a mental map of my next move. Maybe if I could talk to this Tommy So alone . . .

"Nico," I said, ignoring his attorney's glare, "if you weren't at the boat that night—"

"I wasn't."

"Fine. But if you weren't there, then I assume you have someone who can vouch for you, and if that's the case, then it's Tommy So's word against theirs."

"I'd like to reiterate," the lawyer said, "for the record, that this form of questioning by someone unaffiliated with the police is highly irregular."

"I understand that," I said, "but I'm only trying to—"

Straker sprang to his feet so forcefully that he almost toppled his chair. "That was a unit down at the market on Trader Lane." He snapped his phone shut and grabbed his coat. "They say there's somebody down there trying to sell a human tongue."

Chapter Fifteen

The next few minutes of my life fragmented formlessly around me, like bits of the magnetic poetry Isolde arranged on Bella's fridge:

The backseat of an unmarked car. Leo beside me. Wipers thumped. Red strobe flashed from the dashboard.

Rain.

Police radio crackled. Leo whispered my name.

I turned my head toward the window. My reflection, a stranger, looked back at me.

My compass spun.

Raznik drove. Fat freckled hands on the wheel. Straker twisted in his seat. Asked how I was holding up.

I wasn't.

In small increments I began to pull the muddled poetry of my life into sensible prose. But it was a struggle. Isabella's chest had probably been broken open in autopsy, and someone tried to kill me with a car, and everyone I met filled the sky with lies. And if that weren't enough, I always had my Secret Saboteur, which I carried close to my heart like some kind of bad luck charm, and what if the lumpectomy wasn't entirely successful? Would they have to irradiate me until my hair fell out?

Cancer. Jesus.

"Marcy? You still with us?"

Though I heard what sounded like honest concern in Leo's voice, I fixed my eyes on Kyle Straker instead. "I think you need to check on a man named Miguel Saldaña y Hinojosa," I told him.

"And who's he?"

"He owns a shop in Río Piedras in San Juan. Buys and sells books and stamps. He's a real crud. I don't think he liked Isabella very much."

"If mere dislike were enough to warrant murder," Straker said, "I'd have long ago been overwhelmed with work and by now I'd be playing dominoes in an asylum somewhere."

"I think she hit him."

"Excuse me?"

"With that hammer you were talking about. The meat tenderizer or whatever the hell it was. You said she struck her attacker. I think Saldaña might be the one."

Straker's mouth tightened into one of those sad, somewhat condescending smiles that makes you feel like crawling under a rock. "I understand that you want to clear Mr. Murillo's name, but you're barking up the wrong tree on this one. You can't just go accusing everyone who held a grudge against her."

"Why not? I've been finding out that she had a lot more enemies than I ever imagined. Any one of them could've been down there with her that night."

"Maybe so. But Mrs. Murillo didn't hit anyone. At least not with that hammer."

"Well she certainly hit *somebody*."

"Bug blood," Raznik grunted without taking his eyes from the street.

I stared at the back of his meaty head.

"Your friend was squashing bugs," he said. "So just let it go, will you? Drop it."

"We got word back from the lab," Straker said, his tone several shades softer than his partner's. "It wasn't human blood on the hammer—"

The Tongue Merchant

"I don't want to hear this." I turned back to the window.

Straker went on, something about insect blood, probably arachnid, and the radio popped with phantom voices and the queen palms along the sidewalk bowed as if in obeisance to the wind. In my mind I kept hearing the ache in Isolde's voice when she said, *Sometimes I wanted to hold her more than I wanted to breathe.*

The drive to the market seemed like eternity.

The Hozumkur *mercado* never really closed. Even in the rain. Nearly forty stalls and colored tents crowded cobblestoned Trader Lane, which was a pedestrians-only street that stretched between Lionese and the Holiday Inn, a honey pot for tourists. The market was famed equally for the extravagance of its products and the audacity of its pickpockets. Even with the rain coming down like iron rods, business went on. Under a white tarpaulin the size of a galleon's sail, three men in navy peacoats led a coffle of Arabian horses toward a waiting trailer. Most of the other tradesmen were snapping up folding chairs and tying down canvas in expectation of the storm, but a few holdouts kept their lanterns burning and the tent-flaps popping open in the wind. Trader Lane had always fascinated me. Beggars asked for handouts in a dozen different languages, tattoo artists doubled as fences for stolen stereos, and rumor had it that you could find someone who'd sell you a forged passport if your inquiry was discreet and your cash was handy.

But most people knew nothing of the market's spurious underbelly. On the surface it was nothing but your usual mecca of capitalist bedlam, just as it appeared as the four of us got out of the car.

Straker was met immediately by a young uniformed cop wearing a long black slicker and a plastic covering over his hat. While they spoke, I examined the market, as if to chance upon a face I recognized.

He's out there.

Or she.

Yeah, or she. Joe Rotto and the long-suffering Isolde Bancavia were hiding their relationship from me, and God only knew what else they were up to. Neither one of them had an unshakable alibi for the night of the murder, as they both attested to sharing their evening with mute partners—Jose Cuervo and Audrey Hepburn, respectively. But if I thought I'd seen one of them passing like a specter between the tents, I was guilty of honest wishful thinking.

Straker summoned me with a wave.

"The guy we're looking for is evidently some kind of talismonger," he said, loud enough to be heard over the rain.

Raznik turned up the collar of his garage-sale trenchcoat. "A talis-*what?*"

"Talismonger," Straker repeated. "One of those snake-oil salesman who hawks baubles to housewives who've taken up witchcraft as a hobby. Amulets, fetishes, dead scorpions on a string, that sort of crap. It's all the rave in the alternative medicine industry."

"Voodoo bullshit is what it is."

"Could be. Anyway—"

"Where is he?" I asked. "This talismonger. He have a name?"

"I'm getting to that." Straker indicated the officer beside him, who looked about one sneeze away from taking a few days of sick leave. "We've got a solid description of him. Freak like this would stand out in a crowd of circus clowns. Osborne?"

The young cop lifted a hand about two feet over his head. "Guy's gotta be seven feet tall, or so says our witnesses, and as skinny as a tent pole. But he looks even taller, on account of the fact that he wears one of them old Abe Lincoln kind of hats, what do you call them?"

The Tongue Merchant

"Stovepipe," I said.

"Yeah, one of them. Had a coat with all kinds of trinkets tied to it."

"Caucasian?" Raznik asked.

Osborne shook his head. "Black. Probably Jamaican. Junk dealer down on the corner says he came in and said he had a tongue to sell him. To use in black magic, you know. Dealer asked if it was a dog tongue, cat tongue, whatever, and the guy says no, it's a *human* tongue. In our briefing yesterday they told us what happened down at the marina, so I got on the horn while Pollard went to detain the guy, but by then he'd split. Got six or eight of us down here now, but he's just gone. Poof."

Jamaican? I wondered. *What's a Jamaican talismonger got to do with it?*

Probably nothing, gatita. *Don't get distracted. It's just a red herring. A coincidence.*

But of course, I'd already decided that coincidence was illusion. Only motion and perspiration were real. I resumed my study of the street.

"Why don't you and Leo get back in the car," Straker suggested. "Sam and I will poke around for a bit, break a few of the witness's bones, see what we can dig up."

I didn't reply, but Leo said, "Sure thing, Detective. Sounds good to get in out of the rain. As long as you let me turn the heater on."

"There's a thermos of coffee between the seats. But don't touch anything else." He told Osborne to lead the way. The three of them disappeared into the bazaar.

"I'm not getting in the car," I said as soon as they were out of sight.

"I know. So what are you waiting for?"

I shouldn't have been surprised by this, but it was mildly amazing that Leo had guessed my thoughts so accurately. I took my hands from my jacket pockets and flexed my fingers, my knuckles cracking, my pulse ticking excitedly in my wrists. "I want to take a little look around."

"So I figured."

"Are you coming with me?"

"Wild horses, Marcy. Wild horses."

I nodded, more grateful for the company than I wanted to let on. Together we headed toward the nearest stall, where a man with an eye patch was selling windsocks and barometers, as if we needed such instruments to tell us that disaster was on its way.

So began our safari through the wilds of Trader Lane. I asked around about islanders in stovepipe hats. Said a little something about monetary rewards. I got almost nothing in return for my efforts. An unctuous and overweight Kazakh offered to trade me a Persian rug for an hour in the back of his tent. I told him that all I was after was information. Undeterred, he tried to elaborate on his prowess at lovemaking, acquired from years of erudite experimentation, but his accent proved unintelligible the more excited he became. I hurriedly moved on.

A shop called Julabi's sold textiles and rattan furniture, and I ended up buying a Peruvian scarf as payment for what little news the owner could provide. He claimed that the Jamaican called himself Sixbone and peddled heroin on the side. The scarf was a lightweight cotton blend with a hound's-tooth check pattern. Nobody but a tourist would buy a scarf in a place where the daytime temperature rarely fell below seventy degrees, but the thirty-five bucks was worth Sixbone's name any day. Besides, the rain had cooled things off considerably, and the scarf felt good around my neck.

When I looked back for Leo, I found him assisting the men with the horses, incorrigible altruist that he was. As soon as the

The Tongue Merchant

trailer was shut, they got started on the filigreed caroche which served as an expensive taxi for those desiring a horsedrawn tour of the city. The carriage looked like something from the age of Louis XIV, except for the shock-absorbers. We wouldn't want our passengers to suffer the slightest discomfort, lest they give St. Noré a bad report in the next *Fodor's* travel guide.

While I waited for Leo to finish his Good Samaritan antics, I thought about what the scarf salesman had told me of the Jamaican.

That creep? You're talking about Sixbone. He sells paraphernalia.
Like bracelets and elixirs and things?
Yeah, that too. Mainly he's into horse, though.
Horse?
Sure, heroin. H, you know. Brown sugar.
Oh. Right. How much for the scarf?
For you, lady, fifty dollars.
Thirty-five.
Deal. And don't go snooping after Sixbone. He's weird, you know? Way out there.

I stepped under the awning of a small plywood stall that had been nailed shut against the gale. As singular in appearance as Sixbone was—tall, grotesquely thin, with a top hat and an overcoat festooned with talismans—you would've thought he'd be easy to find. But every day was like Mardi Gras in Hozumkur, the walking freakshows benefitting from a kind of kaleidoscopic camouflage. It was the normal people who seemed out of place.

"Learn any deep dark secrets?" Leo asked, joining me under my makeshift umbrella.

"Do you know anything about heroin?"

"Don't tell me. You noticed the track marks on my arm."

"Leo . . ."

"Sorry. Uh, heroin, let's see. Heroin is a semi-synthetic,

narcotic analgesic, which is injected, snorted, or smoked. Its active ingredient is something called diacetyl morphine. In tar form, it's usually packaged in plastic wrap or sandwich bags. But in powder form it shows up in balloons, bindles, and compressed blocks. Its primary effect on the user is a feeling of euphoria, which generally lasts around . . . oh, I'd say four hours, give or take. Points of origin include such drug-friendly places as Thailand, Pakistan, Afghanistan, and our near and dear neighbor, Mexico. Why do you ask?"

I stepped toward him and lifted my chin, so that I was only inches from his face. "Who *are* you?"

"For real?"

"Please."

"My full name is Leonardo. My old man named me after Da Vinci."

"You know that's not what I mean."

"Da Vinci wrote everything in his notebooks backward. Nobody knows why. Maybe just for kicks. Or maybe because he didn't want anyone stealing his secrets."

"And that's what you're doing. Writing backward."

"In a matter of speaking."

"What if I told you that I couldn't care less about your secrets?"

"Then you would be lying." His lips parted in a fugitive smile.

"Get over yourself, Leo. I'm not in the mood for games."

"Fine. So why the sudden interest in dope?"

In my mind, I could hear Saul talking about Corky:

. . . . *if he doesn't stay off the smack while he's on the job* . . .

"Smack is another name for heroin, right?"

"Smack? Sure. Or so goes the slanguage of the drug trade. Why?"

"Because I might know someone who can lead us to Sixbone."

The Tongue Merchant

"Sixbone?"

"The Jamaican. A friend of mine owns a studio at the end of the street. One of his apprentices may be able to point us in the right direction. Come on. I'll introduce you to my favorite potter. You'll love him. He's crazy about cops, so I'm sure he'll get faint in the heart meeting a real live private eye." I set off down Lionese in the direction of Saul's *bottega,* hoping that he hadn't fired Corky yet.

"Okay, I'm with you, but how do we even know that this Jamaican . . . what's his name?"

"Sixbone."

"Right. We don't even know that he's involved with the murder, and if he was—"

"There's no such thing as coincidence."

"So you've said. But if this Sixbone was involved, then he'd have to be some kind of major-league idiot to go around talking about the tongue he'd just cut out of his victim's mouth. I mean, this is a *tongue* we're talking about here."

"I know. And, no, I'm not entirely sure that this isn't a wild goose chase, but I'm out here on the flaky end of things, Leo, and women out on the flaky end have the prerogative to be insane as it suits us. So please, just let me run with this for awhile."

"Hey, fine by me. They're only giving you more rope, you know. And do you have to walk so fast?"

"What are you talking about? Who's giving me rope?"

"The police. The hefty one—"

"Raznik."

"Yeah, Raznik. He hates the sight of you. From the way he was talking, I'm surprised he hasn't burned your house down yet. He's ready to bust you, for sure, but fortunately for both of us, Detective Straker talked him out of it. But Straker only pacified him by telling him that he was just giving you enough rope."

"To hang myself."

"You got it. So watch your step."

"Too late."

We rounded the corner and the rain came at us almost horizontally. The big wooden sign in front of the studio was knocking back and forth in the wind. By the time we blustered inside, I felt like something washed ashore after a shipwreck.

I slammed the door behind us.

"Think this friend of yours has a towel?" Leo asked, shaking the water from his hair.

"I'll see what I can scrounge up."

Though I'd expected to find the *bottega* running a skeleton crew, if not shut down entirely, Saul seemed to take no heed of Bartholomew, other than a token closing of the metal blinds over the windows. The studio itself was more akin to a factory, the vast brick floor occupied by tables for crafting and crates for shipping, plaster molds for casting liquid clay and kilns the size of Volkswagens. The studio was dry and wonderfully warm. It smelled faintly like a bakery. On my left were the wheels, with several potters working industriously over them, while on my right, the room had been subdivided by Masonite partitions, the cubicles serving as offices for administrating payroll, running the Internet trade, importing clay, and exporting the finished product. The twenty-foot ceiling was crawling with a complicated ventilation system, providing the kilns with the proper degree of oxidation.

"Excuse me," I said to a woman with cornrows in her hair who was working on a crate with a crowbar. "I was wondering if you could tell me where I can find—"

"Zo? That you?"

Saul appeared from behind the mountain of crates, wearing a leather apron so big that it had probably been the death of a small herd of cattle.

The Tongue Merchant

I made the necessary introductions, waited while the men shook hands, and then cut to the chase. "Does Corky still work for you?"

"That little cock-knocker?" Saul untied his apron. "If you can call what he does *work,* then yeah, I guess he does. But he's on what you might call probation right now. Why? What did he do to you? If he so much as looked at you the wrong way, Zo—"

"It's about Isabella."

When Saul frowned, it was like a cloud passing in front of the moon. "Tell me."

And so I did. Five minutes later, Saul was current on the life and times of Marcella Paraizo and her misguided attempts to avenge her dead friend.

"Marcy here was hoping your apprentice could give us a lead on Sixbone," Leo said.

Saul barely gave Leo an acknowledging glance. He motioned for me to follow him across the studio. "Not too bad an idea, Zo, picking Corky's brain. Not that there's a whole lot left to pick after all the cells he's fried. Punk's probably been sniffing model airplane glue since he was old enough to twist the cap off the bottle. Miracle he can even feed himself anymore." He led me into one of the cubicles and pulled open the drawer of a steel desk. "Monday morning I went through his locker. That was just a few minutes before you showed up. And you wouldn't believe the junk he's into. You name the crime, Cork the Dork has found the time. I confiscated a bunch of pirated CDs, a phony driver's license, a slim-jim for cracking cars, counterfeiting supplies, lock picks, a piss-ant little .32 revolver—the kid had a Saturday night special *in my place of business*—and a few grams of heroin wrapped up in transparent tape." He removed a paper sack from the drawer and scattered its contents across his desk as proof of Corky's delinquencies. "I've got to give the kid credit. He can throw a pot better than a lot of people with

225

twice the experience. He's got a knack for it, as much as I hate to admit it. And that's the only reason I haven't torn him a new asshole yet. But I never give anyone a third chance."

"So maybe he's got a shot at redemption. Can I speak with him for a minute?"

"I don't know. Do I get to break his thumbs if he refuses to talk?"

"You can break anything you want as long as it gets me closer to Bella's killer."

Saul saluted me, then cupped his hands around his mouth and shouted, *"Corky!"*

By the time I finished with Corky, it was almost noon. My intended schedule for the day was already three hours behind, and I'd need a time machine if I planned on making my appointment back in San Juan. I still had two things remaining on my list, including a heart-to-heart with Tommy So, the prosecution's premier witness, and a rescue mission to the animal shelter. I couldn't let poor Roosevelt remain a convict any longer. I'd have to call Dr. Avundavi and tell her I was running late. I could always blame it on the storm.

Though faced with a disapproving glare from Saul, I'd offered Corky a bottle of *pulque,* a Mexican beer made from plant sap. I had one myself. The booze eventually lubricated Corky's vocal cords. And to Saul's further consternation, there was no thumb-breaking required. Corky claimed that Sixbone was a middleman for a dealer who used a *botanica* on Leeward Street as a front for his heroin traffic. A *botanica* was the island version of a head shop, with more emphasis on sorcerous charms and the herbs central to the practice of black magic.

"But if Sixbone's selling a *tongue,*" Corky had said, "I mean, a real tongue out of somebody's *mouth,* then he's probably already found a buyer. Something like that is heavy-duty mojo to those voodoo people, you get what I'm saying? They call their witch doctors *houngans*. A serious *houngan* would probably give five grand for a real tongue. Hell, they pay five hundred for a person's *teeth*. The only thing they'd rather have than a tongue is a human fetus."

Afterward I thanked him, dismissed him, and then asked Saul if he'd like to act as my chaperone at Bella's wake. He agreed, but only after holding forth with a variety of disparaging remarks concerning the social overachievers that Alonzo Serca was sure to have in attendance.

"Shit-glitzers, Zo. Arrogant shit-glitzers."

I reminded him that one of those shit-glitzers might have murdered Isabella.

He said he'd meet me at the wharf in an hour.

Until then, Leo and I left him to his pots. On our way out the door, I thumbed on my radio and found the news. I wasn't really surprised to learn that my situation was only getting worse.

Bartholomew had been upgraded to hurricane status. Unless it veered north, it would slam into St. Noré in less than ten hours.

Chapter Sixteen

Tommy So lived on a thirty-foot fishing rig named *Seventh Son*. Having abandoned our police escorts, Leo and I arrived at Marina del Sol to find the pier nearly deserted. A few dockhands in soggy white trousers gathered up the buoys and those trendy white parasols someone in the city council had decided to place along the wharf. Many of the boats had been hoisted out of the water. Nearly all of them were lashed with protective coverings and secured to the dock with additional lines strung through their gripes, the metal fastenings which locked the rigs to their cradles. I'm sure their owners all carried hurricane coverage, though, and they wouldn't shed many tears if Black Bart rode into town and forced the insurance companies to ante up a few hundred new yachts.

Mighty Jehovah informed me that it was half past twelve when I stepped up to the *Lynn*.

"Don't do this to yourself," Leo said, gently taking my arm. "It won't do any good."

The yellow warning tape was still stretched across the prow. One strand of it had snapped in the wind and now dragged the choppy waterline. The rain bounced off the waxed wood. I saw the wet remains of Raznik's cigarette on the deck.

"I'm freezing my butt off, Marcy. Let's forget this business for awhile, and I'll buy you a cappuccino."

"I hate coffee," I said, staring at the *Lynn*'s dark portholes.

"You seemed okay with it at Bancavia's place."

The Tongue Merchant

"Just creating the illusion of life, Leonardo. You're not the only one with secrets."

I got myself moving toward *Seventh Son*.

I suppose I expected to find the boat vacant. Nothing had come easily for me up to this point, so why should the cosmos start smiling on me now? But Tommy So was indeed in residence. He was sitting atop the cabin, just as I'd seen him two days ago, although now he had his legs crossed in the lotus position, his skinny chest bared to the elements and a pitcher of red liquid beside him. His eyes were open, and he watched us approach. Across his collarbone was tattooed a series of numbers, perhaps seven or eight in all, a long green procession of 1s and 0s.

"His poor mother," Leo said under his breath.

Keeping my hands in my pockets and my hat pulled over my eyes, I raised my voice above the din of the wind and said, "You do know there's a hurricane on the way."

Tommy So smiled like a seer.

"I'm Marcella Paraizo. You might have seen me hanging around a few days ago. I need to ask you a few questions. Do you mind if I come aboard?"

Tommy tipped his head in a pensive manner, regarding me with his narrow, nut-colored eyes. I stared back at him, growing weary of his silence by the second.

"Kool-Aid?" he asked. He touched the pitcher.

"No thanks. But I'll take that as permission granted." I made the short leap from the pier to the boat. Leo stayed on the dock.

I walked to the cabin. "I know you've already given your statement to the authorities—"

"You're the one in the Navy, aren't you?"

"Coast Guard. So you noticed me."

"One always notices a flower in the midst of a desert."

"I'm flattered. But I'm also short on time. So if you could

dispense with the proverbs, Mr. So, I'd be grateful."

"The name's Tommy." The rain ran down his long hair. His cargo pants were soaked. He wore no shoes or socks. "This is my first hurricane."

"Congratulations. Now tell me about Nicholas Murillo."

"Why? Like you said, I've already given my statement."

"Then you really saw him here Sunday night?"

"Yes."

"Right here?" I pointed toward the *Lynn*. "You looked over and saw him on that boat? Was he boarding or disembarking?"

"Yes, yes, no, and neither."

"Meaning?"

Tommy suddenly looked up at the clouds, as if he felt something staring at the back of his neck. He studied the roiling darkness for a moment, blinked twice, then returned his attention to me. "Yes, right here is where it happened. And yes, I looked over and saw him, but no, he wasn't on the boat, and he was neither boarding nor disembarking. And as for me, I wasn't in this precise spot in the space-time continuum when I noticed him, like I told the police."

"If the man you saw wasn't on the *Lynn*, then where was he?"

"The dock."

"And what was he doing?"

"Messing with some scuba gear."

My heart jiggled a little at that, but I pressed on. "And where were you, exactly, when you saw him. Allegedly."

Tommy grinned at my emphasis on that last word. "I was getting ice. For my party. I know the custodian over at the Rime & Reel. He lets me come over and raid the ice machine. I'd just opened the door to leave when I spotted Nicholas Murillo. Allegedly."

I ignored his sarcasm. "So that would explain why no one

The Tongue Merchant

else at your party saw anything. Had you been here on your boat when you spotted him instead of at the yacht club, one of your friends would have probably seen the same thing."

"I suppose."

"And you're positive about the man's identity?"

"I know him well enough. I'd seen him around. That's his boat, after all. We're neighbors."

"Was anyone else on board the *Lynn* that night?"

"I wouldn't know."

"She was found adrift. Do you remember when she pulled out?"

"Nope. It was a busy night."

"Why didn't you come forward Monday morning, when it was obvious that there'd been an accident? If you'd seen someone hanging around . . ."

"First of all," Tommy said, refilling his glass with a combination of Kool-Aid and rain water, "I didn't think much of it, because the man I saw was the boat's owner, so there was no reason he shouldn't have been there. Second, I try to keep a low profile as far as the local constabulary is concerned. If they want anything from me, they're going to have to ask. The day I come forward of my own volition is the day they legalize weed."

He took a long pull from his glass.

Inside my pockets, I squeezed my hands together so brutally that my nails bit into the flesh of my palms. On the Beaufort scale, my anger was running at force 7 and rising. What it all boiled down to was this: either Nico or Tommy was lying to me. If Nico was the liar, he was probably also the murderer. He brought his scuba equipment out here, used his key to get inside the cabin, killed his wife, took the jewels, motored the boat out to sea, and swam back. But if, instead of Nico, it was my Kool-Aid-drinking Gandhi here who was preaching the canard, then he had to be covering for somebody else.

My forehead wrinkled as I considered that. Covering for who?

Covering for "whom," gatita, *and there's only two reasons for that kind of perjury.*

"One," I said aloud, "you're lying to protect somebody, most likely the real killer. Maybe you owed them a favor. Or two"—my mother's second reason sounded like the more plausible of the two—"whoever killed Isabella said they'd do the same thing to you unless you placed Nico at the scene. Or they threatened you in some other way. Like blackmail. In either case, you know the identity of the murderer."

For just an instant Tommy's eyes lost their insolent luster. But a long pull from his glass seemed to hearten him. The boombox beside him was playing an old Charlie Pride tune. Tommy wiped the cherry residue from his lips with exaggerated indifference. "You've really got a hard-on for all of this, don't you, Navy dame?"

"She was my friend, you shithead."

Tommy's smile reappeared. "There's an ancient Zen saying—"

"Shove it up your ass." I hopped off the boat. "Come on, Leo. Let's get out of here before my urge to kneecap somebody gets the best of me."

But Leo, his eyes still on Tommy, spoke up before I could drag him away. "So, kid. What's the number mean?"

"Sir?"

"That tattoo," Leo said. "It's binary, isn't it?"

I followed his gaze to the numbers imprinted on Tommy's flesh: 10101101.

"Let me see. . . ." Leo rubbed his chin. "That should figure out to be about . . . what? One seventy-three?"

Tommy's thin eyes widened considerably. "Yeah. A hundred and seventy-three. I'm impressed."

"Just something I picked up along life's highway. So what's it's stand for?"

"My IQ."

"No kidding? Why, Marcy, we've a genius in our midst."

"Could've fooled me. Get moving. I've got to make a phone call." As we walked back to the cab which was idling at the curb on Ochoa Promenade, I looked at him askance. "Binary, huh? Is there anything you *don't* know?"

"Well, I don't know how you like your eggs in the morning."

I didn't take the bait. "One of them's lying to me, Leo."

"Appears so."

"I'm tempted to turn around and haul that little weasel below deck, beat the crap out of him until he gives me a straight answer. Something about his story doesn't feel right, but I can't put my finger on it. Where's the nearest phone?"

"Don't you carry a cell?"

"I'm always on the cutter. I don't have much need."

"I'd let you use mine, but it's in the glove box of my truck, which, by the way, we happened to leave sitting at the police station."

"Not a safer place for it anywhere on the island," I said, fighting the wind all the way to Dominique's.

"We're closed for the storm!" a voice hollered from the back. All of the chairs were upside down on the tables. The ceiling fans hung dead in the air. The TV above the bar showed a weatherman standing in front of a spiral of white clouds which was spread across the better part of the Antilles. Just about everything east of St. Croix had been swallowed by the cyclone.

I convinced the guy to let me use the phone, and as I dialed my father's number, I kept my eyes on the boats across the street. Tommy So was still perched on the cabin, staring eastward, his black hair fanning around his head. *What's the wrinkle in his story? What am I missing?* Luckily Bartholomew hadn't disrupted the phone service, so I was able to get the police dispatcher on the fourth ring. I identified myself and asked to be connected with Harry Paraizo. Then I waited for two excruciating minutes before the sweetest sound I could imagine said hello from a thousand miles away.

Almost instantly the winds of anger began to subside. "Hey, Daddy. Are you busy?"

"Lo, and God sent me an angel," he said slowly. "Kitten. You okay?"

"I'm fine, Dad."

"I've been keeping my eye on that spot of weather down your way. I called and talked to your machine this morning. You've got to get yourself out of there, babe."

My father had the sexiest voice in the world.

"Are you listening to me, kitten?"

"Sure, Dad. Hurricanes. Right."

"I can hear you grinning," he said. "You're grinning, aren't you?"

I turned my back to Leo for a little privacy, unable to conceal my smile. Softly I said, "I need to ask you for a favor."

"Uh-oh. Here it comes. Old Harry's life just got a lot more complicated."

"It's not a big deal . . ."

"Escargot is not a big deal? That's what I had to do when you asked me to check on those bogus credit card reports, remember? I had to take Stella down in Bunco-Forgery out to dinner, and she made me eat snails, kitten. *Snails.*"

"This is different."

"Different how?"

"You remember my friend Isabella Murillo?"

"She the deaf one?"

"Yes. She was. Someone killed her." I spent the next five minutes telling him what I knew about the homicide. Being a cop, he asked all kinds of questions I didn't have time for, but I was eventually able to get back to my favor. "I need you to check out a few names for me."

"The pen is in my hand."

"Jan Voorstadt." I spelled it for him, and gave him a quick exposé on ELF.

"Got it."

"Tommy So. *Thomas,* possibly, but I'm not sure. Asian descent. Around twenty years old. He was in trouble here in Hozumkur as a juvenile for drugs."

"Can't promise much on that one, but go ahead."

"Leonardo Kavisti." I figured it couldn't hurt. I mentioned the name Hammersmith and the security firm in the Keys. "And one more."

"Shoot."

"Joseph Rotto."

"You mean the sugar guy?"

"You know him?"

"Know *of* him. There was a piece on him in *Forbes* awhile back."

"Since when did you start reading *Forbes*?"

"I was in the doctor's office, all right? It was either that or *Good Housekeeping.* Which reminds me, the old cabin up in Minnesota's going to need some major renovation before next spring. The caretaker called and said a pine fell and took out half the roof. We're still on for April, aren't we?"

"I wouldn't miss it. But I've got to go now. You don't want me standing around when Bartholomew hits."

"Definitely. Get yourself somewhere with concrete walls and have a hot chocolate on me." He paused for a moment, then said, "You're really doing okay, babe?"

"Yes, Dad. Never been better."

Though I don't think he believed me, he said he did, and

then he told me he loved me, and a second later he was gone.

Roosevelt didn't look happy to see me.

Too bad koala bears aren't like dogs. You always know when your cocker spaniel is singing the blues, just by the look in his eyes and the lonesome droop of his tail. And his happiness is equally easy to read. But koalas . . . well, they just *look* at you, though Bella and I sometimes thought that Rosy was trying to communicate with us. He'd wiggle his little gray fingers, which we swore *had* to be his attempt at sign language.

The folks at the animal shelter didn't argue when I staked my claim on the koala. I explained the situation, left my name and number, and managed to smile politely when they charged me thirty dollars for a boarding fee. Another forty-five bought me a snazzy portable cage. Then they whisked me out the door and shut the place down. Bartholomew had us all running for cover.

Myself included. By the time Leo and I met Saul at the shore, the wind was a monster and the Guard evac boats had arrived. I didn't introduce myself to my brothers-in-arms, not even when a petty officer third class offered to help me with Rosy's traveling condo. I handed over the cage and played like a civilian.

"Am I going to see you again?" Leo yelled above the wind.

I took Saul's hand and allowed him to help me into the boat. "You'll be at Bella's wake this evening, won't you?"

"Joseph never invited me."

"It's a wake, man," Saul said. "They don't send out invitations."

The klaxons began wailing again. The city's storm-warning system was sounding on the hour, just in case there was anyone who wasn't aware that a category 3 homewrecker was on the way. The rain was cold and stung like needles.

"You really believe Joseph had something to do with all this?" Leo said.

"He lied to me, Leo. *Everybody* lies to me. So, yeah, I'm starting to think that he's an asshole. No offense."

"None taken."

The petty officer asked us all to take a seat. The boat throttled up. Leo waved.

I touched the brim of my cap in return.

When the boat began to pull away, Roosevelt made an urgent noise, like a toddler asking for something he couldn't articulate. It almost sounded as if he were trying to tell me something.

The evacuation boat made San Juan in less than an hour, putting a few miles between us and the raw edge of the storm. Though the occasional zipper of lightning still separated the sky, the wind was noticeably weaker and the rain no longer a downpour. We grabbed a cab to Condado Beach, where I'll have lived for two years come November.

The apartment was a gift from the gods. Or Midas Hinojosa, to be specific. Being one of the most popular beaches on Puerto Rico, Condado is dominated by high-rise hotels, glamorous eateries, and rambling megaresorts. In other words, I live in Tourist Hell. Those people are everywhere. All year long. But the beach is clean and somehow maintains its magnificence despite the crowds. The bodies usually thin out at night, and more than once I've had the entire strip of sand to myself. My apartment is actually the corner suite of a beachfront hotel. I'm not aware of anyone else who has a similar place of permanent residence on Condado. But a couple of years ago I managed to bust a credit-card counterfeiting ring, which earned me a promotion from the Guard and the eternal gratitude of local entrepreneur Ricardo Hinojosa, who everyone calls Midas. I probably saved him somewhere in the neighborhood of twenty million. He gave me this apartment in return.

"You want the shower first?" I asked Saul as I worked the key in the lock.

"Nah, you've been out in this muck all day. Just give me a place to hang up this monkey suit and I'll be fine."

I stepped inside and dripped water all over my hardwood floor. "There's a closet there in the corner. And maybe even something to drink in the fridge."

"No thanks. I'm not much into wine coolers."

"Bite me, Saul. There should be a few Heinekens in there."

"No way. I don't believe it." He headed straight to the kitchenette. "I fall more in love with you every day, Zo."

I phoned the clinic on my way to the bathroom. I apologized for my tardiness and gave the receptionist my ETA, but then Dr. Avundavi picked up the line and suggested that we postpone our appointment until Bartholomew made his departure. Just hearing her voice gave me that icky feeling all over again. My old nemesis, reality, returned to kick me in the teeth.

I gripped the phone so tightly that it was a wonder it didn't shatter. "So you're sure it's safe then? To wait a few more days?"

She assured me that the tumor was a tiny and specific mass, with no indication of other lesions anywhere in my body. So the Secret Saboteur was alone in its perfidy. One more day wouldn't give it time to spread. Or so she said.

"Do you have a shelter nearby?" she asked. "Living right there on the shoreline, you certainly have a place to go, somewhere safe."

"I'll be fine, Janice. I'm an old pro at these things." My bravado lasted only until I reached the shower, where I promptly crumpled. I leaned against the wall, letting the hot water do its thing. Though I tried to clear my mind—*breathe in, breathe out*—I found the puzzle pieces presenting themselves for parade inspection.

The Tongue Merchant

Bella hadn't hit anyone. At least for awhile there I'd consoled myself with the thought that she'd gone down fighting. But spider blood. Shit.

Next up: Isolde Bancavia and Mr. Texas, Joe Rotto. One of them admitted a dislike for Bella, and the other one professed to love her, either sentiment being a strong motive for murder. Did Bella hire Jan Voorstadt to foil DCI's oil contracts? And had Rotto retalitated for it? After he read her memo about finding ELF connections in Hozumkur, he'd freaked and gone off to kill her. And how did he get aboard the *Lynn* when the cabin was locked? He got the key from Isolde, of course. They made a cash-for-key switch the night she visited his house. And as for the lockbox, Isolde could have had access to that key as well. Being Bella's lover, she would have known where it was kept, and she could have supplied Rotto with the knowledge of where to find it so that he could swipe the stones to make things look like a robbery. Why else would he lie and claim to have never met her? And hadn't Isolde admitted that Bella was meeting someone at the yacht that night? She'd entrusted me with this detail only to indicate that it was Nico at the *Lynn*, when in actuality it was Leo's boss.

Or maybe Rotto had hired Voorstadt, using Isolde as a go-between.

I uncapped the shampoo and lathered my hair.

And then Tommy So. Assuming that Nico was telling the truth and he'd been nowhere near the marina Sunday night, then Tommy was lying on someone else's behalf. It certainly *felt* like he was lying, though I couldn't say exactly why. Perhaps Rotto or Isolde had paid him off. Either that, or Tommy was entangled in some kind of flagitious business and Rotto had threatened to expose him. They knew that Nico was trained in scuba. Isolde could have learned that from Bella. So they instructed Tommy to sow that little seed in his garden of lies.

It all made an eerie kind of sense.

And the stamp?

Simple. Serca's friend Nathan had knowledge invaluable to Bella's newspaper story, and being some kind of stamp maniac, he'd willingly trade anything for the Adelbert, the acquisition of which would normally be far beyond his financial means. And what was this extraordinary treasure he was bartering for the stamp? Had he dug up the dirt on Rotto? Was Rotto the one who'd hired Voorstadt, and did Nathan have proof of this alliance? I honestly had no idea, but at least I was closer to an answer than I'd been two days ago.

I took my time rinsing my hair.

There was a certain dress hanging in my wardrobe. Black and severe. Very Puritan. There was no way I was wearing it to the wake. The last thing I wanted was Bella's ghost laughing at me for dressing like a middle-school grammar teacher. I've always believed that the spirits of the dead do not entirely forsake this world after leaving the body; the living are too much in need of their psychic advice. So if Bella was out there, hovering somewhere between me and God, I wasn't going to fake anything. I had a simple waist-length jacket and a pair of slacks that would do just fine.

In the meantime, though, I relished the freshness of my bathrobe. It made me feel normal again, just your everyday gal, no longer a comic book crime-fighter. With my damp hair hidden in a towel-turban, I stepped into the living room and almost ran face-first into the phone that Saul was holding out to me.

"It's your pops," he said. "I promised him I wasn't your boyfriend."

"Thanks." I accepted the telephone, and it was nice to hear Dad's voice twice in the same afternoon.

Even still, my sense of unease continued to grow. I grasped the phone with a trembling hand, unable to shake the presentiment that Bella's wake would provide me with more truth than I wanted to know.

Chapter Seventeen

"Jan Voorstadt is a very bad apple," my father said.

"Tell me something I don't know."

"Born in Eindhoven, Netherlands. His papa was a high-profile environmental activist who was KIA while attending a summit in Belgrade. Voorstadt's mother had already passed away, leaving the kid in the clutches of the Dutch foster family system, where he didn't fare so well. Do you want all this childhood trauma junk? I've got a ton of it."

"Right now I'm Joe Friday, Dad. Just the facts."

"No problem. Flash forward to three years ago. Voorstadt's name crops up on Interpol databases as a suspect in several eco-radical attacks, and for the next twenty-four months or so he plies his trade in western Europe, mainly the North Atlantic, which is apparently the Jerusalem of his personal holy crusade. His pet target happens to be petroleum transport trucks and ocean-going vessels, and get this: he's one of the few of his kind who puts himself *out for hire*."

"So he's a mercenary? I thought most terrorists were driven by ideals."

"Most of them, yeah. But not our oil-hating friend Jan Voorstadt. I'm talking eco-terrorism by request. That attack on the Australian oil platform last year? That was our man. They suspect he was flying the chopper that strafed the place, but if you remember correctly, pursuit of the chopper was fouled up by the weather, and the bird was found crashed and empty in

The Tongue Merchant

New Zealand or somewhere."

"And his ties to the Antilles?"

"He was believed to be responsible for torching a bunch of warehouses on St. Noré eight months ago. Several people were killed in the fire, and all of the warehouses belonged to companies with heavy investments in the oil trade. But this was sort of a sudden appearance for Voorstadt in that area. He'd never shown an interest in it before."

"You think he was hired for the job?"

"Just following the breadcrumbs, kitten. And that's where they lead me."

"You heard that his lawyer got him off?"

"So I've learned. You haven't run into this guy, have you?"

"Dad—"

"It's your mother's fault, you know. You've got a nose for inequity sharper than a bloodhound on a muskrat, and it drives me crazy, if you want to know the truth. It really worries me, babe, and old Deadheads like me don't like to sit around being worried. We're too mellow, you know what I mean?"

"Next subject, Dad."

"Sure."

"Joe Rotto."

"Clean. No record of any kind. Just your standard climb-the-corporate-ladder crud."

Damn. "You're sure?"

"I'm not a fortune-teller, babe. All I know is what the paperwork tells me."

I asked myself why Rotto would hire Voorstadt to burn down DCI property.

"Thomas Jefferson So," my father said.

"That's his name? Thomas Jefferson?"

"Again, I'm just reading what's in front of me. Patriotic, huh? Thomas Jefferson So was in and out of trouble as a juvenile.

My guess is drugs. I don't have access to any of the details. In fact, I have nothing on him as an adult except that he's the subject of periodic surveillance by the Federal Narcotics Strike Force out of Puerto Rico. Which means they expect him to cross the line any day now."

"That's all?"

"Hey, you give me this short of notice, you get the *Reader's Digest* version. Now, dearest daughter, being the incorrigible showman that I am, I have saved the best for last."

"You mean Leo?"

"Yep. I didn't find anything by running a check on his name, so I located that Hammersmith place in the Keys, told them who I was and what I was looking for."

"And?"

"And nothing. They threw up a wall. And that made me suspicious. Being a little bit of the bloodhound myself, I kept after it, and ended up on the phone with a buddy in the Department of Justice. Now I've been sworn to secrecy on this, but it seems that Hammersmith is a front for our beloved friends in the Federal Barnyard of Ignoramuses."

I abruptly stopped pacing. *"Leo Kavisti is FBI?"*

"Looks like, though the Kavisti handle is probably just a cover name. Now what kind of mess are you getting yourself into? Terrorists and the feds? The more I hear about this, kitten, the less I'm liking it."

"I've got it covered, Dad. Thanks for the info."

"Don't even think about hanging up this phone."

"They're holding a memorial service for Isabella, and I can't be late. So just tell me you love me and I promise to call you as soon as the storm blows over."

"And that's another thing. There's a hurricane practically on top of your head. Did I mention that it's not good to worry an old man? We're notorious for our weak hearts."

The Tongue Merchant

"Me too," I said, truthfully enough. "Now I've got to go."

"And that wasn't Captain Maddox who answered the phone."

"No, it wasn't. I love you, Dad."

"I love you too, kitten. You're hell on the blood pressure, but I love you too."

My mind went to work the second I hung up.

The best hypothesis I could produce was this: Rotto had a plan to wrest control of DCI from Bella by initiating a terrorist act on company resources. Just how such an operation would serve him, I wasn't yet sure. Maybe there was an insurance payoff of some kind, or perhaps he was just trying to scare Bella into signing away the corporation. At any rate, Bella began to track down Voorstadt's connections in the 'Kur, hoping to find out who was backing him financially. Not knowing that Rotto was the perpetrator, she sent him a memo to let him know that she was on the verge of revealing Voorstadt's employer. All she needed was the proof that Nathan could provide, whatever that might be, and so she bought the stamp from St-Germain as a bargaining tool. But before she made the trade with Nathan, Rotto killed her. He summoned Isolde to his house and paid her for the key to the *Lynn*'s master stateroom, along with knowledge of where to find the key to the lockbox. He took the jewels to lay a false trail, then threatened Tommy Jeff So with God knows what unless he put Nico at the scene that night.

"How does this tie look, Zo? And don't say *dapper* because that's the last thing I want to be."

So my next step? Make the trade with Nathan. And hunt down Sixbone if necessary.

"Zo?"

I snapped out of my daze and inspected him. "Paisleys?"

"What, now you've got a beef against paisleys?"

"No, it's just . . . quaint."

Saul scowled. "I'm not sure which is worse. Dapper or quaint."

I ducked into my bedroom, leaving him there in sartorial distress. As I stood before the mirror putting on clothes that I hoped Bella would find acceptable, I thought about my theory; the puzzle pieces finally started to coalesce. If Rotto was a murderer, I had to get the evidence to Kyle Straker as quickly as possible. My shore leave expired tomorrow morning at 0745, which left me a little more than twelve hours to convince the world that Nico hadn't stabbed his wife to death.

In the meantime, though, I had a hurricane to survive, an angry Coast Guard admiral to elude, and a killer to face. Rotto would be at Bella's wake. He probably knew I was on to him.

The tintinnabulators were screaming.

Saul held the door open for me when we reached the Croesus at quarter after seven.

A DCI security man had directed us to this alternate entrance, which permitted us to access the elevators without having to traipse through the casino. The service was being held in Serca's penthouse above the company offices on the top floor. Folding my umbrella and clutching it like a war club, I stepped into the elevator and saw my wavering reflection in the brightly polished brass.

See there? She seemed to be a sane enough woman. Her suit was classy, if a year out of style. Her hair was thick and enviable. And though a few budding racists in elementary school had gotten their kicks by calling her a half-breed, she had matured into a stunning alloy of her antecedents. Never mind the feral wariness in her eyes or the quickened rhythm of her pulse. For the most part she carried herself like someone in full command of her domain.

If only that were true, I thought.

Maybe that's your problem, gatita. *Stop thinking. Just move.*

That was Alejandra for you, always ready to substitute contemplation with motion.

"You're being kind of quiet," Saul observed.

"Funerals do that to me."

We watched the numbers rise as we ascended.

"This isn't really it though, is it?" he asked. "The funeral?"

"I'm not exactly sure what it is. A hurricane party turned memorial service, from what I gather. I suppose Abdías is in charge of the actual funeral arrangements. I'm sure he'll be here. I'll ask him about the time and place. Tomorrow seems like a likely date."

As long as the police are done hacking her body apart.

I closed my eyes for the remainder of the ride.

The elevator stopped—*bing!*

The doors slid open.

The first person I saw was a ghost.

Not Bella's ghost, thank God, but an apparition nonetheless. He was the croupier I'd seen dealing cards down in the casino last night. The albino. You never realize how eerie they really are until you see one in person. His hair looked like a white dandelion bloom seconds before you breathe on it and disperse it to the wind, with a single forelock hanging between his eyes. His flesh was the color of cheesecloth.

"May I take your coat, madam?" he asked. He stood in front of the cloakroom wearing sunglasses and a suit so dark it only served to highlight his snowy complexion. "And your umbrella?"

"Yes, thank you." I slithered out of my coat and followed it with my umbrella and purse.

"My name is Raoul. If you should need anything throughout the evening, please don't hesitate to ask. You may consider me the genie in your bottle."

"Thanks. I'll keep that in mind. Raoul."

"*Marcus?*" Saul said in his best funeral-voice. Which surprised me. I didn't think he could speak in anything less than a shockwave. "Marcus, don't tell me you've sold out."

I turned to see Saul handing his raincoat to a man nearly his same size, with olive-tinted skin and a mass of black curls. His pectorals bulged the buttons of his green DCI vest. He looked painfully embarrassed. "Evening, Saul."

"You're not free-lancing anymore?" Saul asked.

"It's not paying the mortgage like it used to. A lot of big corps are hiring extra security nowadays. Makes the clients feel safer."

Saul shook his head. "You're a wage slave now, huh?"

"You do what you have to, Saul."

"Yeah, buddy. I guess it happens to the best of us."

"Friend of yours?" I asked as we sauntered across the carpet.

"Name's Marcus. He's the one I told you about who had the gig at Abdías's place. That's how I first met the little pussy and all of his fraternity friends."

"Speak of the devil," I said.

Abdías spotted me from the other side of the room. He looked even thinner than the last time I'd seen him, which might have had something to do with the fact that he was poured into a pair of leather pants, a narrow cummerbund, and a tight silk shirt.

"I should whip his ass right now just on general principles," Saul said.

Abdías started to head in my direction, and in the few moments I had before he got here, I surveyed the rest of those assembled in Serca's posh living room.

There were at least fifty people, with more trickling in behind me. They talked in low voices about things like the New Progressive Party's latest efforts for statehood. The *estadistas* were determined to make Puerto Rico the fifty-first member of the Union, but that would never happen, I heard someone else remark, so long as big business had its way. If Puerto Rico became a state, the Chase Manhattan bank and several others like it would find themselves in violation of interstate banking regulations, and we all knew that the power players weren't about to let that happen. Statehood was a defunct issue, as far as I was concerned. But the locals clung to it for conversational fodder, if nothing else.

A few feet away, Abdías's accountant, Robert Castigere, knocked back a brandy with a trio of oriental gentleman, one of his arms still sealed in a cast and held to his side with a broad sling of black fabric. Evangelina hovered nearby, although her eyes were restless and roamed the crowd. Over by the kitchen was the handsome star of one of the popular Mexican soap operas; I recognized him but couldn't remember his name. He was speaking to a man who I gussed to be the governor of Puerto Rico. No gathering of serfs, this wake.

Alonzo Serca wheeled amongst them.

Like a king on a mobile throne, he wove between his guests, clasping hands and speaking in kind terms of the deceased. I knew he was veering toward me, but there was little I could do to avoid him without being obvious about it. I looked around for Nathan.

He sat behind a cloth-covered table near a framed picture of Isabella. As I watched, he accepted a check from an elderly gentleman and carefully placed it in a coffer on the floor.

What had Serca told me? *Nathan here will be at the door taking donations on behalf of some of Isabella's favorite charities.*

How could I make contact with him without arousing suspicion? And would he even speak with me, or bolt the moment I mentioned Longoria's name?

"Lieutenant Paraizo, is it not?"

The man with the muttonchops was standing in front of me. What was his name again?

"Cicero Horne," he said, guessing my thoughts. "We met at young Abdías's residence the morning after the . . . the accident."

"Yes, I remember. How are you?"

"Deplorable."

"I'm sorry to hear that."

"Death always does that to me, my dear. Nothing is as vexatious as mortality. I've already outlived one cardiac episode, and I've no desire to shake off this mortal coil until I am well into my hoary antiquation." Though Horne's bulk surely could have led to any heart condition he might have had, he appeared otherwise robust and full of old English verve. He had a certain Henry VIII quality about him. "Again, I'd like to extend my utmost condolences on the loss of your friend."

I thanked him for the courtesy, wondering what it was that made me doubt his sincerity.

Abdías and Serca converged on me at the same time, and suddenly I found myself surrounded. Only Saul's presence over my shoulder kept me from retreating.

Keep your eyes open, gatita.

Unnecessary advice, Mom, but thanks anyway.

We exchanged greetings all around. When Serca shook Saul's hand he said, "So you're the man charged with the task of keeping up with Miss Paraizo."

"It's a full-time job," Saul admitted.

"But a rewarding one, no?"

"It has its moments."

Abdías said, "Good to see you, Marcella. Glad you could make it. I wasn't sure if the Guard would let you off to attend."

"The Coast Guard is a reasonable clan," Judge Horne interjected. "And I'm certain that the lieutenant can be most

The Tongue Merchant

persuasive when she has to be."

"I will certainly attest to that," Serca agreed.

I saw Joe Rotto on the other side of the room. He was talking with . . .

Leo.

It took me a second to see past the suit he was wearing—and wearing very nicely, I noted—but it was Leo all right. He was leaning close to his boss and gesturing incisively, as if trying to make a crucial point. The last I'd seen him, he was standing on the docks in Hozumkur. He hadn't wasted much time in getting here. I couldn't imagine what they were talking about.

Rotto saw me watching him and I quickly looked away.

Murderer!

". . . . though I only had the pleasure of meeting her once," Horne was saying. "Your sister seemed to be a unique woman, Abby."

"She was the best." Abdías quaffed the rest of his drink in a single swallow.

"Where did you meet her?" I asked the judge on impulse.

"In court, of all places." Horne's cheeks colored slightly. "She was observing a case over which I was presiding, taking notes for her newspaper. There was a man accused of smuggling exotic animals into the States. He was hiding them in his luggage and had only been caught when one of them suffocated in there and someone at the airport noticed the smell. Barbaric, actually. After my ruling, Isabella approached me and requested an interview. She even took me out to lunch. We had oysters."

Bella loved oysters, I recalled. *And I miss her madly.*

"I had no idea at the time of our lunch that she was Abdías's older sister. But they say it's a small world, eh?"

"To small worlds," Serca announced, holding up his glass.

"Small worlds," everyone chimed.

While they drank, I stole another glance around the room.

Robert Castigere was crouched down beside Nathan, just one more secret conversation I was unable to hear. So they knew each other, Castigere the money-grubbing bookkeeper and Nathan the silent but rabid philatelist. Was there a significance to that relationship I hadn't yet exposed, or was it just as Judge Horne said, a small world where everybody eventually got to know everyone else?

And now Leo was headed this way.

"Excuse me, gentlemen," I said. "I've got to pry myself away from your company for a moment. You going to be okay, Saul?"

"Certainly he is," Horne said. "It's not like you're leaving him among strangers."

"Yes," Serca joined in, smiling. "We're going to gang-tackle him and take his wallet the moment he's out of your sight."

"I'm fine, Zo. Go on ahead."

So I did.

I met Leo midway across the room.

He was grinning.

"Surprised to see me or what?" he asked.

"You lied to me, goddammit," I whispered, resisting the urge to poke him in the chest.

"Whoa, now."

"Private investigator *bullshit*."

"Marcy, calm down . . ."

"I want some answers, *Leo,* or whoever you are, and if I don't start getting them in the next fifteen seconds, this entire room is going to get an earful of just who you really work for, so unless you want your cover blown, you better cut the crap and tell me who it is you're spying on."

"I'm not spying on anyone."

I cleared my throat and made as if to start shouting.

"All right, keep a lid on it, will you? You made your point." He touched my elbow. "You can be a real hard-case when you

The Tongue Merchant

want to, you know that? Let's at least get away from this circus before I spill my guts."

"Liar," I couldn't help but say again.

"Sticks and stones, Marcy."

"Rotto killed Bella."

"*Shhh.*"

"No one's listening, dammit." We stepped around to the far side of the buffet table and tried to look like normal people and not the infiltrators that we were. I kept my voice as low as my anger allowed. "I don't know what the FBI is looking for, but I think you might want to pay a little more attention to Joe Rotto. He's in this up to his red Texas neck."

"In *what?*"

"Bella's murder."

"Says who?"

I looked over at Nathan. Castigere had left. Nathan sat there in his dark wool suit, waiting for the next wealthy donor to happen by.

"Marcy?"

"I can get you proof," I said.

"That would be a very good thing, considering it's required by the Bill of Rights and all. You remember that Tommy So swears he saw Nico there that night?"

"Screw Tommy So. He's a liar, too. Like you."

Leo winced. "I'm just doing my job."

"So am I," I said, and left him standing there.

I pushed my way through the crowd toward Nathan.

Something stopped me halfway there.

". . . . life of a newspaper editor . . ."

Having newspapers on the mind, I immediately thought of Bella's work as a reporter, her part-time passion that had led to her death. If this was one of her associates from the paper, then it couldn't hurt to introduce myself.

"I'm sorry to bother you," I said before I could reconsider, "but do you happen to work for the *Plebiscite*?"

The man I was addressing wore a sport jacket over a frayed sweater. The jacket was one of those corduroy affairs with the leather patches on the elbows. Seeing his five-o'-clock shadow, I could easily imagine him bent over an old Underwood typewriter with a pot of room-temperature coffee and an ashtray full of butts, pecking out pulp horror stories or tabloid gossip columns.

"Guilty as charged," he said. "Mike Moreno. Editor-in-chief."

"You were Isabella's editor?"

He nodded somberly. "And proud of it. She was a fine writer. And a good person."

"Do you know anything about the story she was working on when she died?"

Moreno's eyes did a little dance. He looked over his shoulder, then back at me. "What did you say you're name was?"

I told him my name, and we shook hands. "I was Isabella's friend. And now I suppose I'm investigating her murder. Her husband's been accused of the crime but I don't think he did it, and I'm about one lucky break away from proving it. Can I steal you away for a moment?"

"Consider me stolen," he said.

We spoke for almost half an hour. As privacy was paramount to our continued well-being, we rode the elevator down one floor to the empty DCI offices directly under Serca's penthouse. Once there, we stood in the semi-darkness, talking about trains.

She never informed you of the stamp?

She was working on a project outside the office. I was told to expect the story Tuesday.

Yesterday.

That's right. Is there something you want to tell me, Miss Paraizo?

The Tongue Merchant

want to, you know that? Let's at least get away from this circus before I spill my guts."

"Liar," I couldn't help but say again.

"Sticks and stones, Marcy."

"Rotto killed Bella."

"*Shhh.*"

"No one's listening, dammit." We stepped around to the far side of the buffet table and tried to look like normal people and not the infiltrators that we were. I kept my voice as low as my anger allowed. "I don't know what the FBI is looking for, but I think you might want to pay a little more attention to Joe Rotto. He's in this up to his red Texas neck."

"In *what?*"

"Bella's murder."

"Says who?"

I looked over at Nathan. Castigere had left. Nathan sat there in his dark wool suit, waiting for the next wealthy donor to happen by.

"Marcy?"

"I can get you proof," I said.

"That would be a very good thing, considering it's required by the Bill of Rights and all. You remember that Tommy So swears he saw Nico there that night?"

"Screw Tommy So. He's a liar, too. Like you."

Leo winced. "I'm just doing my job."

"So am I," I said, and left him standing there.

I pushed my way through the crowd toward Nathan.

Something stopped me halfway there.

". . . . life of a newspaper editor . . ."

Having newspapers on the mind, I immediately thought of Bella's work as a reporter, her part-time passion that had led to her death. If this was one of her associates from the paper, then it couldn't hurt to introduce myself.

"I'm sorry to bother you," I said before I could reconsider, "but do you happen to work for the *Plebiscite*?"

The man I was addressing wore a sport jacket over a frayed sweater. The jacket was one of those corduroy affairs with the leather patches on the elbows. Seeing his five-o'-clock shadow, I could easily imagine him bent over an old Underwood typewriter with a pot of room-temperature coffee and an ashtray full of butts, pecking out pulp horror stories or tabloid gossip columns.

"Guilty as charged," he said. "Mike Moreno. Editor-in-chief."

"You were Isabella's editor?"

He nodded somberly. "And proud of it. She was a fine writer. And a good person."

"Do you know anything about the story she was working on when she died?"

Moreno's eyes did a little dance. He looked over his shoulder, then back at me. "What did you say you're name was?"

I told him my name, and we shook hands. "I was Isabella's friend. And now I suppose I'm investigating her murder. Her husband's been accused of the crime but I don't think he did it, and I'm about one lucky break away from proving it. Can I steal you away for a moment?"

"Consider me stolen," he said.

We spoke for almost half an hour. As privacy was paramount to our continued well-being, we rode the elevator down one floor to the empty DCI offices directly under Serca's penthouse. Once there, we stood in the semi-darkness, talking about trains.

She never informed you of the stamp?

She was working on a project outside the office. I was told to expect the story Tuesday.

Yesterday.

That's right. Is there something you want to tell me, Miss Paraizo?

The Tongue Merchant

No. But I guess I have to anyway . . .

And so I entrusted Mike Moreno with my entire stock and store of conjecture, circumstantial evidence, and misbegotten theories. I built the *Lady Lynn Rob* and put Bella aboard her Sunday night. I wrote the poetry on the fridge, I unlocked the door and knocked over the eucalyptus tree and then I murdered her. I interviewed everyone all over again. I found the stamp in the shoe. I drove the car that almost ran me down. I bought the Turkish cigarettes and dropped one on the ground. When I was finished, Moreno promised to full-page such a tale if it indeed turned out to be true. The arrest of a man of Rotto's caliber was a headliner the *Washington Post* would envy.

I'll check her desk at the paper, just in case there's a disk or notes or anything.

Good idea. It seems odd that she never mentioned a lick of this to you.

You're right. But I do know she spent one day last week at the city courthouse.

Doing what?

Something that got her killed, I imagine. Where can I reach you? Do you have a cell?

Just call my house. There's a machine, unless Bartholomew wrecks my house.

We exchanged phone numbers. By then my skin was patchy with goosebumps, thanks to a heady combo of nerves and shadows; the darkness seemed to be encroaching. The only light came from a dull red EXIT sign and the unhealthy glow of a computer monitor somebody had forgotten to turn off.

Like the insurgents that we were, Mike and I thought it best we not be seen returning to the wake together. I guess he didn't fancy the idea of getting run over by a sports car. So I hung back, tapping a fingernail against my teeth, while he slipped upstairs.

I checked my watch. The illuminated dial told me it was straight-up eight o'clock.

I waited three minutes, giving him time to dissolve into the crowd. The soundproof walls made it feel as if I were standing in a tomb. The air-conditioner vent above my head began blowing a cold wind down my back.

When I looked down at myself, I realized I had folded my arms tightly across my chest.

Time to go, for sure.

But when I turned around and aimed myself for the stairwell, I stopped so suddenly that it was like running into an invisible wall.

Joe Rotto stood on the bottom step, cloaked in purple shadows.

Chapter Eighteen

Shit.

I kept my eyes pinned to him because they say that animals can sense your fear and will only pounce on you if you turn to flee. Other than the frigid rush of the air-conditioner, the tiled corridors were deeply quiet, as if silence were a gas that had been pumped into the hall.

He's the one, the killer, and now he's here and I'm alone and—

"Ms. Paraizo."

I didn't move. Couldn't. The practitioners of sympathetic magic believed there was power in knowing someone's true name. More than anything, I wanted to spin around and gallop toward the elevators, but I was rooted to the spot, telekinetically fixed there by the black magic of Rotto's country drawl speaking my name.

He moved out of the stairwell, the gloom sliding off him like a cloak from his shoulders. "Darlin', you and me need to have ourselves a little chat."

You and "I," asshole, I thought, but didn't say.

"Maybe one of these here offices . . ." He gestured toward an open door.

"No, thanks." The words came out brittle. "I've really got to be getting back."

"Not just yet you don't." He stopped about four feet in front of me, thumbs hooked in his pockets. He wore black Wranglers, a string tie, and a blazer the color of smoke. The scent of cigars and Stetson cologne crawled down my nostrils and began fumigating my lungs. "Here I am trying to keep De Casals's house in order, and damned if you ain't right in the middle of things, getting your pretty little self mixed up in matters that ain't none of your concern."

"Isabella is my concern."

"Isabella's dead."

"Thanks for the update."

Rotto snorted, picked at his nose once or twice, and said, "I'm trying like the devil to be polite here, but you're making it a might difficult."

"Obstinate. I get that from my mother."

"Do you now?"

"She's dead too."

"Sorry to hear it."

"Rotto?"

"Huh?"

"Go screw yourself."

He pinched his lips together so forcefully the color fled them.

"I've got to be going." I unlocked my knees and made a line for the stairwell.

He grabbed my arm as I passed him. "Now you look here—"

"Let *go* of me." I wrenched myself free. "Don't you touch me again."

"Now goddammit." He raised his finger to my face, his eyes drawing down to twin slits, his sun-weathered face darkening even more as the anger bubbled in him. "I am a businessman trying to do my job. This is my company, not your dead friend's, and I'm sick of ya dicking around with it. What you're doing could have major ramifications on the company's credibility, and we could take a helluva loss on Wall Street because of it. So butt out. Ya hear me, ya little bitch?"

"Get out of my face."

The Tongue Merchant

"Not quite yet. You're going to stand there and listen to me when I'm talking to you."

For a second the adrenaline overran my fear, and I leaned even closer to him, so that our foreheads almost touched. "I know you met with Isolde Bancavia. You said you didn't know her. Lying prick."

That struck him like brass knuckles across the face.

"Caught you with your pants down, huh?"

But his shock passed quickly, and in a heartbeat he was smoldering again. "Yeah, so what? I called and asked her to my house."

"To get the key, right? The key to the stateroom of the *Lynn*. You paid her for it."

"I paid her for information. I wanted to know if Isabella was in cahoots with that Dutch bastard who burned down my buildings."

"I don't believe you."

"Why don't ya go ask the nigger bitch yourself? I paid her twenty-five grand for telling me that Isabella met with Voorstadt last week. But I don't know anything about a key, and if you're implying that I had something to do with her death, then you're pissing in the wind."

Though my rage only multiplied when I heard him say *nigger bitch*, I didn't have time to fight a war on two fronts. "Isolde told me she didn't know you. Why would she lie about that? What good would it do her? What was she trying to hide?"

"Hell, I don't know. Maybe she was ashamed that she'd sold out her dead lesbo lover."

"Don't you call her that."

"I'll call that stupid tree-hugging whore anything I please."

I swung my fist at his face.

He caught my wrist.

I grunted and tried to pull loose.

He jerked me off my feet.

I landed on my hands and knees, the fear bursting up through the sea of adrenaline like a drowning swimmer crashing the surface for air. Lying on the floor, I felt like time was slowing down around me. In the partial second it took me to catch my breath, I had a flash-fire thought that would have made me laugh had I not been moments away from being killed: I had graduated at the top of my class at the Academy, tied with Steve Yandholf and Martin Leery for the number-one spot. Tonight, Steve was probably teaching a night class in nautical engineering somewhere sane like South Carolina, and Marty was home with his wife and kids after a mundane day of pushing pencils at the State Department. And where was I? Chasing murderers in the path of a hurricane, walking the edge of a court-martial with cancer in my breast, and trapped in a dark hallway at the feet of a killer. If only my co-valedictorians could see me now. I looked up through my hair, and there was Rotto, his fists clenched, his shoulders bent like those of a hunchback, his tongue bit between his tobacco-stained teeth.

"You *will* mind your own business," he said.

I nodded weakly, for self defense.

Rotto wasn't convinced. He shifted his weight to one foot and dragged the other one back.

I saw the kick before his leg commenced a motion that would have shattered my ribcage. In my mind I heard joints breaking, cartilage tearing, vital organs punctured with splinters, and that was all I needed to get myself scrambling to my feet. Once there, I flattened my back against the wall and faced him.

His kick aborted in mid-stride, Rotto settled for grinding his heel into the floor. "You've got a lesson coming to ya, darlin'. Need to learn yourself a few *manners*."

"Eat shit and—"

He slapped me so hard my head struck the wall.

"Isabella paid Voorstadt to torch my warehouses, didn't she? And then the son of a bitch *walked.*" His hand flashed again while my vision was still reeling, this time clamping onto my chin. His hard fingers bit into my jaw.

Oh, God . . .

His face was so close to mine that I could smell his bonfire breath. "And for all I know, you were another one of her gay slut friends, and you were all in it together."

Oh, please, God.

"Now am I right or not? And don't you dare try to scream or I'll give you more than a bruised cheek."

"I . . ."

"Yeah?"

I kneed him in the balls.

It wasn't a dead-on shot, but Rotto nonetheless doubled over like a mannequin struck midriff with a sledgehammer. He made a small, oily noise and stumbled backward.

I ran.

Drunk on a cocktail of fury and fear, I rounded the first corner I saw, forgetting entirely about the staircase and only remembering it after I'd sprinted a good fifty feet deeper into the building. Every fifth fluorescent bulb was lit, the rest of them dark as per after-hours security lighting, so I wasn't able to read any of the doors as I soared past. One of them could've said STAIRS and I wouldn't have noticed.

I slammed against the wall of a T-intersection, and only then did I look back.

Nothing.

The hall behind me was empty and dark and—

What was that?

Footsteps? I held my breath.

From the end of the hall I heard the sounds of a scuffle, like Rotto was trying to drag himself upright and was finding the footing difficult.

Good. Maybe I ruptured something vital.

But that wasn't quite what I heard.

The sound faded. The seconds passed.

More footsteps, these steady and firm, fading into the distance.

What's happening down there?

I hunkered around the corner so as not to be seen, still listening, still feeling my trip-hammering heart.

Breathe!

I let the air escape my body as quietly as I could.

I heard the stairwell door open.

Then the tremendous silence resumed.

Closing my eyes, I leaned my head back and concentrated on staving off hyperventilation.

Holy shit he tried to kill me.

Pull it together, gatita.

"Can't," I gasped.

You must.

I shook my head in denial, even though I knew she was right.

I hung there for three, four, then five minutes with nothing happening but the sweat drying on my brow.

You okay now?

I told myself that I was, but it sounded like a lie.

Yet I was still intact, at least physically. Though the office hallway was dark, there was nothing more threatening here than the alien shapes which the shadows painted on the walls. Joe Rotto was gone. There were no night-things to claw for me from the custodian's closet, no bogeyman plotting sinister revenge in the water fountain. Time to put myself back together, march upstairs, and expose Rotto to whoever would listen.

But if he'd murdered Bella, then why had he let me go?

Witnesses, of course. Someone might have seen him coming

The Tongue Merchant

to meet me. Too bad for him he hadn't been able to bottle his temper; I'm sure I'd have proof on my chin of his savagery.

I had to find Nathan and get my hands on solid evidence of Rotto's criminal undertakings. The clock was running. Time for all good surf soldiers to get their bearings set and their motors on full throttle.

I made my way slowly back down the hall. Had I taken an alternate route upstairs, like the elevator or one of the secondary staircases, I could have avoided a lot of what happened next.

As it was, I retraced my steps, which brought me into the hallway where Mike Moreno and I had made our pact and Rotto had assaulted me. My system slowly returned to its normal operation, though I remained on red alert, all hands at battle stations. I'd been *attacked*. Nearly *killed*. My heart rocked against my ribs. I couldn't gulp down enough saliva to ease my leathery throat.

I came around the corner and Joe Rotto was lying on the floor.

His head was twisted to such an extent that one of the narrow bones in his neck had pierced the flesh and now jutted raggedly from the wound, like a number 2 pencil someone had snapped in half and stabbed him with. Blood covered his face. It ran down his cheek and dripped from his earlobe to the floor. Lying in the gore beside him was a sponge. Except it wasn't a sponge.

I hit my knees as the vomit surged up from my stomach. I bent over, heaving, unable to drag my eyes from Rotto's severed tongue.

I must have screamed, though I don't remember doing so.

Hands pawing at me. A voice whispering my name. Blurry motion. Arms lifting me to my feet. The ship of my equilibrium sinking and sending me down.

When I blinked, all I could think about was spitting. The puke was still smeared over my teeth. I turned my head and hacked so hard the world began to tilt again.

The last thing I saw before losing consciousness was a face as white as the moon.

Raoul, I thought, as I swam back to the light.

Someone had put a cold compress on my forehead. Someone else had called the cops. I could hear the sirens, though my ears felt filled with sand.

I tried to reply, wanting nothing more than to say Saul's name, but the sand was also in my windpipe, jamming everything but a reedy gasp.

"Give the woman a little more room. She'll come around in her own time."

Was that Judge Horne? His voice carried an authoritative tone that sounded judicial.

"Christ, man," Castigere said. "Can't we at least get her out of the hall? The *smell*."

"I suppose that would indeed be for the best," Horne replied. "Alonzo, could you have your men watch the elevators, keep anyone from leaving?"

"Of course."

"Abby, stop standing there like a wooden Indian and begin compiling a list of everyone here. Abdías? Are you listening to me?"

"Uh, yeah, sure. Damn."

"Thank you, Abby. Now then. Saul?"

I felt hands against my face. "Zo? The pigs are on the way. Can you stand up?"

"Never seen a dead body before," I heard Abdías remark. "Is this what that butcher did to my sister?"

"Come, Abby." It was a woman's voice. Haitian accent. Evangelina. "We should do as Cicero asks."

"Zo, please talk to me."

I opened my eyes as much as I could. My head rested in Saul's lap. Raoul stood over Saul's shoulder, looking like someone who'd just showered in Clorox. Leo was nearby, his night-sky eyes haunted with worry. Worry for *me*. Judge Horne knelt beside me.

"Where's Nathan?" I asked, my own tongue thick and swollen.

"Nathan?" Castigere asked.

Horne pulled the spectacles from his face and polished them on his sleeve. "Miss Paraizo, did you see Nathan commit this atrocity?"

"No, it's not that. But he . . ." The darkness started to overwhelm me again. "I've got to talk to him. I think he's going to be the next to die. . . ."

The police kept me there nearly three hours.

Eleven p.m. I did the distances in my head. Bart would be less than thirty miles off the eastern coast of St. Noré, having blasted over the British Virgin Islands and sunk its teeth into St. Thomas, where Bella met Isolde in a theater bathroom during a Wagner intermission and maybe fell in love with her. Eleven p.m. Shore leave expired in a mere nine hours, by which time I would have faced a hurricane and either avenged my friend or gotten killed in the trying. *Eleven p.m.* As I sat there, staring at the glass of water they'd given me but I hadn't touched, I promised myself I wouldn't sleep again until I'd buried the murderer with the murdered.

The woman there was found over the DB., I heard a cop mutter from across the room. My hearing was suddenly that good.

Walking the tightrope turns you into the Bionic Woman. And DB.?

   Dead body.

   She break his neck?

   It could happen.

   Hozumkur says this is her second.

   That doesn't make her the doer.

   Oh, yeah?

   Yeah. There's a shitload of blood around the DB., and she's got none on her.

   But I knew that wasn't true. I felt as if I were drowning in it.

   "I think you're finally finished here, ma'am. You better get yourself somewhere solid and ride out the wind. We'll be in touch."

   I didn't make eye contact with the detective. I didn't have the strength. Alonzo Serca had parked his chair beside mine, lending verbal support when he thought I needed it. Saul orbited me like a planet. Throughout the last three hours I'd been trying to keep track of the faces—Castigere drinking his eyes blurry, Mike Moreno taking notes, Evangelina stealing touches of Abdías's hand, Leo watching me and pretending not to, Judge Horne directing the actions of the police like a king with his royal guard—but it was getting difficult to sort out the facts, such as they were.

   Fact: Joe Rotto had not killed Isabella. So much for my theory. So much for all my work.

   Fact: The true killer was someone I'd seen tonight in this very apartment.

   "He could have run downstairs before we sealed the suite, I suppose," Serca said.

   With supreme effort, I turned my head toward the sound of his voice. "Who are you talking about?"

   "The man who . . . who killed Joseph." Serca's face was

The Tongue Merchant

waxy. His tie was unknotted. He kept dabbing his upper lip with a handkerchief. "I had Raoul and Marcus keep everyone here, and Abdías drew up a list of names, but the suspect could have made it downstairs before we locked the building down."

I wasn't comforted by the thought. I retreated back to my facts.

Fact: The killer had seen me talking with Rotto, seconds before he attacked, yet I hadn't been touched. Was I being set up for something?

"They say we can go now, Zo."

"Take me home, Saul."

"You got it."

I took his hand in both of my own, and he spirited me through the crowd like a bodyguard clearing a path for his client. There must have been two dozen cops and crime-scene workers packed into the suite. Something told me that my buddy Sam Raznik had made sure to tell them all about what a troublemaker I was. Maybe that was why they were all looking at me like I'd just walked out of Chernobyl with my skin glowing green.

Marcus emerged from the cloakroom with our things. It wasn't until I saw my purse that I remembered the treasure it held inside.

"Damn, I almost forgot." I spun around, panning the room. "Have you seen Nathan?"

"Why?"

"Humor me, Saul, please, before I collapse and you have to carry me out of here."

Marcus pointed toward the kitchen. "There he is, with Mr. Castigere."

Five seconds later I'd left Saul at the door and was standing in front of the buffet table.

"Miss Paraizo," Castigere said when he saw me. "How are

you holding up?" He tugged at his coat sleeves and shifted his bad arm in his sling, as if his tailor had stitched when he should have snipped.

"Excuse me, Robert, but I need a minute of Nathan's time. Can you give us a sec?"

"Uh, sure, no problemo. We'll finish this later, Nate."

Nathan, in turn, looked on the verge of ducking behind the table. He didn't acknowledge Castigere's departure, just cupped his hands in front of him and looked at me with his silent gazelle eyes.

And I'm the lioness, I thought, *and this is an African veldt, and if I don't tread lightly, he's going to leap away.*

"I'll be brief," I promised.

Nathan nodded, a quick twitch of his head. His gaze remained impenetrable.

Lowering my voice like an inmate discussing plans for going over the wall, I said, "You know who I am and what I'm after, and the cops are watching, so here's my pitch. Isabella Murillo died trying to expose a crime. They murdered her because she was about to talk, and they just got Rotto for the same reason, because he pushed too hard, or knew too much, or just pissed the wrong people off. And with him dead, my whole half-assed investigation is shot all to hell. The only thing I've got is an upside-down postage stamp, and I think it was intended for you." I slipped my hand into my purse. "It's called an Adelbert. Isabella was going to give it to you in exchange for something. Hard proof, I imagine. So let's finish the deal you struck months ago. What do you say?"

I didn't know what I expected from him. Surprise, maybe, or fear at having been discovered as the keeper of fell secrets. Maybe even outrage at being confronted in such a manner. But all Nathan did was open his mouth and wet his teeth with his tongue and look even more like a frightened gazelle than before.

"Nathan? If you try to run on me, so help me God I'll tackle you right here."

Though my threat was nothing but a charade, the panic in my tone was sincere enough. Either my desperation convinced him, or his desire for the stamp steeled his bones, because he finally bent his head toward me and said, "I didn't ki-ki-*kill* anyone."

"Good for you. Now do you want the stamp or not?"

He nodded again.

"Tell me where you were late Sunday night."

He swallowed twice. "I wuh-wuh-wuh—"

"Hold it. Let me make this easier. I'll just ask the questions and you give me a yes or no. You were in Hozumkur that night, weren't you?"

A third affirmative. *Yes.*

"It wasn't Nico she was to meet at her boat that night. She was meeting you, wasn't she?"

Yes.

A small voice in my heart shouted, *I knew it!* At least I'd made one deduction that hadn't turned out to be fool's gold.

"You were trading for the stamp that night."

Yes. "Buh-but when I got there, the boat wuh-wuh-wuh—"

"The boat was already gone," I supplied.

Yes.

"So you snuck back here to San Juan with whatever it was you had for your end of the trade."

No.

I frowned. "No? Then what did you do with it?"

Nathan inhaled, preparing himself for the half-aborted syllables and stillborn sentences that he knew were to follow. "I had tuh-tuh-tuh-taken a helicopter to Hozumkur, and on my wuh-wuh-way back after I saw that her boat wuh-was gone, I left the puh-package in an airpuh-puh-port locker. Cuh-cuhcan I have the stamp now?"

"The package is in a locker at Hozumkur Municipal?"

Yes.

"I thought they did away with all the airport lockers, as terrorist prevention."

"It's in a puh-private office, where the suh-security guards change uniforms. Very secure. I have a fuh-friend who works there."

"All right. I assume you have the key to the locker with you."

Yes.

Then something else occurred to me. Just how had Nathan gotten his hands on this parcel in the first place? I asked him as much.

He readied himself for another shattered soliloquy. "The bo-bo-board of directors didn't trust the si-si-si-siblings. Mr. Rotto hired a muh-muh-man to watch Abdías. Mr. Serca assigned me to fuh-follow Isabella. This wuh-was six months ago. I ha-had already be-be-been told to find the man named Voorstadt."

That was true enough. I remembered Rotto telling me that both he and Serca had agents doing their dirty work. Those agents were Nathan and Leo . . . who was actually a snoop for the FBI.

"And did you locate Voorstadt?"

Yes. "Shuh-shuh-shortly after the trial."

"And?"

Nathan looked down at his shoes.

"You're not going to tell me, are you?"

"I huh-huh-huh-haven't told anyone but Mrs. Murillo. Not even Mr. Serca. I was too uh-uh-afraid."

My mind ran through the chain of events from there, and *voilà,* puzzle pieces started snapping into place. "Okay, what about after that? You were the first to report Isabella's visits with Bancavia, who turned out to be a link to ELF."

Yes.

"*And*"—spirals of electricity passed down the length of my body—"months earlier you were spying on Jan Voorstadt when he incriminated someone in the warehouse fires."

Yes.

"So you knew that it wasn't Bella who hired him to burn those buildings down. All she ever wanted was to protect her father's company. You knew *that*, as well. So even though you wouldn't give the evidence to your boss, you approached Isabella and offered to give it to her in exchange for the Adelbert, which at the time belonged to a man named St-Germain. Am I getting warm here?"

Yes.

"So this information that Bella died trying to get . . . is it still available?"

"I ha-ha-have it on tape."

I almost hugged him.

"Buh-but she wuh-wuh-wuh-wasn't writing her newspaper story about arson."

"She wasn't? That doesn't make any sense. I read the memo she sent Rotto. She was connecting Voorstadt to Hozumkur."

Yes. "But not for any fuh-fuh-fires. He wuh-wasn't hired by anyone."

"So what the hell was Bella after?"

But the gazelle was about to run. He shook his head. "Just one mo-mo-more thing. He gets his luh-leverage through the dope. Buh-buh-buh-blackmail."

"Leverage? Who gets this leverage? Voorstadt?"

No. "The kuh-killer."

"*Who?*"

But Nathan shook his head, and I could sense that we were under scrutiny from at least a dozen pairs of eyes. If the perp, as the cops called him, was still in our midst—and at this point I had no way of knowing one way or the other—then I was probably signing Nathan's death certificate by talking to him. Nonetheless, there was one more trade left to be made.

    I reached out to shake his hand, the Adelbert scissored between my fingers. Seeing the stamp, Nathan produced a ring of keys and removed one of them. We shook and made the switch. I was becoming such a master of tradecraft, I expected a call from the CIA any day now. This time next week I'd be making chalk marks on embassy mailboxes and taking pictures of dead-letter drops with a telephoto lens. When our hands touched, it was hard to tell whose was shaking with more intensity.

    With a piece of cold brass pressed against my palm, I told Nathan to take care of himself, and when I turned around I tried to look like a normal woman who'd just seen a mutilated body. But, strangely, the trauma of finding Rotto's corpse was rapidly fading, giving way to an acute curiosity. As well as a foreboding certainty that I was now sailing the same waters that had gotten Isabella killed.

    Saul was waiting for me at the door. "Well?"

"I'm leaving."

"Sounds good to me."

"But I'm not going home."

"Zo, don't you do this to me."

"Sorry. But I need to go back to Hozumkur."

"For crying out loud . . ."

"I'm going with or without you."

"Zo, there's a hurricane ready to hit that place."

"I know, Saul. Maybe even two of them."

Chapter Nineteen

The sea heaved against Candado Beach. The scent of salt scoured the air.

"You want to tell me who's going to be dumb enough to give us a lift to St. Noré in this weather? In case you haven't heard, the wind's blowing about ten billion miles an hour over there."

"Only fifty knots," I said, throwing open the door of my house.

"*Only?* Here, let me show you." Leaving the door open and dripping water with every step, he crossed the living room to the TV. But nothing happened when he hit the power button. "See there? Tube's fried. We're probably already getting hit by lightning."

"You might try plugging it in." I dashed into the bedroom and threw off my clothes.

"I take it you don't watch a lot of prime time," he said, rooting around for the cord amongst my stack of Creedence vinyl.

"I'm the XO of a Coast Guard cutter, Saul. I don't really have time."

"Hell, not saying I blame you. I don't even *own* one of these mind-sucking little things." He found the remote under a laundry basket and clicked it on. After a second, he whistled. "There she is. Meanest bitch in the valley, due to stomp us to pulp the moment we hit St. Noré. Thanks for asking, Zo, but count me out."

"Your studio is over there," I reminded him, yanking my rain gear from the clothes dryer.

"So you think I'm going to go over there and *protect* it? No way, *amiga*. The big bad wolf can blow my house down, but this little pig isn't putting up a fight. What's so important about going over there, anyway? What do you expect to accomplish at this hour in the middle of a typhoon?"

"I've got to talk to Isolde!" I shouted between rooms, binding my hair behind my head.

"What for?"

"If she wasn't meeting with Rotto to give him the key to the *Lynn*, then there must have been some other reason they got together. I need to find out what they were up to."

"Need to get your head examined is what you need to do."

I tugged on my hiking boots. "And then there's Sixbone."

"Forget it. It'll be impossible to find him. He'll be hiding from the storm with his head between his legs, kissing his ass goodbye along with every other person on the island."

"So maybe I'm an idiot, okay? I'm hardly going to hang around here all night while that monster is out there. Jesus, Saul, he could have *killed* me tonight. I'm not about to sit and wait for him to come cut the tongue out of my mouth."

"Zo, listen to yourself for a minute . . ."

"And furthermore, I know Tommy So's lying to me. I just can't prove it. Nathan said that the killer was using dope as leverage. I'm betting that Tommy So is being blackmailed. Either he lies and frames Nico, or he gets thrown to the cops."

"Tommy *who?*"

"And then"—I dumped the contents of my purse into my belt pack—"if all else fails"—I strapped on the belt and fastened the aluminum buckle—"I'm going to the airport to see what Nathan has waiting for me in Pandora's box." I wound the hound's-tooth scarf around my neck and went for the door, checking my watch along the way. But the battery seemed to be dead, the hands frozen at twenty till nine. Right around the time Rotto died. I must've broken it during the struggle . . .

I suppressed the memory before it could devour me.

"What time is it?" I asked, fighting a chill.

"Time is a false god," Saul declared, in his usual truculent manner. But despite his belligerence, he was defeated, resigning himself to dragging on his raincoat and attending to my folly. "I haven't worn a watch since I was fifteen."

There was a clock on the wall behind him, but his girth blocked my view. I stepped around him, my compass finally starting to align. "There's a chance I can still catch Wicker Falco at the docks. He owns a powerboat and owes me a favor for not busting him for reckless endangerment a few months back."

"Powerboat. Sixty-mile-an-hour winds. I can't wait."

"Don't wimp out on me now, Mr. Tormé. It's ten-thirty. If we hurry we can—"

I snapped my teeth shut so hard that needles of pain stabbed the backs of my eyes.

Saul was about to turn up the collar of his coat, but his hands stopped moving when he saw my face. "Zo? What is it? You're scaring me."

Why didn't I see it before? How could I have possibly missed it?

"Got you, Zen boy," I whispered. "You can shove your IQ up your ass."

"Pardon me?"

The dawn of epiphany dazzling my vision, I started to explain myself, but then two men appeared in the open doorway, rain bouncing off their white uniforms, flashlights held in their fists like swords.

"Lieutenant Paraizo? I'm Chief Warrant Officer Brady Cox." He held up a wet mess of folded paper. "On the orders of Rear

Admiral Elias Kirkland, I'm hereby placing you under house arrest."

So much in life depends on luck.

At least that's what I used to believe. Cars run off the road and kill families at random. Last-second shots go in from the half-court line. Soda machines give you extra change. Lotto numbers come up. Stocks come down.

Coincidence.

Or so it would seem to the uninitiated. But in the last few days I'd realized that I was the Michelangelo of every circumstance that confronted me; in small and subtle ways, I worked the knife that sculpted the clay, that refined the model of possibility. Chance was an excuse wielded by those afraid of taking responsibility for life. And so when my salvation walked in the door behind Cox and his partner, I was neither elated nor surprised. I simply zipped up my jacket and got ready to leave.

"Excuse me, fellas," Leo said, and when they turned around they were looking at his badge. "Special Agent Kavisti, FBI."

We were alone in my fly-tying room, surrounded by tufts of rabbit fur, phony eyeballs, spools of black 3/0 monocord, and plastic trays of pheasant-tail fibers and hooks from sizes 4 through 12. Home court advantage had never been more distinctly mine.

"What are you after?" I demanded.

"Now Marcy, you don't really expect me to tell you that, do you?" He thought about sitting down, but the only chair was stacked with tackle boxes. With no room to retreat, he could only stand there inches away and have it out with me. "At Serca's place you said you had proof that So was lying. Is that true?"

"Follow me back to Marina del Sol and I'll show you."

"I don't think Abbot and Costello out there will be very keen on that idea. Now what the hell happened with Rotto?"

"You need me to spell it out for you? The person who broke his neck is the same one who stabbed Isabella."

"All right, let's assume that's true—"

"Please, Leo."

"Okay, okay, I believe that it *is* true. It only makes sense. But I take it by that look in your eyes that you know something you didn't tell the police. And that's called obstructing justice, which is an offense I don't think you want added to your ever-growing criminal dossier."

I squirmed under his gaze. "I just need a little more time. I'm so close to this, Leo, you've got to trust me."

"And you were headed back to St. Noré to get your evidence that Nico is innocent."

"Among other things, yeah."

"And why didn't you let the police in on these little details you've collected? Wait a minute, don't answer that. Let me guess. You're not handing over your evidence to the proper authorities because the cops are incompetent, or they won't believe you, or your personal hunger for retribution has gotten the best of you."

"Maybe all three."

"And maybe you better tell me what you know."

"Not a chance. This is not your business."

"It's not? The guy I was assigned to investigate gets his tongue chopped out of his mouth and it's not my business?" He picked up a pair of needle-nosed pliers and used them to emphasize his words. "Marcy, I work counterterrorism. For the last fourteen months we've been trying to get someone inside the Earth Liberation Front. Jan Voorstadt blows up a few warehouses, then finds a get-out-of-jail-free card before we can lean on him. But as it turns out, Joseph Rotto, Alonzo Serca, and one other investor had insured those very buildings against criminal activity six months before the incident. They all ended up making money on the deal. So when Rotto started asking around about hiring a private eye, we seized the opportunity and I went in, hoping to link him to ELF."

"Rotto wasn't involved in ELF," I said. "But he was killed because he was asking questions that would have eventually led him to knowledge he wasn't supposed to have. Just like Bella."

"Think so, huh?"

"Maybe. Give me a few hours in Hozumkur and I'll let you know."

"You know I can't do that. If it weren't for Bartholomew breathing down our necks, I'd already have a dozen more agents down here. Isabella's death was none of our concern, as least as far as jurisdiction is concerned, but now that the subject of an FBI query has been assassinated, all bets are off. We're bringing in a team as soon as the storm passes."

"Too late by then. The killer will already be gone. Bart's the only thing that's keeping him here. I have to find him before morning."

"*You?*"

"Okay, *we* have to find him. Tonight. As in us. Plural, remember?"

He gave me an ephemeral smile. "You don't know how good that sounds, Marcy, but I can't. For two reasons. One, you're not authorized to pursue this investigation, especially now that I know you're concealing possible evidence. And two, I have to stay here and oversee the local dragnet. The hurricane is preventing us from bringing in any reinforcements, not to mention that it's really lousing up our communications. But it's also working to our advantage in the fact that our man's going to have a real hard time getting off the island. If I keep our people on the move, we should be able to seal off all possible points of egress."

"Guess I'll have to go alone then."

"Sure. I may be wrong, but I don't think the Coast Guard is going to be very sympathetic to your cause."

He was right. I rubbed the back of my neck, massaging the oncoming headache, mentally sending Mercator Raznik to a Siberian gulag. I envisioned how it had happened: as soon as the San Juan cops called HPD to compare notes on the murders, my name set off a red flare, and ten minutes later the phone on the admiral's desk started ringing. *Bon voyage* to my promotion to lieutenant commander.

To punish or to save . . .

Before I realized what I was doing, I'd put my hand on Leo's chest. I felt the warmth of the skin beneath the shirt, the rhythm of the heart beneath the skin. At that moment, everything stopped spinning. I read the pressure change in my body as readily as if I'd seen it fall in a barometer. I was *centered*, more than I'd ever been behind the wheel of the Linc or on the bow of a ship.

"Marcy . . ."

"Shhh. Just listen. For one minute. Please. I may have lost my job, which happens to be my life. Getting to Hozumkur is all I have left. The way I see it, you need more manpower, and you're not going to get any until the weather clears, and by then it may be too late. So here's what you do. Are you listening?"

"More than you know."

"You're going to remand me to the custody of Sergeant Kyle Straker of HPD on the grounds that I am an integral part of a priority murder investigation and my assistance is necessary if the joint efforts of the cops and the FBI are to be successful. As a federal agent, you have the authority to overrule the police in this matter. I'm not a flight risk, nor am I just some witless civilian. I've no reason to run, and nowhere to go if I wanted to. I am a peace-keeper. A cop. Just like you." I tapped him lightly on the chest. "Give me till dawn, Leo, that's all I ask. And I'll make you the envy of everyone in the Bureau."

"You sound pretty sure of yourself."

I imagined I could feel the locker key in my pack, burning like a tiny star. I hadn't told anyone about it. Not Saul or Mike Moreno or anyone. "Yes, sir. I am."

"The envy of the Bureau, huh?"

"Maybe even a spot on the evening news."

"Nah, I'm lousy around cameras. Besides, being on TV would blow my cover."

"So does that mean you'll let me go?"

He put his hand over mine. His pinkie ring was cold against my skin. "If it weren't for this storm . . ." His heart beat beneath my palm. "But it doesn't look like I have any better option if I want to catch this guy, now does it?" He removed his hand and ran it through his hair in a teenager's way. "Okay. I'll play along. There's one of my kind born every minute, you know."

I bit back a smile.

"I'll go see what I can do with your two jailers out there. But you have to promise me, and I mean *promise me*, you'll never leave Straker's sight. Got it?"

I held up my right hand. "On my honor."

"Good. I believe you."

The tides of relief washed through me with such force that before I knew it, I was standing on my toes and planting a swift kiss on his cheek. "Thanks. But I do have one more question."

He laughed. "Why am I not surprised?"

"You said there were three investors who made money off the warehouse fires. Rotto, Serca, and one other guy. Who was it?"

"Damn, lady. Don't you ever quit?"

"*Who?*"
"Robert Castigere."
"Bastard."
"Him or me?" Leo wondered.
But I was already out the door.

Chief Warrant Officer Cox used my own phone to report me to Admiral Kirkland's office. The house arrest was in shambles: I was on the move, I'd been commandeered by the imperious FBI, I was not languishing under lock and key, I was a traitor to the Guard and probably the American way of life, to be hunted with extreme prejudice by all creatures of pure heart and pilloried as an example of what happens when good soldiers go bad.

How I was ever going to explain myself, I didn't know.

But then Saul and I reached the docks and found Wicker Falco cheating a group of Pakistani coolies at five-card stud, and whatever doubts I had about my actions were tattered by the shearing wind.

I got everyone's attention by dropping a handful of my best lures atop the pile of money in the center of the table. "So, Wick. A fishing trip next weekend in return for a ride. What do you say?"

As Falco bared his watermelon-seed teeth in a misshapen smile, the clock on the wall behind him struck the hour.

Midnight.

★ ★ ★ ★ ★

Thursday
Barometric pressure 27.01, plummeting

★ ★ ★ ★ ★

Chapter Twenty

Looking back, I'd have to say that the definitive moment—when events began their inexorable spiral beyond my control—was when I set foot in Falco's boat.

He owned a nightmare with a rudder.

The Firefox was a twenty-four-foot supercharged racer known as a cigarette, her name inscribed in slashing scarlet letters across the narrow stern: *Perdition*. Built for nothing but speed, the 'Fox could plane from a standstill in less than three seconds. Riding in it was rather like strapping yourself to a bullet.

The clouds roiled overhead, an iron-black vortex discharging lightning and unending walls of rain. The sea had assumed a sickly green shade, revealed in the jerking light of the weatherproof lamps that Falco had mounted on the boat. I had sailed waters like these before, but never in a fiberglass coffin such as this.

Saul was right. My obsession had suffocated my sense of prudence, and I was risking more than just my career. I was gambling with human lives.

The force 11 wind was so strong that it carved valleys and constructed mountains of water around us, only to demolish them again and rebuild them seconds later. Jurancán the hurricane god had set before us an ever-changing wilderness from which far stronger boats than ours might never return. When the Firefox's engine came alive, the robust growl I'd expected to hear was dwarfed by the cavernous voice of the storm. With sea water splashing over me and salt stinging my lips, I tightened my safety harness and wiggled deeper into my chair, thankful that the restricted seating area forced the three of us to sit with our bodies pressed together—anything to make me feel like I wasn't going to be thrown from this roller-coaster the first time we topped one of those massive crests.

"You sure about this?" Saul yelled in my ear.

In response, I poked Falco in the leg.

His dirty yellow slicker was cinched up tight, revealing only a small oval of his pock-marked face. He'd braced himself with a shot of rum a few minutes earlier, and now his eyes swam in their sockets like tadpoles.

"We can make it, can't we?" I asked him.

"Stranger things have happened!" He grinned savagely.

When he throttled *Perdition* into the tempest, I started to say a little prayer, but it didn't feel quite right in my mouth, so I aborted in mid-supplication. It seemed like the only time I opened up a dialogue with God was when I needed to ask a favor. Instead, I reached out and took Saul's hand in mine. Human hands are our truest rosary, and if we started putting more energy into holding these than a string of beads, this world would be a more heavenly place.

Falco piloted us farther away from the pier. The rain drilled into the hull. Lightning smote the ocean a few miles away, followed by an apocalypse of thunder. Between that and the wind and the churning waves, I couldn't hear the warning knell of the tintinnabulators, which was probably for the best. As we left the city lights behind and the darkness closed in around us, sealing us off from civilization, I was reminded of another of Poe's favorite words: *stygian*. I never really knew what it meant until tonight.

My body shook from the strain as the boat fought off a series of colossal breakers.

Chapter Twenty

Looking back, I'd have to say that the definitive moment—when events began their inexorable spiral beyond my control—was when I set foot in Falco's boat.

He owned a nightmare with a rudder.

The Firefox was a twenty-four-foot supercharged racer known as a cigarette, her name inscribed in slashing scarlet letters across the narrow stern: *Perdition*. Built for nothing but speed, the 'Fox could plane from a standstill in less than three seconds. Riding in it was rather like strapping yourself to a bullet.

The clouds roiled overhead, an iron-black vortex discharging lightning and unending walls of rain. The sea had assumed a sickly green shade, revealed in the jerking light of the weatherproof lamps that Falco had mounted on the boat. I had sailed waters like these before, but never in a fiberglass coffin such as this.

Saul was right. My obsession had suffocated my sense of prudence, and I was risking more than just my career. I was gambling with human lives.

The force 11 wind was so strong that it carved valleys and constructed mountains of water around us, only to demolish them again and rebuild them seconds later. Jurancán the hurricane god had set before us an ever-changing wilderness from which far stronger boats than ours might never return. When the Firefox's engine came alive, the robust growl I'd expected to hear was dwarfed by the cavernous voice of the storm. With sea water splashing over me and salt stinging my lips, I tightened my safety harness and wiggled deeper into my chair, thankful that the restricted seating area forced the three of us to sit with our bodies pressed together—anything to make me feel like I wasn't going to be thrown from this roller-coaster the first time we topped one of those massive crests.

"You sure about this?" Saul yelled in my ear.

In response, I poked Falco in the leg.

His dirty yellow slicker was cinched up tight, revealing only a small oval of his pock-marked face. He'd braced himself with a shot of rum a few minutes earlier, and now his eyes swam in their sockets like tadpoles.

"We can make it, can't we?" I asked him.

"Stranger things have happened!" He grinned savagely.

When he throttled *Perdition* into the tempest, I started to say a little prayer, but it didn't feel quite right in my mouth, so I aborted in mid-supplication. It seemed like the only time I opened up a dialogue with God was when I needed to ask a favor. Instead, I reached out and took Saul's hand in mine. Human hands are our truest rosary, and if we started putting more energy into holding these than a string of beads, this world would be a more heavenly place.

Falco piloted us farther away from the pier. The rain drilled into the hull. Lightning smote the ocean a few miles away, followed by an apocalypse of thunder. Between that and the wind and the churning waves, I couldn't hear the warning knell of the tintinnabulators, which was probably for the best. As we left the city lights behind and the darkness closed in around us, sealing us off from civilization, I was reminded of another of Poe's favorite words: *stygian*. I never really knew what it meant until tonight.

My body shook from the strain as the boat fought off a series of colossal breakers.

Then things really got bad.

Time, as I'd been so recently instructed, was a false god. Seconds and hours and days were units of man's own design, conceived to help break down the universe and make it easier to manage. Whenever I'm up in the Colorado hills with my father, trolling a river as clear as glass, time burns out before I'm ready, sending us back to our day jobs before we've said all we needed to say, or laughed enough, or caught enough rainbow trout. Then there are moments like this, when I'm trying to survive a sea intent on killing me, and time stretches out to infinity.

The Firefox rode the foaming spines of forty-foot green waves and dropped steeply down the other side with such force that we had to support ourselves with our hands on the console in front of us. As if the boat were racing across a war zone, we were battered from port and starboard by mortar explosions that showered us with watery fallout. The thunder sounded like antiaircraft fire. I spit sea water from my mouth and hung on, the backs of my hands being brutalized by the strafing rain.

On my right, Saul vomited over the side of the boat.

The spotlights jerked chaotically through the night sky, giving us glimpses of the tattered belly of the clouds; at some points it looked as if the ocean and the sky almost touched. The air between was filled with foam. I had the impression that if we didn't make landfall soon, we'd be crushed betwixt these two unrelenting forces.

Time passed interminably, if indeed it passed at all.

My watch was broken. I wouldn't have looked at it anyway, for fear that turning my head would bring on the nausea that already incapacitated my friend. Instead, I focused on the bright faces—my dad asleep in the garage on his Army surplus cot, my brother Micah, the fifth-graders I'd spoken to a week ago about life in the Guard—and when Falco touched my shoulder to let me know that we'd arrived, opening my eyes was like coming awake from a dream.

"Poseidon can kiss my ass!" he shouted.

I followed his rheumy gaze. The lights of the marina burned holes through the storm.

"Saul, we made it." I put my arm around his shoulders and gave him a reaffirming squeeze.

He groaned.

Spying the battle lanterns on the wharf caused my spirits to rise like a buoy. Blinking against the onslaught, I watched the marina grow larger as Falco steered us in. He sang lustily as he worked the controls—Elton John's "Rocket Man"—and by the second verse I was almost tempted to join in. Some madman was standing on the docks as we approached, clutching the fisherman's rail so as not to be swept away. Not caring who he was, I hollered at him and threw him the mooring line.

From there time released us, and my life resumed its normal, lunatic pace. I helped Saul to his feet. He struggled out of the boat, his face the color of wet dough. The madman turned out to be Kyle Straker.

"Can you guess where I'd rather be right now?" he yelled.

"Anywhere but here?"

"You got it!"

Between the four of us, we were able to win the tug-of-war with the waves and lash *Perdition* to its berth. I worked my knots in record time, but between the rope and the wind, my hands didn't stand much of a chance. My fingers were raw. I'd never had a professional manicure in my life, but as I tied off the last hitch and blew onto my aching palms for a little bit of relief, I promised my hands that if they got me through tonight, I'd reward them with some serious TLC the first chance I got.

"The feds called half an hour ago!" Straker reported loudly as we hunkered down and put some distance between ourselves

The Tongue Merchant

and the sea. "I don't know if I'm supposed to babysit you or deputize you."

"A little bit of both, I think."

"So what's the plan? Or is that on a need-to-know basis only?"

"Joe Rotto's dead!" I shouted, straining to be heard over the cacophony.

"So they tell me."

"And Tommy So's full of shit."

"I'd like to believe you, Lieutenant, but you're going to have to—"

"Prove it!" I hollered. "Yeah, I know. Come on."

I led them down Ochoa until we reached Marina del Sol. The wharf wasn't as deserted as I'd anticipated. Half a dozen idiots in slickers and wading boots moved amongst the boats, doing a little last-minute belaying, two of them aiming video cameras at the sky. A news van was parked on the sidewalk, its roof bristling with electronics, a reporter in a CNN raincoat standing a few feet away from it, shouting instructions to his sound man. The palm trees along the street were bent to such an angle their fronds nearly touched the ground.

"Yo, Marce!" Wicker Falco jerked a thumb in the direction of the city proper. "If you don't need this old sea dog anymore, I'm skinnin' out! Got this lady friend of mine—"

"Fine, go. And thank you."

"My pleasure." The rain glistened on his face like sweat. "You're *muy loco*, you know?"

"So goes the common consensus."

He chortled. "God bless you, Marce. God *bless* you." He thrust his arm up like some kind of *Heil Hitler* sign, then loped off down the street.

I didn't watch him go. Because I was here. Where it had all started. Ochoa Street at my back, the marina before me.

"Now what?" Saul asked.

I held up a hand for silence.

And remembered.

I'm sitting in Dominique's with an untouched glass of raspberry tea in front of me and villainy in my heart. I'm thinking about dismembering whoever did this to Bella, taking my fists to them until their bones are powder, all the while watching the medics remove a parcel from the Lynn. *Except it isn't just a parcel. It's a bag for a corpse. Inside is my friend, referred to in police lingo as a DB.*

"Zo? We're freezing our asses off here."

I'm seeing the rigs on either side of the Lynn, *one a catamaran with a British flag, one the party boat of the prosecution's star witness,* Tommy Lying Bastard So. *From there my eyes travel to the pilings on the north, encrusted with barnacles, and then to the Rime & Reel Yacht Club on the south. And behold, towering above them all, the ruination of So's story and the next puzzle piece to slam into place.*

Jehovah.

I started walking toward *Seventh Son.*

On either side of me, the men looked at each other helplessly. Straker held up his hands in question. Saul shrugged.

Sure enough, Tommy So had yet to flee to high ground. He stood on the pier wearing sandals and a Mexican *serape,* staring eastward through what appeared to be a pair of night-vision binoculars.

"Hey, Zen boy."

At the sound of my voice, he lowered the binoculars and, after a moment of contemplation, turned to face me, as if he'd been expecting guests. "Why, if it isn't my favorite siren, come to sing me another song." He noticed Straker and smiled. "And she's brought along the Gestapo."

"We need to ask you about a few things, Mr. So," Straker said. "At least"—he glanced at me—"I *think* we do. Would you mind talking with us?"

The Tongue Merchant

"Not at all. I've got a couple of hours before the eyewall hits. Ask away."

The eyewall. For a few seconds there I was so involved with punishing and saving that I'd forgotten that I stood in the immediate path of a hurricane. The eyewall was that part of the storm surrounding the eye. It was the most ferocious region of the storm, with winds that could bend steel girders and hurl Buicks like a child tossing Matchbox cars. I had to hurry.

"This way!" I directed. "To the yacht club."

With the three men chasing after me, I jogged south down the dock, every bit of my body drenched. The rain had penetrated my windbreaker, the cold seeping to my bones. My teeth hurt. My skin was wrinkled from exposure. My back ached from having been bent over for so long in the Firefox in a futile effort to keep the world from tilting. And still I ran on.

I could barely keep my feet in the catastrophic wind, which tore across the marina with such force that it was nearly impossible to struggle against it, much less to see. The klaxons began wailing again. Straker shouted something I couldn't hear. Saul responded. Tommy So rattled off a Chinese aphorism about the medicinal powers of hard rain and a bowl of hot rice.

Jumping up the steps that led to the jetty, I almost laughed when I saw that someone had run the black and red hurricane-warning flags up the staff in front of the Rime & Reel. That was like carrying a banner that read WAR IN PROGRESS onto the battlefield at Gettysburg. I drew up short at the door, my lungs pumping, every nerve ending in my body tingling in anticipation. When the men had gathered around me, giving me looks of varying degrees of skepticism, I took Straker by the elbow and positioned him so that he was facing the closed door of the Rime & Reel.

This is it, gatita. *Are you ready?*

"Call me a simpleton," Straker sighed, "but all I'm seeing

here is a door in my face."

Yes, Mama. I'm ready. I think.

"I assume you have a point," Straker said.

"You ever read Edgar Allan Poe?" I asked him, my mouth inches from his ear.

"Uh, only that one about the raven, and that was in junior high. Is that pertinent?"

"The purloined letter was hidden in plain sight."

"So what? Look, Lieutenant, this is fun and all but—"

I spun him around to face the *Lynn*.

Except the *Lynn* wasn't there.

A sudden nova of lightning froze the scene like a tableau: the soot-colored clouds, the pillars of rain, the roofs of the houses with their boarded-up windows, the boats lashed down to their slips, and the last few frantic souls weaving between them with flashlights. Except only the boats at the south end of the marina were visible. From where we stood in the doorway, where Tommy So claimed to have been standing almost exactly seventy-two hours ago when he spotted Nico with the scuba gear, the entire north half of the pier was blocked from view.

The clock in Jehovah's face glowed like a lighthouse beacon.

Straker pushed the hood back from his face and stared. Just as I had observed Monday morning from my seat under the verandah at Dominique's, the imitation Big Ben stood midway between the *Lady Lynn Rob* and the yacht club. Its base was so broad that the *Lynn* was invisible from this vantage point, along with every rig within forty feet of it. In fact, in order to see *anything* on the pier's north side, I figured I'd have to walk at least thirty feet along the jetty until I was out of Jehovah's shadow, which would put me well away from the door of the Rime & Reel. Though the evidence had been looming in front of me all along, I hadn't caught on until back in my apartment when I tried to peer around Saul's body to get a glimpse of the clock.

Straker rested his hands on his hips. "Son of a *bitch* . . ."

Saul and Tommy So were also gaping at the clock tower, although they were apparently a little slower on the uptake. Neither one of them spoke. I was so elated at having finally scored a point in this dreadful game that I practically floated toward Tommy.

I grabbed him by the shoulders and gave him a little shake. "You lied about Nico."

His mouth moved up and down.

"*Who put you up to this?*" I shouted into his face. "*Who framed Nico?*"

Tommy had lost all of his swagger, as if it had been washed away by the rain and was puddling at his feet as I shook shim. He looked like nothing more than a scared wet kid who didn't know any better.

"Who made you do it, Tommy?"

"He . . . he . . ."

"*Who, goddammit?*"

Tommy shoved me and ran.

I landed hard on my butt. I barely caught myself with my hands and saved my tailbone the brunt of the pain that arced up through my spine. Saul shouted my name and dropped down to help me, then leaped back up to give pursuit.

But Straker said, "Let him go! No use chasing him. He's not going anywhere." He helped me up with one hand and withdrew a walkie-talkie with the other. "You okay?"

Rubbing my backside, I gave him a little nod.

"You can say 'I told you so,' " he said, thumbing on the radio. "I deserve it."

But I didn't feel like celebrating. The feeling of victory was evanescent. When it fled, it left the familiar hollow place in my heart, the cavity that wouldn't be filled until Nico was free and the right man sitting on death row. "Saul? Are you still sick?"

"No," he said, but he looked it. He had paraffin skin and lips as white as his teeth. He stood there flexing his hands, his Sasquatch-sized frame visibly shaking as if he were in the grips of malaria. "I . . . I can't believe this."

That makes two of us, friend. I bent over and braced myself with my hands on my knees, trying to catch my breath. Revealing a man's duplicity takes a lot out of you.

Into the radio Straker said, "Raz, you there?"

After a gargle of static, Mercator's voice came over the line: "Affirmative."

"Our seventh son was perjuring his ass off. Copy that?"

"Ten-one, Kyle. Say again."

Straker shook the walkie-talkie as if that might clear up the interference caused by the storm. "Seventh son is to be considered code 6F. He's on the run. Copy?"

"Ten-four."

"Tell the desk we need whatever units they can spare for roundup duty."

"Roger that. What's your 20?"

"Still at the marina," he said. I looked up through my sopping hair to see him watching me. "Though something tells me I'm going to be jerked all over town before the night's over. Let me know when you've got our man. Straker out."

He clipped the radio to his belt, his eyes never leaving mine. "So. Whose life do you want to ruin next?"

I straightened my back and tried to ignore my protesting joints. "What's a code 6F?"

"Felony suspect wanted, but not armed."

"At least not yet."

"I don't think Tommy So's the violent type, Lieutenant."

"Until recently, I wasn't the violent type either. Do you have a car?"

He wiped his nose with his hand. "Sure, but we've only got two hours at the most before anything left out in the open gets turned into a toy in Bartholomew's sandbox. Including my car and everyone inside of it."

"Then we better hurry. We still need to meet with Isolde Bancavia, find Sixbone, and get to the airport."

"Airport? You know there's not a plane on this island that isn't grounded."

"I'm not flying anywhere, Sergeant. I'll tell you about it on the way."

He'd parked under the carport at Dominique's. The wind harried us all the way there. We were forced to stumble from one solid handhold to the next, a street sign, a phone kiosk, anything to keep from pitching helplessly across the ground. Crates and barrels tumbled down the street. Power lines popped white sparks, and what must have been a dozen panes of glass blew outward from a nearby building, followed by the staccato sound of snapping tree limbs. A dead dog lay in the street.

The closer the three of us got to the car, the harder we fought against the wind, our sense of urgency growing in proportion to the storm. Straker unlocked the doors and fired the ignition with a keychain remote.

"By the way," he said. "The clock tower. Nice bit of police work."

"Thanks. I'll send you the bill."

Straker activated the strobe on the dashboard and slung the vehicle into the street. As we left the marina behind, I couldn't resist one more glance back at the *Lynn,* as if I might see Bella standing on the prow, blowing me a secret kiss.

Chapter Twenty-One

Rolling now, we shot through the empty Hozumkur streets, the windshield wipers not beating fast enough. The puddles were so deep in certain places that the car cast dirty plumes of water at the storefronts. Had there been anyone on the sidewalk, they would have been drenched as we hurtled by. But the city was empty. Man and beast alike had already run for high ground.

His lack of sleep evident in the hollows around his eyes, Straker drove down the center of the road, hands kneading the wheel. He didn't stop for red lights. Each intersection was like a crossroads of the damned. There was no sign of life save the occasional human-shaped silhouette that slipped down an alley or fluttered around a corner, a night-thing attending to some unspeakable business that couldn't wait for the light of day. The rain blasted the car so loudly that Saul was forced to shout when he leaned forward from the backseat and said, "Lionese Avenue is just up ahead! Drop me off there, will you?"

A new flower of fear blossomed in my heart.

"You sure about that?" I asked him. If Saul was out there on his own instead of by my side where I could watch out for him, that was one more worry my already overtaxed system had to accommodate. "I've got a better idea. As soon as we're finished here, we're heading to a shelter. You can come with us. Okay? We'll nuke some popcorn, maybe play a little Scrabble."

"Thanks, Zo, but since I'm this close to the *bottega*, I'm not just going to pass by without making sure those jerk-offs who call themselves employees got everything hammered down tight. I've got over sixty grand's worth of merchandise in there. *But,* and this is a damned big *but,* I don't want to go unless you promise me you're safe. This little mission you're on is getting a bit out of hand. If Straker here wasn't with you, there's no way in the cellar of hell I'd leave you."

"I know." I put my hand on his arm. "It's all right. Go take care of your studio. I'm sure I'll be fine. I've got the whole Hozumkur Police Department backing me up."

Saul glowered. "That makes me feel a lot better."

"Rest easy, Mr. Tunlunder," Straker said, turning the car down Lionese. "I'm watching her back."

"But *you* promise *me,*" I quickly added, "that you'll get in that snazzy ride of yours and get to a shelter with plenty of time to spare."

Saul's iron features melted a little. "You ever meet my mother?"

"You have a mother?"

"Yeah, imagine that. She lives up in Tampa. Last year she sent me one of those Red Cross hurricane kits. The kind that comes in a backpack. Got your flashlight, chocolate bars, transistor radio . . . moms are great, huh?"

"The best," I agreed, trying to swallow the sudden constriction in my throat.

Saul got out of the car, still wearing the same disconsolate expression he'd had ever since he'd stood before Jehovah a few minutes ago, as if something irreclaimable had been lost. I suppose he realized that I'd been right along. Nico was innocent. Real people died for senseless reasons. And only by hanging on to one another like life preservers could any of us hope to stay afloat.

I started to thank him for all that he'd done, just for *being there,* but he slammed the door before I could say a word. He salvaged a smile built of sadness and tumbledown hope, and then turned away into the devouring rain.

Hey You. Watch over him, will You?

The only answer was the wailing of the caterwaul wind.

"Bancavia's place is just down the street," Straker said. "You really think she'll be home?"

I tried to get one last glimpse of my friend, but all I could see through the darkness was the yellow rectangle of light as he opened the studio door. He shut it behind him and the light disappeared.

"Lieutenant?"

"Yes, Sergeant?"

"What exactly are we looking for at Bancavia's place?"

"Just get me there, Kyle."

He gave the car a little gas and chugged us through six inches of standing water. "We checked her out, you know. Bancavia. She's clean."

"I'm not convinced."

"Well, I am. Or at least I was. But off the record, you've got me second-guessing everything right now. I should probably doublecheck my Social Security number, just to make sure it's legit. That's what you've done to me. Ever since I met you, my life has gotten convoluted."

"I have that effect on people."

"I've noticed."

We made Bancavia's Antebellum Books five minutes later. Straker drove up on the curb to avoid as much of the water as possible. I got out and sank halfway up to my knees.

By now visibility had been reduced to about fifty feet, and the gale fought us all the way to the top of the steps. I had to hold on to the doorknob to keep from being pushed back down the stairs. Isolde didn't appear at the door to rescue us, so we set upon it like two people trying to escape a fire. We were

The Tongue Merchant

either getting someone's attention or bloodying our knuckles in the trying.

When our continued screams and poundings elicited no response, Straker reiterated his belief that Isolde had fled her home to seek succor from the storm. But I knew better. It was almost like I could sense the woman's nearness. As if Bella's spirit had connected us with some kind of spiritual telegraph wire. If I listened closely, I could hear a coded warning tapping in my heart.

Fearing the worst, I told Straker to kick in the door.

We found her naked, one arm draped over the rim of the tub.

"Isolde!"

Steam was everywhere. I ran through it without slowing down and almost slipped on the damp floor and *shit*—there was a syringe on the sink and a thin rubber hose and—

"Get her legs!" Straker shrugged off his jacket. "I've got her arms."

I grabbed her by the ankles. Her chin bobbed on her chest when we hoisted her out of the sudsy water and lowered her down. We fell to our knees beside her and Straker put his ear to her mouth, and all I could do was flutter my hands helplessly and wonder if I was somehow responsible for this.

"She's got a pulse. Get some towels and dry her off." He snapped the radio to his mouth and started yelling into it—all I caught was the phrase *10-45*, which I hoped had something to do with an ambulance.

I knocked over the hamper and found a few bath towels. The smell of lilac-scented candles made the moment seem surreal. A tremor passed down Isolde's bare body, the tiny bubbles glistening like diamonds against her black skin.

I did this to her.

After she was swaddled in towels that smelled of stale water from having festered in the hamper, I gathered her head in my lap and pulled the long, honeyed hair from her face.

She blinked when my hand brushed her eyelids.

Straker used a pair of tweezers he found in the medicine cabinet to pick up the syringe and hold it to the light. "My money's on cocaine. Stupid woman."

"Isolde? Can you hear me?"

"I'll get some blankets. Try and get her talking. The paramedics are on the way."

While Straker plundered the covers from the bed in the adjacent room, I stroked Isolde's face and kept saying her name until she finally looked up at me. Her eyes were like those of someone under water.

"You're going to be okay," I told her, trying to sound that way. "Help is on the way."

"What . . ." She swallowed repeatedly. "What are you doing here?"

"That doesn't matter."

"But the storm . . ."

"We'll be fine, all of us. We're taking you to the hospital."

"Hate those . . . damnable places."

"You're not alone. Here. Let's get you wrapped up." I helped lift her head as Straker settled a handmade quilt over her body.

"Ms. Bancavia?" Straker held up a finger in front of her face. "Can you watch my hand for a moment?" He moved his finger laterally, testing her vision.

But she closed her eyes. "Screw you, cop."

"Kyle, please."

He started to argue with me, then thought better of it and held up his hands in surrender. He stood up, backed away, and got Raznik on the radio again.

I took the opportunity to nestle my lips against Isolde's ear and say in a whispered rush, "I know you met with Joe Rotto,

The Tongue Merchant

but I don't know why, and if you tell me now it'll go a long way to getting us both into heaven. So do us a favor and spill your guts."

Her eyes cleared. They jumped toward my face, like quick brown birds.

"Putting Isabella to rest depends on this," I added.

She seemed to understand, seemed, in fact, eager at last to part with her secret. She was a woman coming off a coke high, lying on a bathroom floor with the love of her life dead and her head being cradled by someone who appeared to understand. The words came out like a catharsis.

"I . . . received a telephone call. From Mr. Rotto. He"—another spasm caused her body to undulate—"he said he knew of my involvement with proponents of ELF. He invited me to his home."

"And you accepted the offer."

"Yes, but not the money."

"Money?"

"The money he . . . he wanted to pay me for information on Isabella . . . how she was involved with ELF . . ."

"But you didn't take it?"

The birds of her eyes turned dangerous, baring their claws. "I'd sooner cut my wrists than sell Isabella out to that racist maggot. I was so upset by his proposition that on the way out the door, I stopped at his car long enough to smash in the taillight. A juvenile gesture, perhaps, but I was just . . . overcome."

The warble of sirens grew louder, even through the tumult of the rain.

I weighed Isolde's words on the balance of my heart. Despite my earlier supposition, there'd been no baneful confederation between the two of them, after all. Rotto had learned of Isolde's liaisons with Voorstadt's hoodlums, but she'd turned him down when he tried to barter for information to use against Bella. A simple answer, as well as a logical one. God alone knew the scenarios I'd been imagining—Isolde as Rotto's lover, or Rotto as the third member of a *ménage à trois*—but it turned out he was just a man who'd tried to protect his business interests, just as Isolde had tried to protect her romantic ones.

"I believe you," I told her, remembering the broken taillight. "But if you told Rotto to stick his offer up his ass, then why lie to me and say you'd never met him?"

"I was . . . scared. All that ever mattered to me had been taken away, and misrepresenting myself to you . . . that was simply reflex. I only wished to insulate Isabella from further harm . . . even after she was gone."

Again, the profundity of her love astonished me.

"The EMTs are here," Straker said. "I'll let them in."

At the sound of his voice, Isolde finally seemed to become aware of her condition. "Ambulance . . ." She put a hand to her face, then to her chest, feeling the towels in which she was wrapped as if to confirm the solidity of her own body. Fresh tears clung to her lashes when she blinked her eyes. "My apologies. You . . . you didn't need to see me like this."

"Apology not accepted. If your face had slipped into the water—"

"I understand." She sniffled, grimaced as a new pain stabbed her somewhere I couldn't see, and then touched her hair as if she could return it to its usual sensuous splendor. "It's just so hard sometimes. The stuff . . . it gets me through."

The lights dimmed. A tremor of thunder shook the building. Time to fly.

"I can't stay here any longer." I glanced at my watch, which was still as broken as it was three hours ago. "I've got a lot to do before my charming police escort makes me come in out of the rain. Believe me when I say I'm sorry that things happened like they did. Nobody wants Bella back more than I do, includ-

The Tongue Merchant

ing you. But that's not going to happen. She's not just going to walk through that door, no matter what I do tonight. So this is all I've got. For what it's worth."

For a moment it seemed as if Isolde's lips were touched by the echo of a long-forgotten smile. "Marcella?"

She'd spoken so softly that I had to lean closer. "Yes?"

"It's worth enough."

The paramedics were suddenly amongst us with their radios squawking and their plastic coats throwing off water and their boots making a mess of the bathroom floor. Straker came in behind the stretcher and helped me up, and then there were noisy machines checking Isolde's vital signs and hands in rubber gloves moving along her body, and sheets of lightning blazing the window. Somewhere a shutter banged crazily in the wind.

"Learn anything?" he asked as we made our way downstairs.

"Yeah. Life sucks."

He held the door open for me. "You really believe that?"

I drew my inadequate hood over my head. "No. But the night's not over yet."

We dashed outside, where the rain washed away the lingering scent of lilacs.

"Sixbone," I said.

Straker cranked the car too quickly around the corner, causing the rear end to fishtail and a wave of water to roll over the right front fender. Steam snaked up from the hood.

"Where?" he asked through clenched jaws.

"Leeward Street."

"How do you know?"

"I have my sources."

"Care to elaborate?"

"No."

"Why didn't you tell me this before?"

"Haven't you heard? I'm an insubordinate vigilante who distrusts authority."

"I'll buy that." He leaned on the horn when a motorcycle shot out in front of us, then avoided a fallen palm tree in the street by driving through somebody's lawn, which looked more like a rice paddy in Vietnam.

"Where at on Leeward?"

"There's a *botanica* there. That's all I know."

"And Sixbone will be there."

"Yes. Maybe. I don't know."

"And you think that whoever sold him the tongue—"

"Forced Tommy So to lie about Nico. Yes, that's what I believe."

"Not me."

"Good for you. At this point, Kyle, I don't care what *anyone* believes."

"Think about it. A perp this smart would not be moronic enough to tip his hand to the likes of the corner heroin dealer."

He said something else, but his words were demolished by a wrecking ball of thunder. A sudden cross-stream bucked hard against the car, and Straker fought the wheel to keep us from slamming into a lamppost.

"Kyle?"

"Uh-huh?"

"Let's just get there alive."

"Best idea I've heard all day."

We saw our first looters on Leeward, three androgynous figures climbing from the window of an electronics store. They carried a backbreaking load of amplifiers and car stereos. When they caught sight of the light flashing from our dashboard, they dropped half of their burden and loped off into the night.

Straker just shook his head and kept driving.

"Are you familiar with this area?" I asked, straining to identify the businesses as we slowly cruised the street.

"A little, but not enough to waste time trying to get lucky." He found the walkie-talkie and thumbed the call button.

"I thought you guys used cell phones nowadays."

"Can't count on them in atmospheric conditions like these. Besides, Detective Raznik and I aren't going through the dispatcher with this little escapade. Other than our captain, no one else knows about your extra-vocational activities. So for your information, if you go down because of this, you won't be going down alone."

"But the FBI—"

"The feds'll need a scapegoat if this turns sour in any way, shape, or form. And there's no goat more easily scaped than yours truly." Into the radio he said, "Raz, could you run a weather check for me? We seem to have run into a spot of rain."

"You still with the girl?" was Raznik's only response.

So now I'm "the girl."

"She hasn't run away on me yet," Straker said.

"Too bad."

"Maybe so. I need a head shop on Leeward. One of the local *botanicas* may be harboring our black magic man. Get me an address."

"Roger that."

We drove without speaking, plowing down the center of the street, trying uselessly to see through the rain. Riding in the car was like being trapped in a metal barrel during a hailstorm. Straker used a small spotlight attached near the driver's-side window, playing the cone of light across the shops, most of which were encased in plywood and particle board. I noticed a bicycle lying forgotten on the sidewalk, its rear tire spinning like a roulette wheel.

That made me think about Raoul, the albino croupier. His

skin was so white as to be nearly transparent. I'd been able to see the blue veins under the skin on his hands and the fine tracery of capillaries in his face. Raoul had been the first to arrive when I'd found Rotto's mangled body. Just for paranoia's sake, I wondered if he'd been there all along.

Raoul was Serca's henchman. And Serca was more than he seemed.

Then I remembered what Leo had said: *Joseph's got pictures of the two of them parachuting, weight-lifting, scuba diving . . .*

Scuba diving.

I crossed my arms over my chest and bit my lip.

With Rotto out of the picture, Alonzo Serca was no longer a co-CEO of De Casals International, but the undisputed head man. And if Nathan the Silent had captured the killer on tape, wouldn't it make sense if that person turned out to be someone he was close to, like his boss?

I grabbed my elbows and squeezed tight.

The radio barked.

"What have you got?" Straker asked.

"The eight-hundred block. Place called the Andromeda Strange. Some kind of hippie hangout and voodoo supply shop. Raided last year, owner's name is Buster Ortiz, a parolee out of the can six months now. You copy?"

"Ten-four, Raz. Thanks. Stand by."

He got us there in thirty seconds.

Our doors flew open.

Our shoes hit the water.

We ran toward the shop, the lightning freezing our shadows in front of us.

"Police! Get down on the floor!"

Wild movement, darkness, a bobbing flashlight beam, a lava lamp gurgling—

"Put your hands on your head! You! Get down, or I will *put* you down!"

Glass breaking, someone cursing, the foresty stink of marijuana—

"Shut up and stop moving!"

The metallic ratcheting of handcuffs being locked, whispers, the lava lamp falling over—

"Marcella! Find the lightswitch!"

I groped along the wall.

"And you! I told you not to move!"

A kick, a muffled yelp, a body being dragged across the floor—

"Lieutenant!"

"I'm trying, dammit!"

And then I found it.

When the lights came on, I saw four people lying prostrate, Straker dragging their hands behind their backs one at a time and securing their wrists with duct tape, as he'd been carrying only one pair of cuffs. Trying to ignore the zoo of stuffed animal heads, the faux Aztec artifacts, sitars, tambourines, and bags of incense, I made a hasty study of the prisoners. The first was a Latino with great rolls of flesh on his arms and around his waist. Even his back was fat. Positioned as he was on the floor, his skin pooled around him like layers of melted shortening.

The next two were naked. One man, one woman, both in their early twenties, with bodies like ancient Taíno athletes, brown and lithe. The woman was crying and talking to the saints in Spanish, the man was swearing creatively in English.

The fourth person seemed built of sticks and tar paper, so lean and black was his body.

Sixbone.

He was dressed in torn denim, his feet jutting out of pant legs too short, his shoulders poking as sharp as triangles from a shirt too tight. His hair was a coarse bundle of black snakes, the skin pulled taut across his face. His eyes, sunk deep in his oversized skull, were pits of lurid color. He wore a headband of alligator skin and a dozen glittering rings in each ear.

Every time the fat man demanded to know the meaning for the intrusion, Straker shouted at him to keep his mouth shut. Nothing was said about a warrant. I hoped everyone kept it that way.

I checked the clock mounted in the belly of a ceramic Buddha. Two-thirty a.m.

Straker straddled the Jamaican and grabbed a handful of hair. "You Sixbone?"

"*Si.*"

"In English, please. Your real name?"

"Arthur. Calato. My name Arthur Calato and I done nothin,' mahn, you hear me?"

The fat man started blabbering again but Straker ignored him.

"Word on the street is that you're selling tongues. Human tongues. What of it?"

"Nah, nah! That business, ya know? Tongues belong to chimps. Monkeys, you know?"

"Come again?"

"Animal tongues," I said to myself, shaking my head. I made a fist and slapped it into my palm. *A dead end. Damn.* And I'd been so *sure*.

Straker gave Sixbone a shake. "You lying to me, punk?"

"No, mahn! I tell you they was *chimpanzee tongues.*"

"I don't believe you!"

"Kyle." I felt the heat rising in my face.

"*What?*"

"I think he's telling the truth. He was hawking animal tongues as human ones. No crime in that except for false advertising. You were right. The real killer wouldn't be stupid enough to

The Tongue Merchant

expose himself like that. I was just hoping, that's all. Now let's please just go."

Straker gaped at me. "You're the one who wanted to come here."

"Well, I was wrong. It happens."

"*Marcella* . . ."

"Please, Kyle, this place is freaking me out and it's going on three o'clock and we're running out of time and I really, really need to pee. Can we get out of here?"

"Monkey tongues!" Straker snorted.

"*Sí, sí,* that is all, mahn. Sixbone not sell human tongues."

Muttering a few choice invectives, Straker stood up, unlocked the cuffs and removed the tape, and then elbow-carried me out the door.

"You'll be hearing from my attorney!" the fat man bellowed.

Straker stopped and looked back sharply, his cheeks flushed. "Do you want the destruction of this dope factory of yours to become my mission in life? Well? Do you?"

"No, *señor.*"

"Good. You keep quiet and so will I. *Comprende?*" He dragged me out into the rain.

"You were right," I said again as we slogged through the water. "The killer's not dumb enough to fraternize with those creeps."

"You're forgiven." He opened the driver's door and I slid across the seat.

"I wasn't apologizing. I was just following a lead."

"In the middle of a hurricane," he reminded me.

"If it wasn't for me, you wouldn't have found Sixbone in the first place."

He got into the car and shut the door. "Don't be so sure."

"*Sure* is the last thing I am nowadays."

"Well, you're not alone."

"That's debatable. It sure feels that way."

"For me too. I suppose we're going to the airport now."

"As fast as you can get us there."

"This isn't going to be another false alarm, is it?"

I ha-ha-have it on tape.

"No," I said, thinking about the key. "This one's for real."

The Hozumkur Municipal Airport was under alien assault.

Rain sizzled the tarmac like lasers. The flat expanse that comprised the airfield was a wasteland, like I envisioned the surface of Mars to be, burned flat and raw by the wind. A mothership of clouds carpet-bombed the runways. Every new warhead of lightning revealed an empty parking lot, dark windows, and deserted sidewalks. The only sign of survivors was the searchlight, which swept the skies with its alternating beams of red and white, steadfastly refusing to give up the fight.

We were met inside by a frazzled night manager and a security guard. While Straker displayed his credentials and explained our situation, I cast a longing glance at the door to the ladies' room. *Now or never.* I rushed in and avoided meeting the gaze of the stranger in the glass. On the inside of the stall door someone had written FIGHTING FOR PEACE IS LIKE SCREWING FOR VIRGINITY. That may have been true, but it wasn't the kind of wisdom I needed at the moment.

Straker knocked as I was washing my hands. "You coming?"

"No, I've decided to drown myself in the sink."

And then it was unavoidable. I looked at myself in the mirror.

Whoa. So much for maintaining the illusion of life.

The rent-a-cop showed us the way to the newly upgraded security department. He referred to it as the command center. I'd never before seen an empty airport terminal; it was one of those scenes a lot spookier than you'd imagine. The departure

The Tongue Merchant

and arrival monitors were black. The ticket counters were unmanned. The chairs were uninhabited, except for an old sweatshirt someone had left behind, one worn sleeve dangling toward the floor.

Somewhere along the way I slipped the key from my belt pouch.

"What number?" the guard asked.

Two digits were stamped on the head of the key: 24.

He slotted his passcard in the scanner and the thick metal door clicked open. He led us past banks of closed-circuit monitors to the guard lounge, then showed us to the second bank of lockers. The way they were stacked on top of one another reminded me of the morgue where Bella was lying, even as I shoved the key home and gave it a twist. Bella undressed beneath a sterile sheet. Bella with a card on her toe like the kind they tied on your luggage. Bella with her hands motionless at her sides, unable to transmit to me the sign language that I'd spent the last five years trying to learn.

Chilled by her ghost, dripping rainwater from every inch of my body, I opened the locker door.

Chapter Twenty-Two

I sat in the car with the heater on its highest setting, clutching the videotape in both hands.

It was one of those little micro-tapes they used to use in camcorders before everything went digital. Apparently Nathan hadn't bothered to upgrade. The tape had been wrapped in butcher's paper and tied with red yarn. The wrapping now lay in a bundle in my pocket. The only thing inscribed on the tape's label was the date. Nathan had shot the video seven months ago. Isabella had died trying to find out what was on it. I held it like it was plutonium.

And from here? Straker had asked as we left the building.

We play it. Saul's probably got a VCR. His place isn't far away.

Maybe we should take it to the station . . .

Screw the station. Too many prying eyes. Besides, Saul's studio is closer.

I suppose you're right.

I'm glad somebody thought so. At the moment I didn't feel right about anything. I was riding in an unmarked police car through winds nearing seventy miles an hour, a hurricane no more than forty-five minutes away and evidence of a murderer in my lap. I was so wet that it felt as if I might never be dry again. In a matter of minutes, I hoped to reveal the face of a killer and deliver amnesty to an innocent man. It was all too much. When the lightning revealed my face in the wing mirror, I finally knew what my mother meant by the term *thousand-yard stare.* She said it was a condition which afflicted soldiers too long at war. The thousand-yard stare was not only a vacuity of the eyes, but one of the soul.

Yet I have been a juggler since I was twelve. On his days off, my father had performed as a clown at children's birthday parties. Juggling and close-up magic were his specialties. I used to practice an hour a day, a freshman in high school missing her mother and needing to keep her hands busy to fend off the tears. When I was sixteen I could handle four objects at once. It wasn't until I was twenty-four that I managed five, and then only for a few passes. But sitting in that car on the way to Saul's studio, I found myself performing a bit of jugglery even more amazing than that. Despite the thousand-yard stare, even in the midst of the elemental catastrophe boiling around us, my mental hands were able to keep the puzzle pieces in motion, until at last I caught each one and snapped it home.

There were still a few pieces missing, of course, a few gaping holes in my theory that wouldn't be filled until I viewed the tape. Foremost among them was the key to the *Lynn*'s master stateroom. No one could've gotten in without the key. And if Isolde hadn't provided the killer with one, as I'd first suspected, then it must have been Nico or Abdías, which meant that the suspects were limited to—

Wait a minute.

There was someone else, wasn't there?

When I was thirteen I found my brother in the back of our old man's locksmithing van.

The heater wasn't warm enough to expel the sudden frostbite in my heart.

He was lying in a pile of ten thousand keys . . .

I didn't want to believe it, even though the facts were in front of me. Yes, Leo was FBI, and that would have given him access to Tommy So's criminal history and made it easy to blackmail him. You don't cooperate, the feds make your life impossible. And yes, he'd been at the Croesus when Rotto was slain and hadn't yet mentioned where he'd been late Sunday night. It didn't take a conspiracy nut to imagine a federal agent becoming entangled with an international hoodlum like Voorstadt. Who could guess what kind of black ops our government had its hands in?

But some small part of me wouldn't accept it. Blame it on Leo's eyes.

"Kyle?"

"Yes?"

"Please hurry."

A wave killed the car half a block from the studio.

The water was deeper than it looked. On the corner of Lionese and Conquistador, the street dipped down enough to form a reservoir. The car smacked into a lake and slowed immediately, the water lapping over the bumper and causing parasols of steam to rise from the hot engine.

"Ah, hell," Straker said, fighting the wheel. "We may get a little wet."

A second later a current caught the left front fender, shoving the car toward the curb.

"Hold on!"

Straker twisted the wheel against the stream, but momentum had already done its damage. We sunk even lower as the water deepened. The motor coughed twice and died.

The car began to float.

The river pushed us in a complete circle. We turned helplessly until the back of the car slapped a streetsign, and only then did the car stabilize. By now the entire front end of the vehicle had sunk. The headlights cast a weird submarine shine into the murk. Water seeped across the floorboard.

The Tongue Merchant

"Time to abandon ship," I said, unrolling my window.

"Women and children first." Though he sounded noble enough, Straker didn't waste any time getting his window down. "On second thought . . ."

I shoved the small videotape into my pouch and zipped it shut. Then I hauled my upper body through the window, sat on the sash, and squinted as the rain pummeled me.

Straker exited by the same means, and we looked at each other across the top of the car.

"I thought the captain went down with his ship!" I yelled.

"Times change!"

I tapped a finger on the roof of the car. "So much for police property!"

Amazingly, Straker smiled. "You want to hear something funny?"

"Sure. Why the hell not?"

"This is Raznik's car."

It took me a moment, then a nervous, desperate laugh welled up my throat. Maybe there really was a bit of justice in the world.

Though my hiking boots were insulated and my pants water-resistant, they couldn't account for the sea I found myself standing in when I slid down from the car. The water reached halfway up my thighs, so cold it nearly stole my breath. I had a flashback: *I'm getting out of a pink taxi in this very spot late Monday evening, watching a skinny vein of water trickle into the gutter and never envisioning that my universe would be standing on its head two days later.* Had I been a clairvoyant, would I have still made the decision to press on, knowing that I'd face the knife of a murderer, not to mention a court-martial? I think the fact that God hides the future from us is one of our greatest blessings.

If only He could hide the past.

I grappled with the car until I found a handhold, and then

methodically worked my way around. I'd waded through some fairly active trout rivers with my father, but nothing like this. The wind made things no easier, battering me with such irresistible force that, ironically, if it hadn't been for the water holding me up, I wouldn't have had a chance of staying on my feet.

I met Straker at the front of the car. We grabbed each other like lovers.

"Having fun yet?" he shouted in my ear.

"I'll let you know!"

We turned our faces into the wind. My hat blew off and vanished in a black hole. The water devoured the car's battery, which in turn doused the headlights, leaving us with only Straker's flashlight and the occasional streetlight which hadn't yet succumbed. With my eyes narrowed to mere cracks against the stinging rain, I was nearly blind, and Straker was no better off. Clenching each other, we heaved through the water in what we hoped was the direction of the *bottega*.

The walk was brutal.

I'd scored high on my last physical. My heart rate was under seventy, and I moved a little iron in the *Sentinel*'s gym three times a week. And the moment I met him, Straker had impressed me as something of an athlete himself. But nature makes pretenders of the best of us. The first twenty feet through the water seemed like a nautical mile. The muscles in my legs were burning, and I panted with each belabored stride.

Almost there.

I concentrated on making high ground. When we finally reached the sidewalk, the water was down to mid-calf, and the storefront awnings provided a modest bit of shelter from the rain. My windbreaker was now officially useless. This was not a wind it was going to break. In between the bursts of thunder, I heard the feeble whine of the warning sirens.

The Tongue Merchant

I felt like shouting something profoundly primitive, like *This stinks!* but I figured it best to conserve my breath.

Straker tripped.

He went down with a graceless splash. He nearly dragged me down on top of him, but I stepped quickly enough to catch myself. I pulled him to his feet and we continued without a word.

Was this the same desire that fueled my mother? The same inner furnace that kept her warm? The same unremitting sense of duty?

The same fire that eventually consumed her?

Forget that, gatita. *Better to be burned alive than never have the guts to feed the flames.*

I wasn't sure if I believed that. But here I was, waging war against a hurricane.

The creaking of the sign told me that we'd arrived. Saul's imported slab of teak rocked back and forth in the gale, its joints squealing like they might give way at any moment. The front of the *bottega* was completely dark. Metal louvers had been closed over the windows. I reached for the door even when I was still ten feet away. Straker and I bounced against it, gasping.

"Hope he hasn't left yet," I said, wrenching the knob, "or I'm going to—"

The door opened and we fell inside.

Spikes of rain hammered the tiled floor. We put our weight against the door and outmuscled the storm.

I spent a few seconds catching my breath, then pushed myself away from the door.

"Saul?"

When there was no immediate response, my mouth began to get a little dry. A single lightbulb burned in the office cubicle farthest from the door, but the building was otherwise immersed in gloom. In the dark, the studio seemed as big as an airplane hangar. The dusty smell of clay hung in the air.

"Saul!" We took a few steps into the room. "I know you wouldn't just leave your door unlocked like that."

Straker let go of my arm to unbutton his slicker and clear the way to his shoulder holster.

"Saul, answer me!"

With his hand riding under his coat, Straker led the way toward the light.

I had a vision of Saul sprawled on the office floor with his tongue torn out . . .

"*Mel Tormé sucks eggs!*" I screamed.

A moment of heartbreaking silence, and then:

"Give it a rest, Zo, I was using the john."

He came out zipping his fly.

I sighed so hard I almost collapsed.

"Glad to see you," he said. "I was worried." I met him halfway across the floor and hugged him.

"You talk to Bancavia?" he asked.

I waited for a cavalcade of thunder to pass, then nodded. "We did, but she didn't have a lot to say. She wasn't in the most talkative of moods."

"What about her and Rotto?"

"Believe it or not, they had nothing to do with it."

"You're certain?"

"As certain as anyone could be, all things considered. Do you have a VCR somewhere in this pig sty?"

"Sure, but it's covered in dust. Who uses VCRs anymore? You look like hell, by the way."

"Comes with the territory. Can you load this up for me?" I showed him the videocassette.

"We watching a porno tonight?"

"It's evidence."

The Tongue Merchant

I felt like shouting something profoundly primitive, like *This stinks!* but I figured it best to conserve my breath.

Straker tripped.

He went down with a graceless splash. He nearly dragged me down on top of him, but I stepped quickly enough to catch myself. I pulled him to his feet and we continued without a word.

Was this the same desire that fueled my mother? The same inner furnace that kept her warm? The same unremitting sense of duty?

The same fire that eventually consumed her?

Forget that, gatita. *Better to be burned alive than never have the guts to feed the flames.*

I wasn't sure if I believed that. But here I was, waging war against a hurricane.

The creaking of the sign told me that we'd arrived. Saul's imported slab of teak rocked back and forth in the gale, its joints squealing like they might give way at any moment. The front of the *bottega* was completely dark. Metal louvers had been closed over the windows. I reached for the door even when I was still ten feet away. Straker and I bounced against it, gasping.

"Hope he hasn't left yet," I said, wrenching the knob, "or I'm going to—"

The door opened and we fell inside.

Spikes of rain hammered the tiled floor. We put our weight against the door and outmuscled the storm.

I spent a few seconds catching my breath, then pushed myself away from the door.

"Saul?"

When there was no immediate response, my mouth began to get a little dry. A single lightbulb burned in the office cubicle farthest from the door, but the building was otherwise immersed in gloom. In the dark, the studio seemed as big as an airplane hangar. The dusty smell of clay hung in the air.

"Saul!" We took a few steps into the room. "I know you wouldn't just leave your door unlocked like that."

Straker let go of my arm to unbutton his slicker and clear the way to his shoulder holster.

"Saul, answer me!"

With his hand riding under his coat, Straker led the way toward the light.

I had a vision of Saul sprawled on the office floor with his tongue torn out . . .

"Mel Tormé sucks eggs!" I screamed.

A moment of heartbreaking silence, and then:

"Give it a rest, Zo, I was using the john."

He came out zipping his fly.

I sighed so hard I almost collapsed.

"Glad to see you," he said. "I was worried." I met him halfway across the floor and hugged him.

"You talk to Bancavia?" he asked.

I waited for a cavalcade of thunder to pass, then nodded. "We did, but she didn't have a lot to say. She wasn't in the most talkative of moods."

"What about her and Rotto?"

"Believe it or not, they had nothing to do with it."

"You're certain?"

"As certain as anyone could be, all things considered. Do you have a VCR somewhere in this pig sty?"

"Sure, but it's covered in dust. Who uses VCRs anymore? You look like hell, by the way."

"Comes with the territory. Can you load this up for me?" I showed him the videocassette.

"We watching a porno tonight?"

"It's evidence."

He balked. "Evidence of *what?*"

"Please, Saul, just load the goddamn tape."

He accepted it like I was handing him a water moccasin. "All right. But don't take the Lord's name in vain."

"So I'm a sinner," I said. "Live with it."

We headed for the office, the thunder obliterating the sound of our footsteps.

The TV rested on a wheeled cart. Saul put a battered VCR on top of it and hooked it up.

I stood no more than three feet away. Somewhere in my mind I heard my father telling a little girl that if she didn't move back from the television, she'd go permanently cross-eyed.

Straker blew on his hands to warm them.

Saul pressed PLAY.

I held my breath.

The picture on the video jiggled erratically. The angle was bad. The lighting was nearly too weak to see what appeared to be the inside of a barn. Or a stable. I could make out a line of stall doors, with tack hung on wooden pegs in between. A lantern sat on a shelf between a pair of dented coffee cans. Straw lay in patches on the earthen floor. There was no sound.

The picture banked to the side as the cameraman shifted position. I caught a glimpse of an open window and a giant yellow moon in the night sky before he returned to his original vantage point. He was probably sequestered in a stall on the other side of the stable, shooting his stealthy video from under the door.

Nathan.

I pictured him hunkered down near the floor, reluctant spy and amateur photographer, sent there by Alonzo Serca to get the skinny on . . . whom?

A pair of booted feet appeared.

The camera moved ever so slightly, capturing a pair of European-style men's boots as they walked across the stable floor, looking incongruous amidst the straw and horse-grooming supplies. I could almost sense the quickening of Nathan's pulse. After a few snarls of static, the sound level adjusted enough that we could hear the man's footfalls as he crossed the stable, turned, took two more paces, stopped.

Nothing happened for several seconds, then a cigarette butt landed on the floor between the man's feet. He crushed it with his heel.

Nathan started to move again.

He picked himself up, as if he'd been lying down and was now rising into a crouch. The picture was momentarily blotted out, and when it cleared, it was framed by dark shapes on either side—the stall door on one side, perhaps, and a wall on the other. I could clearly see the man in the center of the frame, the moon filling the window over his shoulder.

"Who is that?" Straker wondered.

"Voorstadt." I knew him on sight.

He wore neatly pressed trousers and a light-weave linen shirt. The tails were loose and the sleeves were rolled up. He was leaning against a support beam, which gave him a look of ease and indifference, if not downright apathy. A gold watch as large as a medallion gleamed on his wrist. His hair was blond, and though I could only see his face in profile, I could tell that he was handsome, probably fiendishly so.

"This would have been shortly after he was released from jail," I said, in case anybody cared.

Nathan zoomed in for a closer look.

Still, it was hard to get a good view of Voorstadt's face, as the video was being shot from almost directly behind him. As I watched, the man lowered his chin and moved his eyes subtly in

Nathan's direction, as if, like some kind of animal, he could sense when he was being stalked.

"I don't like this guy already," Straker said.

"I'll second the motion," I agreed.

Saul said nothing, only stood there and watched.

Nathan's patience far surpassed my own, because it seemed like at least ten minutes passed with nothing happening. Voorstadt scratched his chin, checked his watch, inspected the condition of his fingernails. Once he even yawned.

"This video," Straker said, "how did you know where to find it?"

"Shhh. Later."

"This could be construed as concealing evidence, you know."

"I'm not concealing anything."

"You know what I mean. If a member of the department's narrow-minded upper echelon decides to make an issue of this—"

"Wait! Someone's coming."

A second man appeared in the frame.

The killer, here he comes, he's the one who attacked Bella and—

I inched closer to the television. The chaos intensified outside, but I was oblivious.

Though he wore soft-soled loafers, his footsteps sounded like gunshots to me. In fact, I was now inside the stable: I smelled the damp straw and Voorstadt's expensive cologne; I felt the balmy heat of the night; I heard the swaying of the leaves outside and the quiet rustle of the man's pants as he approached. I was folded so tightly into the moment that I swore I could feel the heat of Voorstadt's breath when he said, "We're quite the weavers of a tangled web, my friend."

"Indeed," said a familiar voice.

"These are the days, they say, that try men's souls. Disturbing, aren't they?"

"Vexatious," the man agreed.

That one word drained the last ounce of strength from my body.

"Judge Horne," I whispered.

"What?" Straker leaned toward the screen.

Jan Voorstadt shook hands with Judge Cicero Horne.

In an instant it all made sense. I cursed myself for failing to see it earlier. Joe Rotto had told me and it had gone right over my head: *The arraignment got hung up on an arrest technicality, and the judge let the scumbag walk.* So Judge Horne had presided over the Voorstadt trial, and wasn't he money-hungry? Didn't he hang around Abdías just to benefit from the steady flow of cash? It only made sense that he'd take a bribe to throw the case out the window.

"Shit." I felt like hitting something. Or someone. "I should've *known.*"

Back in the stable, Voorstadt was handing over an envelope.

"You've got to be kidding me," Straker said.

Horne accepted the envelope and slipped it into his pocket without opening it.

This is the bastard that killed Bella, this man right here!

Through my steadily rising rage, I ran through everything I knew about the murder, just to make sure. And it all worked out. Serca had instructed Nathan to follow Voorstadt, once the trial went south and it became imperative to find out if the warehouse fire had been commissioned by an enemy of DCI. But as it turned out, no one had paid the Dutchman to start the fires. Terrorism and insurance payoffs weren't the catalysts for Bella's death.

Instead, Nathan caught Horne in the act of accepting blood money. But he didn't report his findings to his boss because he was inherently weak-kneed. He'd told me as much at Bella's wake. Instead, he was going to let Bella reveal the videotape to the world, in exchange for the stamp, which she then spent the next couple of months trying to procure. While Paulo Longoria was setting up the Adelbert deal with St-Germain, Bella didn't let any grass grow under her feet. Sensing a news story of galactic proportions, Bella met with Voorstadt at Isolde's shop, perhaps hoping to convince him to talk, or at the very least get a quote directly from the horse's mouth. But someone tipped Horne off to Bella's intentions. Voorstadt's people probably thought she was out to hang ELF.

Upon learning this, Horne panicked. Thinking that he was about to be revealed, he killed Bella and, just like Nathan had told me, he used drugs as blackmail. Either Tommy So would lie on his behalf, or the judge would use the legal system to put So away for peddling narcotics.

Beside me, Straker had been talking into his radio for several minutes now, but I was only just beginning to hear what he was saying. ". . . yeah, Raz, I know he's a federal judge. He worked that racketeering case of ours a couple of years back, remember? Now I don't care if you have to send a car over there to drag his secretary out of whatever shelter she's hiding in, I want to know Horne's itinerary for Sunday evening."

"Ten-four. Stand by."

The camera showed Horne lighting a pipe on his way out of the stable. He was a large man and his fist could easily crack bone. He was probably a robust swimmer and could've made it back to shore from the derelict *Lynn* with little difficulty. But, even as events began to crystallize for me, one piece still didn't fit.

How did he get into Isabella's cabin in the first place?

Voorstadt remained in the stable for a few minutes, smoking, letting the judge put some distance between them. Then he dropped his second butt on the ground beside the first, extinguished it, and strolled from the barn with chilling aplomb.

The video kept running, but there was nothing left to see.

Straker looked at me. "Do you have any idea what you've done?"

"Ask me that tomorrow," I said, pawing for the desk behind me before I crumbled. "Right now I'm sort of in the middle of falling to pieces."

Here at last was the truth. Isabella had been murdered for trying to expose a corrupt government official. On the eve of crucifying him in a front-page story that any newspaper in the country would have mortgaged the masthead to print, she had awakened to find Horne standing over her bed. In her strange, soundless world, he had attacked her. I wondered if the deaf could hear their own screams.

The radio buzzed. "You there, Kyle?"

Straker's stare never left me as he raised the walkie-talkie to his mouth. "Go ahead."

"Sent Collinsworth to find the secretary, but turns out we don't need her. Is this getting through? Reception at this end ain't worth a damn."

"Then talk louder. What've you got?"

I waited for my breathing to resume its normal pace, wondering why I didn't feel relieved.

Raznik's voice came in spurts through the static. "Horne's got a personal assistant. I got hold of him at home. Says Horne left Sunday morning for Miami. Attended midnight Mass at some big damn cathedral there. Repeat: at the time of death, Horne was a thousand miles away, taking communion from the hand of the bishop himself, in front of a thousand God-fearing witnesses. Copy that?"

My legs gave way. I slid to the floor, cupping my face in my hands.

Still watching me, Straker nodded. "I copy. Straker out."

The Tongue Merchant

Just when I thought I'd finally seized it, the truth eluded me yet again.

So I was wrong and maybe Horne took a bribe but he's not stupid so he left town—

"We better get out of here." Straker crouched down in front of me. "Let's worry about finding a cement ceiling. Then we'll talk."

—but if Horne didn't do it then he used somebody else, someone who owed him or—

"Marcella?"

—or someone he could blackmail, but it wasn't Tommy because he was at his party—

"Come on." He took me by the arm and hauled me up.

I knew that if we waited until daybreak, Horne's helper would be gone, having fled the island as soon as the storm permitted. Which meant I had to make a leap of logic, and make it fast.

Fast as in *right now.*

"I've got the tape," Straker said. "I'll call and have a unit meet us out front. The deparment's got vehicles designed to get around in this sort of weather. We'll get our people on this video tonight, just to verify its authenticity, and one warrant later we'll have Horne taking Mr. Murillo's place behind bars. I realize we haven't pinpointed Horne's accomplice, but now it's only a matter of time."

I let him lead me from the cubicle, but everything he said was static. I was as deaf as Isabella. I heard only the voices in my head.

He gets his luh-leverage through the dope. Buh-buh-buh-blackmail.

Maybe Nathan hadn't been referring to Tommy, but someone else. If I could only backtrack, sift through all the events of the last few days, run my fingers along each piece of the puzzle . . .

I leaned on Straker all the way to the door, trying so hard to remember, but I was at the end of my emotional rope and the strands were fraying in my hands. Water dripped from my hair into my face. My body ached. The studio was deep with shadow, the constant din of thunder muffling every noise, so even if I hadn't been preoccupied, I wouldn't have seen the attack coming.

Straker went down without a sound, and even before his body hit the floor, I was being driven off my feet, a black shape riding me down.

Chapter Twenty-Three

Not just anybody could deliver that kind of wallop.

A body fell like an avalanche on top of mine.

The pain streaked beyond my threshold to withstand it, and for several seconds I lost all sense of reality. When I opened my eyes, my arms instinctively covering my head in pitiful self-defense, all I could see was darkness—the dark cavern of the studio, and the darker shape on top of me.

He's all right, Zo. This is the honorable Cicero Horne, federal circuit court judge.

I swung a fist, but something inconceivably strong grabbed my wrist. On reflex I followed my first strike with another, and then both of my arms were locked in what must have been the pincers of some Herculean machine. A tiny cry welled up from the back of my throat.

I confiscated a bunch of pirated CDs, a phony driver's license, a slim-jim for cracking cars, counterfeiting supplies, lockpicks, a piss-ant little .32 revolver . . .

Lockpicks.

Jesus Christ lockpicks.

"Don't try to fight me, Zo."

At the sound of his voice, a part of me shut down and died. The tears that had been held in precarious abeyance finally flooded my eyes, not out of fear, but of sadness. Only now did I understand the look he'd been wearing when he got out of Straker's car, as if he'd lost something that could never be retrieved. That something was me.

"Saul . . ." The word trailed into a sob.

It must have been contagious, because Saul pinched his eyes shut when they filled with moisture. "I'm so sorry . . ."

I tried to move, but I might as well have been pinned under a truck. My arms were locked in place and my heart was about to punch through my ribs and I couldn't see through the tears and—

"Go to hell, asshole."

"Zo, it was complicated. He made me—"

"You killed Isabella, goddammit!"

"*I didn't have a choice!*" He shook his head and sniffed back a bead of snot that was encroaching on his upper lip. "You think I acquired all of this from pottery? Is that what you really believe? You think I make this kind of dough selling stoneware bedpans?"

Another tide of darkness washed over me, my mind responding to the trauma by trying to shut me down. I fought the blackout and tried to wrench myself free.

Saul only tightened his grip.

"It's right there on my car, Zo. I thought for sure you'd make the connection."

I remembered his license plate: POT GOD.

"*Marijuana?*" Bile flooded my mouth. "You killed Bella for goddamn *weed?*"

"Judge Horne didn't really leave me with much choice. He told me to do it that way, to take her tongue, because she was about to squeal, and the sicko wanted to make a point. You've got to believe that it wasn't my idea."

I screamed.

Rage and fear collided. I brought my leg up as high as I could, jerking hard with my arms and trying to hook my foot around his head, yelling senselessly all the while.

For a second I almost had him.

But he increased pressure with his knees, crushing the air from my body. Then he bore down harder on my wrists.

Pain exploded all the way down to my shoulders. My scream melted into a whimper.

"I don't want to hurt you," he said, his voice thick. "You're my *friend*."

"You tried to run me over," I reminded him in little more than a gasp.

"Only to scare you."

"Saul, you're scaring me now."

"I know, Zo. If there were some other way—"

I snagged my foot over his head and heaved.

It worked.

Saul released one of my hands to grab my ankle. In that instant I dropped my leg, pulled myself into a sitting position and, with a howl, drove my fist into his throat.

My knuckles met his Adam's apple. He choked.

The next eruption of thunder felt as if it came from within me. Everything was gone—thoughts, memories, Bella's ghost, my mother's voice—and all I had left was this half second of time which only had room for motion. I didn't consider my actions as they came, but somehow my other hand wiggled free, and I turned that hand into a knife blade and brought the edge of it down against the bridge of Saul's nose. As if from some great distance away, I heard myself grunt as I made contact and felt the crack of bone. Then there was blood, and my heart started beating again, and then Saul's fist was coming—and though I saw it in my heightened state of awareness—I wasn't fast enough to move away.

This was how he broke Bella's jaw—

He punched me in the chin so hard my teeth tore a hole through my cheek. Blood filled my mouth.

I fell back against the floor. Everything turned white. It hurt too much to cry out. Instinctively I touched the injury with my tongue—

Mistake. My tongue poked through the tear in my cheek. I had to swallow the blood to keep from gagging on it.

It was over. Just a little bit longer and I'd be nothing but the next DB.

Saul was still sitting on me, though he wasn't getting much air. He held his throat with both hands and his face was crimson and the foundation of the building shook as Bartholomew at last began to pass over us.

"*Get the hell off me.*" I tried to twist free.

Still coughing, Saul shook his head and reached down for me.

But this time I was faster.

Trying to ignore the napalm in my cheek, I shoved him in the chest with such force that the muscles in my arms flared in agony. Adrenaline did the rest, and Saul tipped backward the slightest bit . . .

I scrambled out from under him.

"Zo!" He crawled after me.

Spitting blood, grunting for breath, I scrabbled across the floor, unable to see where I was going, clawing at my belt pouch, and then my fingers found the zipper in the darkness and—

Saul grabbed my leg.

I screamed and kicked at him.

He was still coughing hoarsely but recovering fast. He got a grip on both of my ankles. I raked open the pouch and everything spilled out. Saul twisted me around so that I landed on my back. He shouted something lost to the thunder and reached for my neck to finish me off.

I found the gun and pointed it at him.

He stopped, poised over me, breathing hotly.

"I'll goddamn kill you," I said.

He seemed to believe me. Slowly he pulled back.

From outside came a splintering sound, then a crash. Saul's sign had hit the ground.

"Kyle!" I shouted. "Are you all right?" My voice sounded like that of a little girl lost in a department store. *"Kyle, can you hear me?"*

"Zo, listen to me."

"Shut the hell up!"

"I've got to show you something."

I was taking no chances. I struggled to my feet and clamped the Walther in both hands, though it was difficult to keep the weapon steady. Blood ran freely down my face. "Kyle has a pair of handcuffs on him," I said. "I'm going to get them, and you're putting them on or I'm shooting you in face. You got that?"

"Okay, sure, whatever you say. But this may change your mind." Holding his right hand where I could see it, he carefully lowered his left to his pocket.

I sighted down the barrel. At only fifteen feet away, I couldn't miss.

He found whatever it was he was looking for, closed his fingers around it, and held his closed fist out to me.

If he opened his hand and there was a tongue lying there, I'd put a bullet in his skull.

But it wasn't a tongue.

He spread his fingers and half a dozen pieces of brass lay on his palm.

Bullets.

It took a few moments to hit me. The logical part of my brain had temporarily given up the helm to the primitive part, and so I had to stand there while this new information was processed. When I finally realized I was holding an empty gun, my body locked up.

"Marcus," I said.

Saul nodded. "He let me rummage through the cloakroom at Isabella's wake. When I found that you were packing, I thought it couldn't hurt to empty the clip."

He turned his hand over and the shells fell to the floor.

The better part of my soul fell with them.

Then I must have blinked, because Saul had a potter's knife in his hand.

"See you on the other side, Zo."

He rushed me.

The door was too far away. I'd never make it. Saul was too big, too fast, too damn unstoppable, he'd murdered my friend to protect his trade, murdered her for *money*, and cut her tongue out and Rotto's too, maybe not with that same potter's blade but close enough, and the gun dropped from my stupid useless fingers and when he was five feet away I did the only thing left for dying people to do.

I fell.

My back struck one of the wooden crates that was probably full of dope, but the pain came as if from a distant continent. My only country now was the contents of my spilled belt pouch, the last little fragments of my life, and what a place to die: lying facedown in a mess of breath mints and emery boards.

And something else.

I grabbed the tongue depressor and snapped it in half.

Saul dropped on top of me, crushing the wind from my lungs and grabbing my hair in one hand, bringing the knife down with the other. He twisted my head to an agonizing angle and tore away the scarf, exposing the white curve of my neck.

Howling, I drove the pointed end of the stick into his eye.

The thunder wasn't loud enough to muffle his scream.

I buried the shaft three inches deep, popping his eyeball and spearing the soft tissue behind the socket. Pinkish fluids spilled over my fingers, followed by a needle-thin discharge of blood.

Saul made a noise that wasn't entirely human.

I let go and shoved him away.

He went into a brutal spasm, raking at the tongue depressor until his fingers closed around it. When he pulled it free, red gelatin rushed from the wound.

I tried to use the edge of a crate to tug myself up, but my hands shook so violently that I couldn't find purchase. My abdominal muscles contracted, and I puked up the last watery remains in my stomach.

I stared at him through my wet hair. He was weeping, lying on his back, his hands clamped over his eye in an effort to keep from bleeding to death. His right leg quivered as his punctured brain fired random alerts to his nerves. A few seconds later, he started to gasp, as if his respiratory system were shutting down.

I closed my eyes and cried.

The hurricane tore at the building. The window louvers banged. One of them tore loose with a shriek. Glass cracked and was blown inward in a thousand diamond shards. The wind ripped shingles from the roof and wailed discordantly across the tops of the kiln chimneys. But it wasn't enough to mask the sounds that Saul made as he died.

He tried to speak through the bloody broth in his throat. "Zo, I can't . . ."

I put my hands over my ears but heard him anyway.

". . . feel anything."

I tried to block it out, to make it unreal, but I couldn't summon an image of my father or remember what Leo's skin felt like, or recall the seriousness of breast cancer or the soothing balm of the sea. All I could do was remain folded on the floor, my face bleeding, vomit on my teeth, one of my friends dead and another on the way because of what I'd done to him.

"Zo . . ."

His body seemed to freeze. Then his hands slipped from his

face, his leg ceased its paroxysm, and he was still. A single red bubble rose up from his eye.

I listened to the storm rage. I don't know how long it beat at the building before I found the will to move.

As barren as a wasteland, I dragged myself toward Straker.

My feet were detached. I had to rely on my elbows. Pull myself a few inches, suck in a breath, try again. A thread of saliva dangled from my open mouth.

There was a hulking shape on the floor beside me. Perhaps it was part of the geography, a low mountain range or some other nameless piece of the landscape. In my stupor, I didn't recognize it, but I veered away from it nonetheless. From somewhere outside came the sound of a streetlamp being bent in half.

Straker was unconscious.

His head was cut and swollen just above his ear. From far away, a voice started talking about checking for pulse and dilation of pupils, though I didn't understand what it was saying. But there was a radio fastened to his belt, and this was an icon that spoke a language the primitive part of me still understood.

It took awhile, but I was able to get the walkie-talkie to my mouth. Using both hands, I depressed the call button. But I had lost the power of speech.

I tried again.

Bending all of my attention on the radio, I pushed out the words, even though it hurt, even though those first few syllables were unintelligible. On my third attempt, I finally produced a coherent sound.

"Detective Raznik?"

Static blasted back at me.

The salt of my tears touched the gash in my cheek and turned it to fire.

I made some indistinct, distorted sound of grief.

Then it was back to the radio.

"Detective . . . if you can hear me . . . please answer . . ."

The seconds passed, the darkness lulling me closer to the void, where the night-things were waiting to claim me.

From the radio: nothing.

"Officer down," I gasped, as the shadows descended. "And so am I."

I sank at last, my body following my mind into the depths. My head came to rest on Straker's chest, my icy fingers letting the radio fall away.

My eyes remained on Saul's body until the night-things dragged me under.

Epilogue

The Florida sun warmed my skin.

Aside from a flight of egrets bound for the nearby wetlands, the sky was empty, a vast blueness unmarred by cloud or passing plane. The air was calm, if a little humid, the forecast free of rain for at least the next week. Mullet and red snapper would be biting, if a person could find the time to cast a few lines.

I stepped between a pair of palmettos and approached the building.

Dad was cooking pasta tonight. Last night I'd tried my hand at a soufflé, and based upon that experience was expatriating myself from the kitchen forever. My father was a sport and traded dinner duties for loading the dishwasher, a task we both felt more appropriately suited to my skills.

I permitted myself a grin. That place on my cheek no longer stung when I smiled.

A week ago I'd had the pleasure of informing Debbie Newcombe that she'd been promoted to petty officer first class, the Coast Guard equivalent of a staff sergeant. We'd celebrated with a weekend at Orlando. But Saturday night she'd run into an old flame, and I'd spent the rest of my shore liberty in my usual state of aloneness. Some things never change.

I reached the sidewalk and followed the fence and its triple strands of razor wire.

I wore my service dress blue uniform, just about as formal as we surf soldiers can get. I'd chosen such a punctilious outfit because it was armor of sorts, as well as a badge. For what I was about to face, I needed every advantage I could muster.

The steel gates trundled open. A sentry beckoned me through. He carried an M16 assault rifle with a folding stock.

From Barrow's shores to Paraguay . . .

As I walked, listening to the sound of my footsteps echoing off the high stone walls, I tried to make at least a tentative plan for the rest of my career. Things wouldn't be the same aboard the *Sentinel*. Admiral Kirkland would have loved to dispense a little disciplinary action in my direction. I'd spoken with him several times in the last few months, and I sensed his chagrin when he was publicly forced to declare me meritoriously valorous. And Lord knows I hadn't made much of a friend of Sam Raznik, or even Kevin Maddox, for that matter. So not everyone was throwing roses at my feet. But I could live with that. At least I knew that I was no longer merely creating the illusion of life.

Great Lakes' or Ocean's wave . . .

I was met at a gray steel door by another sentry. This one greeted me by name. I'd phoned ahead and informed them of my arrival.

He asked me how military life was treating me, and we did the small-talk thing all the way down a corridor with bare concrete walls. A security camera was mounted at the end of the hall, protected behind a wire cage. The next door was wide and had no knob or handle. Beyond the ballistic-concussion glass, several men in uniform were sipping coffee in front of their monitors.

The sentry spoke through an intercom, giving my name to a man with a clipboard beyond the door. I stated my rank and port of call, and then held up my arms in a scarecrow stance while the sentry guided a hand-held metal detector over my body.

He asked me if I was doing okay.

I said of course, as if I did this kind of thing all the time, even though I'd never visited a prison before.

The Coast Guard fights through storms and winds . . .

He led me deeper into the building.

Though over the last couple of months I'd managed to avoid most of the journalists, I enthusiastically relented to a woman writing for breast cancer awareness. The military PR people thought it would be good for public relations, and they didn't even have to order me to sit for the interview. That was one cause I was glad to promote. I'd slain the Secret Saboteur. They'd cut it out of my chest and nuked any invisible remains. Sometimes at night I imagined I could feel that a small piece of me was gone, that I was no longer as whole as I used to be.

The Guard anthem was still running through my head as I entered a large chamber and followed the sentry's pointing finger. The room was divided in half by a series of stalls, each one separated by a window, permitting a person on one side of the booth to see someone on the other. As I made my way along the row, I caught fragments of conversation: faint crying and sad laughter and a wife telling a husband that Brandon had lost his first tooth. At the far end of the room, a guard was having to help a woman up from her chair. Her body was so wracked with sobs that she could barely stand up on her own.

To punish or to save.

The saving part was finally over. Only one more hammer of punishment yet to fall.

I sat down in my half of the booth and met the dusty gaze of the man on the other side of the glass.

"Hello, Navaro," I said.

There was a moment of concentrated stillness as we studied each other.

"Do I know you?" the old man asked.

"You're Isabella Murillo's uncle," I said, switching to his native Spanish without pause. "She was a dear friend of mine."

Navaro de Casals bowed his head. He was entirely bald, his scalp splotched with age marks and knotted little scars. Though he was only sixty, he looked twenty years older, white chest hairs poking through his faded denim shirt, his nose livid with a spider's web of tiny blood vessels.

"My name is Marcella Paraizo."

"I know. I've seen the newspapers. They call you a hero."

"Don't believe everything you read."

"You avenged my niece's death."

"Nothing so noble as that, I promise."

He shook his head. "You are too humble. I'm sure your parents are very proud of you."

I thought about my father hugging me the day of Bella's funeral and my mother saluting me from somewhere above.

"The part I found the most interesting," Navaro said, "was that bit about the bear."

"Pardon?"

"The man who murdered my niece. You killed him. God bless you for that. But with him dead, you would not have been able to prove he was the murderer if they had not found that hair from the panda bear on his clothes."

"Yeah. I guess I got lucky. And it was a koala bear, by the way."

"Right. Koala." He lapsed into a plaintive silence.

"Look, Navaro, I came here to tell you something . . ."

"I was going to make it up to her, you know. When I got out. They put me here for five years for what I did to her. But I messed up. Had to defend myself in here. A man got killed. Now they will never let me out."

Can't say that I'm sorry, I thought. Navaro was right where he belonged. But still, he had a chance for redemption, however small it may be."

"Have you been keeping up with the court proceedings?" I asked.

"When I can get my hands on a paper, yes."

"Then you know that Cicero Horne is going away for accepting that bribe."

"Yes."

"But there was no way for anyone to prove that he ordered Isabella's death. The man he sent after her is dead, so no one could testify against him."

Navaro leaned closer to the glass. "What is it that you are trying to say?"

I lowered my face toward the grille in the window. "Judge Horne will arrive here Monday morning to begin serving a four-year sentence. Your new neighbor is the man who murdered Isabella."

Though his face remained impassive, Navaro slowly closed his eyes. He seemed almost to be meditating. He laced his fingers in front of him and squared his shoulders. When he opened his eyes, they were chiseled to fine points, like pieces of flint. "Is that a fact . . . ?"

"Just thought you might want to make his stay here a comfortable one."

"That will certainly be arranged."

I gave him a curt nod. "Then I'll be leaving."

"I understand. Thank you. For coming here. For giving this to me."

I stood up and pushed in my chair. "Just doing my job." I turned and made for the door.

"*Vaya con Dios,* Marcella Paraizo."

I didn't look back.

All the way out of the prison and back into the street, I kept my mind on trivial things, such as my appointment with the hairdresser, the weather, how badly the Linc needed an oil change, and it wasn't until I was safely behind my sunglasses that I permitted myself to wave goodbye to Bella's ghost and listen to her bid me farewell as she departed. The only thing she left behind was the scar that was sure to linger on my cheek.

So . . . now what?

I was due back at Base San Juan in two days. Time for the cutter's iron-handed XO to indoctrinate a few new swabs. I'd met two of them already. One was fifty pounds overweight and apparently terrified of boot polish and starch. The other, though much more observant of his appearance, was a former ball player with an ego slightly larger than the ship's cargo hold. I wondered about the best way to welcome them aboard. Maybe I'd assign the slob to a marathon laundry detail and make the jock a kitchen assistant. We called the cook's lackey the jack-o'-the-dust, a position only slightly more esteemed than that of an indentured servant. I'd let him buy his way out of slavery as soon as he proved his culinary prowess. But then again, if I were measuring him against my own talents in the kitchen, he'd be a free man in a week.

Savoring a small smile, I walked in the direction of the sun.

"Taxi, ma'am?"

I checked over my shoulder. Leo Kavisti was leaning against a truck.

Though I tried to fold my smile up and put it away, it fought against me.

"Harry told me where to find you," he said. "Are you visiting an old friend?"

"Something like that. What are you doing here?"

"I took a few days off. Work was sort of running me ragged."

"What? The life of a private eye isn't all glitz and glamour?" I hit my forehead with the palm of my hand. "Oh, wait a minute. That's right. You're not really a private eye. You lied about that.

How could I forget?"

"Okay, okay, I'm sorry for the forty-seventh time. You know I was only doing what they pay me to do. But now . . . now I'm going to make it up to you. Finally."

I walked toward him. "So you're driving your truck off a bridge?"

"No . . ."

"Cutting off a finger?"

"Well . . ."

"Or castration? I hear that's how they punish liars in certain parts of the world. I think the least you could do to repent is live as a eunuch for the rest of your life."

He was smiling. "Recently that's exactly how I've been living. Have you eaten yet?"

"I'm on a diet."

"Fine. Salad and water then."

"I'm allergic."

"To which one?"

"Are you ever going to tell me your real name?"

"I don't know. Are you ever going to tell me how you like your eggs in the morning?"

"One thing at a time," I said. "Now open the door. You're buying, and I'm famous for my big appetite and expensive tastes."

I slid across the seat, and he climbed in behind me. He smelled like the sea.

"You seem to know everything about me," I said. "You've read a file that I didn't even know existed. So I have a lot of catching up to do."

"Then by all means, Marcy, the floor is finally yours. You may ask away."

"Okay. Do you fish?"

"Fish? When I was a kid I dug up my grandma's flower garden

looking for worms to use down at the creek, but since then I've never caught anything bigger than my hand. Does that count?"

"Close enough. How old are you?"

"Ever hear of Stonehenge?"

"You're not that old."

"Tell that to my ticker. You almost gave me a coronary a few months ago. You're relentless, you know that?"

"I'm just a poor working girl, Leonardo."

"Are you kidding me? You just made the national headlines. And you're so *nonchalant*. How can you sit there like it was just another day at the office?"

"See no evil," I said. "Just work the broom."

ABOUT THE AUTHOR

Under the pseudonym of Erin O'Rourke, **Lance Hawvermale** published the thrillers *Seeing Pink* (2003) and *Fugitive Shoes* (2006). His poetry and fiction have garnered numerous awards. He is an alumnus of the AmeriCorps program and continues to believe in the power of giving.

A licensed English teacher, Lance travels the American Southwest, speaking to readers and writers about the creative process and espousing the holistic benefits of storytelling, daydreaming, living a vegetarian lifestyle, star-gazing, and make-believing with little brothers. To this day, he continues to trade his hard-earned money for magic beans, trusting that his mother was right when she sent him off with a pencil in his hand and instructions to write about what he found at the top of beanstalks. Visit his official website at www.lancehawvermale.com.